DAUGHTER OF SEKHMET

Daughter of Sekhmet
Copyright © 2024 by Abigail Keyes

All rights reserved under the Pan-American and International Copyright Conventions. This book may not be reproduced in whole or in part, except for brief quotations embodied in critical articles or reviews, in any form or by any means, electronic or mechanical, including photocopying, recording, or by any information storage and retrieval system now known or hereinafter invented, without written permission of the publisher.

Library of Congress Control Number: 2024945507
ISBN (paperback): 978-1-963271-35-5
ISBN (eBook): 978-1-963271-36-2

abigail@akeyeswriting.com

Cover art and spot illustration by Elinore Eden Edge

THOUSAND ACRES

Published by Thousand Acres, an imprint of Armin Lear Press, Inc.
215 W Riverside Drive, 4362
Estes Park, CO 80517

DAUGHTER OF SEKHMET

A NOVEL OF ANCIENT EGYPT

ABIGAIL KEYES

THOUSAND ACRES

For everyone fighting for justice in a world so devoid of it.

In this 20th year of the Good God, I have come here today.
I bind myself to him and to the Two Lands with a light heart.
I fight on behalf of his name, as endures his ka and as endures my own.
I shall not swerve from the Good God on the battlefield.
I smite enemies of the Good God with the potency of Amun.
I act in uprightness for him every day.
I act in accordance with what the Good God asks.
I shall not transgress the command of the Good God.
I emerge from every fire, and nothing evil shall surround me.
I repulse Apep and spit upon his wounds.
I take this oath without coercion, coming to his service freely, and with the priests of the Temple of Sutekh as my witnesses.
I do these things in Truth, blessed by Ptah the Green Lord of Truth, Amun the Hidden One, Sutekh the Lord of the Desert, and Re the Lord of the Horizons.
Ankh. Udja. Seneb.

- A Soldier's Oath

PART ONE:
THE PROVOCATION

CHAPTER ONE

With a swift swing of my fighting staff, I send my opponent to the ground. I hover the end of my weapon over his face, not daring to look away. One last strike and I could end him.

He drops his own staff and waves his hand in surrender. I don't move. It could be a ruse.

When a bull bellows in a nearby field, my opponent and I break out in laughter.

"That's five wins for me today!" I tease as I catch my breath and offer my free hand to Iti, my father, my opponent today and every day.

"And won well, *benret*." As he stands, the ruddy dust makes him cough more than usual. I cup my arm around his bare chest, and he shoos me away.

"I'm fine," he says, leaning on his staff for balance.

With a grumble, I step back and twist my rough linen *shendyt* back to center. Well, truth be told, it's not really mine. It belongs to Iti. And it doesn't quite fit me. It's not a garment meant for women. But the dresses Mawat would have me wear are too delicate for fighting.

So, I wear it, especially when Iti takes me out for my evening sparring lessons and when we hunt together in the marshes.

Iti brushes the dirt from his own *shendyt*, sweat beading at his temples, and beams at me with pride.

"You have the potential to be a fine fighter," he says.

"Potential?" I scoff with a smile. "I've beaten you every day this week."

"Never overestimate your own skill," he warns. "I've seen too many a good soldier let his own arrogance be his undoing."

He knows me too well. The few times I lost to him this month are when I thought I could easily win, only to find his staff a fingertip away from my face.

"But I will tell you . . ." He nudges me with his elbow.

"Tell me what?"

"You fight as well as any of the infantrymen I once commanded in the king's army."

"Iti . . ." I say with skepticism, tucking my black, chin-length hair behind my ears.

"I'd expect nothing less. How many years have I been teaching you?"

"Since I was five, maybe six floods?"

"Longer than most of the king's own men."

Even if I am a decent fighter, I'm not so arrogant that I think I'll ever fight for the Good God.

He puts a rough hand on my shoulder. "Would I tell you anything but Ma'at's own truth, Sati?"

"Maybe?" I say with a playful bump of my shoulder.

"Come on," he says. "Let's go home. Mereyet will start to worry."

Iti tells tales now and again, particularly of his time on the battlefield. What I know to be true is he has seen the Iteru rise and fall over forty times. He served on countless military campaigns in the northern lands of Retenu for both the Wasir King Seti and his son, who now sits on the Horu Throne—King and Good God Ramesses Usermaatre Setepenre. He's not as agile as he was when he first started teaching me to fight, with bones battle-weary and skin scarred by too many blades and the heat of the harsh Shemu sun. And even though I'm not of his or Mereyet's blood, he loves me. This much is true.

Sweat sticks my linen tunic to my back as we begin our long walk

PART ONE: THE PROVOCATION

toward the city. We pass barren fields, patchy with dried, stubborn emmer and barley grasses, and cross dry irrigation channels that should still hold water.

The farmland gives way to a dusty ring road encircling the white walls protecting the heart of Men-nefer, the Black Land's second largest city. It's the only place I ever remember calling home.

Iti greets the gate guards in their crimson leather uniforms and starched *shendytu* with hearty handshakes.

"The girl beat you again?" one of them teases.

"She earned it." Iti gives me a loving pat on the shoulder, and I beam.

Just inside the open gates, a colossal new pylon complex leads into yet another grand temple honoring the Good God and our city's patron deities. Multiple seated figures of the Good God flank its entrance, looming over us with their enigmatic faces and towering crowns.

"The king has been busy," Iti says. "It's just been painted."

In a riot of colorful reliefs carved into the sandstone, the Good God—the largest figure of all—aims his arrows at his Hittite enemies from his chariot. A battle fought sixteen years ago at Qadesh.

"This isn't how you told me it happened," I whisper, craning my neck to read the script.

Iti looks around to ensure no one could overhear and leans toward me. "It's not how I remember it."

"Why would the temple tell a story that isn't true? Isn't that against *ma'at*?" I keep my voice low, as though the Good God himself might hear me through his statues.

"It is *ma'at* to maintain order," Iti says, "and sometimes the Good God has to exaggerate his victories to do so."

He doesn't sound convinced of that last part, and I'm not satisfied with his answer either. He and I both know the danger of images like these. All along the Iteru, the Good God shows himself slaughtering his foreign enemies in the name of *ma'at*: all that is true, just, and balanced.

Meanwhile, people from all over the Good God's domain live packed together in cities like ours. What will it take to set us against each other, putting our tenuous peace in jeopardy?

"You have nothing to worry about, *benret*," Iti says, patting me on the shoulder.

I shake away my scowl and turn to a more hopeful subject. "What about the treaty?"

Iti squints at the relief again. "We can't be at a stalemate forever. Hatti needs our resources just as much as we need theirs, especially now." He taps the pendant hanging around my neck. "In even the bloodiest battlefields, a flower can grow out of the dust."

I'm fidgeting with it, flipping over the corners between my fingers. A small, golden lily blossom, inlaid with red carnelian, blue lapis, and green malachite. Iti gave it to me when I was learning to walk, and I've worn it every day since.

Iti beams. "And what a flower you've become."

"I hope that's not all I become."

"The lily is more than a flower. It's a blessing. It's hope. It's life itself, with the very sun at its center. And the gods have truly blessed your mother and me. We thought we would never have a child to call our own." He flicks my nose with his calloused finger. "Our Sat-reshwet."

Sat-reshwet. *Daughter of Joy.* Sati for short. Iti chose the name, but I don't think it fits me. Just like this *shendyt*.

"Little did we know, back when you were wriggling in a bundle of wool," he muses, "you'd become quite a fighter yourself."

A hint of sadness in his voice hides behind the pride in his face. Even though he loves teaching me how to spar, I suspect he would have preferred a boy child. A child who he could train and send to Per-Ramesses to join the Good God's military, to defend *ma'at* and the Two Lands the way he once did. Sometimes, despite myself, I wish the same.

I smile to reassure him he's doing the right thing, teaching me these skills reserved for men. "There's nowhere else I'd rather be, Iti. The dust in my eyes, and the sun on my face. It's where I belong."

"But I'm not sure how long I'll be able to continue," he says with a laugh, patting his belly. "Your mother's barley beer and honey rolls have made me a bit too round, and certainly not in fighting shape!"

"Oh, you still spar with ease."

"Not like back in the day, like at Qadesh." He looks again at the imposing image of the Good God in his chariot and shakes his head with a shade of disapproval.

We walk through dusty, smokey streets, first passing by the small homes of farmers and herdsmen who wave with a comfortable familiarity. We see them every day; they no longer question the girl in boy's clothing. "That's Captain Paser's girl," they say to each other, proud to have one of the Good God's own warriors in their midst, even if his daughter is a bit strange.

We thread deeper into the city, where the buildings grow taller to two and even three-story mudbrick houses. Awnings stretch from rooftop to rooftop, offering refreshing shade against Re's blazing heat, calming the tensions simmering beneath them.

As the sun barque begins its flaming, orange descent into the Western Lands, the city still bustles with traders and craftspeople. A woman in a linen sheath dress saunters past us with a basket of fresh dates balanced delicately upon her head. A gaggle of children chasing a puppy nearly crash into her, sending a handful of dates tumbling into the dirt. She scolds them as they run off. Another woman settles her baby on her hip as she carries an amphora in her other arm. Men haggle over their last barters of the evening, arguing about whether a bronze bracelet is worth the increased price. A smith hammers in his workshop, sweat dripping off his sooty face. He was here this morning.

If the flood doesn't rise enough this year, we could all be in danger, foreign or not.

When we reach the outer walls of our own home, the oniony scent of evening meals makes my belly rumble.

I turn to Iti before opening the gate leading into our courtyard.

"Umm, Iti..."

"'Umm,' what?"

"I might not have finished my Akkadian lessons last night..." I scrunch my face, waiting for his loving scolding.

"Well, if you don't finish the lessons I give you, you're never going to get better."

"All those little arrow-headed symbols make my eyes cross."

He crosses his eyes at me with a goofy grin. "The more you study, the easier it will be."

"But they all look the same. At least our language has actual figures and pictures."

"Knowledge is as valuable as gold. As silver, even," he says seriously. "It's how I rose so quickly through the king's ranks."

An opportunity I'll never have. That foreign language is for diplomats. Not a soldier's daughter. "When am I ever going to need Akkadian?"

"Languages open doors, *benret*." He leans toward me, resting his chin on his staff. "You must be prepared for what life gives you."

Without warning, he swings his staff. I block it before the end can even get close. A reflex from years of sparring.

"Good girl," he says, stepping back. He lowers his voice. "I don't believe I brought you all the way back from Qadesh for you to be a common *rekhyt* wife."

"Tell that to your mother," I say.

"Perhaps it's not up to your mother at all. Who knows what the gods plan for you?"

Sometimes, I wish they'd tell me.

Iti and I duck through the gate that opens into the small courtyard of the Per-seshen, House of the Lily. From the outside, it looks no different from any other building in Men-nefer, but for our family, it is a blessing from the gods. It's our welcoming refuge. With the gold Iti earned from his loyal service in the military, he built this three-level home, with my mother's significant input, of course. She insisted that we open our gathering room to travelers and traders seeking a fresh meal in exchange for a bit of whatever they carry on their barges or pack animals.

Outside the door to the ground floor, she crouches by a clay pot dangling above a steady fire.

"There you two are!" she says with relief as she stands, dabbing her brow with the hem of her sleeve. She greets Iti with a kiss, then embraces me a little too tightly before planting her lips on my cheek.

"Sounds busy in there," Iti says as the three of us go inside. He leans our staffs against the wall.

With a trill, Maimai, our resident striped cat, rubs her cheeks against my ankles. I scritch her behind the ears, offering her a cube of duck from a cutting mat on a low table. Maimai licks the meat from my fingers with her rough tongue.

"The cat can catch her own meal," Mawat chides. "I need the entire duck for the next batch of stew. Our gathering room is absolutely full tonight." She smiles as she wipes her hands on a rag. "I've already been able to barter for frankincense, a length of linen, and a basket of dried chickpeas. And I've overheard a few of the traders saying they have precious metals and gems—even iron—for the Good God's new capital."

I imagine a city covered in electrum, even more bright and shining than Men-nefer.

She gestures to the cooking pot. "Serve yourself the rest of that stew before I start the new pot."

As Iti hands me a small bowl, a loud, urgent knock sounds from the door to the gathering room.

Iti and I catch each other's eyes. Mawat's eyes lock on the door. That's not a knock from a guest who only wants a refill of beer.

Another knock. This one threatening and violent.

A voice bellows from the other side. "In the name of the Good God in the Great House, Horu on His Throne, Ruler of the Two Lands, we demand to speak with the owner of this establishment."

Iti's unruly brows furrow with wariness. Men in the Good God's service never demand to come into the kitchen. They sit in the gathering room, awaiting Mawat's lovingly cooked meals and a chance to chat with Iti, who regales them with his stories of the battlefield.

I step toward my fighting staff, but Iti darts out a hand to stop me, shaking his head. I grit my teeth in protest.

Mawat looks at Iti, then to the household altar in a niche in the wall where lion-headed Bes grimaces to keep *isfet*—chaos, violence, and injustice—away from our home. She whispers to herself, a prayer probably, then takes a deep breath and opens the door.

Two men the size of oxen fill the doorway, their chests bulging against their tan leather tunics. Their gold pectoral necklaces sway as they saunter over the threshold.

I whisper into Iti's ear, my feet on tiptoe. "No royal cartouche... or red leather." The way he glares at me tells me to be quiet. But these aren't the Good God's soldiers. They can't be. I can't find the royal seal anywhere on their uniforms or jewelry. How can they claim to serve the Good God without any proof?

The larger man scowls down at Iti and rests his hand on the hilt of a sheathed dagger secured to his gilded belt. The Good God's men don't dare threaten former military officers like that.

His companion's eyes scour my face, looking—no, hunting—for something before hooking on mine for what feels like an eternity. The corner of his mouth lifts in a sneer, twisting the angry scar slashing across his cheek.

"Who manages this place?" He keeps his eyes on me while the other prowls the perimeter of the kitchen, fingers tapping on his weapon.

"I do." Mawat steps forward, her voice steady. She gives him a sweet smile, as she would to anyone stopping here for the evening. "If you want a meal, you will need to step back into the gathering room."

"We're not here to eat," the scarred man grunts.

"Then what is your business?" Mawat asks.

The man with the dagger continues his investigation along the walls. He pauses in front of the staffs, and I fight every urge to pull them away from him.

"To keep the peace, of course," the scarred man says, folding his bulky arms.

Mawat forces a laugh in an attempt to ease the tension. "I can assure you our establishment is quite peaceful. Unless a guest has a bit too much beer."

It doesn't work. The scarred man takes a dense step toward her. "And who are your guests?"

"Merchants. Traders. An occasional nobleman."

"None of them ever seems . . . out of place?"

Iti and I glance at each other, neither of us liking where this questioning is leading. I retreat toward the fighting staffs with slow, wary steps.

"Anyone needing a hearty meal is welcome here," Mawat chirps.

Iti puffs up his chest, gesturing toward the beer jars in the corner. "It's no secret the Per-seshen has some of the finest beer in the city."

"By Nefertem, forgive me!" Mawat exclaims. "Would you like a cup? You must be parched!" The sweetness in her voice can't hide the shake in her jaw.

"Sat-reshwet," she calls to me, my full name, which she almost never uses, "pour these fine men a drink."

I reply with an overly enthusiastic nod. The man with the dagger doesn't move as I squeeze past him toward the jars.

As I'm about to pour two cups for these intruders, the scarred man holds up his hand with a scowl. "No. It distracts us from our work."

"And what *is* your work?" Iti presses, standing taller.

Before I know what's happening, the man with the dagger yanks me to him, his enormous hand clamped around my upper arm. The ceramic cup in my hand crashes to the floor.

Mawat's calm facade crumbles to a frantic flailing.

"Let me go!" I wriggle against the man's grip, but that only makes him hold me tighter.

Iti jumps at us. "Unhand her!"

The scarred man answers by drawing a dagger from his belt and pointing it at Iti.

"You dare threaten us in our own home?" Iti says.

Mawat goes still, not even breathing, eyes wide and unblinking. Iti doesn't say another word. I stop my squirming, but my heart beats against my ribs.

The scarred man glares at me, then at Iti. "Is this your daughter?" My belly drops with dread. They don't need to know the true answer to that question. Why are they asking it at all?

"Of course she is." Iti takes a step forward, but the scarred man holds his blade between them. Mawat yelps, retreating to the farthest corner of the kitchen.

My captor leans his crooked face into mine. His breath grazes my cheek as he looks at me the way a butcher looks at a fat goose. If I resist him, he might just gut me like one.

The scarred man circles us, flipping the knife between his hands.

"Funny," he says, examining me and glancing razors at Iti and Mawat. "She doesn't look like either of you."

My guts twist. My light green eyes don't match the deep silt-brown of Iti's and Mawat's, a difference that never gave any of us trouble before. Not like this.

"She's been in our care since before she could walk," Iti says. "And that is all you need to know."

The man's scar lifts with his skeptical cheek. "Where was she born?"

I struggle against my shallow breathing, now sure my heart will pound out of my chest. *No, please, Iti, you don't have to answer.*

"You say you are here on order of the Good God?" Iti asks, deflecting. "And why would he need to search the homes of the *rekhyt*?"

The scarred man huffs. "That's none of your concern."

A spark ignites in me, emboldened by Iti's questioning. I try again to pull free, but my captor wrenches my arm behind my back. I swallow a yelp. I can't let Mawat and Iti see how much it hurts.

"If you will not tell us your purpose here, then let go of our daughter," Iti commands with all the authority of his former military station. Mawat trembles behind him, hands over her mouth.

The scarred man saunters to the storage baskets against the wall, running his hand through the barley grains. "*Isfet* lurks around every corner." He peeks into the basket of lentils, as though Apep himself were hiding within.

Iti stands taller, calling on a lifetime of soldier's strength. "Believe me, I know *isfet* when I see it."

The scarred man darts to him, dagger pointed at his heart.

"Iti!" I lurch forward, and my captor yanks me back against him, wrapping his arm around me so tight I struggle to breathe.

"Then you can swear by the gods," the scarred man snarls, his blade pinching Iti's tunic, "by Re's barque, by the Hapiu Bull, by Wasir's missing flesh, you harbor no agents of *isfet* here?" He takes a threatening pause. "No foreigners?"

My breath trips in my throat. Are they really here for me?

"By the Good God's blue battle crown," Iti adds. "I swear it."

"Would you die by your word?"

I want more than anything to kick against my captor, to throw myself between Iti and that man with the jagged scar. The only thing holding me back is knowing if I do, that dagger would pierce Iti's heart before I even came close.

Iti's voice hesitates. "I would meet Ammit at the scales. My heart is light. We harbor no foreigners here." Dear Ptah, let them not notice the shake in Iti's jaw. He's not telling the entire truth or being completely *ma'at*, because I'm right here in the room with him.

The scarred man takes a step back, dagger still raised. "We will return to claim your oath if we discover you've made your heart heavy with a lie." He nods at my captor, who grunts with dissatisfaction as he tosses me away from him. I stagger, rubbing the burning skin where he held me.

The scarred man sheaths his dagger and pats the hilt, sight narrowed on Iti. A warning. A threat.

The two men shove past us toward the back door. They slam it behind them as they leave through the courtyard.

CHAPTER TWO

Mawat holds me tight as Iti paces the kitchen.

"How dare they?" he barks. "Threatening us like that? In our own home!"

Outside, the stew boils over the edge of the clay pot, and Mawat releases me so she can stir it. My arm throbs and aches, now blooming with a deep red bruise.

"Would the Good God really send soldiers out to search for foreigners?" I ask.

"In Men-nefer? Impossible. He wouldn't do such a thing." He doesn't look at me as he answers.

Mawat regards him with wide, harrowed eyes. "But what if they *are* following the Good God's orders? What then? What happens to our home, our family, our daughter?" Her normally golden cheeks are as pale as fish skin. I've never seen her like this, so vulnerable and scared.

Iti leans down and wraps a comforting arm around her shoulder. "Now, Mereyet, we must not jump to the worst conclusions."

"What's worse? The Good God ordering those brutes to hold a dagger to your chest—after all you've done for him—or a rogue group of men who think they can just barge in here and do the same?" Mawat wrests away from Iti.

"We have no idea who they are. What if they come back?" Her voice shakes, even as she tries to hang on to her motherly authority.

I turn to Iti. "You're a retired captain. You fought for the Black Land, for *ma'at*. Call for the sentries and have those men arrested!"

"Sati, I'm afraid it's not that simple," he says.

"Why not?"

"Those men... We don't know who they are, who sent them, where they came from."

"If we did, we could go hunt them down. Fight them." The words sound far more ridiculous after I've said them out loud.

"Absolutely not!" my mother barks.

"Your mother's right," Iti adds. "They're far stronger than I am."

And stronger than I'll ever be. I couldn't even pull free from the armed man's bronze grip. My incompetence only hardens my resolve.

"I'm no agent of *isfet*. If anyone dares attack me or any of us, I'll break their legs." My muscles tense, and a heat surges through me as I imagine a fray with some ugly, bald, sun-weathered brute. "I swear by Sekhmet's scepter, I'll bring fire upon anyone who tries to harm me or anyone else not born in this land."

Mawat reaches for me, an attempt to calm me. "Until we find out who these men are, who they're working for, what they want, we must be careful."

"What are we supposed to do?" As soon as I ask, I know how she'll answer. And I regret saying anything at all, because...

"If you want to prove you are a daughter of the Black Land, and all that entails, then you need to fulfill your duty as one." My mother's voice is stern and unyielding. "You need to trade that dirty *shendyt* for a dress."

"What temple would take a girl from Retenu? I can't even remember how to recite a prayer to Bes." I brace myself for Mawat's retort.

"Well, you know what your other option is."

"Ugh, Mawat—"

"You're not a child anymore," she says.

Iti steps closer to me. "Mereyet is right."

I can't believe he's siding with her. "Why are those my only options? What if I don't want to do either of those things?" What I want to do is to follow in Iti's footsteps, which is impossible. Maybe my refusal to choose a life in the temples or a husband's home does make me an agent of *isfet*.

"It's *ma'at* to marry," Iti says. "It's *ma'at* to start a family of your own." His voice wavers. "If you wish to prove you are a daughter of the Black Land, which, of course, you are, then you must act and live as one."

"Then why did you teach me how to fight?" I burst out. "Or take me out with you to the marshes to hunt?" An overpowering rush fills my ears. "Or read? Or write? Or learn Akkadian, for Ptah's sake? Why teach me any of it if you both just expected me to become the lady of some man's home?"

"Sati!" my mother scolds. Iti puts a hand on her shoulder to calm her, and she doesn't continue.

"I taught you these skills because you very well might need them," Iti says with a steady voice.

"I won't need any of them if I'm a common *rekhyt* wife."

Mawat ducks away from my father's hand. "You won't need any of them if those men take you, or worse!"

"I won't let them take me. Iti won't either." I tug lightly at the sleeve of his tunic. "Right?"

His shoulders sag. "I'm not in the same fighting shape as my Qadesh days."

That might be true, but how can he resign himself to such an intrusion? Such a violation of our home and our family?

"We can't let them scare us," I say. "Men like that won't tear us apart!"

Mawat shakes her head, forehead in hand. "Please, *benret*, I need you to make a decision. I've been asking you for months. Years, even—"

"Are we really cowering to these intruders? They weren't even wearing the royal cartouche or the red leather of the Good God's elite guard."

"Which makes them dangerous."

My retort sticks to my teeth. She's right. If they aren't royal guards, and instead are armed, bigoted men acting on their hatred and fears, then who knows what they might do next?

"All right, Mawat. If I wear the linen dress you gave me—and the wig—when I go out to run my morning errands, will you give me at least two weeks to decide?" Twenty days to wriggle my way out of this waterway my mother has dredged for me.

Her glare bores into me, stern and unyielding. She nearly speaks, likely to say, *Absolutely not*. Then she sighs. "All right. Two weeks. And remember to wear more kohl."

I wait for Iti to offer some kind of support or commiseration. Instead, he says, "It's for the best."

Not bothering to ask how he could agree with her, I huff up the stairs to my room.

○ ○ ○

The sun's morning rays cut through the window, and I shade my eyes with my arm as I sit up. Maimai is curled like a furry snail at my feet.

I'm still in my *shendyt*. I sigh and wriggle it down my hips and fling it into the dusty corner. There's no point in even adding it to Mawat's washing, because I won't be wearing it for a while. If ever again. Maimai leaps off my bed and trots down the stairs to begin her morning hunt.

Lucky creature.

I, however, have to make myself appear acceptable for going out into the market this morning. Acceptable, yes, but also hiding my true self. I have to be an obedient daughter of the Black Land and put on my linen dress and line my eyelids with extra kohl. And wear that wig. So much work just to prove I belong here, to hide my origins from merchants and traders who see me every day, and from others in the city who don't know me and will never know me.

As I open the acacia wood chest my parents gave me after my first blood, I want to be more grateful for everything in it, for even the rough talismans carved on its surface. The *ankh* for eternal life, an oil lamp for health, and the eyes of both Horu and Re on either side, to keep watch over me. Some protection they're offering now.

Inside, I find the linen dress Mawat gave to me for last year's Wepet Renpet festival. I wore it exactly once before shoving it back into the chest. Today, I wriggle into it, the folds cascading over the bruises and scrapes from yesterday's skirmish with Iti. I have to admit that it's beautiful, even if the hem constricts my steps,

In the distorted reflection of my bronze hand mirror, I paint lamp-black lines along my eyelids. Usually, I only line my eyes enough to shade them from the sun. Today I draw the shape out across my temples to the tops of my cheekbones.

I squint.

Despite my efforts, I've painted the lines crooked. It will have to do, because I'm not starting over.

As I pull the wig over my head, I cringe, the dyed black papyrus locks itching my scalp like a thousand tiny beetles.

Crooked makeup. Itchy wig. My transition into a proper lady isn't off to an auspicious start.

I hold the mirror up one last time, hoping to be at least a little pleased with the image. But my jaw sets.

Even if I wear the wig, paint my face, and hobble my way through the streets in my dress, I can't change the fact that I wasn't born of this land, of these people, no matter how much I try. Fighting the urge to rip the wig from my head, I instead throw the mirror down. It hits the floor with a clang.

○ ○ ○

Mawat is already in the kitchen, chopping the leeks and onions for the day's patrons.

I pass her to grab a large jar of beer for the grain seller and my wide market basket. She looks up and brushes my arm with her palm.

"Your kohl is crooked," she says.

"Good morning to you too, Mawat."

She grumbles. "Well, make sure you fix it before Tahir and Asata come by this evening."

"Neither of them will care if I'm even *wearing* kohl."

Mawat glares at me with the same sharpness as the odor of the onions.

"I'll fix it when I get home," I say, wanting to roll my eyes. "But I need to go before it gets too hot."

"Well, come back quickly," Mawat says as I walk out into the courtyard, "because I need you to help me prepare the evening meal. And no going out sparring with Tahir and Paser while I'm in here stirring the pots and tending to the breads."

I turn. "But Tahir always wants to tell me his stories. Iti too. What if they ask me to go out into the fields with them?"

"Let them reminisce about their military days on their own tonight, all right?"

"But Asata will be here, and she's always glad to cook with you. And isn't little Kala old enough to help in the kitchen?"

Her knife cuts through the onion to the metal tray with a crack. "No more arguing. Just go to the market, and don't make a fuss while you're there, so we can have a pleasant gathering with our friends." Another swift slice through the onions. "And be careful. Iti said he saw those men knocking on our neighbors' doors yesterday evening. If you see them, come home right away."

I clench my teeth. "Of course, Mawat."

PART ONE: THE PROVOCATION

○ ○ ○

"You look quite festive today, Sati!"

I stumble over the hem of my dress, nearly dropping the wide basket balanced on my head as I turn.

"Good morning, Resherem." The grain supplier's ruddy, puffy face greets me as I recover my balance. I force a smile. "May you live forever."

"What's the occasion?" he asks, wiping the sweat from his cheeks with the back of his arm. "Finally getting married? Who's the lucky boy?"

"No one," I say, hoping he won't press any further. So much for blending in.

"Well, whoever he is, I'm sure you'll make him very happy!"

I roll my eyes as I set down the basket.

"Looks like you have a jug of Mereyet's famous beer for me?" He pats his pudgy belly.

I'm relieved to rid myself of the heavy clay jar I carried through the streets to his stall this morning. "Do you have the barley?"

He drops a sack between us.

"Only one?" I ask. For as much beer as I've brought him, there should be two.

"I have to ration it these days."

"Oh, come on, Resherem." I press. "It will break my mother's heart if I come home with only one sack of grain." He's tried to be stingy with me before, but every time, I've bargained him into giving me more.

"It's all I can spare right now," he says with a dry sigh.

"But you said yourself that Mawat's beer is your favorite! Surely it's worth more than just one sack."

"It is," he concedes. Maybe I've been able to break through to him. He leans closer to me. "But it's those damn Hittites. They complain about drought in their own lands, and the Good God insists we help them while we face low waters of our own. What's left for us?"

The vicious tone of his voice makes my skin prickle.

"How could those *mhetyu* be in more need than we are? They take and they take from us."

Against my own instincts, I try to keep smiling.

He takes my silence as an invitation to continue, and his face goes red. "They're behind the drought. They must be. They and their gods are conspiring against Kemet, against the Good God, to stop the waters from returning."

He says aloud what I have feared. That people like him—our neighbors, our friends, our fellow *rekhyt*—blame foreigners for our meager harvests. The flood waters would be low regardless of how much grain the Good God gives away.

Holding my tongue gets a little harder. I hope he can't see the twitch in my jaw.

"The jackals want to take us down with them. If we're weak too, we can't take back the lands in Retenu and Amurru that are the rightful domain of our Good God. Besides, I doubt their harvests have been as poor as their king claims them to be. They're probably hoarding all of our grain in their own coffers, mocking and scorning us."

What a ridiculous idea, fueled by ignorance and a lack of faith in *ma'at*. "Oh, Resherem," I say as sweetly as I can muster, "the Good God would certainly know if the Hittite king were doing such a thing."

His face burns, like the dust in the Western Lands. "You want to know what I think the Good God should do?"

I really don't.

"He should hunt down anyone from that retched land, from all those vile northern places, and rid Kemet of them once and for all!"

With a racing heart, I step back and try not to curse. I've been visiting this man's stall almost every week of my life, first on Mawat's hip, and then by myself, and I've never heard such vitriol spew forth from his mouth. And doesn't he remember where I'm from?

Forget trying to bargain for that second sack of grain.

PART ONE: THE PROVOCATION

"I . . . I need to go." I heave the sack into the basket and the basket on to my head. In my haste, I nearly trip over my dress again as I stand.

He shrugs, the angry pink fading from his cheeks. "Well, watch out for *mheti* scum. I know they're out there."

I wave to distract him from my shudder, and continue through the market, the sharp Shemu heat useless against the chill running down my spine.

◦ ◦ ◦

As I begin my walk home, a man's deep voice sounds behind me, a threat under his calm resolve.

"Do you often speak to good women like that?"

I whirl, still balancing the basket. Tahir?

A few stalls down, a tall, muscular man with silt-dark skin and cloud white fuzz at his temples locks eyes with a younger man with bulky arms and venom in his sneer. Two others—one with a rough head cloth, the other with a layer of fuzz on his head—dressed in the same tan leather tunics, glower behind him.

"Tahir, please . . ." Asata, his lithe wife and one of Mawat's dearest friends, stops short of reaching for him and pulling him back. Kala, their daughter of nearly eight floods—by Nefertem, she's grown—cowers as she tugs on her mother's dress.

"No, Asata," Tahir says. "This man called you a—"

"Please," Asata pleads. "He didn't mean it. Let's just go."

"Oh, but I *did* mean it," the first man says.

I run toward them, but my dress hobbles my steps. And a crowd of onlookers gathers around them, blocking them from my view and hindering me further.

"I served the Good God as a commander," Tahir says. "Is this how you treat the king's own men?"

"It's just like him to appoint a filthy Tanehsi to lead his troops."

How dare he insult Tahir like that? How dare he insult the Good God like that? Who does he think he is?

"Ai, leave them alone," someone in the crowd says. "They're good people."

"Heh. No good people from Tanehsu!"

I hear the sickening smack of knuckles against skin. The crowd erupts in gasps and stifled screams, their curiosity deteriorating into a frantic chaos.

I try to shove my way through the clamor, but my foot catches on a stone. I tumble forward to the sandy ground, the basket and precious grain crashing down before me.

Curse this dress! I tear it apart at the sides and find my footing again. I have more to worry about than Mawat's scolding.

A few merchants and spectators yell at the attackers, but they keep their distance, the cowards.

Trying to get close enough to see what's happening is like swimming against the current of the Iteru.

But when I do, I go rigid.

The first man, his forehead slick with sweat, looms over a writhing figure. Tahir! The man in the head cloth jams his foot into Tahir's belly.

The crowd stares, mouths agape, yelling at the men, but none steps forward to do anything to stop them.

What would Iti do?

I swipe an support pole from the closest merchant's stall, sending the striped awning crashing over his baskets of dried fish. He yells something at me, catching the assailants' attention.

I jab at the largest one with my makeshift staff. "Leave him alone!"

He draws a knife from his belt and jams it at my throat. "You, stay out of it!"

I jump back, and the merchant runs back into his shop.

But I've distracted the brute enough for Tahir to grab his ankles, flinging him to the ground.

The other two rush for him, and Tahir throws a tight, well-trained fist at the youngest man's cheek. He returns the blow with a sickening smack. Tahir falls to the dirt, blood trickling from his nose.

"Stop!" I cry, my feet stuck to the dirt, arms shaking with indecision. Do I run at them and risk being attacked, too?

The first kicks him again, and Tahir moans, his resistance softening.

Finally, a man from the crowd jumps forward and grabs at the closest attacker, who growls and throws his elbow into the man's ribs.

"Please, stop!" Asata yells, her voice shaking, Kala clinging to her leg. The man in the headcloth wrenches her toward him. Kala screams as she's dragged through the dirt.

"We'll stop when your kind goes back to where you came from."

"They're from here!" I yell, my legs trembling as I hold the pole between me and the man with the knife.

He whips around and snarls at me, blade raised. *Please, Tahir, get up and get Kala and Asata out of here!*

Before I can whip his weapon from his hand, another sickening round of bone against bone and desperate moaning sounds behind him.

"No!" Asata can barely squeeze out her words. "You'll kill him!"

"That wouldn't be a bad thing."

The first man lifts his sandaled foot and smashes it against Tahir's chest. Crimson blood spills from his mouth. Kala shrieks, and Asata tries to leap to her husband. The crowd gasps, some screaming and others running from the scene.

I can't make myself move. I don't even know if I cried out. But if I try to stop him, he'll crush me, too.

He doesn't stop. He keeps stomping and kicking Tahir until a river of red runs down the street. Asata crumbles under her sobs.

Before I can will myself to run to her, the man in the headcloth grabs Asata; she struggles against him, a kitten in a crocodile's maw.

Where are the Medjay? Where are the Good God's guards?

I grip the pole, determined to do something. If I don't, I'll never forgive myself. I run toward Asata and Tahir.

The man with the short hair flings me against the wall. My head cracks against the mudbrick. The walls spin, blurry and distorted as my legs crumble beneath me.

"They're coming! Let's go!" A man's voice, frantic and guilty.

My vision steadies enough to see the men pull Tahir's body from the ground while another heaves Asata over his shoulder, and the third carries Kala. The two shriek and kick and pound their arms, but they're like no more than sacks of grain.

I try to run after them, but the pain in my head pulls me down, stabbing deeper, as Asata and Kala disappear into the distance.

CHAPTER THREE

Black clouds swim across my vision like carp. When they part, I realize I'm on the ground. My cough sends a searing ache behind my eyes.

Apart from a piercing ring in my ears, it's so quiet.

"Ai," a gentle voice says as something shakes my shoulder.

A haze of red forms into a tunic of leather. One of the Good God's city guards. He's too late.

"Aren't you Paser's girl?"

I nod and look at my knees. Blood has seeped through the pale linen of my dress, mingling with streaks of red dirt. I don't even care that Mawat will be so mad at me.

"I didn't recognize you in the wig. Let's get you home." The guard helps me to my feet.

As he walks me back to the Per-seshen, my heart shatters into a thousand jagged pieces.

"Who were those men?" I ask him.

He shakes his head with regret. "We don't know."

Of course he doesn't. He wasn't even there to see what happened. Neither were any of his fellow men.

"What in the name of Iset have you done to your dress?" Mawat scolds as I enter through the kitchen's back door. She swears under her breath, then raises her voice. "You think this is how you'll blend in?"

My head still throbs, like a knife is stuck in my forehead. I feel again for a wound, but the wig gets in the way. I tear it off and toss it aside.

"Sati! That wig cost me several jugs of beer! Where's your basket? The grain?" She shoots a hard look at me as the guard steps through the doorway. "What did you do?"

"My apologies, *nebet*," the guard says, his chin down. "There was an incident at the market."

Mawat's mouth gapes. "What? What happened?"

"I'll let your girl tell you. She did her best." The guard dips his head and disappears through the courtyard gate.

I can't force any words out at all as I lean against the wall.

Mawat's eyes widen as she looks at my forehead, then at my legs. "Re in his sun boat above, you're bleeding!"

She guides me to a cushion on the reed mats near the altar. She tries to pull the hem of my dress above my knees, but the blood sticks the linen to the oozing wounds. When she pulls again, the fabric rips away from my skin. I wince at the pain.

"By Ptah's beard, girl, I can't tell what's dirt and what's blood," Mawat says. She takes my chin in the tips of her fingers. "What in the Red Lands was the city guard talking about?"

The words form in my throat, but when I open my mouth, nothing comes out. Mawat rises to pour me a cup of diluted beer. I take a small sip as she rubs my back, waiting. Then she gathers some linen scraps, moistening them with water and honey, and tends to my knees. The white fabric quickly turns ruddy.

When I finally find the energy to speak, I say, "I tried to help them."

"Help who?"

"But I couldn't. They took them, Mawat."

"What? Who? Tell me."

I grit my teeth and pinch my eyes closed. The image of Tahir writhing under that man's foot roars in my memory. "Tahir . . . Asata. Kala." Tears try to force their way through my lashes. "Mawat, I think they killed Tahir."

"Oh, sweet Nefertem." Her face drops from motherly irritation to shock, her breaths turning rapid. "Are you sure it was Tahir?"

I nod. Mawat tightens her hold on me, and she tries to steady a quivering beneath her maternal calm. Her worst fears are coming true.

"No, it can't be," she says.

"I saw it all, Mawat. They took them."

"Who took them?"

I shake my head. I don't know. Not even our own city guards know.

Mawat pulls back. "And I take it from the state of you that you tried to stop whoever it was."

I nod.

"Sati . . ."

"Mawat, don't." My head hurts too much to brace myself for her chiding.

"They could have taken you, too. Killed you."

"I thought I could do something, make it right." And at the time, I truly did. "And no one else really tried." Everyone else just stood there, yelling at the men to stop. They acted tough but did nothing to help.

"Oh, my fierce girl. I know you did." She pulls me in again, closer. And now I'm sobbing. Heaving. I bury my face in her shoulders, the scent of her lily perfume oil a silent comfort.

Guilt twists around me like my mother's arms, squeezing me so I can no longer move. I failed our friends. Even with all of Iti's training, I failed them.

Mawat sighs into the silence, fighting back her own tears.

We hold each other for a long time.

"He won't be greeted by Anpu, will he?" I ask. With no one to prepare his body, to write the spells, to open his mouth, Tahir stands no chance at weighing his heart at the scales.

She pulls away, fingertips firm on my shoulders. "Oh, he will, *benret*. He will."

But I see the doubt in her quivering lips.

○ ○ ○

When Iti returns from hunting not long after, with a duck much smaller than usual, Mawat tells him what happened.

His despairing roar rises into a fury.

"Where were the city guards? Where were the Medjay?" He paces, clenching his fingers into fists again and again. "How could they abandon one of their brothers?"

He pounds the wall, sending up a trickle of dust. I want to go to him, but despite years of sparring with him, I've never seen him so unmoored.

"Curse them!" he cries. "Curse them all!"

"Paser..." Mawat holds out a hand to calm him, but he brushes it away.

"Tahir risked his life for me at Qadesh. And now armed strangers beat him into Oblivion in the clear sight of Re?" His glistening eyes hold on me, then my bandaged knees. "And look what they've done to our girl!"

"I'll be all right," I whisper.

A strangled growl claws up from his belly. "The Administrative Palace will hear of this! Of what happened yesterday and now in the market!"

Before Mawat can stop him—if she even could—he swipes his staff from its place against the wall and thunders through the back gate.

"May Bes protect us," Mawat says.

We're going to need someone more powerful than Bes. His tongue and nether bits aren't nearly terrifying enough to drive away whatever happened today.

Mawat tells me to go upstairs to clean myself up. I change into a clean shift and wipe the kohl from my eyelids. I retrieve the mirror from the floor and regret how I threw it. I'm a mess. My eyes are puffy, and I have a crusty cut on my forehead. A far cry from the lady I tried to be this morning.

When I return to the kitchen, I find it bustling with several of Mawat's friends—all women with children of their own. They insist she sit while they slice the vegetables, skin the duck, and chop the meats. When they see me, they rush over in a cloud of perfume and linen, smothering me in their motherly embraces. At least they think I'm one of their own.

While they fill our kitchen with chirps of the latest gossip and speculations on who's marrying whom and whatever *is* that boy Niankh up to, because they only ever see him with Intef's son, and he really should settle down soon, Mawat and I stay silent. Although I'm sure they've heard of the men prowling the streets, they never mention them. They know better than to talk about it in front of Mawat.

When I try to pour the beer or peek into the clay oven to check on the bread, the women nudge me aside, insisting they have everything under control.

And every time a guest knocks on the door, I hope against the truth it's Tahir. That today was a terrible dream. That he, Asata, and little Kala will visit us tonight, and we'll share a meal together, and Tahir and Iti will reminisce about their military days. But it's only merchant after trader, faces we don't recognize and might never see again.

○ ○ ○

After the evening meal rush, I escape to my room and collapse on my straw-filled bed. I stare at the little five-pointed stars painted on the ceiling. My heart has a gaping, empty place where our friends once were. Friends who couldn't hide their heritage behind makeup and a wig.

I overhear Iti and Mawat talking downstairs, and I creep to the doorway to listen.

"They said they'd look into it," Iti scoffs. "One of the Good God's commanders bled out on our streets, and they'll 'look into it.'"

He must have just returned from the Administrative Palace. From the incessant brushing of the soles of his feet against the reed mats covering the kitchen floor, I can tell he can't stop pacing.

"I warned you about teaching Sati how to fight," Mawat says.

Iti's footfall ceases. "Sati has nothing to do with this!"

"She's going to get herself into far more trouble than just skinned knees. And filling her head with all your war stories? She ripped the dress I made her last year, the one I worked on for an entire season!"

"At least she tried to help!"

"Is this what you want?" Mawat counters. "Our only daughter putting herself in harm's way? Skinned knees and bruises I can heal, but what if . . ." Her voice trails, leaving behind it a thick silence.

"Maybe we've seen the worst of it," Iti sighs. "I'll barter for more linen tomorrow, all right?"

Mawat says nothing, but her apprehension crawls up the stairs.

I slump against the wall to the floor and hug my knees to my chest. I hate feeling so helpless.

The sun barque ducks below the horizon, and the sky burns as Nuit's stars and Khonsu's moon overtake the crimson clouds. If only I could erase what happened in the market, like each night does to the day. To make everything right again.

What did Tahir ever do to those brutes besides be from Tanehsu? And that scarred man and his "friend." What have foreigners ever done to them, anyway?

With a faint mew, Maimai trots through the doorway, her tail as elegant as the royal crook.

"What would you do, Maimai?" I don't expect an answer, but her ears prick up.

A wild, aimless flame grows in my heart.

"I want to destroy those horrible men," I say. "Beat them senseless with my staff."

Indeed, I want to be like Iti. To fight for what's right, true, and just. To balance the scales and bring *ma'at* to those men's already leaden hearts. To be like Sekhmet herself, destroying the enemies of the feather and the double crown of the Two Lands.

To be the fighter Iti brought me up to be.

○ ○ ○

All night, horrifying, violent images flash before me until the gentle glow from Khonsu's moon fades away from the darkness and gives way to Re's sun barque. Maimai stays with me, her body warm and soft against my skin, as if she knows what haunts me.

When a shard of sunlight pierces its way into my room, I give up on any hope of sleep.

I pad downstairs, where Mawat is already dutifully preparing meals for us and the day's guests. Thankfully, Mawat's fussy friends are long gone, but I suspect they'll be a regular feature in our home for some time. She looks up from kneading honey rolls on a stone slab on the kitchen floor. She's been crying.

"My precious girl," she says as she gets up to give me another tight embrace. But she's not saying it to me; she's reassuring herself. She holds firm when I try to pull away. I surrender to her until she lets me go, keeping her hands on my shoulders.

"Where's Iti?" I ask.

"Oh, he's gone out to get more cabbage and turnips, and figs, too. I know how much you love figs—"

"But that's my job, Mawat," I start.

"Well, we wanted to let you rest," she says.

I don't need to rest.

She hesitates and wipes her hands on a rag. "Perhaps it's best you don't go to the market right now, *benret*." She crouches to return to her kneading.

"But Mawat, Iti might have his friends in town, but he doesn't know the city like I do. He doesn't know the merchants. He can't barter like I can. Iti's a hunter, one of the best. Going to the market is my—"

"Sati!" She slams the dough on the stone.

I grit my teeth, preparing for what I fear she'll say.

"You won't be going to the market," she bursts.

"Mawat—"

"You won't be going anywhere for as long as I say!"

My breath sticks in my throat. How could she? Does she really want to trap me in my own house?

"And how long is that?" I counter.

Her jaw trembles as we stare at each other. Mawat returns to her kneading, pounding too hard at the dough. I wait for her answer, but she won't speak.

"For how long?" I press, holding back tears of my own.

It isn't right to push her when she's so vulnerable, but I want an answer. I stare at her, and she only looks at her hands. All I can hear is her short, rapid breaths.

She finally looks at me. "I won't have you ending up like Tahir and Asata!" A tear slides down her cheek, and she wipes it away with the back of her arm. "I just can't."

Before I can say anything else, Iti returns from the market with a basket full of goods. His face is red and swollen. He probably didn't sleep much either. He greets us with terse embraces, an unquenchable vengeance simmering beneath his skin.

I inspect the vegetables. The turnips are too small, and the lettuce leaves are bruised. Iti is always too nice to the farmers and merchants. But I say nothing.

The rest of the day blurs together, like ink under water.

Later that afternoon, Iti takes his bow and quiver from their corner near the courtyard entry. "I'm going out to the riverbank," he says.

My heart wants nothing more than to go with him.

He must see my expression. Iti kisses me on my forehead, where yesterday's cut has scabbed.

"I'm sorry," he whispers. "I'm sure she'll change her mind in a few days."

The shake in his voice betrays his words.

CHAPTER FOUR

Two weeks after the Scarred Man and his brutish friend threatened us, I sit at the edge of my bed, a supper bowl of fresh lentil stew cupped in my hand. As I'm about to roll out the long scroll of papyrus Iti left for me several days ago, my doorway curtain opens.

"What are you reading?" Mawat asks from behind my shoulder.

"*The Tale of Sanehat.*" I try not to glare at her. If it weren't for her forcing me to stay within the confines of our home, I could go have adventures of my own instead of having to read about them. Besides, I know why she's really here. She isn't here to ask about the story. She's here to force me to make a choice about my life.

"One of your father's favorites. I think Sanehat reminds Paser of you," she says.

A warrior and nobleman from Kemet who's trapped in Retenu? I suppose if we flip the settings, he's like me. And if Mawat would leave me alone, I could finally find out whether he returns home. He was about to set sail for Ithtoue, our long-ago capital city, when she interrupted.

"But he's actually from here," I grumble.

"And he is blessed by the gods." Mawat sits next to me, a conspiring smile on her lips. "Perhaps we should ask the gods what they plan for you." She shakes a small leather pouch. Her divination amulets.

I roll my eyes and hold back a sigh. I just want to read and eat my stew.

"Mawat, the gods—they don't speak to me. It's you they love. Before Iti marched to Qadesh, they said you would have a child."

"Yes, a child born of the battlefield, Tawaret said." She gazes wistfully at the starry ceiling. "I didn't believe her. But after several months away, Paser returned with a bundle swaddled in linens woven with royal electrum. My faith in the gods never faltered after that. How could it? They brought you to me."

"That doesn't mean they want to speak to me. They finished their work the moment I arrived here."

She makes a thoughtful sound, the kind she does when she's about to try to convince me of something. "Well, just as your father's last military campaign marked a great change in our lives, perhaps it will take a time of great change for the gods to speak to you, too."

"We tried after my first blood. Besides, why would they care about me, a girl from Retenu? They have temples full of beautiful priestesses offering them platters of dates, figs, and pomegranates to keep them happy. Why would I be anything to them?" Not even Bes speaks to me. He just mocks me every day with that lolling tongue.

And really, all I want right now is to find out what happens to Sanehat.

"Let's at least try. And it's been two weeks since we made our deal."

I was wondering how long she'd sit here before bringing it up.

"I don't want to know what the gods plan for me." Especially if it's more of being cooped up inside, whether it be here or anywhere else.

"If not your future, then maybe the gods will give us some guidance?"

"If they can find Sanehat in Retenu, then why should we have to call on them? They must know where I am. And it's not like I'm going anywhere." I hunch my shoulders over my bowl, as if trying to protect myself from the future, or even from the gods themselves.

"Sati," Mawat scolds. "Let me at least try to pass on this one ability to you. Your father has had so much time to teach you his skills." Indeed, my room is full of slate tablets and unfurled papers. "Teaching you to hear the *heka* is my gift to you."

She pulls a small linen cloth from her waistband and lays it out on the floor in front of us.

Apparently we're doing this tonight, whether I want to or not.

"Finish your stew," she says. "I need the bowl."

I slurp down the remaining broth and meat and wipe my mouth with the back of my hand. She takes the bowl and sweeps out the inside with the edge of a rag.

"And fetch me your lamp."

I place the clay oil lamp on the cloth in front of us.

Mawat pulls a lump of golden frankincense from her pouch and carefully places it in the bowl. She holds it over the lamp's flame, and the resin sputters and melts, bubbles forming at the edge. A thread of smoke reaches up, growing into an undulating veil. Only the gods know what that dollop of sap from the land of Punt must have cost her, or for how long she has been saving it.

The sweet, heady, citrusy smell of frankincense fills the air. Even if the gods never speak to me, something about the incense makes me believe that one day they might. It's no wonder the priests of the Good God prize it so highly. I close my eyes for a moment as its tendrils twist into my chest and head. I sense Mawat rise as she wafts the delicate smoke into every corner of the room, purifying the space and clearing the way for the *heka*. If it deigns to show itself tonight.

As the smoke winds its way around us, Mawat prepares the altar. Eye of Horu on the right, Eye of Re on the left, both a dark blue lapis, the color of the life-giving Iteru and the sky above. She then sets down a small green statue of Ptah, patron god of our city, who through his very thoughts brought the world into existence.

She closes her eyes and takes a deep breath.

"Repeat after me," she instructs. "We call upon you, Ptah, Beautiful of Face. Ptah, the Lord of Truth. Ptah, Master of Justice."

I echo her words with as much enthusiasm as I can muster.

She points to my neck. "We'll need your pendant."

I dutifully untie the cord and hand the tiny flower to her. She places it in front of Ptah.

"We call upon you, Nefertem, the Water Lily of the Sun. Nefertem, whose tears created humanity."

Despite doubting her prayer will work, I close my eyes and repeat her words.

She then draws forth a carving of Sekhmet, Ptah's consort—scepter in one hand, the *ankh* of eternal life in the other, and the sun disk upon her head—and places it at the center.

If Mawat means to ask for Sekhmet's guidance, she must be far more scared for our safety than she wants to admit.

"We call upon you, Sekhmet, Protector of the Black Land. Sekhmet, Enforcer of *Ma'at*. Oh, Sekhmet, Great of Terror and Great of Flame." Finally, a deity I can relate to. "Come to us, Sekhmet, Lady of Slaughter." My spine straightens at the word. *Slaughter*.

But nothing happens.

She returns to my side and holds the bowl over the lamp flame. The last charred remnants of the incense sputter into smoke. A haze hovers in the room, making everything soft and mysterious. Once the resin stops bubbling, Mawat sets the bowl aside and kneels before her temporary altar. She gestures for me to do the same, but I hesitate. She could do this by herself. Why does she have to bring me into it? I kneel beside her and close my eyes anyway.

Mawat continues, her voice solemn and commanding. "We call upon the gods tonight. We seek your wisdom."

My forehead goes warm. Is that the *heka*? Or is it the Shemu heat and a smoke-filled room?

"We are humble in your presence," Mawat says. "Come to us and protect this daughter of the Black Land, saved by the God on Earth, Lord of Fate, in the Red Lands of *isfet*."

Behind my eyelids, I sense the tiny lamp flame growing taller.

Mawat's voice is steady. "Guide us in our time of strife. Show us the way by which our daughter should go forth into her next days."

A burning invades my chest, racing into my shoulders, my arms, my fingertips.

I open my eyes for a moment. A calm engulfs Mawat. She's fallen into a trance.

"We call upon you, oh Sekhmet, woman who plays the role of the male, and whom every god fears!"

The lamp flame explodes, and I tumble back. I hold up my arm to shield my face, squinting so I can see something, anything.

I risk lowering my arm to look for Mawat. Golden, radiating light, as powerful as the sun, fills every corner of my room, while a ring of fire rises around me. But my eyes don't sting, and my skin is cool to the touch. The hem of my shift is immaculate. Not an even a singe.

I need to find Mawat. I cry out for her, unable to see through the blazing inferno.

A purr resounds from all directions.

Your mother is here, and she is safe. A woman's voice, intense and dangerous.

"Where is she?" I cry, my mouth dry with desperation.

I've been waiting for you.

"Waiting? Who are you?"

The confines of my room fall away, the mudbrick crumbling into desert dust.

Brick by brick, stone walls build around me. Temple walls. The electrum plating nearly blinds me as a marsh of columns grows like river sedge, stretching back as far as I can see. Ebony black statues of the lioness goddess appear between each of them.

They speak to me as a single voice.

You know me. You have always known me.

I do know her, but it's impossible. As impossible as the wall of flames climbing as high as the columns themselves, as tall as date palms, as the pyramids of our ancestors.

I knew you would call for me eventually. Her roar thunders in my ears. I need to get out of here. I need to find my way home.

I run down the endless hall, only to find more columns, more statues of the goddess, and so much fire. This hall goes on forever, for eternity. There's no way out. Wherever I run, I find myself in exactly the same place as where I started.

Conceding my defeat, I hunch over my thighs, gasping for air.

Running from me? You might have been born in the land you call Retenu, but you have always been mine. And you have so much to learn. If you heed my guidance, you will.

"Your guidance?" The flames lick against my skin, rough and prickly as cat tongues. "Why now?"

Fate comes as it will. You think you must choose between two paths. But you will take another.

"Another path? What other path is there?"

You will journey far from here. And you will carry out my justice.

"What? How? And what do you mean, 'your justice'?" I hear my own voice blurt out, like it's disconnected from my throat. How can I journey if I'm stuck in the Per-seshen, and can't even leave the safety of our courtyard? "Was it your justice that killed Tahir?"

Patience, green-eyed child.

"I don't have time to be patient."

With patience and discipline, you will be my eye. You will be my flames. You were born of battle and blood. And to battle and blood you shall return.

The goddess herself steps out from the seething wall of fire, her mane flowing forth from under her solar crown. Red stains wind up the hem of her dress, snaking over her thighs. She bares her teeth and growls.

I don't know whether to drop to my knees or run.

Something warm and wet covers my feet. I gasp. Blood. A river of blood runs through the columned hall to an opening no bigger than a flea in my sight, far off in the distance.

The goddess laughs.

Horu on His Throne is waiting. The might of the stars will guide you.

"What stars? Guide me where? Where am I going?"

The temple goes black. My painted ceiling gives way to a river of stars. Maimai yowls as a line of white fire streaks across the sky, bursting into millions of sparks.

○ ○ ○

I'm heaving for breath, doubled over on my knees on the floor. "What in the Black Land was that?"

My mother jumps to her feet. "I knew it was your time!" She picks up the figure of Sekhmet and cups it in her hands. She's smiling, bouncing, laughing. "It finally worked!"

Mawat doesn't notice I'm having difficulty sitting upright. When I press myself to my knees, stars fill my vision. Stars. I look up. But I only see the crude painting on the ceiling.

"What did you see?" she asks. "Tell me. Tell me!"

The snarls and growls of the goddess swirl in my thoughts. What I saw was terrifying, and what the goddess said to me made no sense. I struggle to make myself speak.

"I was in a temple. It went on forever."

"And?"

"And the goddess was everywhere, all around me."

"It was Sekhmet, right?"

I nod, my heart finally slowing. "There were so many flames. As bright as the sun."

Mawat's proud smile flattens.

"We walked through a river of blood." I look down, and my feet are clean.

All trace of Mawat's excitement disappears.

"Did she say anything?" she asks, her voice more solemn. "Did the goddess say anything?"

"She said, 'You will be my flames.'"

For a moment, Mawat's breath stops. "But her flames destroy, they kill . . ." She looks out the window. When she turns back to me, I can tell she intended to say more.

"She said I would journey far. That 'Horu on His Throne is waiting.' It makes no sense."

"No, no, no." Mawat shakes her head. "How can that be true? Horu on His Throne . . . that's the Good God. Why would he be waiting for you?"

Her fingers fidget with the tiny statue. So small, so innocuous. How could a little incense and soapstone be so powerful?

"Maybe it's a mistake," she says as she drops the figure of Sekhmet into the pouch. "How could you possibly go anywhere, let alone to the Good God?"

"That's what she told me." My heart goes light at the mere thought of it. This might be my way out.

"I know, *benret*, I know. You want to go back to the market, to haggle with the merchants, because Iti doesn't do it as well as you do—"

"She said something else."

The color fades from Mawat's face. "What else?"

I pause, knowing what I say next will only make her more frantic, make her want to trap me here further, but it will weigh on my heart forever if I keep it concealed. My fingers reach for the lily pendant around my neck, only to find bare skin.

"'You were born of battle and blood. And to battle and blood you shall return.'"

Mawat's eyes widen. She doesn't even blink.

"She said I would carry out her justice."

"How can that possibly be true? You're supposed to marry or join the priestesses in the temple. That's why we called on her. To reveal your path."

"Maybe I'm not supposed to take either path. Maybe that's not my fate."

My mother's jaw sets. She looks away again. I wait for her to speak. Surely, she's trying to figure out some way to spin my vision into her idea of what my life should be.

After a long pause, she turns back to me. "She said something about the stars?"

I nod.

"What was it again?"

"She said, 'The might of the stars will guide you.' It was the last thing I heard before Maimai yowled."

"But Maimai didn't yowl."

"She didn't?"

Maimai sits like a bread loaf at the foot of the bed, just like when Mawat came upstairs.

Mawat sighs. "Perhaps you were right."

"Right about what?"

"We shouldn't have called upon the goddess tonight." She swipes up my pendant and shoves it at me, and quickly tucks the other amulets and statues back into the pouch, fighting the tremble in her fingers.

"It's getting late," she says, shaking out the linen cloth before tucking it into her waistband. "Finish reading about Sanehat, then get some sleep, and we'll see what tomorrow's sunlight reveals."

She places a pert kiss on the crown of my head before brushing the curtain away from the doorway and going downstairs. Her sadness and confusion linger among the last puffs of incense.

I sit on the edge of my bed. The words of the goddess echo in my ears. *The might of the stars.* As I look up at my ceiling, I search my heart for what that could mean.

CHAPTER FIVE

The next day, I join Mawat in the courtyard. She hands me an ebony-handled knife, and as I strip the skin from the goose carcass, a bit of the remaining blood drips to the dust.

I see myself back in the market, watching the river of ochre spill forth from Tahir's mouth. I try to run to him, but my feet stick to the earth. Blood rises around my ankles. My knife turns into a curved *khopesh*, and a figure with no face walks toward me. He wears the royal seal, but he's dressed entirely in red, the color of the Western Desert, of all things *isfet* and *deshret*. I can't move as the blood continues to rise, over my shins, up to my knees . . .

"Sati?" Mawat says. I shake myself back to the courtyard as a dry breeze blows through the sycamore tree that shades us. Doves coo at each other in the branches.

I'm still holding the goose.

"Are you all right?" she asks.

"I'm fine." I'm not fine. I didn't sleep much last night. These waking nightmares creep into my thoughts again and again. They stalk me at the corners of my sight, waiting to catch me off guard. "Almost finished."

I pull the remaining skin off the goose and put it in a large clay bowl. We'll need it for stock. Maimai threads through my ankles, demanding a handout. I give in and tear off a bit of the skin for her.

Today, Mawat doesn't scold me. Just as well, because she's scolded me enough since those men barged into our kitchen.

Iti returns from the market. The sacks of vegetables are larger.

"You're getting better at bartering," I tease, hoping to shake off whatever darkness just came for me.

Iti chuckles. "But I suspect you could still get better deals?"

I inspect the baskets. Decent onions and garlic, a round eggplant, and a week's worth of lentils. "Hmm." I give him a teasing smirk. "Probably."

He bumps me with his elbow, gives Mawat a kiss, and heads into the kitchen to store the new supplies. He returns to the courtyard right away, holding something behind his back.

"Come with me," he says as he puts a hand on my shoulder.

Mawat nods her approval. "It's all right. I'll finish up."

Curious about how Iti convinced Mawat to let me leave the kitchen, I follow him to the rooftop. Under the linen canopy, I gaze across the city to the river, beyond the reeds, to the fields I haven't visited in days. A hot wind rushes up from between the buildings. Sekhmet's breath.

"Mereyet told me what happened last night," Iti says.

"She did?"

"That the Powerful One finally spoke to you?"

"It wasn't as glorious as Mawat wanted it to be." I flip my pendant between my fingers as I recall the columned hall and Sekhmet's blood-soaked dress.

"It sounds like whatever happened was rather significant."

"If I only knew what it means. None of it made sense." The low waters of the river sparkle . . . like the night sky. "Mawat seemed especially worried about the part about the stars."

"The might of the stars will guide you," he says with a glint in his eye.

"Why are you smiling? How is that a good thing?"

"Mereyet didn't want to consider what it means. She has a specific vision for you. And I admit that for a time, I agreed with her. And while I don't think I can change her mind—not yet anyway—I convinced that her I should give you this." He presents me with a bundle of rough, woven wool. "For you, my little lion cub."

"What is it?"

"Unwrap it. You'll see." He puts his hands on his hips.

I pull back the first layer of wool, then another, uncovering ebony, carnelian, malachite, and gold, and a sheath of blood red leather. A dagger?

I hand Iti the fabric wrapping, and pull on the hilt, revealing a glimmering blade as long as my forearm. I turn the weapon over again and again in my hands, enraptured by the jewels and color of the inlay. My eyes travel to the blade itself. I can hardly believe it.

"Is this iron?" Iron is legendary. I've read about it in stories, but I've never seen it, let alone held it. It's nearly impossible to find, and even more difficult to smith. Only royalty and noblemen ever get near it.

"Yes," he answers, beaming. "Ore from the heavens themselves."

"The stars." I wrap my arms around Iti, smiling for the first time in what seems like an eternity. "It's so beautiful," I say as I pull away and continue to marvel at the dagger.

"It served me well on the battlefields of Qadesh. A gift from our Good God."

I imagine a younger Iti on the battlefield, Tahir by his side, defending the Good God, fighting for *ma'at*. That will never be me.

"I'm not sure what I'll do with it," I say. "It's not like I'm fighting anyone."

"Well," Iti says, "what else did the Powerful One tell you?"

"There was so much."

"Something about a journey? Blood and battle?" The corner of his mouth turns up in a grin. How can he possibly be happy about that?

"It can't be true." I shake my head. "I'm supposed to stay here, in Men-nefer. Get married. Or serve in the temples."

"But what if you *do* have another path?" His satisfied smile widens.

"Iti, don't make it seem possible." I don't understand why he's pressing me.

"The Powerful One herself told you it's possible."

"Why are you even saying that? Mawat won't let me leave the Per-seshen. I haven't even gone out to the gathering room to serve beer to the guests. And we haven't sparred or hunted together in so long."

My cheeks grow hot, and it's not the sun or the winds blowing across the city from the Western Lands.

"I can't accept your dagger, Iti," I say as I return the blade to the sheath. I hold it out to him, hoping he'll take it back. The possibility of what he's hinting at is too much, too strange, and too fantastic for me to even entertain.

I keep my arms out, the dagger in my palms, but he refuses to take it back.

"It's yours." He folds his arms sternly.

"What in the Red Lands am I going to do with it?" I ask.

We stare at each other in a stalemate.

Finally, he puts his hands on my shoulders.

"Sati," he says, "you are a better fighter than so many I shared ranks with. Your wit, reflexes, and intuition have always been superior."

"What does it matter?"

"You're quick and smart," he continues. "More so than some of the greatest warriors I've known."

I want him to stop. For days, I've pushed away this ridiculous idea, despite every bit of my skin wanting nothing more than to be a fighter like him.

"I can't be a warrior," I say. "No woman can. And you told me not to become too sure of myself."

Women aren't allowed to be soldiers. And even if they were, I'm still not allowed to leave the house. I just started to accept my fate as a domestic woman, and he plants this seed in my mind that I could be something different. How could he when he knows my future is to be confined, painted, and dutiful?

"Well," Iti says with a glint in his eye. "I've heard my fair share of stories about fierce young women like yourself fighting alongside our kings."

"It's not *ma'at*." And it's an utterly ridiculous idea. Sometimes I wish he'd stop telling me these tales of wonder.

"*Ma'at* isn't always as clear as we would like it to be," Iti says. "Remember the temple walls? Just as our Good God portrayed himself as the victor at Qadesh, the truth is far more complex and hidden. Just like Amun in his temple."

"What are you saying?"

He smirks and folds his arms. "There's a reason I had you read about Hatshepsut and Sobeknefru when you were still a girl." Women who acted as kings. They wore the royal headcloth and the blue war crown. But their successors tried to erase them from the temple walls, and some even doubted, and still doubt, their womanhood. Others deny their existence, because women in positions of military power court the dark waters. But *isfet* never came for us. In fact, their rule made us stronger, more prosperous.

Even so, I'm not a royal daughter. I'm not a Great Wife with aspirations of kingship. Women like me, *rekhyt* women, are never allowed to fight alongside the Good God.

But maybe...

"So, you're saying women have fought alongside the Good God? That women have fought for our kings? For the Black Land? It can't be true."

"Why would it not be? If women can become the Good God, then why can't they fight for him?"

I can't believe what he's saying. I can't believe he dares say such things at all.

"But common women? Daughters of soldiers? Like me?"

"Indeed, I have heard tales. I suspect some even snuck their way into our ranks." His conspiratorial smile grows wide.

But I am not smiling. "And you never told me."

"I never thought I had to tell you," he sighs.

I doubt that's true. He knows if he had told me, I'd get ever more ideas about leaving, pulling away from my duties to the family, and not following the path Mawat wants for me.

"But Sekhmet seems to have greater plans for you," he says. "And I have witnessed her power many times, healing the ill, punishing transgressors, protecting the Good God himself."

A tiny hole of betrayal bores its way into my heart. Years of feeling alone, strange, and maybe even a mistake, and he never once gave me hope of doing the one thing I've dreamed of my entire life. Becoming the one thing he's been teaching me to be.

"How could you teach me to fight, to read?" I burst out. "And expect me to be content with marriage or the temples?"

He doesn't reply.

I look out across the city, seeking answers that aren't there. I pace the rooftop, flipping the dagger over and over again in my palms.

"I wanted you to be educated," he says after I've crossed the roof several times, "the way a boy would be."

"And for what? How could you never tell me there are other girls out there who've fought in the name of the Good God? And now you give me a dagger, after I haven't seen anyone except you or Mawat in two weeks? You even agreed with Mawat when she told me I had to marry."

I search his face for an answer, but he looks to the floor with remorse.

"Admit it, Iti," I say. "You would have preferred a boy child."

He doesn't answer. He doesn't even look up.

"Sati—"

"But I'm not a boy. And I'm stuck here. With a weapon I can't use."

I turn away, cradling the dagger, not knowing whether I should keep it. I suppose I could use it if that man with the scarred cheek and his friend return, not that Mawat would even allow me to be in the same room with them if they did. But all other times? Such a precious object would be useless in my hands. I turn back to search my father's face for some sort of guidance, that he'll know what to do. He must know giving me something so valuable will only fan the fighting flames in me.

He stares off into the distance, his arms still folded across his chest, as if to protect himself from the truth. He's partially responsible for this mess we've found ourselves in, having taught me skills women so rarely learn. And when we do, we are suspect, agents of Apep.

The two of us fall so quiet that I can hear the footsteps of passersby bouncing off the walls of the buildings below.

I finally decide to break our silence. "I can't be your daughter and a daughter of the Black Land at the same time."

Iti turns to me, the grin long erased from his face.

"If you could have your way," I continue, "I'd be like a son, carrying on your legacy. But I can't do that. And Mawat . . ."

"She wants you to be happy," Iti interjects. "And to be safe."

"Well, it doesn't seem like I can be both." I examine the weapon; it's more than iron and gold. It's my father's history of service to the Good God, of battle victories, and of protection and honor. It has certainly spilled the blood of enemies and worthy warriors. And all of them were men.

I offer the hilt to him. "I can't keep it. What am I going to use it for?"

He keeps his arms folded, and he shakes his head.

"Why won't you take it?" Tears well in my eyes.

"Because it's yours now."

"Augh!" I growl at him. But he stands there, unwavering, unmoving.

He finally approaches me and places his rough hands on my shoulders. "Both of us want to make your mother proud."

I run my fingertips over the inlaid lily flowers that adorn the hilt, the base formed into the head of a falcon. Re. Protector of the King. Giver of life.

"But she doesn't know you the way I do," Iti says.

"What way is that?"

"That you'll do what *you* wish to do, regardless of what we say."

"And what about what the Powerful One said?" I ask.

"If I were you," Iti says as he heads back downstairs, "I would listen to her."

CHAPTER SIX

I slash the dagger in front of me. In the days since Iti gave it to me, the heat has grown more intense. Even under the shade of the rooftop canopy, the sun is unyielding. Sweat trickles down the back of my dress and onto the roof.

"Sati!" Mawat's voice calls me from downstairs.

I turn and volley, ducking and attacking, imagining those men in the market before me. I stab and thrust my weapon, envisioning it piercing their leather tunics. With my feet close under me, knees bent, I prepare for the next strike.

"Sati!" Mawat calls again. "I need you down here now!"

I advance and launch one final slash. The fatal blow. I can practically see the dust rise around the fallen body.

"What are you doing? Are you ignoring me?" Mawat's voice grows louder. "Don't make me come up there!"

When Mawat's sharp footsteps approach, I sheath the dagger and tuck it into the folds of my leather waistband as quickly as possible. Mawat stands at the base of the stairs, her arms folded, and glares up at me.

Some warrior I am, flinching at my mother's scolding.

As we head to the kitchen, I expect a reprimand, but she doesn't deliver one.

"Take those onion rolls out to the guests," she says, to my surprise.

She hasn't allowed me to serve the guests since that horrible day in the market. I raise an eyebrow at her.

She sighs. "I know I've been harsh, but what could happen if you're only in the next room?"

I can't help but bounce on my heels with joy. It's not total freedom, but it's more than I've had in what feels like forever.

I arrange the breads on a wide metal tray, taking care to arrange them in an artful way, the way Mawat does. Then I saunter through the door and into the gathering room to serve our guests.

Every manner of man sits on our cushions this late morning. Wealthy merchants, their upper arms ringed in gold. Sun-wrinkled traders with skin tawny and stretched. A few men who might have been soldiers back in their younger days. I recognize their confidence, but also their weariness. Iti has the same.

Mawat has served some of them already; they're slurping stew from clay bowls and popping dried figs and dates into their mouths. Others await their meals patiently, chatting with old friends, and making deals with new connections.

But an agitation slithers between the tables.

A few merchants lament the low waters, saying how it made their ships' passage difficult, particularly farther up the river. Some comment that the Good God has been demanding enormous building projects, both down in the delta and up in Tanehsu, honoring none other than himself. They ask how he could focus on such grandiosity, dipping into a dwindling treasury, while the *rekhyt* must ration their grain.

Without a word, I walk my tray around to the guests, one by one. Most give me pleasant thanks as they take a roll, while others are too rapt in their conversations to notice. Just as well.

An older man, his head shiny and mottled, scowls at me as I approach. He turns to his dining companion, a skinny man, his head bald with short grey stubble.

"I can't wait to get home," he says, taking a roll from my tray without even making eye contact with me. "How long have we been away?"

"It feels like years," the older man says, taking a roll of his own. "Didn't we leave at the end of the last harvest? Or was it two harvests ago?"

"I don't even remember," the skinny man replies with an exaggerated sigh. "My baby son is probably walking already."

"All this searching, and that bastard has likely been in Hatti this whole time."

My ears prick at the mention of the kingdom in the north. And what do they mean "that bastard," and why are they looking for him?

As I move on to the next table, the older man leans toward his friend. "Did you hear what happened here a few weeks ago?" he asks. "A man from Tanehsu assaulted a Medjay soldier, right here in Men-nefer."

Man from Tanehsu? They couldn't possibly mean Tahir... could they?

I try to keep moving from guest to guest, but I realize I've paused to listen. I risk a glance their way.

The older man takes a sip of his beer. "He got his wife and little girl in on it too."

They do mean Tahir, and they have it all wrong. Those men attacked Tahir. And they weren't Medjay. They weren't even city guards. Just *isfet* criminals.

"Those dogs!" The skinny man holds an offended palm to his heart.

"And in the light of Re's sun! In the middle of the market! They didn't even try to hide it."

"Well, I hope the Good God's forces arrested them right away," the older man says. "He should feed them all to the crocodiles."

How could he say such a thing? He doesn't know what happened. He's just repeating some rumor that isn't even true.

The skinny man leans back against the wall. "I heard the Medjay

killed the Tanehsi, and who knows what they'll do with the women."
He lets out a short, cruel chuckle.

"I can think of a few things." The older man chuckles, too, making an obscene gesture with his fingers.

My hands would ball into fists if I weren't balancing this tray on my shoulder.

"Three less foreigners is a good thing," the older man says, his voice quieter. "They call Kemet home and claim to pledge their loyalty to our king, but how can we be sure? And who knows who they pray to behind the walls of their homes? It's bad enough the king is letting northerners build temples to their gods in our cities."

I circle back to their table. They're in our home, eating our breads, drinking our beer, and I can't stand back and let them continue their insults.

"More bread?" I ask with the sweetest voice I can muster.

"No, we're fine," the older man says with a dismissive wave of his hand.

"I heard you talking about what happened in our market," I say. "I was there."

"We didn't ask you," the skinny man hisses.

"Well, if you're telling stories, they should at least be *ma'at*."

"Oh?" The older man glares at me. "And what *did* happen, serving girl?"

Serving girl? I try to hide my indignation behind a smile.

"Ta—The man from Tanehsu was attacked. He didn't start anything. Neither did his wife or daughter."

I fight back the tears that sting at the mention of our friends.

"Hmph," the older man grumbles, returning to his plate. "If the Medjay attacked them, then they probably still deserved it."

"That's not what happened," I protest. "And the Medjay weren't even there."

"Doesn't matter."

"How could you say that?" My belly twists like it's full of tiny snakes. "You didn't know them."

"And you did?"

I nearly quip back but stop myself.

"Foreigners are foreigners," he says. "They serve Apep. Everyone knows that."

Please, let my face still be pleasant, because I want to throw my tray right in this man's face. "Anyone can be loyal to the Good God, no matter where they're from."

The older man snaps around. "I know the king's domain better than you ever will, girl. Tell me, how many times have you even been out of this city?"

My jaw sets. "I don't need to leave the city to know not all foreigners are *isfet*."

"Doubtful. I've been a merchant for the Good God for more floods than you've been alive." He rises to his feet. He's... much taller than I expected.

His skinny friend bolts up next to him, folding his arms across his bare chest. "Heh. You're serving dinner rolls while we sail the length of the Iteru year after year." He leers down his nose at me.

I roll my shoulders back. "Well, if I were in your place, I'd pay more attention to the people I meet instead of saying anyone who's different is *isfet*."

"Everyone who is different *is isfet*," the older man growls, as if it were Ma'at's own truth.

The skinny man scoffs. "Even *rekhyt* girls like you should know that."

"I'm more than a *rekhyt* girl. And I know quite a lot. More than you, apparently."

The older man looms over me. I stare right into his muddy eyes.

"A *rekhyt* serving girl needs to learn her place. Didn't your mother teach you to respect the men who serve the Good God?"

"My mother has taught me what's *ma'at*," I say. I close the gap between us, holding the tray of breads out to the side. "Maybe *your* mother needed to do the same for you."

Something snaps in him, and he lurches at me.

I step back, and my heel catches on the edge of one of the reed mats. I stumble. My tray and all the rolls on it fly into the air. They suspend for a moment before the tray clatters to the floor, the cascade of bread in its wake.

Strong arms pull me against a bare chest, and I struggle against them. "Let me go!" I kick and thrash. My blood races through my ears, sharp and tingling.

If both men are in front of me, then whose arms are these?

"Sati, no, it's me!"

Iti? I stop struggling and find my footing. The arms release me and push me back. The older man glares at me and Iti, and the skinny man does his best to do the same.

Iti looks at them, then looks at me, his arm a protective barrier. "What in the name of the Beautiful Face is going on?"

The older man opens his mouth to speak, but I jump in before he can get in a word.

"These men said Tahir attacked a Medjay soldier, and it's not true!"

They puff up and stride toward Iti.

The older man shoves his own finger in Iti's face.

"You need to teach your serving girl to keep her mouth shut."

"I'm not a serving girl!" I say. "I'm a military captain's daughter!"

The entire gathering room falls deathly silent. Everyone's watching me.

The two men shoot looks like daggers at my father. "Even more reason for her to be quiet."

"She will say what she wishes to say, and I will not discourage her," Iti says, to my surprise. He steps forward. "And if that doesn't please you, then you are free to leave."

I scowl at the men. My hand wraps around the hilt of the dagger tucked in the folds of my waistband.

We stand, locked on each other. The other guests continue to stare.

"Great Mother Iset!" Mawat storms into the gathering room from the kitchen. "What is going on in here?"

Iti turns to her, his hardened jaw softening. "It's all right. Just a little misunderstanding."

She pauses where the serving platter lies upside down on the floor, surrounded by a mess of rolls. She grits her teeth at me with fire in her eyes. Then her expression softens, and she forces a light smile.

"I'm so very sorry," she says to the two men. "I'll fetch you more bread."

She burns a glance at Iti, grabs my wrist, and pulls me back into the kitchen. The door slams shut behind us.

"What in Ptah's name were you thinking? I can't even leave you for a moment before you get yourself into trouble?"

"I didn't do anything! They threatened me!"

"And why would they do that?"

"They were telling lies about Tahir!"

Mawat presses her palm to her forehead.

"They said Tahir attacked a Medjay solider," I say. "But they weren't there. They didn't see what happened. But I did! I know what's *ma'at*."

Mawat's mouth tightens. "You can't pick a fight with every guest who says something you don't like."

"They said Tahir and Asata and Kala deserved it!"

Mawat's granite face squeaks with shock. If I'd blinked, I would have missed it.

"People will tell stories," she says with a sigh. "And sometimes you have to let them."

"But they also said all foreigners serve Apep. That we're *isfet*. But Tahir wasn't *isfet*." My teeth set, and I look at the floor. "I'm not *isfet*."

Mawat takes a deep breath, her head in her hand.

"Go upstairs," she says. "Now."

○ ○ ○

As Re descends into Duat, I sneak to the roof with my dagger, assailing imaginary foes. The men in the marketplace. Those merchants in the common room with their shiny bald heads and infuriating smirks.

Each strike stokes the growing fire in my heart. With each stab, it burns brighter.

It becomes violent. A roaring lion clawing at its tiny cage.

I bristle when Mawat calls me down for the evening meal, making it clear that under no circumstances am I allowed in the gathering room.

When I'm finished, Maimai follows me upstairs, as she always does, tail pointed upward. I light my lamp and sprawl out on my bed, staring at the stars on my ceiling. My hands find the dagger in my waistband.

With a sigh, I set it on the floor. Why do I even bother to keep it with me if I can't use it? It almost compels me to fight.

Maimai settles on my belly, her claws poking me as she kneads my skin like honey rolls. I can't muster the energy to remove her, so she keeps on.

Eventually, I fall asleep. I wake up some time later. Maimai sleeps next to me, and the lamp has gone dark.

The full moon's light paints the walls in a silvery haze. These four walls that have been my childhood sanctuary, my haven, are now nothing more than a prison. And if it weren't these walls, it would be someone else's. A husband's home. A temple. Anywhere to keep me safe, or to keep others safe from me.

An impulse overtakes me. An impulse I've ignored and pushed down for far too long. It's time to become what I've always wanted to since Iti taught me how to hold a fighting staff.

PART ONE: THE PROVOCATION

I remove my sheath dress and slip a tunic over my head.

I retrieve my *shendyt* from the floor. It's been in the corner since the day I abandoned it. Red dust has accumulated in its folds, and I stifle a cough when I shake it out. I secure it around my hips with the same sand-red leather waistband I've worn every day. Iti's belt, from his military days. From my storage chest, I retrieve a wide, wool shawl and toss it over my shoulders.

I run my hand through my hair, smoothing it down along my scalp. No wigs today.

With the back of my arm, I smear away the script of my last writing lesson from a clay tablet. With a stub of charcoal, I scribble a message. I set the tablet near my headrest.

Then I crouch, feeling for the dagger. My fingers find the handle, and I slip the sheath into my belt.

Maimai is still curled at the foot of my bed. When I pet her, she wakes with a chirp.

"Look after Mawat and Iti for me," I whisper. "I'll see you soon."

I slip down the stairs to the kitchen. A dish of uneaten honey rolls sits on their metal tray on a small table in the corner. I take one and find my fighting staff at the wall where it has been leaning, neglected, for weeks.

As I walk through the door to the courtyard, a few stars hold fast against the faint light emerging in the east. Soon, the Shemu morning will surrender to the harshness of the sun.

Then I open the gate, the one that separates the Per-seshen from the rest of Men-nefer. I haven't even been near this entry in so long. I pause. Down the alley, an oil lamp gutters in the window of a neighbor's home.

There, on the threshold, I take a deep breath. I glance back at the courtyard one last time.

And I pass through the doorway.

PART TWO:
THE OFFER

CHAPTER SEVEN

My feet keep moving, one in front of the other.

I pass through sleeping streets, narrow and dark. The last stars of the night fade as Re begins his daily journey across the sky. The residents of Men-nefer will be waking up soon, starting their work in their homes, workshops, and on the docks. And in the morning sunlight, they'll see me, the girl in a man's *shendyt* whom they haven't seen in over two weeks. Those who know me will have questions. And I don't want to answer.

I fidget with my lily pendant. Despite the encroaching heat, I pull my cloak around my shoulders to keep out prying eyes.

A lone stone worker leads a donkey up the street, wider here than near the Per-seshen, with an enormous block of pink granite in his cart. He barely looks at me as I pass. A good sign.

The buildings grow taller, and the red and green flags of the Temple of Ptah across the river billow in the breeze. The pungent smell of fish fills the air, along with the mustiness of wet earth and decaying plants.

The streets open into avenues, and the city's sprawling port rises from the maze of whitewashed mudbrick. Masts bob above the light morning mist hanging over the water, sails rolled up tightly against them. In the distance, men on the banks cast nets into the shallow waters, praying to the fish god Rem, who fertilizes the land with his tears.

Here, where the city meets the harbor, I pause. Now is my last chance to turn back. No. No turning back. I need to keep going.

Re has fully risen above the horizon. Sailors, traders, and merchants heave baskets of minerals, whole cedar tree trunks, and spices on to the shores and banks. They don't seem to notice me. I pull back my shoulders and walk a little taller along the docks.

I pass cargo barges adorned with spells and protective symbols to guard against hippopotamuses and crocodiles, and small fishing skiffs appealing to the waters for a bountiful catch. Along a short canal, humble reed boats, woven together with papyrus fibers, huddle like ducks. I keep going, searching.

But that ship is too short. The next is too modest. Another is too old. And that one is, ugh, too crowded.

Downstream. What I'm looking for will be downstream, where the water is deeper and the docks are closer to the temples and away from the *rekhyt*.

My feet carry me along the river, passing bustling crews, and the ships grow taller, larger, and more elaborate.

Finally, at the end of the harbor, at the most northern pier, a lily-shaped stern plated with electrum flashes in the sunlight.

I try not to seem too eager, but I quicken my pace. This ship, the size of the Per-seshen and its towering cedar mast reaching to the sky, is the one. It has to be.

If the Powerful One wants me to journey, I won't travel on anything less than a vessel fit for the gods.

I stride toward the ramp.

A man with a weathered, tawny face peeks over the railing. "You better not get near my ship."

"Excuse me?" I haven't even reached the short wooden dock that stretches along the side of the ship's hull.

The man stands, and although he's wearing simple linens, two wide gold bracelets cuff each of his wrists. "I said—"

"I heard what you said," I call back. He can't deter me so easily.

"Then step away from my ship."

"But maybe you can help me?"

He grumbles. "Dressed like that? You look like trouble." He points at my staff. "And I know a weapon when I see one."

Did I think that because the goddess told me I had to take a journey that it would be easy? And I want to tell him I'm not trouble, but after last night, I'm not sure that's *ma'at*.

"What do you want, girl?" He tromps down the ramp, thick ropes coiled over his shoulder.

"Are you sailing to Per-Ramesses?" I ask as he winds his ropes around a mooring.

"I wouldn't tell you even if I wanted to. Go annoy someone else. And put on some proper clothing."

His oblique insult raises my hackles, but I brush it aside.

"So that's a yes? You are sailing for the capital?"

He grunts and continues to wind his rigging. Of course, the ship I need to board has a grumpy old captain. A dark little flame kindles in my belly. Is that you, Powerful One?

The man disappears up the ramp and into the ship again. He barks out orders to his crew, and I catch a glimpse of sun-weathered and shaven scalps above the boards.

I want to follow him, but I stop myself. He'd be justified in calling the Medjay on me if I came too close to what is obviously a royal vessel. So, I step up right to where the gangplank meets the pier. "What would it take for me to gain passage on your ship?"

His head pops up again, eyeing me as though I were a jackal trying to steal his lunch. "From a *rekhyt* girl? What makes you think you have anything I can't get already?" He gestures to his ship. "If you haven't noticed, I have everything I could possibly want."

The flame inside me burns brighter. No, I can't get angry, not over this. "Maybe that's true, but this is important."

"Important, hmm? Whatever it is, it's not important enough for me. Now step away from the *Nebkhepri*, or I'll have the Medjay arrest you right here!"

My cheeks grow hot, and against my own judgement, I grip my staff readying for a fight.

"Khefer! That's no way to speak to a stranger!" A younger man's cheerful voice sounds from behind me.

I spin around, and a man of about twenty floods saunters toward us, an enormous clay jug in one arm and a covered basket balanced on the opposite shoulder.

The sheer abundance of riches he wears so casually makes my breath catch. Gold encircles every part of him, from his beaded broad collar to the braided human hair wig woven with electrum to the filigree rings on his fingers. His immaculate *shendyt* is made from the finest linen I've ever seen.

"Don't mind him," this golden man says to me as he gets closer.

His inlaid pectoral necklace nearly blinds me in the sunlight. Even his sandals have blue and green glass beads . . . or are they more rare and expensive lapis and malachite?

"He's just protective of his ship," he adds. "It's been in his family for three generations."

He continues up the ramp and sets the jug and basket on the deck. Someone wearing that much gold wouldn't even design to consider helping load cargo, as though he were a common crew member. People like him give the orders, a servant on the right with a fan and another on the left with a sunshade.

He gives the old man a familiar pat on the shoulder. "Would it send you to Ammit you to show a little more hospitality?"

Khefer grunts. "No place for hospitality when we have goods to deliver to the Good God."

I knew it. They *are* on their way to Per-Ramesses.

The younger man comes back down the ramp, brushing his palms together to rid them of dust. He squints at me with dark, kohl-lined eyes as he wipes the sweat from his brow with his forearm.

"Why would Khefer want to set the Medjay on you?" His soft, rakish smile catches me off guard.

"I need to board this ship."

"*This* ship?"

"Well, I need to go north, to the capital. And that's where *this* ship is going."

He studies me for a moment. When I'm sure he'll order me to go back to where I came from, he turns and calls up the ramp. "Ai, Khefer! Why would you turn away a young woman in need?"

"Another mouth to feed and another *ka* to protect." Khefer barely peeks his head over the boards.

"We have plenty to go around," the young man replies. "I just refilled our bread baskets."

Khefer doesn't answer. The young man gives me a little lift of his well-groomed black eyebrows. "He's considering it."

He holds my gaze, and I look away. A *rekhyt* girl shouldn't be staring at someone so above her status, but he doesn't appear to mind. "I swear by the feather I won't eat all your food."

Khefer grumbles and steps to the railing again. "All right, but if she comes with us," he barks, "she's *your* responsibility. And she better stay out of the way of my crew."

The young man's cheeks quirk. "That's Khefer's way of saying 'Yes.'"

Oh, thank the gods. Again, I find myself looking at this man a little longer than is proper. Everything about his adornment screams wealth and high status, but nothing about his mannerisms whisper anything of the sort.

"But I can't promise Khefer will be any kinder," he adds.

"I don't need kindness," I say. In fact, I'd be happy if they all left me alone for the entire journey.

He leans in closer to me, and I catch the scent of expensive resins and spices—frankincense, cinnamon, and cardamom. Even his perfume is rich. "He'll get used to you being on board soon enough."

"I can hear you!" Khefer yells over the railing. "And I'm *not* responsible for keeping her safe. Thieves have been much bolder this year."

"But didn't you see?" The young man points at my staff. "She's armed!"

"Just temping *isfet*, if you ask me," the old man grumbles.

The younger man must see my face fall at the mention of the word. "I'm sure he didn't mean it."

"It's all right," I say, hoping my voice doesn't betray my offense. Will there ever be a day when I'm not accused of courting the dark waters?

"Well, it's pretty unusual to meet a young woman with a weapon."

"Believe me, I know." And neither of them seems to have noticed I'm doubly armed with my father's dagger.

"Hopefully, you won't have to use it." He gestures to the ramp. "Let me be the first to welcome you aboard the royal barge, *Nebkhepri*."

I almost turn to walk onto the ship. But I stop and take a long look at this man who wears more wealth than any *rekhyt* could ever dream of, and for some reason, who decided I'm worth convincing his grumpy friend to allow me to travel with them to the capital. How much should I trust him, if I should trust him at all?

"And who *are* you?" I ask.

"Oh, of course." He clears his throat, and stands straight, adjusting his wig. "I am Lord Ahmose, son of the Wasir Lord Useraasen. Newly appointed overseer of relations between the Black Land and kingdoms in the north, in service of the Good God in the Great House."

He enunciates every syllable, as though he has been rehearsing the words his entire life, but only now started to use them. But those words explain all the gold. He's not just a highborn man. He's a nobleman in the Good God's immediate service. Now I'm really trying not to stare.

He spins the gold cuff around his wrist. "You can call me Ahmose."

"Am I allowed?" I say, half-serious.

"Of course, of course. And you are?"

"Sati. Just Sati. I mean, it's Sat-reshwet if we're being formal, but I don't have any fancy titles."

"No need for titles here, at least not until we arrive at the Great House. Besides, they get in the way." He gestures to the immense, grand, and gilded *Nebkhepri*. "After you . . . Sati."

○ ○ ○

After the crew has loaded and unloaded all manner of crates, baskets, and ceramic jars, they guide the *Nebkhepri* from the docks, through the narrow canals, and to the Iteru. The ship picks up speed, the oarsmen pushing through the waters in unison, hoping to catch what little current the low river offers. The port of Men-nefer, with all its barges, gleaming mudbrick, and bustling merchants recedes away into the hazy air. Only a few modest homes remain along the river's edge now, scraggly fields stretching out behind them, and a humble fishing boat or two bobbing along the banks.

Fluffy tufts of papyrus dance in the breeze, and lily blooms of purple and pink float gracefully on the river's surface. I breathe in the damp air, reveling in the sun's warmth on my shoulders and the fresh wind on my cheeks.

By now, Mawat and Iti will have found my note. And they'll be worried sick.

But I couldn't stay there. I need to go be who I've wanted to be for as long as I can remember. And the farther the *Nebkhepri* sails down the Iteru, the more I realize I can't go home. Not yet. Not for a long time.

A crocodile slides into the water, sending a ruffle of ducks into the air, when I feel someone looking at me. I glance back at the center of the ship, where Ahmose slips into the captain's shelter.

"Why did you make me let that girl come with us?" Khefer says from inside.

The crew is too busy with their rowing to notice me sidle up to the shelter. I lean against the wall and pretend to gaze out at the riverbanks.

"I didn't make you," Ahmose says, almost laughing. "You said"—he drops his voice in an exaggerated imitation of Khefer—"'She better stay out of the way of my crew.' I'd call that as much an invitation as you've ever given anyone."

I strain to hear Khefer as he quiets his voice. "We've got a full cargo hold. She could be a thief. A criminal."

"A criminal? Really, Khefer."

"You saw her. She's got a weapon. And not just the one." My fingers find the hilt of my dagger. It's not as concealed as it should be.

"If it concerns you so much, you should just *ask* her why she has a staff," Ahmose suggests with a hint of sarcasm.

Khefer huffs. "I need to stop letting you push me around."

"What? Me?" I can hear the smile in Ahmose's scoff.

"If you weren't Useraasen's boy, I wouldn't let you get away with half the things you've coerced me into doing."

"Oh, like what?"

"Sailing to the edge of the first cataract at the height of flood last year, just so you could see the water spilling out of the rocks."

"You say that like you didn't have fun," Ahmose teases. "Admit it. The rush of the waters? The mist in your face? Witnessing the work of the gods themselves?"

"Nearly capsized us against the boulders!"

"That was the best part!" Ahmose lets out a proud laugh, and I press my palm over my mouth to stifle a laugh of my own.

Khefer grumbles. "Could have lost our entire shipment of frankincense."

"But we didn't," Ahmose says. "You and your crew delivered us safely to Waset. A few days early, if I recall correctly. Besides, if I weren't good at convincing even one of my dearest friends to do something harmless, what kind of negotiator would I be?"

"You certainly are your father's son," Khefer grumbles.

"I'm not so sure about that." Ahmose's voice flattens. Something shuffles inside, like the lid of a basket. "I'm going to go check on our guest."

For a moment, I consider running back to the stern to pretend like I wasn't listening. But it's not as if the crew members around me couldn't hear most of what they were saying, either. Well, apart from what Khefer failed to whisper.

Ahmose stops mid-stride as he steps through the doorway, basket in hand. The brief surprise on his face yields to a confident facade. "I was just coming to find you."

"It's for protection," I say, leaning against my staff. I hold his gaze, and one side of his mouth pulls up.

"That's what I wanted to say, but the old man is more stubborn than the river at Akhet."

"I heard that!" Khefer barks from inside.

He opens the lid of the basket, releasing a faint smell of yeast.

"And because Khefer won't ask you," he says, glancing back through the doorway, "I will. Why do you need to protect yourself?"

He hands me a flatbread, but I don't take it. I catch myself staring at him, my eyebrows raised in disbelief. I can't tell if he's feigning ignorance to make conversation or if he truly doesn't understand. But the look on his face appears genuine, which only puzzles me further.

"You haven't heard what's been happening in Men-nefer?" I ask.

I assumed that the men in charge—because they're always men— knew what was happening. Iti even went to the Administrative Palace to tell the city officials, to warn them, and request more guards to patrol the streets. And more guards did, or at least, that's what Iti told Mawat. And these kinds of attacks and intimidation must be happening all along the Iteru, not just in Men-nefer, or in any of the cities where peoples of Retenu, Tanehsu, Ribu all live together. Where temples of Amun and Astarte stand beside each other in an uneasy coexistence.

He shakes his head, the gold beads on his wig glinting in the sun. "I'm afraid I haven't. I've been on the river with Khefer for the entire season."

I find my gaze trailing over his jewelry again. What did he say he was? A diplomat? Wouldn't he want to know if sentiment against foreigners in one of the Black Land's largest cities has turned from tenuous to terrorizing?

The confusion on his face unwinds. "It's a bit much, isn't it?" He glances at his adornment and spins the gold bangle around his wrist again. "If I change out of all this, will you join me under the awning at the stern of the ship for a little midday meal?"

If only out of sheer curiosity, I nod. "I'll meet you there."

CHAPTER EIGHT

When Ahmose emerges from the captain's shelter, he's shed his jewelry and wig, wearing a *shendyt*, a light tunic, and a few weeks' worth of fuzzy curls on his head. If I didn't know any better, I'd think he were just another member of the crew. He seems lighter now, unfettered by his bangles and bracelets. He bounces a basket in one hand.

As he approaches, I look away to the riverbank. Why do I keep staring at him? Khefer would be right to call the Medjay on me if I continue to show such disrespect to someone so far above my status.

But Ahmose himself doesn't abide by the formalities I'd learned as a child. Demanding that *rekhyt* must always defer to anyone highborn, bowing and keeping our gaze cast at the ground in their presence, while they glare at us from their litters.

He sets the basket between us, steps next to me, and leans against the railing. I brace myself for a comment about my appearance, my weapon, or that my *shendyt* is dirty and losing its pleating.

A hippopotamus wriggles its ears in the distance, snorting as it comes up for breath.

"I've sailed these waters for almost my entire life," Ahmose says dreamily after a long pause. "Yet on every journey, I still feel like I'm seeing the river for the first time."

He takes out a flatbread and tears it in half, offering one side to me. The emptiness in my belly twists, and I take it. When I take a bite, it melts in my mouth. Not even Mawat has ever made bread so soft and fine.

"And," he says, "it's the first time I've seen a woman in a man's *shendyt*."

Ah, there's the first comment. I turn away. I don't need a rich man to tease me about my clothing.

"Or armed with two weapons," he adds.

And there's a second comment. Now I understand why he wants to talk to me. I'm a curiosity to him. Something to be marveled at, like a dwarf or wild creature from the southern lands.

"So," he starts, "our agreement was that I'd change, and you'd tell me more about yourself and what's happening in Men-nefer."

"The agreement was that I'd eat with you." I finish what's left of my bread before reaching for a second.

"Ai, you are right." His face goes serious. "Look, while I was replenishing our supplies in Men-nefer, I saw nothing unusual. But it's clear that you have."

Of course he saw nothing unusual. Dressed the way he was, no one would dare doubt his power or status. Not only is he obviously not foreign, but he's also one of the king's officials. Neither Tahir's attackers or the Scarred Man and his friend would have any reason to give him even a sideways glance. And if they tried, I'm sure the most well-trained and lethal Medjay would be there to protect him in an instant. The Medjay who failed to protect my friends. Not even the city guards came to their aid until it was too late.

"You weren't there long enough," I say.

"Perhaps. But part of my work for the king is to report to him on anything that might be a threat to *ma'at* in his domain."

I expect him to imply that I am a threat to *ma'at*. The girl dressed in men's clothing. At least he doesn't know I'm foreign-born.

"And if a young woman finds herself needing two weapons to protect herself," he continues, "then clearly the scales are unbalanced."

I'm about to spew my defense against his accusations that I'm an agent of chaos when I realize he didn't imply that at all.

But the Scarred Man and his brutish companion most certainly did. How hasn't this nobleman heard anything about them or the simmering tensions in our city? They even harassed our poor neighbor, who walks with a cane and worked the emmer fields as soon as he could walk. He has the mud of the Black Land flowing through his veins.

"The scales *are* indeed unbalanced," I say. "How don't you know about the rogue men that have been prowling through Men-nefer?"

He opens his mouth to speak, like he'll ask another question, like he knows more about it all than he wishes to admit.

"I saw my father's best friend attacked in the streets," I say. "Under Re's light. For being from Tanehsu."

He swears under his breath and pinches the bridge of his nose. "The rumors are true?"

I can't tell whether he's asking me or the wind, but I answer anyway. "The rumors are wrong."

"Wrong?"

"If what you heard is that Tahir threw the first blow, then yes. They're wrong." Those two men in the gathering room heard rumors too, and they had it all backward.

His gaze drifts out to the river again. "Another attempt to undermine the king," he mutters.

"'Another' attempt? How long has this kind of thing been happening? And under the Good God's own foot?"

He responds with a nod. "Believe me, he has been trying to root them out."

"But not trying hard enough if his own subjects are assaulted in the streets, and the attackers flee with no consequence, no judgement, no punishment."

A heat grows inside my ribs and into my throat. I try to control myself, contain my words, but they push forth from my mouth. My feelings of helplessness, of grief and anger, become too heavy to bear. I've been holding them in for too long.

"The *rekhyt*—all of us, regardless of where we were born—have been struggling a long time," I say. "After another year of low floodwaters and meager harvest, we can't grow enough grain, most of which goes to the Good God and his temples. Many are afraid of leaving their own homes. Sometimes those aren't even safe."

I recoil at my words. Surely this nobleman will admonish me now. He'll have me removed from the ship at the next docking, or he'll tell a crew member to toss me overboard.

When he doesn't do any of that, the heat in me burns stronger, emboldened by his silence.

"Have you ever worried if you'll have enough food?" I ask. "Or whether you'll make it home alive after visiting the market?"

Ahmose straightens his back. "We know the *rekhyt* are struggling. A poor harvest affects us all."

There it is. The distinction between his kind and mine. The fathomless gap separating highborn men like him and commoners like me. A gap widened further by my blood.

A bitterness floods through me, like a poison. An arrow seeking any target near enough to strike.

"While we go about our daily lives just trying to survive, men like you wear your riches, your gold and jewels, living in enormous, idyllic estates, with servants attending to your every need."

By all the gods, Sati, what are you saying? Stop talking before this man tosses you from the ship himself. And if he doesn't, then surely Khefer will.

But I can't stop.

All the brutal memories, all the fear, the anger, resentment, and betrayal I've been carrying leaps out of me. Besides, he asked. If he didn't want to know, he shouldn't have been so insistent, offering me his expensive bread and standing next to me, too close to me, as though we were equals.

"While we *rekhyt* dream of entering the Field of Reeds after our *ka* has left our bodies, you live there already, in this life, right now!"

It's only when I bite my lower lip that I notice it's trembling. I pivot from him, hunching my shoulders, expecting him to wield his status over me like the weapon it is.

For an eternity, I wait for his retort.

My heart beats fast against my folded arms.

"I—" He reaches his hand out to me but pauses when I shrink away.

I sense him stepping back, the way one would from a hissing desert cat.

"It's true that I serve the Good God," he says softly. "But I also serve all the people in his domain, no matter where they were born. And I'll do whatever I can to root out the *isfet* men who've caused so much harm."

Out of the corner of my eye, I see him dip his head before he walks back to the captain's shelter.

When I turn, he's already gone.

◉ ◉ ◉

We moor outside a small village for the evening, and overnight I sleep in the cargo hold with nothing more than an itchy wool blanket atop a pile of furs in scratchy sacks. A few crew members do the same, their snores knocking me from my dreams more times than I can remember.

I spend the second day at the stern, watching the banks narrow into the distance, running my palms over the worn leather wraps of my staff and fidgeting with my pendant, waiting for Ahmose to admonish me for being so bold. And if not him, then Khefer.

Mawat would be furious if she knew how I'd behaved. "Did you just forget all I taught you?" she'd scold. "It's a wonder you still have your head!"

Not only do I still have my head, but Ahmose also hasn't said so much as a word to me all day, not even to warn me never to speak like that to him again.

Mawat would be wrong.

Isn't that why I'm on this ship? To escape from Mawat's hold, no matter how protective she claims to be?

When I imagine how Iti would react to what I said to the nobleman, I chuckle. He'd probably be proud. "Fierce and quick like a caracal cat," he'd say. Or, at least, he does in my imagination.

My heart aches when I think of how Iti and Mawat must have felt when they found my message.

For now, I remain perched on this small platform at the back of the *Nebkhepri*, watching my old life pull away from me.

And as one would regard a wild animal, Ahmose—and everyone else—leaves me alone. I keep my distance too.

He and Khefer eat with the crew, chatting and reminiscing about past trade missions, and congratulating themselves on their current shipment. When they've finished, Ahmose catches my attention with a friendly wave and gestures to the basket and the beer jar. As soon as the crew returns to their posts at the oars and sails, and he and Khefer wander toward the captain's shelter, I dart in to see what's left.

Two whole flatbreads and at least two full cups of beer. And a clean ceramic cup to drink it from.

After my insolence yesterday, I don't know why he'd bother. I try to show my gratitude with a little wave of my own, which Ahmose returns with a dip of his chin.

"She doesn't need your help," Khefer grunts.

"But she does need to eat," Ahmose says. "Besides, she's our guest. *Your* guest."

"Only because *you* insisted."

I pour the remaining beer into my cup, watching the two lean against the railing.

"I heard how she spoke to you," Khefer says. "Admit that I was right. She's nothing but trouble."

"Troubled, perhaps. But not trouble."

"What's the difference?" Khefer scoffs. "You're too kind for your own good. Always have been."

"I see *ma'at* in people. You should try it."

Ahmose looks back in my direction, and that's when a glint of metal flashes behind him.

○ ○ ○

A bald man with a scarf wrapped over his face climbs over the boards and raises his blade over Ahmose's head.

A million thoughts flash before me.

The Scarred Man threatening Iti.

The men in the gathering room telling their lies.

Tahir's blood in the market.

And in every instance, my feet stuck to the earth. I wanted so much to do something, but when it really mattered, I couldn't defend myself, my family, or even Asata and Kala.

I won't let it happen again.

I raise my staff and race forward.

Khefer pushes Ahmose out of the way, drawing a dagger from his belt and whirling on me.

"I knew it!" he yells. "You *hiyut*!"

Before I can even think to explain, I jam the end of my staff at the masked man's chest, thrusting him back into the black waters of the river.

Khefer growls and stomps at me, an untethered rage on his snarled lips. "You! I'll kill you myself!"

"We're under attack!" I yell, pointing behind him where one, two, three—more than ten men with covered faces crawl over the railing.

Khefer swears as the ship erupts into chaos. The crew scrambles, grabbing daggers, staves, and any makeshift weapons they can find. The men collide in a mess of clanging metal and groans of effort.

Dear gods. Is this what Sekhmet meant when she said I'd return to blood and battle?

And if it is, then Iti prepared me for this moment.

I swing around when I sense a presence behind me. An attacker slashes his dagger at my neck. I duck and whip my staff at his knees. He crumples like a rag doll. I wail on his head, and he collapses, blood pouring out of his nose.

Another appears behind him. He slices his blade at my belly. I jump back, striking the soft spot just under his breastbone. He doubles over, gasping for air.

By Sekhmet, I think they're looking for me.

Something hisses by my ear, and my attacker tumbles to the deck. He grips at an arrow in his chest, its white feathers in stark contrast to his grey tunic.

I risk a backward glance. At the opposite end of the ship, Ahmose draws an arrow, taking aim at the men flooding the ship. He lets it loose, and another attacker falls at my feet.

A rough hand pulls my shoulder back right before a dagger finds my neck.

Khefer shoves me aside before driving his own blade into my attacker's side.

I try to make sense of the fray, but Re's light fades too quickly. The agonized cries of men fill the air in the growing darkness. Dear Nefertem, I can't see a thing.

Another appears out of the shadows in front of me. I throw myself at him with every bit of force I can muster. I won't let them take me, not without a fight.

Before my staff makes contact, he slashes his blade across my upper arm.

I cry out and fall back, gritting my teeth against the searing pain.

He sneers, but another arrow rushes past, sending him to the deck.

A splash echoes against the cries of fighting men, and a horrific scream erupts from the waters. Crocodiles.

"Find the negotiator," a man commands from somewhere in the clamor.

The negotiator? They're looking for Ahmose?

I struggle against the twilight to find him, to warn him. But I can't see anything past the writhing, brawling bodies.

The tiny moment of distraction is too long. A dagger slices too close to my face. I whip my staff at its wielder.

He sneers at me a savage cruelty. A cruelty he seems to enjoy.

Ahmose yells out in pain behind me. I try not to look in his direction, lest this man with the cruel eyes hunt him down.

My attacker arcs his dagger at me again.

"You know where he is," he growls as I dart back from another stab.

I risk a glance at his weapon.

I've seen a dagger like this before. It's like the one the Scarred Man had.

My heart races. They couldn't possibly be the same men. It's just a dagger. A plain, common dagger.

But that poison in his stare is just the same.

"You're one of them, aren't you?" I say.

Around us, metal clashes against metal above the sickening sound of bodies falling and weapons cutting across flesh and bone. A stream of arrows falls on our attackers.

I look up to where they come from, and the masked man does the same.

"Found him," he says with a predatory sneer.

Curse my eyes!

He tries to throw me aside, but I push myself into his hulking body. Surprise grazes his brows as he falters.

The might of the stars . . .

I toss my staff to my left hand and draw my father's dagger with the other.

The man lunges for me. With all the strength I can muster against the shrieking wound in my arm, I jam the blade into his side. I twist the handle into his flesh, and hot blood streams over my fingers.

He limps back, swinging his blade without aim toward me in the darkness.

An uncontrollable, savage force overtakes me. I pounce on him, bashing his temple with the hilt of my weapon. His body hits the deck with a thud.

For a moment, he's motionless. Oh, Sekhmet, have I killed him? But he starts writhing, clutching at the open wound in his side.

"Apep curse you," he snarls, blood oozing out of him.

I rip the scarf from his face. I expect, almost hope, to recognize him from the marketplace. Or that he's the Scarred Man himself. But he's neither.

"Who are you?" I press the sole of my foot on his chest, pinning him to the deck.

He laughs, and dark liquid bubbles from his mouth.

Around us, the din of fighting has quieted, but I don't dare look.

Under my foot, he lets loose a gurgle of cough.

I should be disgusted. I should feel sorry for him. Have some sense of mercy. But a vicious fire burns in my belly. It makes me want to do terrible, violent things. Instead of holding it back, I let it overcome me.

I push harder. He winces and gasps for air.

"Sati, no!" Ahmose calls through labored breath. His *shendyt* is completely crimson, with blood running down to his feet.

"But he wants to kill you!" I say.

The man wriggles beneath my weight. "There he is." He grins, his teeth red. "The king's new peacemaker."

Ahmose pulls an arrow from his quiver and aims it at the man's throat.

"Not so peaceful now," the man chuckles through his cough. With every breath, his resistance weakens.

"Do not try me," Ahmose says, his voice low and harsh. His eyes dart to the dagger near our feet. "Take his weapon."

I swipe it away from the man's feeble reach.

The sinew of Ahmose's bow creaks as he focuses on the man under my foot. "Return to your men. Tell them that the king will find you and destroy all of you."

"What?" I shoot a glance at Ahmose. "Why not just end him?" How could Ahmose let him go?

Ahmose gives me a withering glance, the one I've expected since our failed conversation my first day on the ship. And behind it, the pain from his wound churns.

My jaw sets. Rage burns across my cheeks, down my neck, and into my limbs. Why not send this man to Ammit now?

"May the Devourer have you," I snarl.

"What are you doing?" Ahmose yells.

"Ensuring he can't attack us again."

With everything left in me, I drive my weight into the fallen man's ribs.

"Stop!" Ahmose's order is no match for this rage that overcomes me.

Something cracks beneath my foot. Bone. The man yowls.

I feel no mercy, no sorrow, no concern for him. And it scares me.

Ahmose lowers his bow and pulls me back. But the damage is already done.

"Leave now," Ahmose says to the man writhing in pain before us. "And be grateful for my mercy."

The man groans and struggles to his knees, the gash in his side a shredded mess of linen, leather, and flesh. He wraps his arms around his chest and spits blood at our feet.

"Mercy is for fools," he says, glaring at Ahmose. He crawls to the railing, pushes himself upright, and scrambles over the side.

His splash crashes against the silence.

Ahmose and I run to railing. I see nothing. Just blackness. As black as the waters of Nu.

Perhaps Sobek has already claimed him, but whoever these men are, they'll come for Ahmose again.

The thought of it unsettles me, and I don't like that it does.

CHAPTER NINE

"Why did you let him go?" I yell as I chase after Ahmose.

The silence of the night fills with the groans of wounded men. Crew members tend to each other, and Khefer curses as he runs between them with rags and water. He barks orders at the ones still well enough to stand.

I want to scream at him, for thinking I'd dare attack Ahmose or him unprovoked. But to my surprise, he nods at me, as if to apologize for his mud-headed assumption. It's not enough, but for now, I'll accept it.

I wonder for a moment what Khefer will think of Ahmose's foolish choice to let that last attacker go. Surely he'd be just as confused as I am. Maybe that's one thing we have in common.

If we're lucky, the attacker will bleed out in the waters.

But luck has not been on my side lately.

I follow Ahmose into the captain's shelter. He strikes a flint and lights an oil lamp hanging from the ceiling.

He says nothing as he sits on a small stool.

"They attacked a royal barge," I say. "They need to be brought to justice. They need to know *ma'at*!"

Ignoring me, he grabs a strip of linen from the nearby table, a napkin from the last meal, probably. When he lifts the hem of his *shendyt*, his face twists as he sucks the pain back through his teeth. I can't even see the gash in his thigh through all the blood.

But he dabs at it as though it were nothing more than a skinned knee.

"I already took enough lives tonight," he says, his voice like the rumble of a distant storm.

"What's one more?" My words almost shock me. "They would have killed you!"

"You are a brutal one, aren't you?"

His words and the glance he gives me—full of curiosity and awe—knock me off balance. It's like he can see right into me. All the angry and confused parts of me. What's more mystifying is that he doesn't recoil.

"I just . . ." My tongue stumbles.

"Too many deaths," he says, "add too much weight to our hearts."

Before I can concede that he's right, my arm seethes. I wrap my hand around the oozing wound.

As I'm about to ask him for bandages, Ahmose crumples over his legs. The rush of energy from the fight seems to have faded, and the pain overtakes him. Fresh red liquid trickles from his leg every time he wipes it clean.

"By Sekhmet's mane," I mutter. "You need to put pressure on that."

I rummage through the baskets and jars, looking for linen, honey, flaxseed oil, water. Anything to help clean and wrap his injury before the *shema't* take hold.

Finding enough of what I need, I tear a large swath of linen into long strips, moistening the scraps with oil and honey.

A pin prick of a thought scolds me for my impropriety, questioning Ahmose's decision to let the attacker go, and now, for touching his skin.

What does that matter now? If he won't treat himself, then I will.

"This might hurt," I warn before squeezing together the two sides of his wound.

He sucks in through his teeth and swears by Wasir's lost flesh. I push my weight into his thigh, and he gulps back a deep growl of pain. Carnelian blood seeps through the layers of fabric.

"Just a bit longer," I say. "Breathe."

He gives me a puzzled look, then takes my advice. And after a few deep breaths, the wound bleeds a little less. Enough for me to wipe away the clots and dirt.

With most of the bleeding finally stemmed, I take his hand and push it against the linen. "Put as much pressure on it as you can," I say. "Otherwise, it will open up, and we'll be starting all over again."

As I wind a long linen strip around his leg, I notice one gold ring on his smallest finger. The only jewelry he seems to be wearing. It must be important. But now isn't the time to ask him why.

My thoughts turn to Sekhmet and her healing power. *Please, Powerful One, care for this wound and protect it from festering.*

I press my palms on the bandages, hoping I can channel her might into Ahmose's skin. When the blood has abated, I release my hands and tuck in the one last dangling end.

My own arm screams out, and I grasp at it.

"I hope you didn't use all the linen on me," Ahmose says, trying to stand, reaching for the pile of makeshift bandages.

"No," I say, nearly pushing him back on the stool. "Don't get up. Your leg will start bleeding again."

"Then bring me that linen, and sit here."

"I can take care of it myself," I say, defying his command.

"Please," he says calmly. "I insist."

He's not commanding me at all. He's offering.

I swallow back my pride as I let him wipe away the clots and crust, revealing a long, but not deep, gash.

"Praise Anpu," he says. "It's not so bad under all the blood."

Indeed, there's only flesh, no bone. But it will scar.

After he has wrapped my arm, a smirk tugs on the corner of his mouth. "Khefer is going to be so mad when he sees what we've done to his sheets."

My cheeks heat. I tell myself it's just the rush of the fight and the pain in my arm.

"I should go see if the crew needs help." I gather the remaining linen and grab the bottles of honey and oil.

"When you see Khefer," Ahmose says as I'm about to head out to the deck, "tell him I was right."

"Right about what?"

His crooked smirk gives way to a soft smile. "Letting you aboard the ship."

○ ○ ○

Several of the crew members are seriously wounded, with yawning gashes in their sides, across their backs, arms, and legs. Khefer has done a decent job caring for them, but he leaves me to tend to them while he checks on the cargo hold.

When he returns to the deck, he scans his men and turns to me. "Not bad."

What I want from him is an apology, but for now, I'll gladly take his gruff acknowledgement.

As soon as we have enough sunlight to navigate the low waters safely, we continue down the river. Not long after, we anchor in the city of Per-Bast. A few of the less scathed crewmen take a reed skiff to the shore. They return with essential provisions like beer and bread, as well as a heap of scrap linen and a few jars of honey. Behind them, a small boat with two Medjay follows, assigned to travel with us the rest of the way.

Ahmose mostly stays in the captain's shelter, but not without protest. Khefer insists he give his leg a chance to heal. He also insists

Ahmose partake of his personal stash of poppy tincture to ease the pain. Or, at least, that's what Khefer tells him. After the poppy tincture pulls the nobleman into a deep sleep, Khefer admits to me the tincture also ensures that he stays on his bedroll.

That evening, I tend to Ahmose's injury.

"Where did you learn?" he asks hazily.

"Learn what?"

"The bandages? The honey, the oil?"

"My mother taught me. I used to get scraped up a lot when I was younger."

He chuckles. "I'm not surprised." He reaches a listless hand to me before his eyelids grow heavy and the poppy tincture takes hold again.

○ ○ ○

While checking on the crew keeps me busy enough, the time between stretches out forever. One little village tucked amongst the reeds and sedge blends into the next.

On the fourth evening since we left Men-nefer, I sit at the bow, my vision wary.

The buzzing in my bones from the attack hasn't abated. Even the splash of a fish or a heron taking flight sends me reeling, and I expect another masked man to confront me with his razor eyes and even sharper blade.

Even still, do I regret my decision to leave Men-nefer?

I take a deep breath, savoring the taste of the river in the back of my throat. My fingers trace over the bandage on my arm.

No. I don't.

If I hadn't left, if I hadn't taken this chance, my life would have been lived for me. And I already feel like I've lived a thousand lifetimes since my first step on the *Nebkhepri*. My heart is light. Happy, perhaps.

I whirl at the sound of sandaled footsteps.

"You shouldn't be up," I say.

Ahmose limps beside me carrying a beer jar and two cups. "Are you giving me an order?"

By the Hapiu Bull, he's stubborn. I'm still so angry at him for letting the attacker go. But what can I do about it now? He made his decision. The decision of a diplomat. I would have made the decision of a warrior.

"No, but don't blame me if your leg refuses to heal."

"I would never." He grins as he fills the cups and hands me one. As he settles his weight against the boards, he sips from his own and regards me. "In fact, I wanted to thank you. Properly. So, thank you, for taking care of me."

I stare at him again. How many times will this man will surprise me before we reach Per-Ramesses?

"You're welcome," I say, taking a drink and turning to look back at the glistening waters. Lush, green marshes stretch out before the ship all the way to the horizon. "I only did what needed to be done."

We stand in silence for a moment. One of the crew members starts singing a rhythmic song, and the others join him, their oars moving in time.

"The men who attacked us," I say after a while. "They were looking for you. Why?"

"Ah, well." Ahmose pinches the bridge of his nose. "Probably because I'm my father's son."

"What did he do that they'd want to kidnap you? Kill you?"

"He was the king's chief diplomat, but he became Wasir last Peret."

"May he live forever," I say in polite response.

"Indeed," he says with an enigmatic resentment. I note he doesn't raise his cup in honor or say any other words of blessing.

"But I don't understand," I say. "Why would a diplomat make such enemies?"

"He believed that for the Two Lands to prosper, we must make peace with our rival kingdoms and welcome any who wished to live along the Iteru, so long as they lived by *ma'at*. And word must have made its way down the river of my return and of my taking his place."

My heart threads together the pieces, revealing an image I feared to be true. The brutes in Men-nefer and the men who attacked the ship must be connected.

And from the look on Ahmose's face, I see he's thinking the same.

"These men who attacked your friend," he says. "What do you remember about them?"

"Big, brutish, cruel. But the men who came to our home—"

Ahmose's eyes grow wide. "Your home?"

"Not just ours. Our neighbors' too. All the neighbors. They said they worked for the Good God, but they didn't wear his name." No matter how much his presence calms me, I don't dare tell him that the Scarred Man certainly suspected my foreign birth.

He scowls with thought and mutters something under his breath.

"You know who they might be, don't you?" I ask.

"I have my suspicions. Quite a few career military men don't like the idea of peace. It might rob them of their usefulness."

"It's not as if the Good God would disband his forces in the wake of a peace agreement," I say. "They wouldn't be useless."

"Indeed, most wise soldiers would take any chance to avoid death on the battlefield. But these men. I fear they're not so wise. But they are powerful."

My shoulders tense. Iti would never have dreamed of being so insolent while in the Good God's service.

"If they pose such a danger to you," I ask, "why are you taking your Wasir father's place at all?"

"While Khefer and I were in Punt, the king sent a messenger calling me back to the capital. The negotiations must really be going poorly for them to ask me to help."

"With Hatti?"

He whips back to me. "You know about that?"

"My father . . . he told me."

I wait for him to ask what Iti might know about the negotiations, but he doesn't.

He raises his brows in some kind of understanding, then slumps against the railing, rolling the cup between his hands. "I'm not sure what I'll be able to do unless they find Urhi-Teshub."

"Who?"

He opens his mouth but hesitates. I say nothing, waiting for his answer, even if it's to tell me I'm not allowed to know.

After a moment, he heaves a long sigh. "Hattusili—the Hittite king—swears by his gods that his nephew, Urhi-Teshub, the prince that he himself deposed, is hiding in the delta. In Per-Ramesses, no less. And he refuses to sign any agreement with our king until we return him to Hatti. How can we return him if he's nowhere to be found?"

So that's what those men in the gathering room were talking about.

"And if you can't find him?" I ask.

"Our negotiators continue pushing forward, hoping our king is more stubborn than theirs."

"Our Good God does seem like the stubborn type. I've seen what's on the temple walls."

"You mean the images of him trampling the enemy?" The way he says it hints that he knows the conflicting stories as well.

"Well, that and what's written around the images . . ."

"Oh, yes, of course," he stifles a laugh, then narrows his eyes at me. "Wait, you can read?"

Another thing I learned from Iti that makes me ever more unusual. I nod and take a large drink from my cup.

"You can fight, and you can read." He beams that vexing and warm smile again. "You call yourself *rekhyt*, but *rekhyt* girls don't usually know any of these things."

"And *rekhyt* girls usually don't end up on royal barges tending to wounded noblemen, but here I am."

He breathes a chuckle. "Here you are."

A cluster of white egrets bursts into the sky from a tree along the shore. "At least now I know who to call on if I need a peacemaker when I return home."

His eyebrows lift in curiosity.

"I nearly knocked out a guest with a tray of honey rolls for calling me a 'serving girl.'" And for daring to suggest that Tahir would even dream of attacking anyone in the market. For saying that foreigners serve Apep.

"You did?" Ahmose laughs. "Oh, excuse me, I mean, how dare he!"

I let myself laugh with him.

"Is that why you're running away?" His voice softens, like downy duck feathers, but his question tightens my chest.

"I never said I was running away."

"Hmm." He purses his lips in doubt. "I suspect it has to do with the men who came to your home. But there's more, isn't there?"

I almost tell him without a second thought. Something about his countenance, his casual stance, the way he speaks to me as an equal, makes me want to tell him everything. About how Mawat wouldn't let me leave the house. About where I'm really from, and how Iti lied to protect me. But how long has it been since we met? Four days? Even as the tension at the back of my neck abates as he leans a little closer to me, I can't tell him.

The longer I hesitate, the longer he looks at me. I wonder if he can see Retenu in my features. The light malachite green in my eyes, my narrow nose, the angle of my jaw.

I turn my back to the river, leaning against the railing. The crew still rows in unison as Khefer directs them and calls out orders to the two men climbing the center mast. I fold my arms and run my fingers along my bandage again. Tears sting my eyes.

"My apologies," Ahmose says to my surprise. "I've been too forward."

"I just needed to get out."

The winds shift around us, both prickly and tender. Ahmose turns to face the deck, and as he does, he edges closer to me. "Whatever it is you're seeking—and I'm not asking you to tell me—why not seek it from the Good God himself?"

I give him a confused look.

"When we get to Per-Ramesses," he says, "would you allow me to escort you to the Great Royal Hall, for an audience with the king?"

I haven't even thought through what I would do once I set foot in the capital. Find my way to the military garrison, walk to the gates, and say, "Hello, my name is Sati, and I wish to join your ranks." They'd laugh me away.

But what about that sounds any less preposterous should I say the same thing to the Good God?

To make matters more complicated, men in the king's own military might be connected to the attack two nights ago, even to Tahir's assailants and the Scarred Man. If they are, what serpent's nest will I find myself in if I get what I want?

Ahmose leans closer to me, his shoulder nearly touching mine. "Consider my offer a gesture of gratitude, for defending our ship so valiantly."

Against the cooling evening, the wind turns hot, and a lush purr resonates in my ears. *You would be a fool not to take his help.*

I take a deep breath. "Yes," I say, feeling as though I'm floating above my body in my *ba*. "I'd like that."

His smile widens. "I would too."

PART THREE:
THE COMMAND

CHAPTER TEN

The morning of our fifth day on the Iteru, I awake to the noise of men shouting. With a racing heart and bleary sight, my hands fumble for my staff.

After climbing up to the deck, the air sticks to my skin. I try to make sense of the commotion.

We're not under attack at all. We've almost reached Per-Ramesses.

Here the river gives way to small passages, flat and wide, some with tiny islands made of nothing but sand and a few grasses, and others large enough for towering temples and manicured villas. Great white ibises poke about in the mud, and a pair of ducks lifts off into the haze.

Just beyond the harbor, the city appears, shimmering in the heat like a dream. Gold-capped obelisks stretch to the sky, blindingly bright in the morning sun. White walls of mudbrick and polished limestone wind off in every direction. Red, blue, and green royal flags lilt in the gentle breeze. I thought Men-nefer was beautiful, but this city is indeed fit for a god king.

The crew guides the barge to the docks under Khefer's rough command. In an intricate dance, they offload the cargo to the carts and porters waiting on the shore. Several scribes stand with their pens and papyrus ready to note each and every item.

Khefer grunts at me with something like approval as he passes. "Ahmose *was* right about you."

He returns to his crew before I can reply.

As I walk down the plank, my legs wobble. Being afloat on the Iteru for five days has played with my balance, and I try to steady myself with my staff once I'm on the docks.

There, Ahmose meets me, now clad again in his jarring collection of gold. Such a contrast from the humble linens he's worn since we first met, and even more so from when his *shendyt* was soaked with blood. A bruise still graces his cheek, just below his thick kohl.

I should have applied kohl of my own. At least I've managed to wipe most of the evidence of the attack from my skin, apart from my own bruises and my bandaged arm.

A bald groom in quite a bit of jewelry of his own leads an almond-colored horse pulling a chariot, itself gilded and shining. Ahmose jumps into the carriage.

He holds his hand out to me, and I hesitate.

"The Good God awaits your petition," he says.

I take a breath, and I place my hand in his. It's soft and inviting. I try not to notice as I step up. The horse adjusts its weight, the platform shifting with it. So much for returning to solid ground.

"Lean into the front," Ahmose says. "You'll be more steady."

The groom hands him the reins, and Ahmose clicks between his teeth. My shawl nearly flies from around my neck as the chariot lurches forward, away from the *Nebkhepri*.

The scent of wet earth and marsh yields to dust and frankincense. The verdant harbor disappears behind us, and brilliant limestone walls rise around us on every side. Everything here looks like it was built yesterday. And maybe it was.

Ahmose turns the horse down a grand avenue lined with more carved sphinxes than I can count, one after another, each as large as a hippopotamus.

A few people stroll, enjoying the morning sun, chattering in pairs and trios about Djehuty knows what. Their sandals shimmer with beads and precious metals. Servants trail behind them, carrying sunshades, feathered fans, and fly whisks. And even the servants' ankles are bound with gold.

What do these people talk about, clad in fine linen, their hands and arms encrusted with jewels?

Part of me resents them, and part of me wants to *be* them.

The horse turns a corner, where we approach what must be the walls of palace. A pair of obelisks reach to the sky. Granite statues of the Good God himself sit at the entrance, draped with garlands of flowers. I wonder what hides behind that content grin I've seen so many times in Men-nefer. But never so many times as here.

The walls cast a shadow over us.

Here, the Good God aims his arrows at his foreign enemies, crushing them under the wheels of his chariot, his horses trampling over their chaotic cloud. Soldiers march into battle, counting the severed hands of the defeated. Prisoners of war in shackles trail behind them.

The Good God projects his power on these walls, to strike fear into those who dare oppose him and those who want our wealth and the grain from our fields. Fields already struggling against the burning Shemu sun.

But is this what I want to become? Is this what Iti wished for me to be?

Indeed, I am foreign born. But Kemet is the only home I've ever known. In that way, I'm no less Kemeti than this nobleman beside me. So why not join the Good God's forces? I can think of no better way to prove I belong here than serving the Good God, defending *ma'at*. And when I do, I'll train with his most elite fighters, so I can protect those like me. My legs won't become granite as they did in the market, and I'll have the conviction to destroy men like those who attacked the *Nebkhepri*.

"Are you all right?" Ahmose asks, his voice low and careful.

I swallow and nod quickly. "I'm just . . ."

"Nervous? I assure you the Good God is just and will be keen to hear your petition. As am I."

He guides the horses toward a pair of immense cedar doors flanked by guards with bronze lances. The doors to the Great House.

A groom takes the reins as Ahmose steps down from the chariot, offering his hand to me again. I take a deep breath, my legs finally steadying on solid ground.

The doors open, and we pass through together.

○ ○ ○

I've read about forests, where the trees grow so tall and dense that they block the horizon and even the sky above. But I've never walked through one, until now.

These vibrantly painted columns surrounding us, reaching up to a cedar beam canopy, are how I imagine a forest to be. Their lily-bud capitals make me feel as tiny as a beetle in a cypress tree.

While my eyes must be as wide and round as the full moon itself, Ahmose takes to these halls as though he has never left. All of this is normal for him.

As we walk, the guards never once stop us, ask why we're here, or question Ahmose about why I'm with him. When he passes, they just nod. And he nods to them in return.

We pass through yet another hall, even more dense and colorful than the first.

Finally, we reach an antechamber, its walls again showing scenes of the Good God's triumphs in faraway lands. He holds a trio of people from Tanehsu by their braids. In the next panel, he crushes Hittites beneath his feet. That sick, twisting feeling in my belly returns.

But I can't turn back now. I tell myself to stay strong and ask for what I seek. This may be my only chance, and if I don't take it, I'll go back to Men-nefer, where Mawat will have already chosen my fate. Where those *isfet* men are still prowling the streets.

I may be walking into a serpent's nest, but at least I'm making that choice for myself.

Ahmose turns to me. "I regret to say that I must leave you here." He looks at his wrist and spins his gold bangle. "And the court is expecting me."

"Will I see you again?" I ask, stepping closer to him.

Behind me, the sound of footsteps and conversation shuffles into the antechamber. Two noblemen in long robes and sandals follow, chatting about the process of their tomb building.

Ahmose looks straight into my eyes. "I certainly hope so."

My cheeks go warm again.

"Go with Ma'at and her feather," Ahmose says. "May your voice be true, and may the gods grant you eternal life."

After a deep bow, deeper than a man of his status dare give a *rekhyt* girl like me, he disappears down the side of the chamber and through a narrow doorway. I want call after him but think better of it. He promised to bring me this far, and he did. His obligation to me has ended.

A trio of women as old as Mawat bursts into the antechamber, chattering like doves about how they suspect the smith lied about how much gold he really used in their new rings. They carry on as though an audience with the Good God is just another daily errand for them, like baking bread or pouring beer.

I pace, and my fingers fumble with my necklace.

The court. On the other side of those doors is the entire court. The Good God, the Great Royal Wife, the high priests, the *tjati* . . . all of them. It doesn't even seem real.

Soon, the antechamber fills with petitioners, including a few *rekhyt* farmers in their rough headcloths, lamenting the low waters and even lower emmer yields. Despite their fretting, I feel a hair calmer in their presence. At least their concerns are real. Those women can live without their jewelry, but none of us can live without bread.

The doors open.

A trumpet's abrasive call pierces through the murmurs and mumbles.

A man laden in gold strides through the doorway. He holds his head high, looking down at all of us. He strikes the base of his tall standard against the floor, and the chatter hushes in an instant.

"The Good God Ramesses the Second, Usermaatre Setepenre, Lord of Fate, the Justice of Re, the Ruler of the Two Lands, will now hear your petitions."

He motions to me.

"Me?"

The man responds with an annoyed nod of his chin.

Before we cross through the doorway, he points to my staff.

"No weapons," he says, his voice commanding and cold. "I'll take it."

I sense the disapproving glare of those noblewomen who couldn't stop talking about their jewelry.

The standard-bearer gestures to my waistband. "The dagger too."

"You'll give them back, right?" I ask, ignoring a gasp from the women behind me.

He flicks his fingers at me with a scowl. "When you leave."

I reluctantly hand him my weapons. Watching him take my staff is like watching him take my arm off my body.

The doors open wider.

"Keep your head down," the standard-bearer says. "Do not look at your Good God without permission. When I tell you, you will kneel before him."

The doors shut behind us with a boom, and I step into a heady haze of lilies, frankincense, wine, and spice. I struggle to keep my sight on the floor, keeping the standard-bearer at the top of my vision.

He clears his throat. "Your Majesty, presenting Sat-reshwet of Men-nefer."

Ahmose must have told him my name. It doesn't feel real.

"Let her approach Horu on his Throne," a man's voice says. I don't dare try to see who spoke.

But I can't help but notice courtiers and attendants lining the walls, adorned in their glistening jewels and neatly pleated robes. If Ahmose, who has actually traveled throughout the Good God's domain, hasn't heard much of what troubles us in Men-nefer, these people must know nothing at all.

I sense kohl-rimmed eyes narrowing at me, evaluating me, already questioning my presence. Some whisper to each other in hushed voices, cupping their hands at each other's ears.

Under my shawl, my fingers flip my pendant. My skin feels too tight for my bones.

The standard-bearer stops in front of the tiled dais. The crack of his standard against the floor ricochets through the hall.

His feet turn toward me. "On your knees."

I fall to the marble tiles, trying to steady my breath.

For an agonizing moment, I wait, motionless.

"You may gaze upon us," a man's deep, buttery voice says.

I hesitate.

"I insist," he says again.

When I do, I'm sure this is a dream. Time itself stops.

The Good God sits tall and proud on his golden throne, the red and white crowns of the united Two Lands upon his brow. He doesn't move, wrists crossed in front of his chest, hands holding the ceremonial crook and flail, all plated in gold and electrum. His nose arches down his face like Horu's beak, and the beard of Ptah graces his jawline, inlaid with malachite.

Beside him sits the most beautiful woman I've ever seen. Proud and poised, her dark eyes twinkle like Nuit's starry belly. Golden vulture wings drape over her elaborate braided human hair wig. This must be the Great Royal Wife, Nefertari Meritmut. As she looks at the Good God and takes his hand, he softens with adoration. I know he has other wives, even a second Chief Wife, but apparently none are as dear to him as she is; none of the others are here.

And at their sides, bald men, their faces stern and unyielding, hold their forked scepters. Priests.

I stop short on a young woman in a linen shift holding a palm frond fan behind the Great Royal Wife.

Her expression widens before she averts her gaze.

If I didn't know better, I would think she looks a lot like me. A few years older than me, but her nose, her chin, her eyes . . . No, that's impossible. The fatigue of the journey must be settling in, or the gods are playing tricks on me.

The Good God and the Great Royal Wife look directly at me.

I drop my forehead to the floor.

"Please," the Good God says. "Raise your head."

I raise my head, not sure where to settle my gaze.

"Tell me," he says, "what has brought you to the Great House?"

Where do I start? I can't just blurt out what I've really come for, or the Medjay will drag me across this floor before I can even blink.

But I want more than to follow in Iti's footsteps. My thoughts flash with the gathering room at the Per-seshen. The Scarred Man in the kitchen. The attack on the ship. The market.

Murmurs from the court swirl along the walls.

I take a deep breath. To my surprise, the Good God regards me with kindness, nothing like the vicious warrior on his temple walls.

"Your Majesty," I say, steadying my voice. "There's been trouble. Trouble in my city."

"Your city? And which city is that?"

"Men-nefer."

He tilts his head.

"Something there isn't balanced," I say. "Men who say they're acting in your name have been intimidating us. And some of these men . . ."

PART THREE: THE COMMAND

The court's chattering falls to a deathly hush. I hold my breath.

"Go on," the Good God's soft voice encourages.

"Some of them—they attacked our friends." I push back the tears that creep just from the mention of it. "They were from Tanehsu, but they were loyal to you, to the Two Lands. Tahir . . . He fought for you at Qadesh."

The murmurs of the court grow louder, agitated.

"And these attackers claim to be acting under your command."

Gasps and shouts erupt around me as the young man holding a brightly painted ostrich feather fan steps forward from his place at the right side of the Good God, a sharp scowl on his face.

"Your Highness," he says, "I believe she is accusing you of ordering such acts. You cannot allow her to continue with such slander."

The Good God waves the back of his bejeweled hand at him. After he steps back, the Good God focuses his falcon's gaze on me. "Please, continue."

I take a deep breath, but it does nothing to quell the tremble in my belly. "Your Majesty, I don't believe you sent these men. But I do believe your justice can protect us."

The Good God calls over an older man in a long kilt. The ties of his green and blue beaded belt brush over the tops of his feet as he scurries to the throne. He must be the *tjati*; he's almost as powerful as the Good God himself. He leans to the Good God's ear. The Fan-bearer rushes in front of them, hiding their faces with his billowing ostrich feathers, as white as the feather of *ma'at* itself.

I can't hear what they're saying, not even a whisper.

When the Fan-bearer pulls away, the Good God addresses me. "You are from Men-nefer? Our enduring and beautiful city up the Iteru?"

I nod.

"Tjati Hatiay has confirmed with me that there has been trouble there, indeed. But is it not true the men you speak of were provoked?"

Curse these *isfet* rumors.

"No," I blurt. "I saw what happened. Tahir didn't start it. These men, they insulted him. They punched first."

Again, more hushed whispers behind the ostrich feathers and wine goblets.

The Good God's rehearsed calm falters for a moment. Just like Ahmose, he knows more about these men than he wishes to admit. "The Good House will send more Medjay to Men-nefer," he says.

"My eternal gratitude, Your Majesty," I respond, forehead to the floor again. The Medjay might help, but I fear they won't be enough.

The Good God speaks again. "But you are here for more."

Is it that obvious? "Yes, Your Majesty. I do wish for something else."

"I suspected as much," the Good God says with a close-lipped smile.

This is it. My only opportunity to ask for the life I want, no matter how outlandish, unlikely, or unbelievable it may be. If I don't do it now, then when?

Dear Sekhmet, I could use your wisdom now. Give me your strength here in the Good God's home, in the Great House, in the temple of the king whose life you protect. For it is you who brought me here.

I listen for her, for the *heka*.

"What is it you seek?" the Good God asks.

Oh, Powerful One, you told me Horu on his Throne is waiting, and I don't want to make him wait any longer.

The air around me purrs. *Yes, my child. Ask for what you seek.*

I raise my chin and straighten my back. The words form in my throat, and I finally speak.

"Let me serve you in your military, as my father did." My voice fills the chamber, bouncing off the columns. "Let me be a soldier."

The chamber erupts, but I hold my gaze firm on the Good God. He sits calmly, observing, allowing his court their moment of dissonance. Laughs and jeers bounce through the throne room. What did I expect? I know how strange it sounds, but no amount of insult from these highborn sycophants will deter me.

The Good God raises the royal crook and flail, and the hall falls silent. He glances at the Great Royal Wife, and her eyes dart to the girl beside her, then back to the Good God.

"A noble request indeed," he says softly.

The courtiers whisper to each other again, and the ladies behind the dais shoot each other looks of disbelief. But the Great Royal Wife leans forward.

"If I may speak," she says, her voice as strong and regal as her presence.

"It would make me glad," the Good God says, and the Great Royal Wife turns her attention to me.

"Tell me again," she says. "What is your name?"

"Sati, Your Majesty. Sat-reshwet." My heart races. Will she be the one to tell me that what I ask for is impossible?

"Tell me, Sati, the soldier's daughter, what skills do you bring with you to this great hall, to the service of your king and a God made flesh?"

"I can fight," I say, my voice firm.

The Great Royal Wife raises her painted eyebrows. "And?"

"And I am literate. In both our native tongue and Akkadian."

The whispers in the hall build into a rush. They don't believe me. And why would they? But they'll believe one of their own.

I raise my voice, hoping to be heard above them all. "And a nobleman in your court can testify to my claim."

As the courtiers jeer and laugh, I search the court for Ahmose, but I can't find him. I've said too much. The Good God and the Great Royal Wife will think I've been possessed by *isfet* demons. That I've been imagining everything, even my own abilities.

The jeers turn to surprise as Ahmose steps forward.

The Great Royal Wife and the Good God share another look

before he holds up the crook and flail again. The room falls into an obedient hush.

Satisfied with the quiet, the Good God turns to Ahmose. "Is it true, Lord Ahmose?" he asks. "Do you know this young woman? Does she speak *ma'at*?"

Ahmose walks to the center and kneels beside me on his uninjured leg. The faint scent of myrrh and cinnamon follows him.

"Yes, Your Majesty," he says, bowing his head. "Every word is *ma'at*."

"Every word?" the Good God asks.

"Yes, I swear by the feather. And she might have even saved my life. The *Nebkhepri* was attacked on our journey here—"

"Attacked?" The Good God's eyes widen with fury.

"Yes, Your Majesty. Sati fought alongside me and our crew. And she also tended to this wound." He pulls up the hem of his *shendyt* to reveal the linen bandage. A few people around us gasp. "It would have festered without her attention and care."

The Good God leans back in his golden throne. "Far be it from me to question the son of Useraasen. May he live forever."

The court echoes the words in a reverent whisper. Ahmose says it too, but with less conviction.

The Good God beckons to Tjati Hatiay, and the Fan-bearer hides their faces once again.

Finally, the Fan-bearer pulls away and the *tjati* steps back. The Good God and the Great Royal Wife have an entire conversation with only glances and share an almost devious grin. The Good God continues with a commanding voice that fills every corner of the Great Hall.

"My half-brother," he says, "has been lamenting to me for months about how none of his scribes have even a modicum of fighting skills. And here you are, Sati of Men-nefer, brave and loyal and literate."

Will he truly grant my request? Will he go against all tradition and welcome me into his ranks?

"It would be a shame to let your gifts be wasted," he continues. "After all, you have come all this way."

My chest tightens.

"I shall grant you what you seek. You will join my military as a scribe and soldier."

He said it. If my ears don't deceive me, he actually said it. And not only will I become a soldier, but a scribe as well!

The court erupts again with astonished voices, their protests on the edge of decorum.

The Fan-bearer steps forward. "Your Excellency, I urge you to reconsider."

The Good God narrows his sight at the younger man. "You question my wisdom? Please, explain yourself."

"If I may," the Fan-bearer says, "but a woman in the military? It's not *ma'at*."

The Good God's lips purse. The *tjati* rolls his eyes. But the Fan-bearer keeps talking.

"If what this girl says is true, that there are men stirring the waters of Nu already, you would tempt the Serpent further by placing her in the role of a man?" Several of the attendants on the dais nod their heads in agreement.

The Good God's angled face sharpens. "You claim to know *ma'at* as well as I do?" It's not a question to be answered. "Observe, and perhaps someday you will, Son of My Body."

The voices quiet once again as the Fan-bearer drops his head, and he falls back behind the royal retinue. The Great Royal Wife gives him a dagger-like stare. I know that look. Mawat gives it to me when I've let the bread burn. The Fan-bearer must be her son.

"I have made my decision," the Good God booms. "Sat-reshwet of Men-nefer, I welcome you into my service."

My heart stops. Somehow, I've done it. The Good God himself

has decreed it, spoken my dreams into existence. The air around me heats with a satisfied purr.

The Great Royal Wife holds up her hand. "May I offer some advice to the young woman?"

The Good God nods to her, and she leans forward.

"Sat-reshwet," she says, as though we are the only ones here. "Life as a woman in the Black Land already presents its challenges. And now, you must bear an additional burden in the service of our king. The officers and their men will question your presence. They will test your strength, perseverance, and intelligence. Far more than if you had been born a man. But if your fellow soldiers should doubt the decision to place you amongst their ranks, remember the Good God made that choice. They have no authority to challenge it, now, or in the Field of Reeds. And you serve us now, for it is the Good God who is a deity among men."

I bow, unsure of how to thank her. How does one thank the God's Wife?

"I can see you have a greatness you have not yet realized."

My head darts up in disbelief. Has the goddess spoken to her, too?

Ahmose turns his head to me. "Well deserved," he whispers against the chattering of the crowd. "Now is when you praise the king and his wife for their wisdom."

My fingers fumble over each other. "Serving the Great House, defending *ma'at* in the name of the Good God, Amun, Mut, and Khonsu, and the patron gods of my city would be my greatest honor."

The Good God calls a young man to the foot of the dais. He must only be twelve floods old, a page for the court.

"Take this new recruit to General Setankh," the Good God says. "Ensure he understands that at my special request, Sat-reshwet now serves him as a scribe, and she is to be trained in combat with the infantry. And emphasize that she is to enjoy all the privileges afforded to her as a scribe."

The young man nods in obedience.

"And if he objects," the Good God continues, "let him know I will act accordingly."

Those words sound like a threat.

The Good God beams, but there's something else behind his lips that I can't make out, something shrewd and scheming. How I play a role in whatever he plans, I can't tell. Whatever his intentions, the wheels are in motion, and I have no choice but to turn with them.

"May you serve with a light heart and may you live forever, Sat-reshwet from Men-nefer."

The Fan-bearer narrows his gaze at me, his eyebrows furrowed in disapproval. But the Great Royal Wife lifts her chin in pride.

And the young woman behind them stares at me with what I see now are wide, green eyes.

CHAPTER ELEVEN

As the page leads me back through the antechamber, the standard-bearer stops me. "It sounds like you'll be needing these."

I swipe back my dagger and staff, wrapping my fingers around the worn wood and leather.

As I tuck the dagger back into my waistband, I follow the page through the crowd of petitioners, then through the forest of columned halls, one after the other, until we exit into the midday sun.

We pass lush gardens crowded with sycamores and acacias and palms expectant with dates, around the imposing walls of villas and vibrant temples. The sweet smell of myrrh and pine resins gives way to the musty scent of the riverbanks. The sun burns stronger here. In the distance horses neigh, and the sour reek of manure wafts across the dust.

Then I hear it. The familiar clacking of staffs, the shuffle of feet in the dirt, and the wail of a man who failed to dodge his opponent's weapon. It's been so long now since I've heard those sounds, since I last sparred with Iti. While my heart misses him, I know now I'm in the right place.

We approach a larger building, its exterior armed with that now familiar scene of the Good God riding into battle on his chariot. But here, a man in scaled leather armor rides beside him, his axe raised. He's painted the same size and height as the Good God himself. If he's so important, why have I never seen him before?

Before I can read the name, a voice calls out behind me.

"Oh, thank the gods." Ahmose jogs up to greet us. "I hoped to get here before you meet the general."

"What are you doing here? Don't you need to be at the Great Hall?" Not that I object to seeing him one more time before my training consumes me. I catch the scent of myrrh and cinnamon again.

He flicks his hand at the page. "Tell the general his new scribe will see him in a moment."

The page nods dutifully and slips through the doorway.

Ahmose lowers his voice to a whisper and steps closer to me. "I wanted to give you a word of warning."

"I know what I've gotten myself into," I start. "I know I don't belong—"

"No," he says. "It's General Setankh. He harbors a resentment for the king."

"But he's the Good God's brother."

"Half-brother. A fact he won't let the king forget. So, be vigilant. If you see anything that seems, well, unusual, tell me."

"How will I do that?" I'm not even sure what might be unusual for this place.

He hands me a small, long box. I instantly recognize it as a scribe's kit, complete with finely made pens, new cakes of black and red pigment, and even a few strips of freshly pressed papyrus. A kit like this one must have cost a month's worth of grain.

"I can't take this—"

"It's yours. You'll need it." He clasps his hands around mine, and my breath hitches. "Leave any notes under your headrest. Remember, the Good God has given you his blessing, and although you serve the general, your duty is to the Great House."

"Of course."

"You will do right by the feather, I'm sure of it."

Ahmose loosens his hold when the page reappears from inside. I roll the kit back up and hold it close to my chest.

"General Setankh grows impatient," the page says in a boyish voice on the verge of adulthood. "He demands to see the new scribe."

"Go with the feather," Ahmose says, his eyes intent and warning.

After I watch Ahmose disappear into the dusty haze, I take a deep breath and open the door behind me.

An imposing man, completely clean-shaven, sits alone at a table in an ornate chair. He's engrossed in the papyrus scrolls in front of him.

"Let me guess," he says without looking up. "You have no combat experience and are just as weak as the rest."

I tread across the reed mats, past the walls painted with brutal battle scenes. Here, only the mysterious man with the axe leads the soldiers, with the Good God nowhere to be found. I find his name. General Setankh.

I stop in front of his table, and I hold my head high, my staff in one hand and Ahmose's scribe kit in the other. "I'm here on appointment of the Good God, Usermaatre Setepenre, the Lord of the Sedge and the Bee."

The general's painted eyes widen. "Is this some sort of joke?"

"No, *imyr*," I say, recalling what Iti called his own commanding officers. "My instructions come directly from the Good God himself, *imyr*."

"The page told me the king was sending me a scribe."

"Yes, *imyr*."

"A scribe with combat abilities?"

"Yes, *imyr*, that's me."

"You? A girl?" He laughs, his mouth wide. "Ramesses has lost his mind."

Despite the fact he wishes to dismiss me for not being a man, it's his use of the Good God's name that unsettles me, even if they are half-brothers.

The general returns to his papyrus.

I clear my throat. "With all respect, *imyr*, the Good God has placed me in your service, as both soldier and scribe."

"I heard what the page said, and I do not accept. Leave my office." He flicks his hand at me as though swatting away a gnat. It stuns me that he would question the Good God at all, especially with such blatant disdain.

The little fire in my heart ignites, and I take a step closer to his desk. "*Imyr*, the Good God has commanded me to serve you."

He glares at me as he rises to his feet. My palms go slick with sweat.

The top of his head nearly touches the ceiling, and his neck bulges under his broad collar. Wide gold bands strain against the muscles in his upper arms. He's at least a head and a half taller than me.

Just breathe. Stand firm. He must accept the Good God's order. Who would be so insolent to dare do otherwise?

"I said, leave my office."

We stare at each other, locked into a test of wills. I've come too far to turn away now. I know my standing here is an act of disrespect, but if I leave, I'll be disobeying the Good God. I tighten my grip on my staff and the scribe's kit.

He folds his arms and sits back in his chair. "You do have spirit, I give you that."

He was bluffing. Perhaps he's not that intimidating after all.

"Most of the other spindly scribes my brother appoints to my military would have run away scared by now."

I note that he says "my" military.

He tilts his head as he evaluates me, as though I were a weapon, and makes a shrew, thoughtful sound. "Your muscle tone is good. But you've recently been injured." He points to my bandaged arm.

"It's not that deep, *imyr*. And almost healed."

"How did it happen?"

"We were attacked on our journey here, *imyr*."

He lifts his chin. "Oh? Who is 'we'?"

"The crew aboard the royal barge *Nebkhepri*, *imyr*."

Not a bit of surprise shades his sun-weathered face. "And you fought with only your staff?"

I nod. "And a dagger, *imyr*."

His gaze drifts to the side, sharp eyebrows furrowed, then darts back to me. "Did you kill any of these attackers?"

"To be *ma'at*, *imyr*, I'm not sure."

"You're not sure?"

"Yes, *imyr*. But I'm sure I broke one man's ribs, after stabbing him in the side. He jumped into the river."

The general's brows lift for a moment before he leans forward, resting his elbows on the desk. He folds his hands under his pronounced chin.

"If what you say is *ma'at*, then you might be worth my time."

Oh, I'll be more than worth his time, if he would give me a chance.

"If you fail, if you are even one grain of sand in my teeth, I won't hesitate to send you back to whatever hovel you came from."

"I assure you, I won't fail, *imyr*." I have too much to prove and too much to lose. I give him a small bow.

He returns to his papers. I try to peek at what's on them, but I can't make out any of the writing from where I stand.

"Tonight," the general says, "you will report to the mess hall with the rest of the infantry. You'll need to earn your place at the scribes' hall, so don't think you'll be enjoying any lavish meals with those spoiled flamingos yet. Tomorrow morning, you will take your oath of loyalty in service of the king. When you have finished, you will begin your training in combat with your unit commander. And in the afternoon, after the midday meal, report to me."

He raises his head and glares at me with his deep-set, black eyes.

"If you are even the slightest bit difficult, insolent, or disruptive,

I will dismiss you and never think twice about it, despite whatever the king promised you."

"Understood, *imyr*."

The general calls for his page.

"Find this girl a room." He looks me up and down again. "And a uniform."

The page nods in obedience and darts away.

"You are under my command now, girl. Don't make me regret it."

○ ○ ○

The general's page leads me past the humblest barracks, and I can't get General Setankh's stony face out of my heart. He didn't seem shocked at all that anyone would dare attack a royal cargo barge. Perhaps such a thing is more common than I thought. But if it were, Khefer and his crew would have requested Medjay guards as soon as they left Punt.

"Your quarters, *nebet*. I'm told you'll be staying on the first floor."

Where it's dirtier, hotter, and more likely to attract pests.

He points to a straw mattress on a plain bed frame. "Your uniform is there."

A new *shendyt*, a carnelian leather tunic. The color of the Good God's own warriors. The color Iti wore when he fought alongside the Good God.

At the far side of the bed stands a small headrest. Where Ahmose said he'd find my messages should I need to write them. And in the farthest corner, an unadorned wooden chest to store what little I have with me.

"May you be in favor with Amun." With a bow, the page ducks away, closing the door behind him.

I can't believe it. I'm here. I did it. My first step in truly becoming a soldier.

And leaving even more of my home and my old life in the past.

I lean my staff against the corner wall and pull my father's dagger from my waistband. I conceal it among the folds of my shawl, tucking them both deep in the storage chest. If I am, indeed, in a serpent's nest, I'll certainly need them again. But not now.

After peeling off my linen tunic, I draw the leather one over my head, smoothing it down with my palms before tightening the lacing at the sides. I shuffle out of my rough, dirty *shendyt* and wrap the new one around my hips with a tight knot in the front.

If only Iti could see me now. If only *I* could see me now. Without my mirror, I can't even see my own transformation, the one I've imagined and dreamed of for so long. Even Mawat might be proud. That I came this far, that I've stayed true and strong. How could she not?

As I fold my old clothes away in the chest, the front door opens with a rush.

A tall, skinny man with gangly limbs, maybe only a few years older than me, stands at the threshold. He's sliding a reed pen into his ebony writing kit, a delicate box gilded in electrum, which reflects the physical appearance of its owner. The glass beads of his chin-length wig clink against each other in a bubbly chorus.

"By Djehuty, I must be in the wrong building!" he exclaims in an airy voice, painted eyes still cast on his kit.

"I wouldn't know. Are you?" I ask.

After he slides the lid back onto the box, he blinks at me in disbelief.

"Oh, I certainly am in the wrong building! I'll leave you to . . . whatever it was you were doing." He flaps his long, ink-stained fingers at me.

"Changing. For the evening meal."

"Right." He doesn't sound convinced. "Good evening. May you live forever." He leaves in haste, closing the door behind him.

But the door opens as quickly as it had shut.

"Back so soon?" I chuckle.

"It seems this is my building after all." He strides in with a new-found sense of purpose, then scrutinizes me. "Are you sure *you're* in the right building?"

"General Setankh's page brought me here."

"General Setankh, hmm? Well, if you say so. Are you staying long?"

"You could say that. I'm a new recruit."

"An infantryman?" He shakes his head, and the thin mustache on his upper lip twitches. "No, no, no. An infantrywoman! Is the king conscripting women now? This is the first I've heard of such a thing, and believe me, I would know before anyone."

"It's a new policy," I say with a little laugh, and he gapes at me. "Starting today. And only for me. And you're a scribe, I see." I point to his kit.

"Ah, yes, very perceptive. Which is why I live here, and not in the filthy infantry barracks. So, why are you, a soldier, in a scribe's house?"

"I'm both."

"Both? The river is truly running uphill today, isn't it? Well, your skills will be in demand if you can show it can be done."

"So I've been told."

"We'll know soon enough if you're up for the task. The general doesn't take kindly to, well, unusual recruits. Have you met him?"

I nod. "Just before I came here."

"Then you've had the pleasure."

"I'm not sure I'd call it that."

He quirks a thin smile, then points that long, ink-stained finger at my bandaged arm. "How did that happen?"

I run my fingertips over the linen wraps. "A blade got in my way."

His painted brow quirks. "You might survive here, yet."

He turns and strides toward the stairs.

"Ai, you didn't tell me your name," I call to him.

The beads on his wig clink together as he spins to face me and presses his palm over his heart. "Djedi. Scribe to the Commander of the Chariotry Host. And you?"

"Sati," I say with I dip my head. "Newly appointed scribe to General Setankh, I suppose."

He purses his lips. "Well, I hope your pen is faster than your arm."

"I'm sure I'll be just fine," I say through a tight jaw.

"The evening meal will start soon," he says, "and you best not be late. Let me put my kit upstairs, and I'll take you to the meal hall."

"But if you're a scribe, why would you eat with the soldiers?"

"Oh, I didn't say I'd *stay*."

He turns to the stairs again. Before he goes up to his room, he points to my staff. "You best bring that weapon. I have a feeling you'll need it."

CHAPTER TWELVE

As Djedi walks me to the meal hall, we find ourselves behind a cluster of young men, all clad in the same red leather and *shendytu*. Some wear no tunics at all, sporting the bruises on their chests like trophies.

One rams his elbow into another's rib cage, and they laugh from deep in their bellies. Linen wraps calves, wrists, and ankles, some stained with ruddy, dried blood. I recognize those injuries. Whenever I returned home with a cut or even a minor scuff, Mawat insisted I cover it right away. But these men wear their wounds with pride.

As we pass, they keep their distance, glaring at Djedi and sneering at me.

At first, they whisper. "What's a girl doing here?"

I hold my head high. I'll be defending my place more often than I would like, and I'm confident I can do it.

"Go back to the kitchen!" one yells at me.

"Do you know how to use that staff?"

"I've got a staff you can use right here!" One of them gestures to his crotch. Delightful. Little does he know that I could hit his "staff" before he could even think to defend himself.

Djedi darts between me and them, and the men fall back, looking vaguely apologetic.

"Typical boys," he grumbles. "Just ignore them. Besides, when they learn you are a scribe, they might leave you alone."

"I'm not counting on it," I say.

The meal hall sits on the edge of the river, and here the air is cooler and fresher than near the barracks. My belly snarls at the yeasty scent of baking bread.

The gaggle of men leer at me as they disappear through an entrance of simple lily-capped columns.

"Keep your weapon close," Djedi says. "And tell me all about it later!"

He flits away before I can even say goodbye or ask what he means by "it."

I let out a long exhale and enter the meal hall.

The reeking scent of stale beer and sweat slap me in the face. I don't know what I expected, but whatever it was didn't smell so bad. But I pull my shoulders back and hold my chin higher. And I grip my staff tighter.

Along the wall, tables are spread with beer jars, simple clay cups, and worn baskets of bread and dried fruits. The walls, of course, brandish scenes of great military victories, soldiers marching in unison, weapons and shields at the ready.

I join the line of chattering men waiting to fill their plates. Dozens already have, sitting on sparse cushions around low tables throughout the hall, devouring their meals.

My belly rumbles again. I grab a few dried dates and several onion rolls from a fraying basket and pour myself beer from the jug. I wince at the smell; it's far more pungent than my mother's brew.

I find one of the few empty tables, tucked in the farthest corner. As I sit, I realize why these seats were empty. Heat from cooking fires in the kitchens sends sweat dripping down the back of my tunic. But from here, I can see every man in the hall, some of whom lock eyes with me as I take in the scene. Other men watch me, resenting my presence with my every move.

As I shove a roll into my mouth and crunch against the sand in the flour, a man twice my size approaches my table. At least five rolls balance precariously on his plate, and his tunic stretches over his round belly.

"Can I sit here?" he asks, in a voice much lighter than I expect.

I wait for him to comment on me being a girl, or worse, to say something leering or lecherous. But he just flashes me a toothy grin. And he's missing a tooth.

"Sure," I say, sidling over to make room for him.

"I'm Rahuti," he says as he sits. To be *ma'at*, I don't really care who he is. Especially if he's like the men who "greeted" me outside.

But because Mawat raised me to be polite, I lift my cup to acknowledge him. "Sati," I say, and take a drink. I almost spit it out. The beer is so sour and bitter it puckers my mouth.

"You'll get used to it," Rahuti says.

"I certainly hope so."

Three sharp hand claps silence the rumbling hum of men's voices.

"The general!" Rahuti says.

On a raised dais at the opposite end of the hall, General Setankh stands, surveying us like a vulture gliding for carrion.

And his sight lands on me. I stop short of shoving another roll into my mouth and quickly set it back on the dish.

"Let us welcome our special new recruit," he bellows. "A scribe here on order of the king." He gestures to me with his broad hand.

The hall rustles and creaks with the sound of bodies shifting to face me. And when they do, most of them snicker.

One man yells from behind the others. "Are you serious? A girl?"

I find him. He leans back against the wall, muscular arms crossed over his leather tunic. Even from so far away, he stares down his jackal's nose at me. I hope my face is behaving itself and isn't sneering at him in return.

"Indeed, Commander Hani," General Setankh says, his voice oily and contemptuous. "Shall we see if she is deserving of the king's post?"

Commander Hani grabs a staff from beside his table; the ends glimmer with lines of gold leaf. My heart races, not out of fear, but to prepare for a fight, and my hand darts to my own staff.

"You! Girl!" Commander Hani yells, pointing the end of his weapon at me, and my belly drops. This must be the "it" Djedi wanted to hear about later.

Rahuti glances at me with apprehension. "You don't want to spar with him," he whispers.

"I might not have a choice," I say, tightening my grip around the leather wraps.

"Yes, you!" Commander Hani calls again. "Outside."

"You don't have to," Rahuti says. "He does this to everyone he doesn't like." The look on his face tells me when he arrived, Commander Hani challenged him to a spar, and he didn't fare all that well.

"He doesn't even know me enough to dislike me." But I won't let this commander intimidate me. If I fail, I'll do it fighting. "And he'll like me less when we're done."

"I'm not sure that's a good idea . . ."

In the sand between the meal hall and the officers' quarters, the commander draws a rectangle with the end of his staff, no more than ten cubits on each side.

I know this game. The House of Battle. After my first blood, Iti drew the same shape in the dust, carefully measuring the sides with a length of yarn. He told me how he and his fellow soldiers would spar to pass the time between battles and convoys, and how whoever stumbled out of the House first would have to clean the kitchens or muck out the stables for the next week. The first time he and I played, he shoved me across the line in three blows. The last time, the one just before the Scarred Man showed up, I had sent him across in two.

A sea of soldiers gathers around it, hungry for what they think will be Commander Hani's inevitable win. General Setankh pushes his way through them, joining his commander at the narrow side. Commander Hani must be at least one head taller than me, yes, but Iti always assured me that my strength is in my speed and agility. I hope he's right.

"Since you claim to be so experienced," the general says to me, "we don't have to explain the rules to you."

"So long as you haven't changed the rules," I say.

The two men sneer.

"Last fighter in the House wins," I say.

"Last fighter in the House wins," the general repeats. But I suspect he's keeping something from me. I'm sure I'll discover it soon enough.

A wisp of hot air brushes against my neck and shoulders. Is that you or just the late Shemu breeze? Or my empty belly? Oh, Sekhmet, give me strength to fight, and to be powerful enough to prove my worth to you and the Good God's army.

"Soldiers at the ready." General Setankh steps back, and the men part for him, keeping their distance. Behind them, Rahuti peeks over their heads.

As I take my place opposite Commander Hani, my foot catches on something, and I tumble into the House. A soldier behind me releases a wicked laugh. The piece of *hes* tripped me!

Commander Hani steps his sandaled foot on the end of my weapon, pinning it to the earth, and sneers.

I wrap my hands around my staff and jerk up the end, sending the commander lurching backward. When I take the opening to wheel my weapon at his shin, he nearly steps over the edge. Ptah's beard! So close.

He finds his balance, standing with his chest puffed like a partridge.

He didn't even start this fight properly. We were supposed to stand facing each other, staffs crossed in the center. That's what Iti taught me.

But the crowd cheers for him, this cheater.

"Hit her, Commander Hani!"

"She's just a girl!"

"Are you going to let that *ka't* beat you?"

Commander Hani goads the men, arms out wide. They chant his name. "Hani! Hani! Hani!" He basks in their adoration. They don't even address him by his title, another show of strange insolence against everything Iti taught me. General Setankh beams at them with his vulture's eyes.

Resolve brews in my belly. If they think they intimidate me, they're wrong. I widen my stance and straighten my back. If these men don't regard him as their superior, then neither will I. Not until I've won.

The commander takes a weighted step toward me, more might than grace.

My attention narrows. What they say doesn't matter.

Toe, ball, heel, I tread nearer to the commander, sensing the earth beneath my bare feet. Each step leads me closer to victory or defeat as I reach the center of the House.

To my surprise, Commander Hani lingers near the edge. He'll have to defend himself now.

But he only smirks at me. I take one more step, now squarely in his half of the House, shrinking the gap between us to no longer than our weapons.

I swing.

His weapon blocks mine, and he whips the opposite end at the back of my legs. The searing pain knocks me to my knees. The crowd roars.

Commander Hani laughs, holding his arms out to encourage them.

I press myself to my feet, but he strikes me again, right under my ribs. My breath leaps from my lungs, and I double over.

Another across the middle of my back. I lurch forward, pain engulfing me.

The men around me spin and wobble. I can't see where they end and the sky begins. I try to use my staff for support, like an old man. The scales aren't balanced. And neither am I.

PART THREE: THE COMMAND

This is all wrong. It's not supposed to be like this. I'm supposed to hold my own.

Come on, Sati, stand up.

"Seems like this won't be much of a fight," the commander says, turning to the crowd of soldiers. They erupt in vicious laughs.

Tears well in my eyes as the throbbing ache from my back overtakes me. My resolve begins to crack. The insidious sense of being an outsider multiplies in me. You don't belong here, it says. You need to go home. You're weak and an imposter. You're nothing but a stranger here, and they'll find out. You are the enemy. They'll find out you're from Retenu. When they do, they won't hesitate to kill you. They're going to kill you. They'll even kill Mawat and Iti.

"No!" I hear myself yell.

Commander Hani gives me a puzzled look. I press myself upright, widening my stance, centering my weight. I've traveled too far and sacrificed too much for him to knock me down so easily. If I'm going to fall, it's not going to be fighting a man like him.

"No? No, what?" Commander Hani snarls.

"No." I repeat. "You haven't won. I'm still inside the House."

I flick the end of my staff at his waist. His quick reflexes block me, and we fall back from each other, measuring instinct against instinct, each tiny move a signal of the next.

"Ai, Commander! Hit her again!"

The commander grunts as he swipes again, this time at my feet. I jump and he misses. He curses.

With my aching arms, I strike. Wood cracks against wood, again and again, neither of us getting in another hit against flesh.

We're in the corner of his side of the House, eyes locked, close enough to each other that one strike would knock the other across the line.

But something catches my eye. Thank Sekhmet! He attempts

three strikes, and before each one, the gold on his weapon glints in the fading evening light, with a shake no larger than a mosquito's wingbeat.

He sneers, anger clouding his sight. He tries to slide past me, pushing me back, but I maneuver in front of him so he can't get closer to the center.

The end of his staff trembles before it even gets close. He suppresses a curse. Only a foot's length remains between him and the edge.

The prickling in my skin calms. I can do this. I can beat him. He's burly and strong, but I'm quick and clever. And his rage is getting the better of him.

He lets out a satisfying wail as I jam the end of my weapon into his toes. He limps back, nearly over the boundary of the House.

I lunge forward, striking the same foot again, this time at his ankle. He cries out and his weapon grazes my skull as I duck. I have no choice but to jump back.

But I shouldn't be this close to the edge.

I glare at Commander Hani. Iti told me that the boundaries were set, in accordance with *ma'at*. The commander made this House smaller than it's supposed to be, smaller than Iti's careful measurements.

Vile, *desher* cheater!

The crowd erupts around us.

"Finish her, Commander!"

"Defeat that she-jackal!"

"Can't you beat a snake, Hani? Crush her!"

How can they cheer for a man who laughs in the face of *ma'at*?

Stay focused. Stay strong. I can't let them bring me down. I've only just arrived here.

And when I win, I'll do it with the feather.

I roar toward Commander Hani.

My staff takes on a life of its own, hitting his belly, chest, and feet.

He attempts another strike as he tries to find stability, but he misses, which only throws his balance off even more.

With a swing, I send him reeling backward on his rear.

The crowd hushes to shocked whispers.

Commander Hani growls, and his staff hits the back of my ankles. The searing pain races into my head and knocks me to the ground.

"You think I haven't fought warriors twice as experienced as you?" he snarls.

Of course not. But every strongman has a weakness. They must. I reach deep within me, past the exhaustion, the heartache, and the ridicule, and I hit the side of his ribs with all the force I can muster.

When I strike at the crease between his leg and hip, the commander doubles over to his knees and collapses to a crawl. I take the chance to stand again.

"If you're so experienced," I taunt through clenched teeth, "then why am I the one standing?"

He tries to hit me again from below, but I block him. I push forward, and he crawls back.

The way he hunkers down doesn't give me any opening for a worthwhile hit. I take a chance and step back.

The men around us cheer for him as struggles to stand. Yes, Commander, take the bait.

He reveals the tender, vulnerable front of his chest. With my tiring arms, I ram the end of my staff below his ribs. His mouth opens as if to cry out.

Time stops as he wobbles.

He teeters, rage and humiliation overtaking him.

The men cease their yells. I feel them watching me.

The commander reaches his thick arm down, palm splayed.

And he stumbles back over the boundary and falls to the dust.

The men become as silent as a sealed tomb.

That's right. Watch your man fall.

"Daughter of a jackal! May Ammit devour you!" Commander

Hani bares his teeth, and I jump to the side as he hurls his weapon at me. He brushes the dirt from his skinned knees. "You filthy, dirty—"

A few daring soldiers laugh at his taunts but stop when the commander burns a glance at them. Some whisper to each other. The rest say nothing. Eyes dart from me, to Commander Hani, to General Setankh, and back to me again. I let the stares wrap around me, an invisible cloak of victory.

As I catch my breath, dust still swirling around me, I turn to face General Setankh, my stance wide. I played his game. I fought his mighty warrior. And I won by his rules.

Judging from the way he stares down his vulture's nose at me, my success wasn't part of whatever he'd planned for me. I was supposed to lose. I was supposed to be humiliated. I was supposed to be so defeated that I would give up and leave, and he could prove that the Good God's decision to assign me as scribe and soldier was a terrible mistake.

The others shift awkwardly around us.

Finally, after what seems like an eternity, the general speaks.

"Perhaps," he admits, "you are as good as you claim to be. As my half-brother claims you are." His upper lip curls. "Or maybe you were just lucky."

"She won't be so lucky next time. Next time, we'll fight with actual weapons." Commander Hani limps past me to retrieve his staff. He wags the gilded end in my face. "If you step out of line," he says, "I'll rend you limb from limb. We'll feed your fingers and toes to our dogs, and we'll burn the rest of you so you never even make it to the Field of Reeds, even if you could make it past Djehuty's scales. Don't think you've escaped me because you won this round."

Contempt seeps out of his pores with his musty sweat.

"You don't scare me," I say as a cloud of soldiers gathers behind him. "Neither do your men." I tighten my hands around my weapon, trying to hide the tremble in my fingers.

"Well, they should." He turns. "Come, men. We have real battles to prepare for."

Even as several of them spit at my feet, I make sure to look directly at them as they pass.

After the commander and his men leave, the others disperse, and my heart slows. The ache of my grumbling stomach and a new crop of blossoming bruises and welts replaces the rush of the fight. I call on every grain of strength I have left to keep myself upright, but I stumble, catching myself with my staff.

A sturdy hand appears before me.

"Rahuti?"

"You were right," he says as I take his hand and he gives me a honey roll. "He's definitely going to like you less. A lot less."

I grab the bread and tear away a bite, like I haven't eaten in weeks.

At the sound of forceful, sandaled footsteps, he hops back. "General Setankh."

"Fill your belly while you can, girl," the general hisses. "Because tomorrow, you'll be reporting to Commander Hani."

CHAPTER THIRTEEN

As Re's barque peeks its prow over the eastern horizon, ten other recruits and I gather on the southern edge of the garrison in the courtyard outside the Temple of Sutekh. A few shuffle their feet nervously, while others, like me, hold their chins high and proud.

A priest, his scalp polished and shiny, adjusts the leopard skin draped on his shoulder. He looks at me askew for a moment.

I'm sure I look unusual, not just being a woman, but now a woman with only a little layer of fuzz of hair on her own head. Before we came to the temple, two military pages woke me and the other recruits and delivered us to the barbers. They quickly cut whatever hair we had and shaved our heads. And as they did, I sat tall, welcoming that essential moment of transformation. Iti told me that when he was a soldier, the barbers would shave his head at least once a week.

I run my hand over my scalp, soft like the belly of a cat. I wish Iti could see me now, about to devote myself to the defense of the king's domain, just as he did when he was my age.

The priest stamps the end of his scepter against the ground.

"Enter!" he says, "and bow before your gods."

We line up side by side in front of the altar, where figures of the four gods of the Two Lands—Sutekh, Amun, Re, and the familiar green face of my own city's god, Ptah—loom over us, at least two men tall. The priest at the center, the one wearing the most gold, holds up his own scepter.

"Kneel!"

As I keep my eyes on the cedar floor, I inhale the purifying frankincense. Sandaled feet stop in front of me, and something wet and cold sprinkles on my neck. It smells of cinnamon, anise, and salt.

The sandaled feet return to the altar.

"In this twentieth year of the Good God, you have come here today to bind yourself to him and to the Two Lands with a light heart."

A lightness flutters in my chest. I'm here, saying my oath of service, dedicating my life, my body to the Good God, to be a soldier for him, just like Iti. Like Iti wanted me to be, even if he never actually said so. I made it happen. I'm here because I fought for it.

"Repeat these words, swearing your fealty to the military of the Good God, Lord of the Sedge and the Bee, King Ramesses Usermaatre Setepenre."

With each line I devote myself to the Good God and the Two Lands, vowing to uphold his order, smite his enemies. I promise with my *ka* I will repulse Apep, emerging from every fire, and nothing evil shall surround me.

The sandaled feet step down from the dais.

"Rise, for your oath is not yet finished."

The chief priest unrolls a sheet of papyrus as large as ox hide on the floor.

"Come forth to crush Apep," he says, "rendering him powerless under your foot, driving him back to Duat where he shall remain, and so he shall never bring temblors of *isfet* to the Two Lands."

The priest calls us, one by one, to stomp on the image of Apep. Some curse it. Others are more tentative, and I wonder how long they'll last here.

By the time I'm called to the Serpent, the paper is torn and covered with dark footprints.

PART THREE: THE COMMAND

As I lift my foot, I see the man on the ship beneath me again. His vicious scowl, the blood gurgling at the corner of his mouth. I would have crushed him completely if Ahmose hadn't stopped me. But Ahmose was right. We didn't need to make our hearts any heavier than they already became that night.

But the Serpent before me is no man. It is the harbinger of the destruction of this land I love, that took me in, provided for me, and loved me. It is everything I will devote myself to fighting.

I stomp on the image, grinding the ball of my foot into the very face of the Serpent, tearing its head from its body.

The chief priest gives me a surprised, yet impressed, glance as another draws a *sa* knot on the center of my forehead in red paint and gives me a ceramic cup of amber-colored wine.

After all of the soldiers return to our places facing the priests and the altar, the chief priest lifts his arms and speaks.

"May you live forever, with a happy heart, serving the Good God in this world and the eternal Field of Reeds," the priest says. "Raise your cups, and be blessed with life, prosperity, and happiness."

With a sip of spiced and honey-sweetened wine, I am officially a soldier of the Good God.

○ ○ ○

"You! Girl!" Commander Hani points his finger at me. "Come here."

I take a deep breath and step forward from the crowd of soldiers gathered on the training grounds, a broad stretch of land between the barracks and the stables. "Yes, *imyr*."

The moment I've separated myself from the others, something wrenches my shoulders back, and now I'm face down in the dust. I cough, spitting the dirt out of my mouth.

Another hulking man, one who was by the commander's side yesterday, glares down at me. The jackal snuck up on me.

Commander Hani's sneer is vinegar in a cut.

"See, men?" Commander Hani says. "You must be prepared for anything."

He puts his fists on his ox-like hips. The man who pulled me down does the same.

Several of his men laugh as I try to stand. By all the gods, my legs ache. But when I see the wide green bruise splaying out over the commander's foot and wrapping around his ankle, I find some satisfaction that he's probably feeling yesterday's fight, too. I hope he has an even larger bruise on his rear and that it hurts for him to sit.

I brush what dust I can from my leather, not daring to look away from either of them.

"A weapon might serve a warrior well," Commander Hani says, "but nothing is as valuable as his own hands. Lieutenant Wefer, show this new recruit what I mean."

That's Commander Hani's lieutenant? He circles me, as ugly and conniving as a hyena. I turn with him, making sure he can't even so much as grab me.

Men like this rely on their size, their strength. And intimidating their opponent.

I hear Iti again in my heart, my heart that hasn't had a chance to rest since the attack on the ship. "Be quick, light, and flexible," he'd say.

Lieutenant Wefer chugs forward. I duck, leaving him wrapping his arms around empty air. He scowls back at me.

A few *oohs* sound as the lieutenant grunts.

Just when I think he'll lurch at me again, Commander Hani says, "That's enough!"

The muscles around the lieutenant's neck release, and he folds his bulky arms.

Intimidation. That's all this is. Intimidation to convince me to give up and leave. But I can take whatever they throw at me. I have to.

"Let's get started," Commander Hani says to the others. He walks so close to me that I can smell the sour beer on his breath. "You don't belong here. And I'll make sure you don't forget it. Every moment. Every day."

"How could I?" I say, glaring at him. "Shall I return to my follow recruits, so we can begin our training?"

His jaw sets. "You will call me *imyr*."

"Shall we begin our training?" I pause, letting contempt seep into my voice. "*Imyr*."

He grunts, and I return to my place in the bundle of men.

"All right, you fleas," Commander Hani says. "Watch carefully, because I won't demonstrate again."

He calls Lieutenant Wefer forward.

"Run at me," the commander says to him.

The two collide, equally matched in size and strength, grabbing at each other's limbs and shoulders. Commander Hani ducks his head under his lieutenant's armpit and loosens the lieutenant's grip around his waist. The commander sends Lieutenant Wefer tumbling over his back. He hits the ground with the grace of a sow.

A few men snicker behind me. I grumble. I was hoping both of them would end up on the ground.

"Quiet!" the commander barks. "You laugh now, but we'll see who's laughing when you're covered in dust and bruises after you miserable gnats can't do the same thing."

Lieutenant Wefer stands, only a little humiliated, and returns to Commander Hani's side.

"Split them into pairs," the commander tells him. As he whispers into his lieutenant's ear, the lieutenant points at me, then to someone behind me. The two share a conspiring grin.

Of course, the lieutenant pairs me with Kahuti, the largest, tallest man here. He matches the others with men of a similar frame and size. Why couldn't I wrestle that boy over there who can't be any older than thirteen floods and is only a hair taller than me?

"All right, fleas! Use the technique I demonstrated with Lieutenant

Wefer, and throw your partner to the ground as many times as possible before the midday meal. Losers have to line up last to eat."

The soldiers spread out throughout the training grounds, some throwing themselves against each other without second thought.

Rahuti fiddles with the knot on his *shendyt*.

"So, we meet again," I say.

"I can pretend," he says with an apologetic wince. "To lose, I mean."

"You think I can't do it?"

He shakes his head quickly. "No, it's just . . ." He gestures to himself, as if I can't see he's so much larger than me.

"What are you waiting for?" Commander Hani yells at us from a few paces away. He strides between the sparring men who now grunt and groan, sending up clouds of dust.

I back away from Rahuti and widen my stance. "Let's do it."

"All right . . ." He sucks his teeth as he takes a few steps back and crouches, shifting his feet.

"Now!" I yell, and we run toward each other.

But right before we collide, I spin under his arm, avoiding him completely. My instincts darted me away from Rahuti before I could stop myself.

The commander yells at us. "I saw that!" Or, rather, he yells at me.

Rahuti turns, panting. "We're supposed to wrestle. Throw each other down."

I groan and roll my eyes. Rahuti looks almost offended that I would dare.

"You heard Commander Hani," he says. "You don't want to be last in the meal line, do you?"

I shake my head before we try again.

I think I duck in time to grab his legs, but he slams into me. My breath leaps from my chest before we even hit the ground.

He gets up and reaches his hand down to help me stand. "Are you all right?"

Before I can take it, Lieutenant Wefer fumes up to him and smacks Rahuti's arm. "You idiot! Don't help the enemy!"

Rahuti pulls back, looking at me and the lieutenant. "Sorry, *imyr*."

"You better be," Lieutenant Wefer says before stomping away.

As I stand, I hope my ribs are all where they're supposed to be.

Somewhere behind us, the commander's laugh cuts through the dust.

As the morning continues, I lose count of how many times my body hits the ground. My backside and shoulders ache even more every time I fall. With each attempt, my legs shake more, and my attacks and defenses only get worse and worse.

Maybe I should let Rahuti pretend.

Relief overcomes me when Commander Hani releases us for the midday meal, even if I'll be met with the most stale bread and sour beer, if there's anything left for me at all.

○ ○ ○

Commander Hani lines us up in order of wins. Because I have none, he makes me stand last in the meal line.

The other men sneer as they pass. "Weak," and "pathetic," they say as they laugh at me. Others say worse things, making foul gestures with their hands.

With each insult, I pull my shoulders back and hold my head higher, somehow stopping myself from kneeing them all in the crotch.

I tell myself that it's only the first day. I beat Commander Hani yesterday, and I can beat Rahuti too, or whoever Lieutenant Wefer pairs me with tomorrow. Even with my staff, I struggled with difficult parries and techniques. But with time and practice, I mastered them.

I can master this wrestling thing too, if the commander gives me a chance.

But Iti never taught me wrestling. Not like this, anyway. Ruthless and with no rules other than to throw your opponent down first. I wish he had.

Down the line, Rahuti stands nearest to the front, likely because he had so many wins. As he takes his dish, he glances back at me, then tips his head to the corner table where we sat yesterday.

When I finally reach the serving tables and take what's left—and thank Nefertem there's anything left at all—I join him.

"I'm sorry," he says, to my surprise.

"For what?" An abrasion on the back of my thigh burns as I sit, and I wince.

"For that."

"I've had worse," I say, as a trio of men, ones I recognize from Commander Hani's little entourage yesterday, make a point of walking past us. They have no reason at all to be back here in our corner, other than to make the trouble I see on their faces.

"Oooh! Rahuti's got an *idet*!"

Rahuti keeps his head down, pretending to focus on what remains on his dish.

"Can't even look up at the real men, can you, you big pufferfish?"

"Let him be," I say, pushing down the little angry flame burning in my belly. I can't fight back here, not where Commander Hani watches us all, waiting for any one of us to slip and lose control. Especially me. Iti told me many a story of his fellow soldiers being beaten, or worse—expelled—for throwing a fist at another in the meal halls. And General Setankh warned me as such yesterday. I'm not going to throw everything away over these pieces of *hes*.

But the three men step closer. "Heh. The bitch is defending him."

I can't punch him, but I can't let him stand there and insult us either. Rahuti tugs at my arm as I stand.

"Sati, no, please." From his tone, this must not be the first time these men, these boys, have harassed him at a meal.

"But these dogs"—I look right into the closest man's beady eyes—"are insulting you."

He tilts his head. "What are you going to do about it, dirty *ka't*?"

I let out a hearty laugh and fold my arms. I know how boys like them think. I've known too many boys like them. "You're hilarious."

Their faces quirk in confusion.

"You think that's an insult? I doubt you've ever seen a *ka't*, let alone touched one—"

The man in the center lunges at me, but his friends grab his elbows before he can stumble across the low table and even dream of striking me.

"Stop, 'Awi," one of them says as they pull him back.

"The commander's coming!" the other warns.

"What seems to be the trouble?" Commander Hani asks, his hands on his hips.

If they dare say Rahuti started it, or I started it, I swear I'll—

"Nothing, *imyr*," 'Awi says with a squeak.

Commander Hani scowls. "Then return to your table and finish your meal, because the day isn't finished, is it?"

The men reply with quick bows, saying, "Yes, *imyr*," and "Of course, *imyr*," and scurry back to their seats.

The commander scowls at me as I sit, hoping he can't see the pain in my face as my abrasion meets the leather cushion again.

"You," he says.

"Yes, *imyr*?" I wind my fingers together as I await his misplaced punishment.

"General Setankh is waiting for you."

CHAPTER FOURTEEN

I stand in the general's doorway, holding my new scribe's kit close to my chest.

"Sit." He gestures to a mat next to his table. He is again preoccupied with a document on his desk.

I sit beside him on the floor, folding my legs and smoothing my *shendyt* out over my lap. I managed to clean some of the dirt off after the midday meal, but not nearly enough.

"And how was this morning's training?" he asks, otherwise not acknowledging me at all.

"As good as expected, *imyr*," I say, hoping to obscure just how much I failed. I pour a bit of water from a small jug into my ink palette and stir it into a thick liquid.

"I'm sure you performed to the best of your abilities."

I can't tell if that's an insult or a compliment.

He looks up from his paper and down at me. "Why are you here?" he asks with a sandy voice.

"Because the Good God ordered me to work under your command, *imyr*."

An irritated sound rasps in his throat. "Why are you really here?"

I'm not sure what he's trying to get me to say. But I answer, "To serve and defend the Good God and his domain, *imyr*."

He grunts and returns to his papers, shuffling through leaf after leaf of papyrus. From where I am, I can't see at all what's on them.

"Shouldn't a girl like you be married? Making stew and honey rolls and tending to children?"

My lips tighten.

"Or perhaps a priestess? You have a way about you."

"I'm not sure what you mean, *imyr*."

"Of course you don't."

I don't know what he's getting at, and I'm not sure I want to know right now. I need to focus on proving I deserve to be here, showing the Good God I'm worthy of his decision. After this morning, I have a lot to make up for.

"Did you wish for me to record something for you today, *imyr*?"

Another grunt. He sits back in his chair and tosses a blank sheet of papyrus at me. "Write exactly what I say. Word for word."

I pull the paper on to my lap, pen at the ready.

He clears this throat. "Your Majesty, Great God of the Two Lands, Protected by Horu and Beloved by Sekhmet..."

My hand races, pen flying across the paper to keep pace with the speed of his speech. He doesn't give me any time to consider what he says, only enough to commit it to ink. I don't even have a chance to get frustrated with how fast he speaks.

He talks and talks until I've filled an entire side of my paper with writing.

Finally, he stops.

After I finish the last symbols, I'm shocked at what I've written.

On this 2nd day of the fourth month of Shemu, I wish to complain to you regarding a decision you made just yesterday morning. It is paramount that only the best and strongest soldiers serve in our forces as we prepare for future battles against our enemies on the frontiers of our empire. While you have been instrumental in our victories, your soft heart will surely lead us to defeat on both the northern and southern fronts.

We must remain as vigilant as Horu in the Horizon and as strong as the Hapiu Bull as we face the vile foreigners and Agents of the Nine Bows who dare tread across our lands and lay claim to our territories. The enemy prepares without mercy, and we must do the same.

Our soldiers must be of the highest caliber, the strongest and fastest in the land. To achieve this noble aim, I strongly suggest that you give me—general of the Black Land's elite fighting force—and only me, the final say in who serves in your name. Your failure to heed my warning may lead to the fall of the Two Lands itself, forcing it back into the waters of Nu and the mouth of Apep.

Perhaps it's normal for someone with such a prominent position as the general to question the Good God's decisions, but it feels unbalanced and insolent. Not only that, it's clear this isn't a message just for the Good God, but to scare me into making mistakes the general would most certainly use against me.

"Is that all, *imyr*?" I sit taller to hide the apprehension coiling up my spine.

"You can't possibly have recorded everything I said." Contempt drips from his voice.

"I did, *imyr*. Every word. Exactly as you spoke."

He swipes the papyrus out of my lap with a crack. He scans the page, symbol by symbol, line by line, mouthing the words as he reads.

I swallow, trying to moisten my dry throat.

When he reaches the end, he says, "Seems you *can* write."

Of course I can write. I told the Good God, and the Good God himself believed me.

"The script is quite accurate," he continues. "And legible."

Oh, thank Djehuty for that, because I had to write so quickly. I allow myself to beam a bit.

The general makes a low noise and signs his name at the bottom in red ink.

"Should I deliver it to your page, *imyr*?" I ask.

"No. I'll have it delivered myself. Now, sit, until I need you again."

○ ○ ○

Finally, as the light tints orange in the west, General Setankh dismisses me for the evening meal.

Thankfully, I'm not too late, with plenty of bread, beer, and a bland duck stew left at the serving tables.

'Awi and his cronies already sit, cackling like the hyenas they are as they point at other soldiers and make mocking faces. When they see me walk toward the table in the corner, where Rahuti sits alone, they do the same to me, repeating their rude gestures and even cruder insults. I keep an eye on them, in case they make the mistake of coming near us. But Commander Hani, who sits near the general's dais next to Lieutenant Wefer, also keeps watch, and I suspect 'Awi doesn't want to be on the commander's heavy side. I do note that the commander lets 'Awi insult his fellow men on a regular basis. What has that fly done that affords him such a cruel privilege?

"Thank you for eating with me," Rahuti says as I sit, the abrasion on my thigh a little less tender, thank Sekhmet.

"Why? Because of those fools? You could beat them up in two flicks of a viper's tongue if you wanted."

He shrinks a bit in his seat. "They've been awful to me since I first arrived."

"Well, *they're* awful." I glance over at them, and 'Awi makes a face at me that's supposed to be intimidating. I turn back to Rahuti without acknowledging them. "I knew boys like that when I was younger. They laughed at me when I asked to spar with them."

Except, unlike 'Awi, those boys were dangerous, and they did more than laugh at me. They were a few floods older than me, and even after I stopped trying to join them, they'd follow me back to the Per-seshen, calling me awful names and sometimes throwing rocks at me. Iti would threaten them, and they'd retreat until the next time they saw me. One day, when I was around six floods old, Iti decided to teach me how to defend myself, and he gave me my first sparring lesson.

They only left me alone after I fought back. Fought back and won.

"If those boys saw you fight the commander," Rahuti says, "I don't think they'd laugh."

I rip apart a stone-hard bread roll at the memory and change the subject. I don't want to talk about those boys back in Men-nefer. "When did you get here?"

"Only two months ago."

"And 'Awi?"

"I'm not sure. But he and his friends were already Commander Hani's favorites."

"They're certainly reaped from the same crop." A crop rotten with blight.

"Ai, where did you go after the midday meal?" Rahuti asks.

"General Setankh's offices. For scribal work."

"No wonder Commander Hani doesn't like you."

"Why would that matter?"

"He doesn't like scribes."

"I'm sure he dislikes me for more reasons than just me being a scribe."

"Well, I think you're all right. You're the only one who'll sit with me."

○ ○ ○

That evening, I collapse on my thin straw-filled mattress and stare at the ceiling. My legs, my arms, my back, my feet ... Everything's so sore.

I'm not sure what I expected. I've never trained so hard and for so long, and in something I'm so utterly terrible at doing. Iti and I never spent this much time sparring and certainly not throwing each other to the ground over and over again. And sitting on the general's floor for the afternoon made my legs feel as lifeless as lead.

"Your first day went well, I see." Djedi saunters through the front door in a crisp ankle-length *shendyt* and a delicate beaded belt.

"Everything hurts," I say. "Even my toenails hurt. I didn't know my toenails could hurt."

"I hear you'll get used to it. That's what the other men say, anyway." He stops at the foot of my bed and raises his brow in disgust. "Wrestling training?"

"How did you guess?"

"You're as dirty as a donkey's hooves. You worked for the general looking like this?" He points a disapproving finger at me and perches on the edge of the mattress.

"I didn't have a choice," I say as I sit up. "I wasn't even finished with my midday meal when he summoned me."

"And how did *that* go?"

"Hours of dictation and record-keeping. I sat so long my legs went numb. And he had me write a rather scathing message for the Good God, scolding him for allowing me into service."

"Unsurprising, really," he says. "The two of them have been at each other's throats for years now. Some say since Qadesh."

Everything can be traced back to that cursed battle.

"And you still have the *sa* on your face." Djedi disappears upstairs and returns with a large square of linen and a small, blue and white striped glass bottle. "Let's get you cleaned up."

He pours a viscous, greenish liquid on to the linen and wipes my forehead.

"By Min's member, how many times did you fall into the dirt today?" he asks, showing me the linen. It's as black as kohl.

"You mean how many times did I get thrown into the dirt today? Commander Hani paired me up with the biggest man there."

He makes a disapproving sound. "Of course he did. Your win yesterday almost guaranteed it."

Djedi continues to wipe my face, meticulously and carefully, like Mawat did when I was a child, when I came home from sparring with Iti covered in red dirt and black mud.

"Well, tomorrow is another day." He pulls back to examine his work and crinkles his nose. He must have missed a spot, because he goes for my cheek and rubs it a bit more. "That's better."

"You didn't have to—"

"Oh, believe me. I did. Besides, I remember how lonely I was when I first arrived here." He points at my headrest. "But it looks like you might already have some friends here?"

I lean over to see what he's referring to. Ahmose. How could I forget? I pluck the folded piece of papyrus from under the base.

"It must be quite important to be delivered directly to your quarters." He stands, handing me the bottle and the linen. "You'll want to keep these. You're still utterly filthy."

After Djedi pads up to his room, I unfold the paper.

The 2nd day of IV Shemu, 20th year of our king
Sati,

It is my eternal wish that this message finds you and finds you well. My page, Ubenu, uncovered your whereabouts far faster than I expected him to, and for that, I am grateful. I have instructed him to come by your quarters to retrieve messages you might have for me or the Good God. Anything you say is safe with him and completely confidential. Please leave for him your reply, so I know you are in good health, and that you have triumphed today.

May your hearing be beautiful.
Ahmose

Iti once told me he could tell quite a bit about someone by their writing. Ahmose's hand flows over the paper, elegant and practiced, with each figure in perfect proportion to the others.

And it lifts the heaviness of the day from my shoulders, dissipating the aching soreness in my legs and back. Reading the letter again is like stepping into a refreshing Akhet breeze.

He writes to me only to ask if I've seen anything unusual, as he told me to do before I met General Setankh. But there's more between his words, something enticing and warm. I'm not sure if I should trust it. But what's the harm in writing back to him?

I prepare my inks, and I write my reply.

CHAPTER FIFTEEN

The morning trumpets shock me out of some of the deepest sleep I've ever had.

When I take my first steps of the day, my muscles are so stiff I can hardly walk. The backs of my legs are like dry clay, and my arms are buckets of water hanging from my shoulders.

And by Sekhmet, my poor feet. The soles of my feet are more tender and beat up than the rest of me.

I pull on my uniform and trudge to the meal hall, all while telling myself this pain will be worth the suffering.

During morning training, Commander Hani gives us the barest of instruction in wrestling before pairing me with Rahuti again.

"My offer's still good," Rahuti says softly, looking back to make sure the commander isn't within earshot. "To pretend."

I consider it. "No. I need to learn. Really learn."

We take our fighting stances, and he tosses me down again and again. Commander Hani berates me every time he strides by with that infuriatingly smug look on his face. Lieutenant Wefer is never too far behind.

"Not looking good, flea," Commander Hani says to me with a sneer.

Rahuti offers his hand to help me, and the commander smacks it away.

"Any soldier worth their place can stand on their own," he says.

From across the field, 'Awi points at me and laughs.

That alone fills me with enough spite to get up and keep fighting until the midday meal.

As we're in line, 'Awi and his friends—they're always together, hovering around him like flies on *hes*—throw their insults at me and Rahuti again.

Despite the rage they incite in me, I hold back. They're not worth risking being reprimanded or expelled. I just tell them to leave us alone, or we'll call the commander on them. And for some reason, that's enough to drive them away. For now.

During my service to the general that afternoon, he doesn't ask me to write anything for him at all. I sit cross-legged beside him, my legs growing numb.

He pores over another stack of papyri, grumbling under his breath.

What could possibly be so important on those pages that he's not out supervising the training of his soldiers? Training I should be a part of so I can become as strong and fierce as the rest of them.

I almost think he's trying to sabotage me, keeping me here doing nothing, so my skills will always be inferior. When he thinks I've failed, he can justify discharging me.

Another meal swatting away 'Awi and his flies.

Another evening when my legs and arms feel like stone.

When I return to my quarters, Djedi has already returned from eating with the scribes. Oh, I wish I could eat with them every night. Even if I were allowed—and didn't the Good God say I was to enjoy all the privileges of being a scribe—I'd be leaving Rahuti alone to face 'Awi's flies, and I can't do that. Besides, I haven't yet "earned" my place among the scribes, despite sitting on the general's floor for hours. I don't even know what doing so would entail. Waiting on the floor in silence for a week? A month? Writing out a minimum number of papers, if I ever get the chance to write anything else for the general?

I'm sure if I did ask when I'll be permitted to dine with the scribes, he'd say, "When I say you can."

Djedi glides down the stairs.

"I procured a little something for you," he says, pointing to a small, shallow washbasin filled with clean water.

"Oh, thank Nefertem," I say.

"Nefertem? Oh, *bitbit*, he had nothing to do with it. Besides, I know how smelly you soldiers can be, and I will *not* have that kind of stench in my house."

"A gift from the kindness of your heart," I quip.

"Just be grateful," he says.

"I am. Thank you, Djedi." I let out an embarrassed chuckle.

He beams and flicks back the braids from his face. "I'll let you get to it."

Even though I scrub my skin of the dust and the sweat, I can't rid myself of it all entirely. The dirt has become one with me, hiding under my fingernails and between my toes. I'll never be clean again.

When I'm finished, the water in the basin might as well be mud. But I find a folded square of paper under my headrest.

> *The 3rd day of IV Shemu, 20th year of our king*
> *Sati,*
> *Your reply has lightened my heart, but I am sorry that your first day was not the triumph I hoped for you.*
> *The* tjati *has requested you keep a particular eye on your commanding officer. When I asked him why, he wouldn't tell me, but I suspect he knows something* desher *may be afoot, beyond the general's disdain for our king.*
> *Wishing you victory this day and all days.*
> *May your hearing be beautiful.*
> *Ahmose*

○ ○ ○

Morning trumpets pierce through my meager sleep.

Sore everything. More failed attempts at wrestling. Dodging 'Awi and his flies. Sitting in silence beside the general.

Attempting to wash off the day.

And another kind reply from Ahmose.

Perhaps I don't have any reason to be suspicious of him at all.

○ ○ ○

4th day of IV Shemu, 20th year of the Good God
Ahmose,
May you be in favor of Amun.
You asked how I was finding life at the garrison. Well enough, I suppose. The commander has not taken kindly to my presence, which I suppose was to be expected, especially after my victory over him the night I first arrived. That victory was short-lived, as I have yet to find success in our daily wrestling exercises. The scribe with whom I share a house has kindly provided me with a washbasin, but even if I can scrub the dirt from my skin, another morning of training leaves me covered again. What I wouldn't do for a dip in a bathing tub full of warm water!
In peace, health, and goodness,
Sati

○ ○ ○

The same routine for a week, and that week becomes a second. Sometimes, instead of beginning the day with wrestling, Commander Hani makes us march back and forth in unison across the training grounds as Lieutenant Wefer beats on a double-headed drum the size of a calf.

PART THREE: THE COMMAND

I chuckle when Commander Hani yells at 'Awi several times for being out of rhythm with the men at his sides. Surprisingly, he never once shouts at me. At least this is one thing I'm good at.

But we always return to wrestling. After fifteen days, I haven't thrown Rahuti to the ground.

The commander saunters up to me. "Seems like you could use a little . . . motivation."

What I need is more time and a partner closer to my own size. Or for my pride to retreat and allow Rahuti to pretend.

"Every time you fall," Commander Hani says, "run one lap around the training grounds."

After ten laps, I stop counting.

○ ○ ○

12th day of IV Shemu, 20th year of the Good God
 Ahmose,
  May you be in favor of Amun.
  Despite transcribing the general's missive my first day in his service, he hasn't yet asked me to write for him since. He is consumed by stacks of paper on his desk, never tending to his soldiers, or asking me to write. I haven't been able to investigate the subject of these papers, seeing as the general is always there while I am in his office. But the cruelty he shows his young page more than unsettles me. The boy arrived late today, and the general beat him over the back with a fighting staff.
  Apart from wishing to avoid a similar fate, what I want most of all is a decent meal. I am so weary of sour beer and gritty bread. Perhaps you can save me from this wretched food!
  In peace, health, and goodness,
  Sati

The next day, I find his reply, neatly tucked under the base of my headrest, along with a roughly woven pouch about the size of my fist.

> 13th day of IV Shemu, 20th year of our king
> Sati,
> May you be in favor of Sekhmet.
> It is indeed strange that the general who'd lamented for so long about his lack of a scribe with fighting skills has you sit all afternoon and write nothing. If Djehuty allows, I would very much like to know the content of those papers that have so captured his attention. But I implore you to investigate only with the greatest of caution.
> While I cannot provide for you a basin of warm water and soothing oils, nor can I send you a full meal, perhaps the small gift that I had Ubenu deliver with this note will please your ka. Freshly dried dates from trees in my own gardens. This harvest was particularly sweet.
> May your hearing be beautiful.
> Ahmose

After letting myself daydream for a moment about a perfumed bath, I untie the twine along the top of the pouch. Inside are ten plump, mouthwatering dates. I take a bite, and the sweetness glides over my tongue. I savor this tiny, almost illicit, indulgence, knowing tomorrow I'll again have to face Commander Hani, 'Awi, and the *desher* training field.

○ ○ ○

Rahuti prepares to run at me.

I've been here twenty days, and today I'm determined to get it right. Something in my balance and timing has shifted for the better.

PART THREE: THE COMMAND

The sun disk bears down on the dry training fields and has nearly reached its highest point in the sky. Sweat runs down the sides of my face.

"Come on, Rahuti!" I yell. "Attack me like you mean it!"

He settles his feet into the earth and puts on his fiercest scowl.

"Just do it!" I say.

He hurtles toward me, and we collide.

My backside hits the dirt. Again. Rahuti spins away from me. Even he's getting faster and more agile. Why can't I? I was so quick on my first evening here, but that was with a weapon I've been wielding for years. After being tossed, thrown, knocked, and hurled to the ground, again and again, even my bruises have bruises. I'll have green skin like Ptah for the rest of my life.

Ptah. Sekhmet's consort. I haven't heard the faintest of rumbling purrs since I started my training. If she wanted me to come all the way here, then why hasn't she helped me master any of this cursed wrestling? Don't I have more important things to do for Horu on His Throne than letting Rahuti throw me around?

I grumble. This is no time to get distracted by cryptic messages from a goddess or wallow in my own self-pity.

Rahuti reaches his hand to me, but pulls it back, probably remembering the commander's constant reprimands. "You did say I should mean it."

"And you certainly did," I say as I stand.

Commander Hani and Lieutenant Wefer saunter over to us, scheming sneers staining their faces.

"Run your lap," the commander says.

When I've finished, now drenched in sweat, he waits for me by Rahuti. I brace myself on my thighs, recovering my breath.

"If you don't win at least one round by the end of the day," the commander warns, "I'll expel you."

"What? But you can't—"

"I can do whatever I deem necessary for the strength of my unit, and the failure of one soldier drags us all down." Scorn fumes on his face. "And you will call me *imyr*."

He's determined to rid himself of me. And I won't let him. I can't.

"Yes, *imyr*."

"Get on with it," the commander growls.

I turn to Rahuti. I can tell he wants to let me win, to ensure Commander Hani doesn't expel me. I give him a little shake of my head. No, don't be easy on me. I want to succeed with *ma'at*, not with cheating like the commander did my first night here.

"Let's try again," I say.

Commander Hani and Lieutenant Wefer laugh.

I walk back, putting the requisite space between myself and Rahuti.

Focus. Aim for his legs. Use his momentum against him. I just need to crouch at the right time. All the other new recruits have toppled each other with ease. I can do this. I need to do this.

Rahuti stares me down. His form is more hippopotamus than jackal, but the hippopotamus is far more dangerous than even the most vicious predators.

Rahuti yells out and hurls himself at me, faster than he ever has.

He gets closer. And closer.

The commander yells at me. Something meant to distract me, but I don't even know what he says.

Wait for it. Wait for the perfect moment.

Not yet.

Still not yet.

Trust your heart.

Now!

I dip to my knees and wrap my arms around Rahuti's calves. As I duck my head forward and hunch my back, I release him and jump up.

Rahuti tumbles over me, trying to brace himself against the fall. He rolls to a standstill several cubits from me.

I stare at him in disbelief. Then I toss a smug look at Commander Hani. He saw the entire thing. When it counted the most.

"You did it!" Rahuti yells from behind a cloud of dust.

I stride up to the commander, leaving only a hand's width between us.

"Are you satisfied now, *imyr*?" I raise my chin and put my hands on my hips.

The commander's upper lip curls. Lieutenant Wefer looms behind him. I stick out my elbows as wide as I can, waiting for his concession.

"Consider yourself lucky," Commander Hani says.

That was far more than just luck.

Rahuti comes to my side, dust caked on his sweaty skin.

"Good work!" He pats me on the shoulder, but it's more of a slap.

Commander Hani and Lieutenant Wefer shoot dagger-like looks at him, as though they think he's betraying them.

A few other men compliment and congratulate me. Most of them speak in hushed voices so Commander Hani and Lieutenant Wefer won't hear them. 'Awi and his flies hover behind them.

The commander's nostrils flare at their every word.

But he recovers his composure and claps his hands.

"That's enough!" he yells. "Get back to work!"

The men disperse and return to their wrestling partners. But I stay behind. And Rahuti stays with me.

The commander glares down at me again. "I don't know what game you are playing, but don't think I won't crush you if you give me even the slightest reason."

"Then I won't give you a reason . . . *imyr*." I turn to Rahuti, who's still at my side. "Come on. Let's get in a few more matches before the midday meal."

○ ○ ○

My victory isn't without repercussions.

As Rahuti and I stand together in line for the midday meal, 'Awi and his flies swarm at the entrance.

Rahuti turns away, pretending to ignore them. But I fold my arms and face them as they get closer.

"Letting the girl win, now?" 'Awi says, trying to get Rahuti's attention.

"Leave him alone," I say.

"I wasn't talking to you, *ka't*."

He shoves past me and punches Rahuti's arm.

I want to smack him away and push him into the dirt where he belongs. The little flame within me burns, hungry to balance the scales against these pieces of *hes*. I tell myself I can't, that even after my success today, Commander Hani would still expel me without a second thought if I so much as dared touch another soldier outside of training. Especially his pet 'Awi.

"Ai, big boy," 'Awi says. "I'm talking to you."

Rahuti keeps his eyes down.

"Some warrior you are," 'Awi continues. "Especially if we fight the Hittites again."

What a fool. We won't be fighting the Hittites again, not with the treaty so close.

One of 'Awi's flies steps up. "Heh. He might as well grow his hair long like them, like a woman."

"Ai, that's enough!" I say, hoping my voice is loud enough to intimidate them, but not to catch the commander's attention.

"He won't even stand up for himself," the other fly says. "Letting his little *ka't* do it instead."

Despite trying to steady my breath, to contain the flames in me, the heat in my belly flushes into my neck and cheeks.

"I said, leave us alone!" I yell louder than I intend. The loathing that filled me when I finally stood up to those boys in Men-nefer floods through my limbs. When I pressed my foot on the murderous man's ribs.

"Ooh! She's getting angry," 'Awi taunts.

I step up to him, keeping my fists at my sides to ensure no one can accuse me of touching him. "I swear to Sekhmet, I'll beat you like I did to those—"

"The commander!" Rahuti gasps and tugs me away from 'Awi. He points down the line where Commander Hani strolls toward us, hands clasped behind his back.

'Awi and his flies snicker, but when they see Commander Hani, they fall quiet and wisely turn away.

"Don't do anything foolish," Rahuti says as he releases me. "Not for me, anyway."

The heat in me subsides, and my heartbeat returns to something akin to normal.

"Thank you," I say.

And I think I hear the distant echo of a purring laugh.

CHAPTER SIXTEEN

On my twenty-fourth day of service, I report to the general, as I do every afternoon. The Shemu heat grows scorching and relentless, with the waterways around the garrison as cracked and dry as my rough feet.

The whitewashed mudbrick has, thankfully, kept his office somewhat cooler than outside, but not so much that I stop sweating. Why couldn't we work under a sunshade near the river? At least there, we'd find relief from a breeze or two.

"Sit," the general says, as he always does.

"Yes, *imyr*." I take my time, watching for anything suspicious. I have every day since Ahmose asked me to.

But today, like all the others, I only find what I'd expect on an officer's table. Records of how many shields have been made, or how many arrowheads the smiths have forged, or how many horses have been trained for service. I tell Ahmose, of course, just in case any of that information might interest the *tjati*, but he replied saying none of it was out of the ordinary for a man of the general's position.

So, I take my place on the floor, expecting to do nothing more than sit and sweat until the evening meal.

When the heat and days of training pull me nearer to an illicit nap, the general's page enters, a roll of paper in hand.

I straighten my back. I can't let the general see me dozing. Besides, this message could prove useful.

After the general takes the paper and dismisses the page, he scans the document with an intensity I've never seen from him. He holds it closer to his face, furrows his brows, and lets out a sour chuckle.

I'm supposed to remain quiet, but I want to ask him if the subject displeases him, or if whatever it is he's reading warrants some kind of reply for me to write. Anything that could tell me more about what consumes him so much. But I don't, even as the words dance on my tongue.

The sunlight from a small window behind him hits the paper, silhouetting the writing enough that I might be able to decipher the figures. I attempt to read it, trying not to make it obvious I'm sneaking a glance. What I can see appears to be in a language I've never seen, with not a single familiar figure.

His eyes dart to me, one corner of his lip twisting. The expression he flashes feels like ants crawling up my neck.

He strikes a flint, lighting a lamp on his desk, and holds the corner of the paper over the flame. The fire leaves nothing but ash.

He does the same with several other documents.

Hes. I'll never find out what's on them now. Worse, he must know I've been trying to steal a look at them.

He lets out a satisfied huff and flips to the next page.

○ ○ ○

25th day of IV Shemu, 20th year of the Good God Ahmose,

May you be in favor of Amun.

Today I might have some information of value for you and the tjati. The general received a message, that after reading, he burned. Then he did the same with at least ten other pages. I regret I couldn't read any of them before they went up into flames. What I could see looked nothing like Kemeti script or even Akkadian.

What's more, there was nothing ma'at *in the twisted smile he gave me after he finished. I will remain vigilant, but I fear even if I could see his papers, I would not be able to read whatever strange language has been penned upon them.*

In peace, health, and goodness,
Sati

◉ ◉ ◉

Ahmose replies the next day, urging me to stay vigilant. But I'm not sure what I'm looking for. He doesn't seem to know either. But we both know something *desher* is afoot.

◉ ◉ ◉

As Rahuti and I line up for the evening meal, the sun has started its descent into the Western Lands, setting the sky on fire with a vibrant orange glow. It only makes the low waters even more ominous.

'Awi and his flies must be late, because they're nowhere to be found. Just as well. I could do with a respite from their incessant biting and swarming.

"Ooh, lentils!" I scoop a hearty spoonful into a small wooden bowl. They're thick and mushy, like Mawat makes them. I take a sniff. Onions, gristly meat, and that's about all. Mawat would have at least added coriander and fennel. I miss her cooking, the care she put into her meals, and even the way she would fuss over me as I helped her in the kitchen.

But they'll have to do.

Rahuti plops a spoonful on his own dish.

We take our dishes to what is now firmly our table in the back corner. I sit against the wall, so I can watch the other soldiers, in case I need to swat away 'Awi and his flies.

I take in the hall. Men laugh, toasting each other for a successful day of training, jabbing their elbows into each other's ribs, and shoving their food into their mouths as though they'll never eat again.

None of them even glance back at us. For once, Rahuti and I are just fellow soldiers, not outsiders to be jeered at or insulted.

While I welcome the respite, that maybe I've earned my place among them, I'm uneasy.

'Awi and his flies never appear.

"Things are a little too quiet tonight," I say to Rahuti as I tear off a half of bread and take a bite.

"You're right," he says. "Where's 'Awi?"

"I was going to ask you the same thing."

"Wouldn't be a meal without him getting in our faces." Rahuti washes down his food with a clumsy swig.

"The commander isn't here either," I say.

"That is weird," Rahuti says, his mouth still full. "He hasn't missed an evening meal since I got here."

Indeed, he wouldn't miss a chance to intimidate us soldiers.

"As long as they're gone," I say, "let's enjoy tonight's meal, because you know the commander and the rest of them are going to make our lives miserable again tomorrow." I raise my cup. "To peace."

Rahuti's mouth widens in relief. "To peace!"

○ ○ ○

When I was a little girl of only six or seven floods, Mawat told me tales of the *shuyitu*, the shadows who come alive at twilight. She said they are the spirits of those who have died but weren't granted a proper burial.

She said it didn't matter that their bodies weren't embalmed and wrapped, the way the elite do for their own. So many *rekhyt* can't afford such a luxury, and most of them never become *shuyitu*. Rather, Mawat said, the *shuyitu* never crossed the threshold into Duat. No one prayed over their fallen bodies, reciting the spells to ensure their hearts be light. They stand no chance of ever meeting Djehuty. Not even Ammit will devour them.

They wander among us, seeking vengeance, lifeless and silent, at this time when the light plays tricks on us. They make us believe a mere shrub is a *hiyu* or a tree is a man lying in wait with a dagger to attack. They're too tortured to let us forget them. Sometimes, they even attack the living.

As a child, I believed Mawat and stayed close to the Per-seshen when Re sailed his barque into the west.

As I grew, after my first blood, and after countless evenings walking home with Iti as the daylight faded, I stopped believing her. No *shuyitu* stalked us as we strolled through the fields, through the city gates, and down dark and arrow passages. Every day, we made it home, safe and sound. Not a *shuyitu* to be seen.

I told myself it was just a tale Mawat told me to keep me from straying too far from home or from Iti.

But these figures on the edge of the scribes' quarters look like the *shuyitu* of my girlish imagination.

Shendytu so long that when they walk, they appear to be floating. Shrouds so dark that their faces fall into shadow, even in the light of the braziers lining the path.

I know they're not the creatures my Mawat warned me about. They're just men. They must be.

But what are they doing here, just a few houses away from mine? And why would they want to cover their heads with such dark cowls when the heat of the day is barely abating?

I edge closer, keeping my back pressed against the outside wall of my quarters.

The men whisper. I creep toward them, hoping to hear their conversation.

With every step, I risk them seeing me. And with every step, I wonder more and more if my Mawat was right about the *shuyitu* after all.

I hold my breath, so even the sound of my own air doesn't betray me.

They float around the corner. I follow them, winding between the grid of buildings, hoping I'm far enough out of their sight.

When they approach the outskirts of the scribes' barracks, they stop. I pray to Nuit for her darkness to shield me.

"The master says it's almost time," one of them says.

"Before the floods return."

"But Sopdet will appear in only a few days."

"Then we only have a few days."

I think I recognize one of the voices, but the riotous chorus of frogs from the nearby rushes drowns them out.

The group splits, each man going a separate direction. As one walks down the path right past me, I slip into the alley between the two houses.

He keeps his head down, his cowl obscuring his profile.

When I can't see any of them at all anymore, I make my way back to my quarters. Even in the abating heat, my skin is like gooseflesh. I wish Mawat never told me those tales at all.

When I reach my quarters, I take a long look up and down the path, making sure they didn't follow me, and slip through the doorway.

◦ ◦ ◦

Before I begin my feeble attempt to wash up, I light a lamp and find a reply from Ahmose.

What is this between us, this daily correspondence? Sometimes I have nothing interesting to write. Just a recounting of the day's exercises or lamenting my sore muscles and the mediocre food. But he responds to me without fail, with words of encouragement, sometimes telling me

PART THREE: THE COMMAND

of his own struggles with the negotiations, and reminding me to report to him anything that seems unbalanced.

Oh, those men I saw tonight were certainly unbalanced. Heavy with suspicion and secrecy.

Before I prepare my inks and papers to tell him, I sit on my bed and unfold today's reply.

> The 29th day of IV Shemu, 20th year of our king
> My dear Sati,
> May you be in favor of Sekhmet.
> The Great God—Beloved of Horu, Protected by Sekhmet—and his High Priests will mark the First of the Five Days on the End of the Year, birthday of Wennefer Wasir, and return of Sopdet's star, with a grand ceremony and banquet the evening after tomorrow. Nothing would bring me more happiness than if you would honor me with your companionship at the celebration.

It must be my exhaustion, or training in the late Shemu heat for hours. Or maybe the *shuyitu* are playing tricks on me. I can't believe what I'm reading.

His message continues on the back.

> Should you accept, leave me your reply, and wait at your quarters just after midday on the birthday of Wasir. Ubenu will come for you, and my attendants will attire you. I will also secure any necessary permissions for you to attend.
> May your hearing be beautiful.
> Your Ahmose

"Your Ahmose." I breathe the words, as though bringing them into my mouth will make them more real.

Indeed, I read the note at least three more times in disbelief. A highborn man is inviting me to a royal banquet. And he began his letter with "dear." *My dear Sati.*

I imagine myself there, beside royals and nobles, and I'm weightless. Me. A *rekhyt* girl! With a nobleman, as though I were highborn myself. And in the presence of the Good God, not as a subject, but as someone in his service. If only I could tell Mawat and Iti right now.

I can almost hear Mawat's gasp of amazement and feel Iti's proud hand patting me on the shoulder when the front door opens.

"Someone looks like they've received beautiful news!" Djedi says, closing the door behind him.

He sits at the foot of my bed, eager with anticipation. "It must be good, because I've never seen you smile like that! Or your cheeks so pink."

I curl the paper in my hands so Djedi can't read it. "Have you ever been to the Wepet Renpet banquet at the Great House?" I ask.

"Oh, I go every year, *bitbit*." He points at Ahmose's message. "Is that an invitation?"

Another smile bursts on to my face again as I nod. "What is it like?"

"Well, *bitbit*, I'll tell you what it's not like. It's not just some priests saying prayers, waving incense over the crowd, and blessing the Black Land for the New Year. Oh no." He flashes a mischievous grin. "It's the most glorious, extravagant, and utterly indulgent event of the year. Pure, unabashed revelry. The wine flows like the river at the height of Akhet itself."

"And what about the food?" The mere thought of a royal feast makes my belly rumble, the lentils and bread from earlier no longer satisfying my hunger.

"Some of the finest and rarest dishes you'll ever have the pleasure of tasting."

"Praise Nefertem," I say, falling back on the bed. "I've been dreaming of a proper meal since I first arrived."

"Oh, is that all you're dreaming about?"

I nudge him with my foot, and he lifts his delicate eyebrow. "So, who is this mystery correspondent? They've written to you every day. And I know you write back. I see your inks out in the morning."

I gaze at the ceiling beams. "Just . . . a friend. Someone I met on my way here."

"Hmm." He doesn't look convinced. "A woman's heart is not mine to read. I'm sure you'll tell me in time."

"Will we see you there, at the banquet?" I say, sitting up again.

"Ooh, well, that would be quite the reveal, wouldn't it? Your secret correspondent in all their festival finery?" He points at me with a raised brow that says he's going to make some comment about my appearance. "You don't expect to go in your uniform, do you?"

"No! He said his attendants would give me something to wear."

A grin brightens his face. "So, now I know it's a 'he.'"

I reply with a little push of my elbow.

"I have faith you'll clean up well," he says.

"Umm, thank you?"

"Oh, *bitbit*, I mean that as a compliment. Some people, though." He clicks his tongue. "No amount of gold in the king's domain can save them from their impropriety."

"What do you mean?"

"I've seen the highest-stationed men in this city lose themselves at the Wepet Renpet, behaving like fools, putting their positions in jeopardy, sometimes losing it entirely." His tone lowers in warning. "These are the most dangerous days of the year, you know. And people here talk. Don't give them anything to talk about."

"I'm sure I'm already in the mouths of the people who saw me in the Great Hall on my first day here."

"Then keep your eyes and ears open. You, and your . . . companion."

CHAPTER SEVENTEEN

The 29th day of IV Shemu, 20th year of our king
My dearest Ahmose,
May you be in favor of Amun.
Yes! Yes yes yes! A thousand times, yes!

What am I writing?

No.

No no no.

I can't say that. It's too eager. Too improper.

I tear the writing away the paper, hold the scrap over the lamp flame, and start again.

In a second attempt, I say I'll absolutely go to the Wepet Renpet with him.

And I tell him all about the shrouded men I saw outside the scribes' quarters.

○ ○ ○

During morning training, Commander Hani makes us march across the field carrying sacks of sand the size of large cats. As the sun grows ever more intense and the ground burns under my feet, I can almost ignore my faltering shoulders, because I can't stop thinking about Ahmose's invitation.

At the midday meal, Rahuti notices my lightened mood.

"You seem happier today," he says as we eat.

"I've been invited to the Great House for Wepet Renpet," I say, unable to contain my excitement.

"So you won't be at the garrison's own celebration?"

The slack look he gives me makes me realize I'll be leaving him to face 'Awi alone.

"It's only one night," I say, hoping I'm reassuring enough. "Maybe they'll actually behave themselves."

"I'm not sure about that."

"If they start anything, you're stronger than all of them combined. Don't let them push you around. I'm half your size, and you see how they wobble when I stand up to them."

His face twists with doubt.

"And," I add, "if that doesn't work, remember: for some reason, they listen to Commander Hani."

After another sweltering morning of training and a few successful wrestling bouts with Rahuti and other soldiers, I finish my midday meal and report to the general's office. I turn the last corner, and something blunt strikes me under my ribs.

I double over, unable to breathe. I try to stay on my feet, wrapping my arms around my chest, coughing, and trying to recover my breath.

A man's voice chuckles.

The shadow men. They must have known I was following them.

My vision blurs. Lieutenant Wefer?

He sneers at me, punching his palm as a threat.

I try to speak, but I can only groan. My ribs ache from the effort.

"Go back to where you came from, girl," he taunts.

Through the blaze of pain, I struggle with what he might mean.

That I should just leave the garrison, or to go back to where I truly come from? And if so, how would he know?

I brace myself against the mudbrick.

"No," I eke out. "I'm earning my place here."

"There *is* no place for you here."

I will myself to stand straight. The pain from my belly spreads, radiating through my back and into my shoulders.

He lifts his fist.

"Well?" I say, hunched over in anticipation. "If you're going to hit me again, do it."

But the blow never comes. He lowers his hand and grunts. "Consider this your warning. If you won't leave on your own, we'll make you leave."

He spits at my feet before lumbering away.

I hug myself tighter, taking a moment to crouch with my back against the wall. The pain shifts from piercing to aching. But if I spend too long here, I'll be late for my work. And the general will certainly reprimand me the same way he does his page if I'm late. And I've been beat up enough today.

○ ○ ○

Setankh's page announces my arrival.

"Greetings, *imyr*," I say as I enter, trying to act like his sandal-licking lieutenant hadn't just pummeled my *ka* out of my body.

He says nothing when I stop midstep just inside the doorway.

I've never seen so many weapons, and certainly not in one place. I sit beside him a bit more hastily than I usually do.

As I set out my papers and palette in anticipation of work that won't happen, I take in the arsenal.

Spears, lances, axes, clubs, *khopesh* swords, and dozens of ox-skin shields line the walls, stacked in neat piles, nearly covering the mural of the general in his chariot.

The metal shines, and the leather is immaculate. The craftsman in the military's workshops must have just finished making them. They must have been working for weeks to create so many.

The mere existence of these weapons doesn't unsettle me; this is a military garrison, after all. What's unusual is they aren't in the armory storehouses near the stables. What are they doing here, in General Setankh's office?

"I see you admiring my new delivery," the general says.

I try to suppress a cough as the pain from Lieutenant Wefer's attack heaves through me again.

"They're beautiful, no?" he continues. "All ready for the battlefield."

"Indeed, *imyr*." I nod in obligate agreement.

"We will use them soon enough," he says. "Of course, what I have here is only a small fraction of our stockpile." He leans back in his chair, hands behind his head. "It will be glorious. Don't you think?" He slides an expectant gaze to me.

My heart beats faster. Why is he asking me anything at all, especially about a suspicious collection of weaponry? Quick, Sati, say something.

"What do you mean by 'it,' *imyr*?"

"Ah, you're still so naive. Exactly what I'd expect from your kind."

My kind? Does he refer to my being a woman, or something more? I'm feeling less like a dutiful official and more like a duck in a cage. Breathe. Breathe so he can't see how his words intimidate you.

"But," he says, "you are under my command, which means you should know the ways of our world. And any warrior worth his bread must understand his foreign enemies."

I run my fingertips over the edges of my scribe's kit, wondering where all this is leading. He's always been so quiet, rarely speaking to me at all in the nearly three weeks I've been in his service.

"As one of *my* warriors," he continues, "you will soon be sent to the northern lands for a final and definitive battle against those vile Hittites."

Can that be true? Have the efforts to settle the treaty failed? Surely Ahmose would have told me. Or perhaps he wouldn't. He has no good reason to keep me appraised of the negotiations. But even Commander Hani has said nothing indicating we'd be deployed soon, and he's the type to use any hint of an impending campaign to rile up his men.

The general watches for my reaction. Although my the skin on my neck bristles and my heart drums in my ribs, I try not to show any at all.

"It is a battle long overdue," he says. "It was only a matter of time before the king realized he must make real what he's carved on his temple walls. Such an offense against *ma'at* can't stand any longer. In the sixteen years since Qadesh, even the *rekhyt* are seeing the truth through the paint." The corner of his mouth tilts up. "You're a *rekhyt* girl. Is this true?"

The question sends a creeping feeling over my skin. I know the story the Good God tells is, well, not exactly *ma'at*. But do I dare admit it to the general?

"I have heard rumors, *imyr*," I say, hoping that will satisfy him.

"Well, we must quash the rumors by quashing the Hittites."

But the Good God can't possibly mean to send us to war in the north. Commander Hani hasn't even started us in any kind of weapons training. Just days and days of wrestling and marching. How can we battle the Hittites if we haven't even learned to wield lances, spears, or *khopesh*?

"What do you think?" He narrows his eyes at me.

"Pardon me, *imyr*?" He must know I'm stalling and holding back. The general doesn't strike me as an ignorant man. Arrogant, yes, but he observes and watches and waits. An ambush predator.

"What do you think of crushing the Hittites once and for all?"

Quick, say something. "I believe whatever the Good God decides will be for the best . . . *imyr*."

He grumbles. If he wants to convince me the Good God intends to bring us back to the battlefield, then he can't argue with me saying I agree with the Good God's decision. But I'm not convinced the Good God will do anything of the sort.

The general stands. "Record these numbers."

"Yes, *imyr*," I say as I scramble to mix my inks and prepare my papers. Finally, some scribal work. And an end to his questioning.

He sorts through the bundle of arrows. "Two hundred arrows." He moves to a stack of *khopesh*. "Fifty *khopesh*."

I write each amount with careful precision, taking note of what the general has stored here today.

"Twenty-five throwing sticks."

As the general approaches the axes leaning against the wall beside me, he stops.

He squints at my neck. "That necklace."

My free hand reaches for my pendant. "Yes, *imyr*?"

"Where does a *rekhyt* girl get such a piece of jewelry?"

Iti told me over and over again how he found it and why he gave it to me.

When the Good God realized the battle at Qadesh was a stalemate, and he and his soldiers stood no chance at vanquishing the Hittites, they retreated.

As they did, a few officers and their closest men scouted ahead to a nearby village to ensure the Hittites weren't lying lie in wait for them.

Iti told me that by the time he walked down the streets between the huts and hovels, the damage was done.

Everyone there had been slaughtered.

But he heard a cry in the haunting silence.

When he tried to find the source of the crying, he found a woman, her belly ripped open, and a child no more than two floods old, clutching her breast, covered in blood.

As Iti took me from her, he saw that she wore a single piece of jewelry. A gold pendant, inlaid with gems, in the shape of a lily, no bigger than a man's thumbnail.

It's not an unusual shape, even so far from the Iteru. The lily graces all manner of jewelry, walls, pottery, and embroidery. Even weapons.

But the way the general waits for my answer makes me wonder if he recognizes my pendant from that day.

No. That's impossible. How could he distinguish this necklace from any other? And if he does recognize it, does that mean he knew my father?

"It was a gift, *imyr*," I say.

"A gift you wear every day. It must mean quite a lot to you." He counts through the axes. "Fifty axes."

"Yes, *imyr*, it does." I hope he can't see the shake in my fingers as I write.

"A gift from whom?"

Do I tell him? If he knew my father, then what would be the harm in telling him? I wouldn't be revealing anything he doesn't already know. Right? By Ptah, Sati, you need to say something.

I hope I'm not making a deadly mistake.

"My father, *imyr*."

He lifts an eyebrow at me. "He still lives?"

"Yes, *imyr*, praise be to Wasir."

I try to catch the flash of expression on his face when I answer. It's something between revelation and irritation.

"To teach his daughter how to read and write. And fight. He must be a remarkable man, indeed."

"Yes, I think so, *imyr*."

"Of course you do." He steps to a stack of shields. "Twenty-five shields."

As I write, he approaches an unadorned box on his desk and opens it. He pulls out a plain dagger, turning it over in his hands as he gives me a sly grin. "He must be very proud of you."

"Yes, I'm sure he is, *imyr*." The dagger looks familiar. No markings, no inlay, no precious metals. Like the one the Scarred Man held against Iti's chest.

He returns the dagger to the box, but he doesn't tell me how many there are.

"Pardon me, but the daggers, *imyr*?"

"Hmm?" He closes the lid.

"The daggers, *imyr*. How many daggers, for the inventory?" I gesture to the paper in my lap.

"No need. These have been made especially and only for me."

○ ○ ○

At the evening meal, I don't dare tell Rahuti about the weapons in the general's office. And I definitely don't tell him how the general asked about my necklace, or about that dagger that looked far too familiar. I don't even mention how Lieutenant Wefer attacked me after the midday meal. Not that I don't trust him. Strangely, I do. But I don't want 'Awi and his flies overhearing any of it.

Instead, I ask Rahuti how afternoon training went, hoping to keep him talking, so he doesn't ask me about *my* afternoon.

"So much marching," he says. "I thought my arms would fall off. Those sandbags are so heavy!"

"Well, at least we have the next five days off to recover," I say.

His expression brightens. "Thank Sobek! I can't wait. I'm going to sleep late every day, eat as much as I can stand, and go swim in the river. Maybe I'll go explore the city. I haven't even left the garrison since I started training."

"That sounds like a marvelous way to open the new year."

He lifts his cup. "To the new year!"

CHAPTER EIGHTEEN

My skin buzzes in anticipation of the arrival of Ahmose's page. It's finally Wasir's birthday.

Yesterday, I didn't write to Ahmose about anything that happened outside of or inside the general's offices. Something about all of it feels so *desher* that if my message ends up in the wrong hands, it could prove dangerous to both me and Ahmose. I might be on the brink of discovering a conspiracy that isn't just a threat to the two of us, but to the Good God's realm itself.

Would the general incite hatred against foreigners in the streets of our cities only so he could justify starting a war in the north? And if so, what might he do to me if he finds out I'm the baby Iti saved, if he does recognize my necklace?

And now, waiting for Ahmose's page to arrive, I can't sit still. I fold and refold my *shendytu* and shawl, stacking them in my chest, only to remove them and start over. I sort through the stack of letters from Ahmose, aligning the corners, glancing through them, reading them over and again.

Djedi saunters down the stairs, wearing a wig I've never seen him in before. Each braid is capped with a gold bead. And his long linen robe is so pristine and clean it's practically glowing.

"Still waiting for your mystery suitor's page, I see."

"For an eternity. Wait. Suitor?"

"Well, that's what this is all about, isn't it?"

"I . . ." I never thought of it like that. Sure, there might be something between Ahmose and me, but we haven't seen each other since my first day here. And our correspondence has been mostly formal. I report to him on my day; he tells me about mine.

"Someone writes to you every day and has their page leave the letters under your headrest? Then you blush when you read them? That's a suitor."

My face goes warm. That would explain the dried dates, the *Dear Sati*...

"You're blushing now!" Djedi teases.

"Well, you never told me who you're going with." I try to deflect the attention away from me and my flushed face.

"You'll have to wait until tonight to find out. Besides, it's not who you arrive with, but you're with at the end of the night."

"Djedi!" Now I'm definitely blushing. Even under a layer of his gold-flecked face cream, I think Djedi is too.

Someone knocks on the door.

Djedi raises an eyebrow at me.

The knocking repeats.

"Well," Djedi says. "Go see who it is."

My belly feels as though it's full of kittens as I open the door.

A clean-shaven man of about thirty floods greets me with a bend at the waist. "Ubenu, at your service. May you live forever. I am here to retrieve Sati."

So this is Ahmose's page.

Djedi's grin stretches between his ears like the crescent moon.

I turn back to Ubenu. "I'm Sati."

"My heart rejoices in meeting you," Ubenu says. He almost sounds bored. "My lord awaits your arrival."

My heart pounds.

"Ooh, a lord, is it?" Djedi teases.

"Oh, hush."

Ubenu clears his throat. "My lord's house anticipates your arrival, to prepare you for the evening's festivities."

"Sounds like you'll indeed be wearing something quite appropriate," Djedi says. "I can't wait to see."

I shoot another glance at Djedi.

"Remember what I told you," he says. "Don't lose yourself."

"Of course, of course," I say, brushing off his words. He has no idea what might be at stake for me, for our Good God. "May your *ka* rejoice at the return of Sopdet's star."

"I'll see you on the other side of the resurrection," he replies with a suggestive grin.

I shake my head and stride through the doorway with Ubenu, feeling as though my feet aren't even touching the ground, and I close the door behind me.

○ ○ ○

The grand cedar doors open with a creak.

A woman perhaps only a little younger than Mawat greets me with a kind, round face.

"You must be Sati," she says with a chirp. "We are so thrilled you're here!"

She takes my elbow and leads me through the entrance hall into a grand room, the ceiling vaulted and as open as the sky itself, supported by green and gold lily-capped columns. A life-size painted image of a young man in the rushes along the river holds up his hunting stick, ready for the next flock of spotted ducks. Perch and carp swim in the waters, and butterflies float around him. Above me, the ceiling is a deep lapis sky, covered in twinkling, golden stars. This must be what the Field of Reeds is like, surrounded by beauty and the gifts of the Black Land for all of eternity.

We enter a smaller chamber, just as richly painted as the previous.

Here, the great goddesses greet us. Iset and Hat-hor bless two figures, a man and his wife, from what I can read. Useraasen. Didn't Ahmose say that was his father's name? And Siyanofret. This must be his mother.

A second woman, close in age to Mawat, approaches us with a serene smile. Fine lines stretch from the corners of her eyes.

"It's such a pleasure to meet you and to dress you for the birthday of Wennefer Wasir tonight," she says.

She wraps her henna decorated hands around mine. "I'm Nehemet, and Beket accompanied you here. It's been so long since we've helped dress a woman for a royal festival."

Beket claps her hands together. "We're so excited!"

Nehemet squeezes my hands, and her familiarity gives me a start. "Your first banquet, I'm assuming?"

I nod. My dirty uniform and impressive collection of bruises make it obvious.

"Well," Nehemet says, looking me up and down, "Ahmose said you might not be accustomed to such gatherings."

"Where is Ahmose?" I ask.

"With his own attendants, of course! So much to prepare and so little time!" Her necklace of large turquoise baubles dances along the base of her neck.

She leads me past a brazier in the center of the room sending up threads of frankincense. I close my eyes and take in the smoke. It reminds me of Mawat. If only she could see me here now.

"First things first." Nehemet gestures to a stone basin by the wall. And beside it, a large clay bowl filled with steaming water. A real bath!

"Oh, thank Nefertem," I say.

"Lord Ahmose did tell me you might appreciate it. Now, let's take off these, um, clothes." She *tsks* and reaches for the laces at the sides of my tunic.

Instinctually, I pull away from her.

"It's all right, dear!" Nehemet chirps. "But you're not used to having help like this, are you?"

"No, not at all." Maybe the highborn are used to attendants undressing them, but only Mawat has ever done that for me. And not for a long time.

"You have nothing to worry about," Nehemet says.

If these ladies are in Ahmose's service, then he trusts them, and I should, too. I should learn to accept help a bit more often. I drop my shoulders and step closer.

With their deft hands, they undo the laces, and they lift the leather over my head, setting it aside. I wrap my arms around my chest, which does me no good in any attempt to cover myself when they untie the knot of my *shendyt*, unwrapping it from my hips, and set it beside the tunic. From here, I can see just how dirty they are compared to the pure white of Nehemet and Beket's own linen dresses.

Nehemet holds out her hand. "In you go."

I step into the bowl and sit, pulling my knees into my chest. The cold marble against my skin makes me only pull myself in smaller. But when Nehemet and Beket pour a basin of warm water over my shoulders, my muscles relax. My apprehension dissolves away with the scent of jasmine and lilies. Beket scrubs my underarms, neck, and shoulders. I revel in the sensation. This is the cleanest I've been since my arrival in this city.

They scrub my entire body, and I surrender to finally being cleansed of days and days of dust, dirt, and blood. I'll be clean again after all!

But it all ends too soon, and Nehemet helps me out of the basin, with Beket ready to wrap me in a linen sheet.

As Nehemet dries my legs, she *tsks* at me again.

"We have wrestling training every day," I say.

"And apparently no way to remove this hair!"

I laugh. That's what she sees? I thought she was disapproving of my bruises and cuts.

"What a sacrifice you've made to serve the Good God," Nehemet says. "No razors. No wax. I couldn't stand one day of living like that!"

Oh, if only that were the worst of it.

She brings me to a raised wooden table with gold inlay, near the wall with the mural of Ahmose's family.

"I see you admiring the mural," Nehemet says.

"Ahmose's father and mother, yes?"

"Useraasen and Siyanofret, yes. Both have since passed into eternity, may they live forever. We served them both, and I even helped raise Ahmose. He was quite the handful as a little boy. I could never keep up with him."

I'm not surprised. "Does he have any other family here?"

She shakes her head. "Just us attendants, and the rest of the staff, of course. We're the only family he has left now. At least, here in Per-Ramesses. Now, sit back."

She and Beket smear a warm wax on my skin, following with strips of linen. Without warning, they rip the linen away. I can't hold back my yelp.

"Oh, my dear, has it been that long since you had this done?"

Before I can answer, they do the same . . . everywhere else.

This is worse than being tossed around by Rahuti. And I don't want to admit to them I've never been waxed so completely like this. When they finish, they rub a lily-scented oil over my angry skin.

"I would never forgive myself if you went to the Great House with so much hair!" Nehemet declares as Beket slips a dress over my head. It's made of a linen as sheer as mist. Djedi was right; this banquet must be quite the uninhibited event. I twist side to side, reveling in the sensation of it brushing over my skin.

"It's like wearing a cloud," I say.

"Oh, just wait," Nehemet says proudly, raising her eyebrows at me.

I hold my breath as she helps Beket unfurl a mesh of beads down my body, revealing an ankle-length dress.

"Please, breathe!" Beket tugs on the fringed hem and giggles. "The strands are strong."

The ladies sit me on a stool, and Nehemet applies kohl to my eyes and a shimmering green powder to my eyelids, followed with a salty red paste on my lips.

Nehemet steps back, tapping her finger on the side of her cheek. "Yes, yes," she says after a moment of examination. "The malachite brings out your eyes."

Beket combs my short hair—only a fingernail long now—with oils scented with myrrh and what I think are roses before slipping a wig made of human hair over it, each braid wrapped in gold and glass beads of every color imaginable. I expect the underside to itch like my wig at the Per-seshen, but it's as smooth as my freshly waxed legs.

"Now for the finishing touches," Nehemet says, her smile even wider.

She brings over a small wooden box with glass inlay and tips open the lid. She pulls out four gold bangles with bands of green, red, and blue glass, and two golden hoops. Beket slides one of the bangles up one arm, and Nehemet does the same on the other, and the upper one covers my fresh pink scar. After adding one to each of my wrists, they fasten the gold hoops on my ears.

"One last thing." Nehemet drapes a wide beaded collar around my neck, fastening it in the back.

Beket bounces with joy as she hands me a large hand mirror. "Look!"

I hesitate. The last time I wore anything similar was the day Tahir and his family were attacked in the market. When Mawat made me wear a dress and wig, so I wouldn't stand out as foreign. When I drew on my kohl crooked and my wig made my scalp burn.

But today, I almost don't recognize my reflection. The girl—no, the woman—I see is elegant. Refined. Regal, even. She doesn't have to attempt to appear like she's from the Black Land. She simply just is.

Has this woman been a part of me all along?

I turn my head side to side, watching the shimmer on my eyelids dance in the light.

"Like the *heka* of Iset herself," I say.

"Oh, I'm no priestess," Nehemet says. "I just knew that underneath the dirt and military uniform was a stunning young woman. And here you are!"

As Beket laces fine leather sandals around my calloused and sunburned feet, Nehemet squeezes my shoulders then adjusts the braids in my wig, ensuring none is tangled or out of place.

"Iset has truly blessed Ahmose on this day," she says.

My cheeks go warm, and I look away. "I don't know if it's like that," I say.

She shares a playful glance with Beket. "Oh, it will be after tonight!" They laugh.

Curse my cheeks. They must be as red as desert sands.

A sharp rap on the door echoes against the walls. Beket flits to the door, and a young page steps through. "Lord Ahmose waits for the lady Sati."

"Lady?" I mouth to Nehemet. She nods with confidence, and Beket giggles.

"Enjoy tonight, little kitten," Nehemet says as the two of them wrap their arms around me in a warm embrace.

"I can't thank you enough," I say as I pull them closer. I never thought I would miss the company of women, but right now, I do. I even miss Mawat's friends fussing over my hair and swarming around in our kitchen.

"Go celebrate the return of the star," Nehemet says. "And tell us all about it when you return."

PART THREE: THE COMMAND

◎ ◎ ◎

As the page and I pass through a grand hallway, I'm a swarm of butterflies. My fingers feel for my lily pendant under the beaded collar.

Worried I'll snap the delicate threads on the dress or the laces on the sandals, I take careful steps. I find myself moving in a lighter, softer manner than I would in my *shendyt* and leather. Is that because of the clothing, or because I know all eyes of the court will soon be on me? Or because I'll see Ahmose in only a few moments?

The page holds open a final door. He bows and gestures for me to pass through.

And on the other side, Ahmose meets me. He seems to be holding back a smile, but I can't keep mine from dancing over my face.

How long has it been since we last saw each other? Three weeks? Enough time for the gash in my arm to heal, for the late Shemu sun to have toasted my skin, and for him to grow into his office as a negotiator. Enough time for us to forget the details of each other's faces, but to learn the quirks and flourishes of each other's writing.

But the sight of him now—even as he adjusts his wig, as he pulls up the gold bangles on his upper arms, straightens the electrum pectoral pendant gracing his chest—is oddly familiar.

No, that's impossible. We only spent five days on that ship together. And he's a nobleman. I'm a *rekhyt* girl. We are born of different worlds. How could walking toward him now feel like walking through the courtyard of the Per-seshen after an afternoon sparring in the fields?

As he approaches, the scent of cinnamon, myrrh, and pine sends me right back to the first moment we met.

He fidgets with his jewelry. "You look . . ."

As he hesitates, I expect him to say something polite. Some platitude about beauty, embodying everything *neferet*. Something his mother and father taught him to say to a woman dressed in her finery.

"Different?" I say, unsure of how to respond to the soft vulnerability in his expression.

He lets out a faint laugh. "In a way, yes. Stronger, taller, more confident. Like you could take on an entire army."

That's not at all what I expected. And after so many unsuccessful days of training, hearing his words makes my heart dance. I look at my sandals and press my lips together. "In a dress like this?"

"Even in a dress like that." His voice is as rich as river silt.

I twist my pendant in my fingers again.

He steps closer. "It's all right if you're nervous."

"I'm not . . . Well, yes. I am a bit nervous."

"I admit these gatherings make me a bit uneasy, too."

"Really?" If he feels out of place, then I'm not alone.

"All the rules and decorum and etiquette. It doesn't come naturally to me."

Without thinking, I reach for his hand, holding his gaze.

"You'd rather be on the *Nebkhepri*?" I say.

He places his other hand on mine. "Only if you would come with me."

The wings on my heart flutter. By Hat-hor's horns, Nehemet and Djedi are right. It *is* like that.

"But tonight, I only ask that you accompany me to the Great Hall." He offers me his arm. I think first to place my hand in the bend of his elbow, but I thread my arm through his, closing the space between me and the warm skin of his torso. He turns his gaze to meet mine, and for a moment I forget to breathe.

"I would be a fool to say no," I say.

"Good," he says softly, "because I wouldn't have anyone else on my arm tonight."

A kindling warmth in my belly winds its way into my cheeks, and my heart now feels as though it will flutter off into the evening air.

We walk together through the receiving room into the villa's grand entrance. A footman waits with a chariot led by two horses as black as a moonless night.

Ahmose jumps into the cab and offers me his hand. I take it and step up with care, so not to pull on the threads of my beaded dress. As Ahmose takes the reins in one hand, he wraps his other arm around my back.

I inhale as deeply and fully as I can, as though I can somehow preserve this one moment in my lungs forever. I release it as Ahmose clicks his tongue against his teeth, and the horses trot toward the palace grounds.

CHAPTER NINETEEN

In Men-nefer, the streets fill with revelers during these five days at the end of the year. The entire city rejoices, praying for the waters to return. Before long, they become drunk on beer and, if they're wealthy enough, on wine from the delta or even the northern lands. Drummers pound on their instruments all day and night, followed by musicians blowing into buzzing flutes and strumming their lyres. Dancers clap and prance around them, beckoning anyone and everyone to join them. The neighborhoods come alive with bakers selling honeyed breads and tiger nut cakes drenched in date syrup, woodcarvers convincing parents to buy dolls and toys shaped like animals for their children, and weavers showing off their most expensive shawls and dresses. Mawat always dressed me in fine linen and drew on my kohl thick and sharp. Iti would spend the holiday with his military friends, and we'd often bounce from house to house so Mawat and Iti could reminisce about their younger days with neighbors and distant family. I hope Mawat and Iti are celebrating now, finding the joy they deserve, even if this is the first new year in sixteen years without me.

But we *rekhyt* aren't allowed in the temples. Only the elite gather there, in the houses of Sekhmet and Ptah, offering piles of the land's bounty to call back the flood. I've seen them enter with dishes towering with ripe fruits and vegetables, entire legs of ox, draped with lapis blue lilies.

I always wondered what happens behind the closed temple doors, because whatever they do never fails, even if the waters are low. But I never thought I'd witness it with my own senses.

I don't know how many people serve in the court of the Good God, but it seems every single one of them has crowded into the main chapel of the Temple of Amun. Perfumes with flowery notes I've never smelled before mingle with the haze of frankincense pouring forth from braziers and censers lining the temple walls and hanging from the wide cedar ceiling beams.

Ahmose and I arrived early enough to be close to the altar, but I strain to see over the sea of bewigged and bald heads surrounding us.

The crowd shifts, their shoulders bumping and jostling.

"He is coming," Ahmose says in an excited whisper.

Before I can ask who, a drum beats three times, followed by a chorus of men's voices.

"*Ankh, udja, seneb!*"

The entire court repeats it to the high priests, their words bouncing off the limestone walls. A rush of rattling and clapping follows with the ululating cries of women. The haze of incense thickens.

I stand on my tiptoes while Ahmose steadies me with his hand on the small of my back. I could balance well enough on my own, but the warmth of his palm is nearly as intoxicating as the perfumes and incense. It doesn't even matter if I can't see what the crowd so eagerly anticipates, so long as we can linger here like this.

But I can see.

A life-sized statue of the green-faced god Wasir appears at the far end of the hall above the heads of the crowd. His feathered crown glows in the light of what must be a thousand braziers and lamps. As it shuffles closer, I see he stands in a gilded barque, balanced on the shoulders of ten high priests.

As the god approaches, the crowd moves around his barque like a school of fish, holding up their arms and murmuring prayers.

The cacophony of claps and rattling grows louder and louder. A cloud of priestesses follows in the god's wake, shaking their sistrums and slapping their ivory clappers. Others strike their hands together with wide open palms, chanting, "*Ankh! Udja! Seneb!*" between their ululations.

We step back for the god and his retinue as a group of young women wail behind them, tossing dust over their heads, pulling at their hair. Some even beat themselves with flails in grief. The first time I saw professional mourners, I was still a little girl. Their pained cries and their kohl-streaked cheeks scared me so much that I hid behind Mawat's leg as they passed. But when Mawat told me they were paid to cry like that, I was never scared of them again.

The mourners fall quiet when the priests raise their scepters and the god's barque stops in the middle of the temple hall, just in front of me and Ahmose.

A trumpet blasts through the expectant silence with a piercing note, and a priest steps forward. "O Wasir! We call upon your son Horu to guard your body!"

The priestesses follow with a clattering of percussion.

"O Wasir, we bless your *ba*, exalt your *ka*, and open your mouth to give you breath!"

A cacophony of prayers bursts out, calling for Wasir to return, to bless the Black Land with the waters, to be resurrected so we all might see a prosperous and fruitful year.

The priest raises his hands. "O Wasir, we call upon your wife Iset, who completes you!"

Everyone hushes again as a reed flute plays a delicate, haunting melody, and a young priestess wearing the throne-shaped headdress of Iset steps in front of the barque, flanked by two others.

"O Wasir, the Perfect One, Beautiful in Eternity," she says in a voice trained from birth. "I, your sister, your heart's desire, flood the land with tears. Come to your house. Come to your body!"

She shakes her sistrum, and a second priestess steps beside her, in a headdress shaped like a temple. Iset's sister, Nebet-het. A harp follows with melancholy notes.

"Come to your house," Nebet-het calls. "Drive all pain from our hearts!" She beats slow and steady on the skin of her frame drum, and the metal cymbals on the edge shimmer and rattle in time. "We ward off Sutekh, and the two sisters protect your body."

Through the smokey haze of perfume, incense, and belief, a burgeoning energy builds. These priestesses become the goddesses, and the goddesses are the priestesses.

"No evil befalls gods and men when you shine," Iset says, shaking her instrument in time with Nebet-het's drum. "Jubilation is in your temple, you being protected, protected in peace."

Iset and Nebet-het sing out, "Come in peace and ascend with the sun!"

The other priestesses and priests join in the rhythm, clapping, chanting, banging on their drums. The entire band of musicians plays together, repeating the same melody again and again. Something takes hold of me, and I lose myself, clapping and ululating along.

A priest comes forward from behind the god, holding a large tray of bread and a jug of beer. "We promise you bounty for your body, and you will be satiated. We await your return!"

The rhythm and chanting grow faster. The crowd sways in waves, overtaken by the entrancing rhythm. The harp and flute compete with the wailing of the trumpet, all playing the same rousing song. Iset and Nebet-het shake their sistrums furiously.

The bodily separation between me, the revelers, and even the gods falls away. And then I sense it. The *heka*. It swirls around me, around Ahmose, around everyone here, distorting the light like heat over sand.

A burning wind scrapes across my face.

And the crowd vanishes.

"Ahmose?" I call out. "Ahmose!"

But he's gone, and I'm alone.

Until I feel her presence. It's been so long since she's revealed herself.

Because you have failed to call on me. Do you not trust me to guide you?

"Where are you?" I search for any sign of her. And I don't know if I can trust her. If I can trust myself, my senses.

I've always been here. Especially for you, little cub.

The fires in the braziers burn taller.

"I still don't understand. Why have you brought me here?"

A threat lurks on the horizon.

"You mean the general? And those men outside the scribes' quarters?"

You will soon know.

"But these are your days. Loose your arrows on them. Why bring me into any of this at all?"

Be my eyes. Her voice purrs, soft and soothing.

"Your eyes?" I ask.

Remember the might of the stars. And to battle and blood you shall return...

Before I can ask any more questions, her presence vanishes, and I'm surrounded by the worshipping crowd again.

I swear I spoke to the goddess out loud, but no one around me seems to have noticed. Not even Ahmose, who sways beside me in blissful reverie.

The quickening, urgent pulse sweeps through us, and the goddess' voice resounds in my ears. A threat on the horizon. A threat I'm meant to uncover.

The repeating chant of the priests and priestesses shakes me from her words. "Raise you up, O Wasir! Raise you, raise you up in peace!"

"Lo!" the high priest calls. "He comes!"

The drumming, clapping, and chanting boils to an urgent,

churning roll. The nobles hold up their hands, rocking and shifting with the beat, crying out Wasir's name. I find myself doing the same.

Wasir in his barque blinks his eyes open and holds out his arms.

"Wennefer Wasir is reborn!"

We erupt into cheers and piercing ululations. The priestesses rattle their sistrums, pound the drums, and the clatter of clapping fills the hall. The trumpeter repeats a triumphant note. The mourning women call out, reaching for the god.

"The waters will return!" the high priest proclaims. "Let the Wepet Renpet celebration begin!"

The high priest holds his scepter to the sky, and the doors alongside the temple wall burst open. The crowd roars and the revelers flood the doorway.

Ahmose, now released from his trance—as though this were another normal evening for him—offers his elbow to me.

"Are you ready?" he asks.

"Ready for what?" *Ma'at* be told, I haven't been ready for most of what I've seen tonight.

He gazes at me with those rakish mud-black eyes. "The fun part."

I thread my arm through his, pressing myself close to him.

"Yes," I say. "A thousand times, yes."

○ ○ ○

Sentries at the entrance with their feathered standards nod at us as we pass through the double doors into something from my most extravagant dreams.

The aroma of roasted meats, rare spices, and floral perfumes washes over me. Garlands woven with lilies and jasmine line the walls and arc gracefully from column to column over our heads. Sweet incense puffs up from braziers, obscuring the opposite side of the hall. Musicians pluck grand harps and delicate lutes, blow into reed flutes, and tap on frame drums, playing enchanting songs. Enjoy tonight's earthly riches, the harper sings, for tomorrow they may all vanish.

Clusters of richly adorned people chatter together in excitement, while others let their eyes wander.

They're watching me. Even in all my new trappings of sophistication, the nobles must know I'm out of place here. Not just as a *rekhyt* girl, or even as a soldier, but as someone born in the northern frontier.

A few of them must recognize me from my petition. If they don't, being linked with Ahmose will give me away, because he stepped forward to speak on my behalf.

A tinge of nervousness buzzes in my heart.

No. Release it. Ahmose asked me to join him. He said there's no one else he wanted to accompany him tonight. And I'm here in the capital because the Good God himself determined I stay and serve him. Even the Powerful One herself guided me here. Was tonight part of her plan as well?

I swallow into my dry throat, pull myself closer to Ahmose, and look directly into anyone's eyes who dares to stare at me. I belong here as much as they do.

Let them see the *rekhyt* girl from Men-nefer. The girl who, in the finest linen and purest gold, looks as though she were born in Kemet. I've already overcome more challenges than these people in their walled villas and gold sandals could ever imagine.

A servant—a young man, probably about my age, with long limbs and a crisp *shendyt*—approaches us with turquoise-colored cups in the shape of lily blossoms and a jar painted with dark purple grapes and a vine winding around a trellis.

Ahmose takes two cups and hands one to me. "Only the best for the New Year celebration," he says as the servant fills it with a rich, crimson liquid. "From grapes grown in Retenu, of course."

My heart goes cold at the name.

"What's wrong?" Ahmose asks. He must have noticed my expression change. "Do you not like Retenu wine?"

Oh, if that were the problem! I wouldn't even know the difference between wine from my homeland and wine made here in the Black Land.

"I've never had much wine at all," I laugh away my discomfort. "And I'm not sure temple wine counts."

"You're in for a special treat." He lifts his cup and dips his chin. "To your first taste of wine from the north."

He holds my gaze as we both take a sip. It's warming, sweet, spiced, like the *heka* itself.

"Let's see what the kitchens have prepared," Ahmose says, as though he has attended celebrations like this a thousand times. "I haven't eaten a proper meal since morning." He takes my hand with an ease and familiarity that diffuses any lingering feelings that I don't belong here.

Every dish I could ever dream of, and even some beyond my wildest imagination, covers the serving tables. It's impossible to see and believe famine threatens the Black Land just outside these walls.

Arranged before us are whole roasted ducks garnished with leeks and green onions. Perch stuffed with barley and kamut, spiced with cumin and coriander. Hammered metal platters piled with steaming slices of beef and lamb, drizzled with vinegars and sprinkled with dill and sesame seeds. Enormous bowls filled with lentil stew, teeming with chunks of roast meat and dotted with pomegranate seeds. Loaves of bread baked in every shape imaginable: lilies, stars, fish, hedgehogs, even full oxen. A few noble ladies tear off some for themselves, leaving two legless cows.

"Tell the servants what you want, and they'll bring it to us when we sit," Ahmose says.

My mouth waters, and my belly rumbles so loud I'm sure Ahmose can hear it over the bubbling conversations of the crowd.

"You should try the honey-basted gazelle." He points to a whole roasted beast at the center of the table. "And these," he says as he plucks a small dark fruit from a bowl with human-shaped feet, "are the best olives you'll ever have the pleasure of eating."

I scrunch my face.

"What? You don't like olives?" he asks as he pops it into his mouth.

"Ugh, no. Weird, bitter things!"

Ahmose laughs. He takes another and grins. "More for me."

When we approach a steaming tray of baked figs served with honey and yogurt, my mouth really waters. I tell servers I want extra helpings.

"No olives, but extra figs," Ahmose notes, as though he's saving his observation for the future.

He points his way along the tables and stops at one of the most modest dishes there.

"No matter how rare the fruits or how large the ox," he says, "these are always my favorite."

"Plain honey cakes? But that's *rekhyt* food." I stifle a laugh at the irony. "My mother makes those."

"Ah, but they remind me of when I was still a boy."

"And what were you like as a boy?" The wine gives me the courage to ask what would otherwise be too intimate a question.

"According to my father, I was incorrigible, reckless, and a trouble-maker." He smirks in a way that tells me he agrees with the assessment.

"Mawat would say the same thing about me."

We share a spark of recognition, as though our *ba*s are fluttering together over head.

At the end of the spread, he takes my hand again. "Come, let's sit and watch the dancers while we wait for our meals."

Ahmose leads me to a short table along the wall, surrounded by low benches covered with embroidered cushions, laced with gold and electrum in bold geometric patterns. The revelers around us have already grown louder, their gestures bigger, less refined, and far less self-aware. And fewer of them notice me as I pass by. It must be the wine.

"Looks like everyone's getting into the spirit of Sekhmet's days," I chuckle.

"Ah, yes. Someday I'll tell you what I've witnessed in these days of drunkenness."

"Any about yourself?" I tease.

"Perhaps." His grin sends a rush through me.

A dancing girl prances past us, the fringe of beads on her belt tinkling as she goes. Another follows, bending back so far her hands touch the tile floor, tumbling feet over head, then upright again. A few more behind them kick their legs in unison to the beat of the drums, reed flutes calling out in a searing melody above them.

As we're about to sit, a familiar face approaches.

"Djedi!" I say.

"Sati!" He greets me with a grin and a kiss on my cheek. "Aren't you just a goddess among us! I knew there was elegance in you all along."

"I'll take that as a compliment."

"And who is your . . ." Djedi regards Ahmose as he pauses.

If he says "suitor," I'll spill ink all over his kilts tomorrow.

"Your companion?" Wise man. His kilts will survive another day.

"I'm Ahmose, son of the Wasir Useraasen. May you be in favor with Amun," Ahmose says. "You look familiar. A scribe, yes?"

"Yes. My name is Djedi. Scribe to the Commander of the Chariotry Host. Pleasure to meet your acquaintance."

I jump in before Djedi can say more. "Djedi has the unfortunate distinction of having to share a small house with me," I say.

Djedi chuckles. "Oh, now, you're not too terrible! At least you keep your quarters neat, and I can't say that for some I've shared space with in the past."

Ahmose gives me an ember of a glance. "I'm sure it's not terrible at all."

A young man walks up behind Djedi, two full cups of wine in hand. He gives one to Djedi; ink stains the fingers of his right hand.

"And who is this?" I ask.

"This is Tay," Djedi says. "Scribe to the Master of Horses."

Tay places a hand over his heart and dips his bald head. "May the gods bless you on this happy day."

"Peace upon you," I say.

"A pleasure to meet you both," Ahmose says. "Will you eat with us?"

Tay defers to Djedi. When Djedi says he's meeting with the scribes at night, he probably means just this one.

"Only if the lady wishes it," Djedi says.

"Oh please, of course," I say. "Pshh. 'Lady.'"

Ahmose sits on the cushions, and I take my place beside him.

The servants bring over our heaping plates of food, the abundance of the meal overflowing before us. Everything, every drizzle of vinegar, every lump of cheese, every chunk of meat, makes my belly growl in anticipation.

But what I want are the figs. I can't help myself. I pluck one from my dish, dip it in the yogurt, and take a slow, luxurious bite.

Djedi raises his delicate eyebrow at me.

Ahmose just smiles. "Dessert first?" he teases.

I relish the sweetness of the fig and the honey and the cooling of the yogurt. After I've finished the juicy and luscious fruit, I say, "If Djehuty and Anpu deem my heart light enough so my *ka* can travel to the Field of Reeds, then I'll eat honeyed figs first for all of eternity."

CHAPTER TWENTY

"They aren't feeding you well in the barracks, are they?" Ahmose says as I wipe the remaining juices and spiced sauces from my dish with a wedge of soft bread.

"I can't bear to waste any of it," I say. "Maybe it's just a habit, especially at the end of the year."

He gives me a sympathetic look.

"There have been years where every crumb mattered," I say. And I'm still hungry.

Beside us, Djedi and Tay are in a rapt conversation about which inks they prefer, how best to cut a reed pen, and they've disagreed on when to use black and when to use red in a manuscript. This must be what companion scribes talk about over wine. Scintillating.

I stand, smooth out my beaded dress, and offer Ahmose my hand. "Come with me. I want to get more figs."

Thankfully, there are still plenty left, and a server hands me a fresh bowl. As I immediately bite into one of the fruits, Ahmose spins away. He takes a deep bow, bending to one knee.

I nearly choke on my last bit of fig when I see why.

"Great Royal Wife," I say as I dip my head.

My wig slips forward, and I catch it with my free hand, trying to slide it back into place without anyone, especially the Great Royal Wife, noticing.

"Abundance and blessings on you both on this day of Wasir's birth," she says, her voice like a falcon's wing. I never expected her to leave her seat on the dais, let alone roam around the ever more boisterous party.

"May you live forever, Your Majesty," Ahmose says. He doesn't appear to be phased by her presence.

The Great Royal Wife turns her elegant face to me. The light of the hundreds of lamps along walls glints off her gold-dusted cheeks.

"Lord Ahmose," she says, "if you don't mind me briefly taking your companion away from you."

Ahmose dips his head again. "Anything the Great Royal Wife wishes," he says. His palm lingers on my shoulder as he passes, slipping into the undulating crowd.

"Please," the Great Royal Wife says, "remind me of your name."

"Sati," I stammer.

"Ah, of course. Sat-reshwet, from Men-nefer." What is happening? Why does the Great Royal Wife, the most powerful woman in the Good God's domain, wish to speak to me?

"Seems you are settling in well," she says.

"Um . . ." My tongue stumbles. "Yes, Your Majesty."

"How has your time been here in our glorious new capital?"

What do I say? I could respond honestly, telling her of 'Awi's bullying, my struggles with training, and the general's stockpile of weapons and his pile of enigmatic papers. All that doesn't seem like a proper topic of conversation with the King's Wife at a grand celebration. But to tell her everything has been wonderful would be so far from *ma'at*.

My fingers find my lily pendant. "It's . . . much different from my life in Men-nefer."

"I would hope so," she says, the corner of her painted lips turned up. "That is what you wanted, is it not?"

"Indeed, Your Majesty." I take a larger sip of my wine than I have all evening.

"And your time as a soldier. I trust you are doing well in your training?"

"Well enough, I suppose." As we speak, the Great Royal Wife glides through the crowd. The people part and bend to her like shafts of emmer in the breeze, and I follow beside her in her wake.

"Well enough that the general has kept you in his employ. He has discharged many a scribe who didn't please him."

I suppose that's something. But why would he want me to serve him if he rarely has me do any work for him at all?

Servants rush to refill the Great Royal Wife's electrum-plated goblet, and we walk to a corner near the dais, away from the dancing revelry.

"Now," she says after taking a delicate sip, "you should know while it is true Lord Ahmose wished for you to be his guest tonight, I expressed my own wishes for your attendance."

My heart startles. "Me, Your Majesty?"

"You have a way about you I so seldom see."

I give her what must be a very puzzled expression. Especially because General Setankh said something so similar only yesterday.

"A wisdom most highborn ladies will never have, or need." She leans closer, her floral perfume washing over me. "In fact, when you first stepped before us, you reminded me of Aya, my handmaiden." She gestures with an upturned palm to a woman standing on the dais beside the Great Royal Wife's throne. The one who stared at me after my petition.

The handmaiden dips her head in reverence.

"Something happens when a woman enters a realm where others think she doesn't belong," the Great Royal Wife says. "She will either triumph . . . or be consumed."

"What do you mean?"

"Well, Aya was plucked from the aftermath of battle. My husband's generals warned him and me to not place a foreign child beside the throne of the Great Royal Wife, but I insisted. I understand what it's like to have all eyes on you, hearing whispers around you saying eventually your blood will betray your loyalty. You see, I am one of the last descendants of the heretic's dynasty. Yet, here I am, the king's favorite. And there Aya stands, one of my most trusted attendants. And here you are, at the royal New Year feast."

"That's very kind of you to say, Your Majesty, but I'm still not sure I *do* belong."

"You speak with the King's Wife now, do you not? Certainly that must count for something."

"Yes, of course, Your Majesty." I run my fingers along the rim of my cup, unsure of how to respond.

"I'm confident you'll find your place. I did and made myself invaluable. And so has Aya."

The handmaiden stands almost motionless, watching the Great Royal Wife's every move with the care of a mother cat.

"Ah," the Great Royal Wife says. "But you are far more fierce than she, and I suspect your fates will be quite different. While she has been blessed with the comforting shade of Hat-hor's sycamore, I sense the flame of her sister Sekhmet in you."

The word burrs into my ear. Sister? This time I can't deny she resembles me. Were two daughters spared in that village outside of Qadesh?

"And with that flame," the Great Royal Wife continues, "it is no wonder you have captivated the wild heart of our young negotiator."

All thought of Aya being of my same blood diverts to wondering if I should hide the flush in my cheeks.

The Great Royal Wife chuckles knowingly. "Don't be shy about it. In fact, I can't recall the last time he was so happy, especially since his father passed on to the Field of Reeds. He was always running off on some new trade or diplomatic mission with that old captain. Since your arrival, he has settled into the role he was raised to fill."

"He told me he has work to do. For the parity agreement."

"Ah, that is the issue at hand. And why your journey here was attacked, yes?" She raps her ringed fingers against her goblet.

"I think so, yes." She must see the confusion in my face, no doubt exaggerated by my dark makeup.

She allows her lips to quirk into a tiny smile. "From the moment you set foot in the Great Hall, I sensed you could be valuable to the Two Lands. And we need all our ears open in these next few days. The end of the year is always tenuous."

"I've already seen things that seem heavy. Unbalanced."

"Have you told our nobleman?"

I nod. But I haven't yet told Ahmose what I saw yesterday. What was too risky to put into writing.

"Good," she says wryly. "A woman who has the ear of a man of noble birth has great influence. No weapon in the world will ever give you that kind of power, even while you learn the ways of the warrior. Now, I'll leave you to your wine and figs. May you live forever, Sati of Men-nefer."

I bow to her, but not so much that my wig slips again.

Her gold-threaded gown flutters in her wake as she turns toward the dais.

○ ○ ○

I return to the table with my refreshed dish of figs.

Never in my most wild and wonderful dreams would I have imagined speaking with the Great Royal Wife, let alone her telling me she sees something valuable in me.

Even more unbelievable is the possibility I could be related to her handmaiden, the woman named Aya. She might even be my sister.

I try to push all those thoughts from my heart with each delectable bite. What if all of this is a dream, and tomorrow I wake in my quarters, dirty and bruised, covered in hair, only to face another disheartening day?

Ahmose sets his second helping of honey cakes on the table before sitting beside me again.

"What did the Great Royal Wife say to you?" he asks between mouthfuls of the dessert.

I pause, taking in the dancing revelers, rapt musicians, contorting acrobats, and servants bustling about between them all to keep everyone satiated and their cups full. Far past the sea of linen-draped bodies, Djedi and Tay move together in time with the music. And the Good God and the Great Royal Wife observe it all from their dais.

Even through the pulse of the drums, the sweetness of the incense, the dizzying effect of the wine, I know in my *ka* this can't be a dream.

"Is everything all right?" Ahmose asks.

I shake myself out of my thoughts. "Yes, yes, of course. But I need to tell you what happened yesterday. I didn't want to risk writing to you."

Ahmose leans closer. "What was so bad you couldn't even commit it to ink?"

I take a final glance around the hall. I see no signs of General Setankh, Commander Hani, or any of their men. And I hope the din of the celebration will cover my voice from any prying ears.

"My position here," I say, "and your safety, could well be in danger."

"Just look like you're enjoying the festivities," Ahmose says, gazing out on the swirling bodies, smiling to acquaintances and nobles as they pass.

I keep my voice as low as I can, and tilt my head to his ear. "The Good God isn't planning to wear the blue battle crown again in the north, is he?"

"Not at all. In fact, we're creeping ever closer to an agreement with our brother kingdom."

The space between our shoulders grows narrower, and he waves at an older nobleman dressed in his most glimmering finery. The man looks as though he might approach us. I take Ahmose's hand, hoping to signal we don't want to be disturbed. It works, and the man inclines his head and strolls away.

I gather the thoughts that the softness of Ahmose's skin against my palm has too easily unraveled. "So why did the general tell me as much? He even has an armory of weapons in his office."

Ahmose doesn't even glance at me, masking any apprehension or worry. "An armory?" he asks. "What did you see?"

I lean my shoulder against Ahmose's as though I might have had too much wine already.

"Hundreds of weapons. Direct from the garrison's workshops. Spears, axes, *khopesh*, arrows. Everything you could possibly imagine. He claimed they were for an upcoming campaign against the Hittites."

"The king plans no such campaign," he says, his voice low with resentment.

"That's what I thought. The strangest part was the box of daggers on his desk. They looked exactly like the ones used by the men who threatened my family. Like the ones the attackers used on the *Nebkhepri*."

"Do you mean to suggest the general ordered the attack?"

"Perhaps? He didn't want me to record the daggers. He said they were for his own use."

Ahmose pauses, letting out a long exhale. "Our suspicions seem to be true. The king's own brother, conspiring against us. Against our own people."

And I see now why the Good God, the Great Royal Wife, and even Ahmose himself were all so eager to secure me a position so close to the general. I've become a spy for them all.

For a moment, I doubt Ahmose's affection for me. What if all of this—his letters, his gifts, inviting me to this banquet—has only been to win my trust? After I've given him the information he wants, will he even bother to write to me, let alone invite me to another celebration?

As if he knows my troubled thoughts, Ahmose interweaves his fingers with mine. Was that a little squeeze of reassurance? A warmth spills over me. I want to believe this is real.

"You were wise not to write to me," he says.

"How far do you think he'll go?" I ask.

"He could drag us back to battle, yes. But his insolence, as well as these 'shadow men' you've told me about, tells me we must prepare for Apep himself to rise from the waters. The Horu Throne itself may be in danger."

"The shadow men said they had until Sopdet appears."

"Then we only have four more days." Ahmose leans his temple against mine.

There's also the matter of the general possibly recognizing my necklace, of knowing who I am and where I'm from. If he's sending men up the Iteru to hunt foreigners, to foment bigotry and hatred amongst the *rekhyt*, then what dangers await *me* when Sopdet's star rises?

I should tell Ahmose. Perhaps he could offer me some additional protection.

No, it's too risky, especially here. I fear I've already let myself become too close, trusting him too much.

And the way his perfume mingles with the aroma of the wine, the way he traces his fingertips over my hand . . . I don't want to break whatever *heka* this is that has come over us. Not while the drums grow ever more urgent and the crowd more raucous and the effects of the wine ever more exhilarating, even if the general courts the waters of *isfet*.

"The general underestimates you," Ahmose says, turning to me. "But I don't."

His eyes sparkle in the light as he kisses the back of my hand.

My breath catches in my throat.

Dear Sekhmet, please let his affections be real, for my heart will surely shatter if they aren't. Let me have this one intoxicating pleasure while I navigate this serpent's nest you've led me into. Let the stars in his eyes be the ones that guide me, if only for tonight.

Ahmose points at my dish. "You still have one fig left," he says. "After you finish, let's go join the celebration."

○ ○ ○

As we pass from conversation to conversation, Ahmose chats effortlessly with nobles, musicians, and servants alike. If he feels even a little awkward or out of place here, I can't sense it at all. He introduces me to officials and nobles and princes as simply Sat-reshwet from Men-nefer. They respond kindly, asking if I've enjoyed my evening or what dish was my favorite. Tonight, they seem to accept me as their own. I'm sure I won't remember their names, and after this wine, maybe not so many of their faces either. But I remember the harper's song. Enjoy this moment today, for it could all end tomorrow.

The rhythm of the drums and harps and flutes washes over me, and I find myself rocking to the pulsing beat, as though watching myself from a soaring vulture above.

A servant refills my cup, and as I sip, the hall, the music, the people, the noise all fade away as Ahmose's presence intensifies in my awareness. He holds me close as we stroll.

After days of brutal training, watching behind my back in this treacherous and unfamiliar place, surrounded by even more treacherous men, I grasp at the shred of ease that replaces the spiny vigilance I've needed just to get through my days. And I wrap my arm around Ahmose's waist.

For the first time in so long, I feel safe.

Sure, some here will gossip like Djedi said they will. They'll sneer at the *rekhyt* girl who dares to spend an evening in their presence, and worse, still dares to march alongside the men who defend this land. Let them all talk tomorrow so I can enjoy tonight. Their gossiping will never be any match for the dangers that face me.

For now, I'll revel in this moment as though it will last forever. Soaking in the music and the incense, the perfume and the wine. I will live by the harper's song.

I turn to rest my cheek on Ahmose's shoulder. He draws me in closer, and we sway together into the night.

◌ ◌ ◌

We're some of the last people left as the braziers are extinguished, the tables are cleared, and the musicians cease their playing.

Ahmose drives us back to his villa where Nehemet helps me change into my *shendyt* and tunic. She wipes the kohl and color from my face with sesame oil, and returns the wig to its delicate storage box. How she's still awake, I don't know. In fact, I don't even know how soon Re's barque will rise. I've lost all sense of time.

After changing, I meet Ahmose in the entry hall, where he, too, has returned to more humble clothing. Gone are the gold pendants and bracelets, and he's only wearing his own *shendyt*, a light tunic, and that single ring. Even without the trappings of wealth, he's so regal and poised, with an air of calm that eases my heart.

"The short hair suits you," he says. I run my hand over my head. I nearly forgot he hasn't seen me like this, with hair barely the length of a thumbnail.

He takes my hand and leads me out through the grand doors. A chariot waits outside, a young groom holding the reins. The lithe horse snorts against the bridle.

"I'll take you back to the garrison," he says. "Not that I want to."

Not that I want to go back, either. I could lose myself here, with him, if I'm not careful. And I need to be careful.

He cups his arm around my waist as he drives us across the city to the garrison gates.

There, two guards stand motionless, spears in hand. I feel their eyes on us, even if they pretend not to notice.

Ahmose steps out of the cab and helps me follow.

"When will I see you again?" he asks.

"I wish I knew," I say. "They keep us well contained here."

He takes my hands and closes the space between us. I sense the guards watching us a little too intently. They might even be working for the general, waiting for my return.

"If you find yourself contained," Ahmose says, "then we must resort to our pens."

He's so close now I could kiss him. And I want to. And the way he tilts his head . . . By Nefertem, what's the harm in just one kiss—

But my eyes dart to the guards, and his follow. He steps back, spins the ring around his smallest finger, and looks east, where the sky has already begun to brighten.

"Write to me?" I say.

"Of course. Every day."

He brings the back of my hand to his lips. His breath floats on my skin as he releases my fingers.

"May your hearing be beautiful," he says as he jumps into the chariot. "And may your heart be just."

He clicks his tongue, and I linger at the gate as I watch him drive into the purple glow of morning.

PART FOUR:
THE SERPENT'S NEST

CHAPTER TWENTY-ONE

Re's light cuts into my quarters like a razor.

My body aches and my head throbs.

It must be the blow to the belly from a few days ago.

Or it could be the lingering effects of the wine.

And if it's the wine, that means last night was real. It was all real. The beaded gown. The honeyed figs. Speaking with the Great Royal Wife and witnessing the rebirth of Wasir himself. And dancing with Ahmose. I try to remember the spice of Ahmose's perfume and the softness of his skin under my cheek.

But that also means Aya is real. And the Good Good's plans for peace are in danger. That the general is plotting something that could tempt Apep out of the waters, dragging us all into *isfet*.

A wave of pain clobbers through my forehead again.

Ugh. No wonder the elites take this time off from, well, everything. How do they celebrate like this for five days? I need a resurrection ceremony just to get myself out of bed. Thank Hat-hor I returned before this headache started. Not that I wanted to leave. If I could have held back the sun, I would have.

But I should go eat something. I rub my eyes, smearing what's left of last night's kohl and shimmering green from my lids on to my fingertips. Last night wasn't a dream at all.

Which makes me wonder, where's Djedi?

I call up to his room, but he doesn't answer. He must still be with his scribe. And well-deserved, I think.

I tie on a clean *shendyt*, slip on the tunic I brought from home—which Djedi had washed for me—and head to the meal hall. But before I close the door, I rush back inside, open the cedar chest, and pull out my father's dagger. Just in case.

◎ ◎ ◎

The meal hall is mostly empty, with a few men playing a lively game of senet at a low table, and a few others taking slow bites of bread. They probably indulged a bit too much themselves. But the mood is lighter, hopeful. Soldiers laugh together, teasing each other, and recalling follies from last night's revelries. Even if the waters haven't returned yet, Wasir has been resurrected. The first ritual is complete.

And my skin feels less prickly when I see neither Commander Hani nor 'Awi and his flies. They've might have already eaten, considering it's well after midday.

As I pluck a few loaves from the serving baskets, I sense a hulking presence behind me. I whirl around, my hand on the hilt of my dagger.

Rahuti beams at me, and my fingers relax. I bump my elbow into his belly, laughing a sigh of relief.

He shoves a dried date into his mouth and leans down to me. "What was it like?"

Where do I even begin? "It was like a dream."

"Maybe one day I'll get to go."

"We just need to find a highborn woman to ask you next year!"

He looks up dreamily. "Wouldn't that be something . . ."

"Did 'Awi leave you alone last night?" I ask.

"Mostly," he says. "I did have to threaten to call over Commander Hani right before the garrison priests led the prayer to Wasir. Thankfully, it worked."

"Good. Because if they did anything more, I'd have to have a word with him." I pat my dagger. Rahuti's eyes widen.

We finish our meals and head back out into the scorching afternoon.

I turn a corner around a storage shed and shove Rahuti behind me.

"What was that for?"

"Shh!" I scold, and I pull him against the outer wall of the white mudbrick.

A group of men in long *shendytu* and heads covered with shawls hurry past us. They're out a little early for *shuyitu*, but they're dressed like the men I saw the day before last. Thankfully, they don't seem to have seen me or even Rahuti, who is rather difficult to miss.

"Why are we hiding?" Rahuti asks.

"Hush! We can't let them see us."

"Who?"

I swear I'll call Ammit up from Duat to make him stop talking.

"Wait here."

I creep around the corner. There are more of them today. At least ten. And they're in a hurry. Something in my heart knows General Setankh is involved, and I need to find out how.

I pull on Rahuti's arm. "I hope you didn't have any plans today."

"What? Why?"

"You're coming with me. And don't say anything!"

◦ ◦ ◦

I leave an entire building's length between their strange group and the two of us, taking soft and careful steps. Rahuti tries his best to do the same, but I worry his clumsy footfall will give us away.

We follow them through the alleys of the scribes' quarters, where we tuck behind the buildings, but they keep heading south. I hold us back even more, hoping we won't attract the group's attention.

They head into the open fields, toward the walls surrounding the Temple of Sutekh.

We stay under a cluster of date palms as the men enter through the towering temple gate. One of them, his cowl shading his face, keeps watch until the last of them has disappeared into the courtyard. He takes one more look around before going in himself.

The door starts to close.

I dart forward, catching it right before it shuts, peeking into the narrow opening. The men are still entering through the doors of the temple itself, and none seem to have noticed that the gate never fully shut.

"What if it's official military business we're not supposed to know about?" Rahuti asks.

"Whatever this is, it isn't official. And we're definitely not supposed to know about it."

"We're going to be in so much trouble if they know we're following them."

"Then let's make sure they don't know."

And we'll be in far more trouble if I don't try to uncover whatever it is they're plotting.

Rahuti and I wait for a moment after the last of the men enter the temple; they'll surely see us if we follow too close. But if I wait too long, I might lose them. So we creep through the temple doors as the men head back toward the chapel where I took my oath of loyalty. That seems so long ago now.

Darting from column to column, I keep my sight on them. At the altar, they light their lamps and vanish into the floor.

"Where did they go?" Rahuti whispers.

"Let's find out."

"But that's Sutekh's sacred space," Rahuti says, appalled.

"If they're planning what I think they are, then Sutekh will forgive us."

I listen for any others who might still be lingering, then enter the chapel. When we approach the altar, we find nothing.

"How could they just disappear?" Rahuti asks.

I grunt in frustration. "I don't know!"

"Maybe we should leave."

"No," I say. "I'm not letting those pieces of *hes* get away." I run my hands along the base of the altar and the wall behind it, searching for any sign of the cloaked men. It's as though they were never here.

I swear through grit teeth and stomp the cedar plank floor.

It shifts under my heel with a clunk.

Rahuti and I look down. One length of wood is cut out at the end, with just enough of a gap for my hand.

I creak open the trap door and wince, hoping the sound doesn't betray us, waiting a moment in case one of the men has heard us. But we're only greeted with a rush of cool, musty air. And a narrow staircase leading straight down into a black void.

"We need to follow them."

"I'm not going down there," Rahuti whispers.

"Well, I'm not going alone. And I *am* going down there."

"What if they catch us?"

"If you listen to me and stay quiet, they won't."

"All right . . ."

Step by step, we pad down the narrow shaft. Rahuti has to crouch so he doesn't hit his head on the ceiling. As we go, it becomes ever more difficult to breathe. I can't see my feet.

I run my fingers against the walls. Stone.

We reach the bottom, where the floor is damp, the air stale and fetid. In the dim light, I can see the bulbous bellies of wine jugs stacked along the walls. We must be in the storage cellars.

Men's voices and sandaled footsteps bounce against the walls.

I point to a passage that leads to another chamber. Rahuti's eyes go round with fear, and he grabs my shoulder hard. I shake my head at him. No, we can't leave. Not when I'm so close.

I press my back against the wall as we slide into the second chamber.

Rahuti tightens his grip on my shoulder, and I hold back from scolding him.

We hide behind a stack of chests when one man steps forward, his head covered in a linen shroud, features obscured by the shadows. He looks out over the gathering of cloaks and hoods and holds up a scepter.

"I have called you here on this day," he says with the cadence of a trained priest, "because the reckoning is upon us."

The others murmur in agreement.

"But first, let us pray."

The men bow their shrouded heads.

"Oh, Apep, Serpent of Chaos, enemy of Re, the light-bringer. We serve you as you rise from the dark waters."

Apep? What priest would dare call upon Apep, and with such praise?

Rahuti shivers beside me. Please, Sekhmet, make him keep quiet.

"We call on you, oh Great Snake, to rest your head of flint and stone upon the scales to tip them in our favor. Widen your mouth, which is more vast and consuming than the floods of the Iteru, than the sky itself. Widen it to devour our enemies. Oh, praise Apep, so you may favor us with your might."

"Praise Apep!" the men call out with a nauseating enthusiasm.

The priest raps his scepter against the floor. "Now, for why I have gathered you here today. I have received word that the Good God and the Hittite are ever closer to a peace agreement. Is this true?"

"It appears so, *wabuir*," a man says, his voice weak with regret.

"An unfortunate consequence of your failure to capture the negotiator while you had the chance."

Hes. They *were* behind the attack on the *Nebkhepri*.

I barely dare to breathe. At my side, Rahuti looks as though Apep himself has just slithered over his feet.

"We could try again, *wabuir*—"

The priest flicks his hand at the man. "The time for trivial action is over. You failed, and now we have a much wider river to cross. Besides, why set our sights on such an inconsequential and inexperienced man when we could be hunting far more valuable prey?"

I'm all at once wildly relieved it seems they won't go after Ahmose again, offended at how they speak of him, and dreading whatever they plan next. I squint into the dim lamplight, trying to find General Setankh's face under the dark shrouds. But I can't make out any of the men's features at all. It's as though some dark *heka* has cast them all into shadow.

"But if he's anything like his father," the first man says, "he'll have a treaty signed before—"

The priest snaps his fingers in the air, and the man falls silent. "If you wish to be promoted to general," the priest hisses, "you will do as I tell you."

After a stark silence, the man asks, "And what will you have me do, *wabuir*?"

"Prepare your men. Gather your weapons. It's time for us to take what is rightfully ours. The Serpent demands a sacrifice."

The men cheer and yell, raising and pumping their fists in a bloodthirsty throng.

I try to press myself into the darkness and hold an arm over Rahuti who takes in shallow, short breaths.

Rahuti's foot slips against the stone floor, and he squeaks.

"Silence!" the priest roars.

The men hush as I pull Rahuti down so we're both on our hands and knees.

One man prowls along the edge of the chamber, right toward us.

I tug on Rahuti's *shendyt*, crawling into an alcove stacked with crates, but Rahuti is so terrified he doesn't budge.

The man stalks closer to Rahuti. In the light of his lamp, I see his profile.

Commander Hani.

CHAPTER TWENTY-TWO

Commander Hani creeps closer to Rahuti, holding his lamp along the wall.

Just before the commander reaches him, Rahuti darts over to me on his knees. I press my hand over his mouth and pull him back behind the stack of boxes. We try to make ourselves as small as possible, avoiding all flickers of light that might betray us. I hold my breath as Hani passes us.

Don't move. Don't breathe. Oh, please, Sekhmet, let the commander pass without seeing us.

He prowls by, never peeking into our hiding place. The Powerful One must have heard me. But I never took Hani for being a particularly smart man. Just one who follows orders and loves ordering others around.

He grumbles, taking one last look near us, and turns back to his men.

"Come, men. We have a battle to prepare for."

The men cheer and praise Apep, rejuvenated by their violent mission. The light from their lamps fades as they move closer to the stairs.

Rahuti and I hold as still and quiet as the dead until they leave the chamber. After I hear the doorway close at the top of the stairs, a suffocating darkness engulfs us. Rahuti whimpers.

I crawl out from behind the storage boxes, across the damp floor, toward what could be the center of the cellar. Rahuti keeps a hand on my back, and it's shaking.

I strain to see even a hint of light, but all I see is black. Rahuti scrambles behind me. We brace each other as we stand. Up feels like down and right feels like left. I fear my feet won't even find the floor. This is what Oblivion must be like.

I hold my hands out in front of me and step forward.

"Keep your hands on my shoulders," I whisper back to Rahuti.

My palms find the wall, and I heave a sigh of relief.

But the air only grows denser with every exhale. We need to get out of here before there's nothing left for us and we suffocate.

"Why did I let you talk me into this?" Rahuti whines.

"Don't let go. Eventually, we'll find the stairs."

"Eventually?"

"This place can't be that large. There was one entrance and this chamber. We'll find our way out."

"And if we don't?"

"We will. Trust me." Because I don't want to die down here. Not before telling Ahmose what Commander Hani plans. Not before trying to stop them. If I'm the only person standing between the general and the throne, then by all the gods, I will get us out of here.

I run my palms along the walls, with Rahuti clinging to me like a child on his mother.

"We're never getting out of here," he says.

"I think we're close."

I keep running my hands along the stone, but it goes on forever. My chest tightens. Are there multiple passages, and I've led us astray?

But I feel a chiseled corner of stone. I crouch, hoping to find a step. Thank Ptah!

"We're at the stairs," I say. "Stay low, and keep going up."

We climb, step by deliberate step. Fatigue takes hold of my legs, and I fear Rahuti will need a break before we reach the top. But soon, little slivers of light penetrate through the wooden trap door above us. We're almost out.

I push against the door, but it doesn't budge. I try again, and again, and it doesn't move even so much as a finger's width.

Now I'm beginning to worry. But I can't let Rahuti know. He's frightened enough for both of us.

"We're going to die down here," he says.

"We won't. I'm close. I know it," I say, hoping to reassure him and myself.

I push with my shoulder, and my feet slip against the stone stair. Rahuti braces me before I tumble back down the shaft.

Panic twinges in my belly, but I try to shove it aside. I need to stay calm. But the light creeping through the slats mocks me.

"Let me try," Rahuti says. He wriggles past me and shoves his palms against it. Still, nothing.

Did those men know we followed them, jamming the door to trap us down here? They won't rid themselves of us, of me, so easily.

"Together?" I suggest.

I count back from three, and with all our might, we shove our shoulders into the wood. It squeals as the door flies open, cracking back against the temple floor above us.

The light nearly blinds me.

"Run," I say.

We race past the altar, through the columns, to the temple doors. If there are priests attending to the sacred space, I can't focus enough to see them. We push our way through the exit and into the even more searing sunlight.

I run toward the gates, with Rahuti close behind. Following the outside of the walls, I turn the corner, and finally let myself stop.

Rahuti's chest heaves in deep wheezes, and we slump against the mudbrick.

"That was utterly horrible, and I'm never following you ever again," he says.

As I catch my breath, I sit and stretch my legs out. In the clear blue sky, the sun barque looms over us, its intense rays cutting through the shimmering heat.

"You say that now," I laugh, hoping to lighten his mood. But he's not wrong. That was horrible.

"They almost saw us. What would have happened if they did?"

"Thank all the gods they didn't, because I don't want to find out."

"This isn't what I imagined I'd be doing during my festival days," Rahuti says.

"If it helps at all, it's not what I expected either."

Rahuti wipes the sweat from his bald scalp with his forearm. "Was that—"

"Commander Hani? It definitely was."

"Praying to the Chaos Serpent?" Rahuti's voice quivers with horror. "He's so much worse than I thought!"

I draw my knees into my chest. "And they're planning something that could destroy us all."

"What?"

I can't protect him from the terrible truth any longer. "They want to put General Setankh on the Horu Throne."

Rahuti's jaw drops. "But how? He can't do that! Ramesses Usermaatre Setepenre is our king. He's our Good God, the Bull of the Two Lands."

I shake my head. "With the sheer number of weapons I saw in his office several days ago, I'm not so sure the throne is safe from him."

"What weapons?"

"Every kind of weapon you can imagine. The general's office was full of them. Bows, arrows, lances, spears, *khopesh*, axes."

"Maybe those are for us? I mean, we are soldiers."

"I don't think they are."

"We should tell someone," Rahuti says franticly. "But who? We can't tell the general, or the commander, or . . . anyone!"

I put a hand on his shoulder, and he calms a little. "You won't be telling anyone. No matter what, act like you saw nothing. You know nothing."

"But we need to do something." He looks at me with the urgency of a child.

"Oh, I will. I know exactly who to tell."

◉ ◉ ◉

But this is far too urgent and sensitive to commit to writing.

I need to tell Ahmose now, myself. I need to tell him my suspicions are true. They're all true. The general *did* order those men to attack the *Nebkhepri* and means to usurp the Horu Throne.

But I don't know the way to Ahmose's villa. Besides, would that be too forward, showing up at his gates with no invitation?

I pace my quarters. Am I even allowed to leave the garrison at all? Surely the general wouldn't confine us during these days of celebration. Didn't Rahuti say he wanted to explore the city? He wouldn't have said so if he wasn't allowed. He wouldn't dare break any kind of rule, no matter how small or inconsequential.

The light goes golden outside.

I can't sit here anymore. The longer I wait, the longer the general has to plan his takeover. I'm going to find Ahmose's villa myself. How hard could it be? I could even ask people along the way.

As I grab my shawl and head to the door, Djedi bursts through, a little more disheveled than normal.

"What are you doing here?" he asks with surprise. "I thought you'd be spending the day with your new *ibib*."

"I thought you'd be doing the same thing," I say.

His wig sits askew, and his *shendyt* is twisted off center. Even his usually neat kohl has smeared. He must have had quite the evening and morning. And afternoon.

"I'm just here to grab a few things before going out to celebrate again," he says, turning to the stairs. He's a bit more hasty than usual. Like he's hiding something. "You really should be doing the same!"

"Maybe you can help me."

He whirls to face me, bright with intrigue. "Oh?"

"Do you know the way to the villas?"

"Of course, *bitbit*," he scoffs. "It's where you should have stayed last night, anyway!" He makes a disapproving face. "It's a shame you couldn't keep that beaded dress."

"Djedi..." I grit my teeth.

"All right, all right! I'll take you to him."

CHAPTER TWENTY-THREE

I follow Djedi through narrow dirt pathways, some I'm sure will become creeks and channels when the waters return. Is he even taking me the right way?

"This isn't the way Ubenu took me yesterday," I say.

"I've been here long enough to learn all the best shortcuts," Djedi says proudly.

A pair of women in elegant dresses strolls past us, arm in arm, giggling to each other. One looks at me and Djedi, and upon seeing Djedi's delicate braided gold wig, they nod their heads in recognition.

We wind between tall mudbrick walls, and just above them I see the top stories of elegantly painted villas, rooftops shaded with colorful canopies.

He stops at an imposing walled entrance with wooden double doors, painted in multicolored repeating patterns of flowers and curling vines. Two guards stand motionless on either side.

"Here we are," Djedi says.

"What do I do?" My heart is full of bees. I can't believe I'm doing this, that I'm here again, unannounced and uninvited. Will the guards even allow me in?

"Let me handle it." Djedi strides up to the guards. "The Lady Sati is here to see Lord Ahmose, son of the Wasir Useraasen. She was his guest at the royal banquet last night." He winks at me.

The guards squint at us for a moment, then knock.

After what feels like a year, the door swings open.

"Sati!" Beket's braids swing around her round face. "May you come in peace!"

"You're in, *bitbit*," Djedi says, patting me on the shoulder. "And I have a party to attend, so I'll leave you to it."

"Thank you, Djedi."

He gives me a wry grin. "I'm very happy to help. May your bodies rejoice in the return of the green god."

"May your evening be beautiful," I say, ignoring his insinuation. What I have to tell Ahmose weighs so much on my heart that I can't even spare a moment to be embarrassed or quip back at him.

"You know it will be!" Djedi waves his skinny fingers and saunters off between the date palms.

I take a deep inhale and turn back to Beket. "Is Ahmose here?"

"Yes, he is," she says. "Is he expecting you?"

I shake my head, hoping she won't turn me away. "I'm afraid he isn't."

"Oh, but he'll be so delighted," she says. "Come in, come in!"

The tension in my shoulders releases, and I find myself once again in the receiving room of Ahmose's villa. Between the inlaid benches and tables, extravagant arrangements of rare and strange flowers line the walls as though they were the most normal thing in all of Kemet.

"I will tell you though," Beket says with a quiet giggle, "he has been a bit out of sorts. Last night must have been quite the celebration."

I chuckle, remembering how my own head throbbed this afternoon.

"Wait here," she says. "I'll go fetch him."

Beket bounces through the columned entryway of the villa and turns down a hall.

Not long after, Ahmose greets me with a wide smile stretched across his face. My heart flutters at the sight of him.

He embraces me in his warm, strong arms, then pulls back, his hands still on my shoulders. "I didn't think I'd see you again until after Sekhmet's days. What did you have to do to sneak away from the general?"

"I didn't have to. The Good God must order him to give us the days off. I don't think he would otherwise."

"As well he should." He turns to Beket. "Please bring some refreshments to the garden."

He offers me his arm and leads us through this palace he calls home. We pass lily-capped columns that open to a raised patio, with stairs leading into a lush, green courtyard.

It's a different world from the one outside the walls, and certainly from the one at the barracks. Gasps of warm wind rustle through the tall sycamores and around pomegranate trees dotted with deep red buds.

He leads us to a granite bench beside the rectangular pond at the garden's center, where blue lilies open their golden hearts to the sky. The chirps of crickets and frogs bob on the breeze. When I sit, the stone still radiates heat from the day's long sun.

I wiggle my fingers above the water's surface. Carp with long whiskers swim up to greet me. I laugh to myself as their fins splash beneath my hand, their mouths round and hungry like a full moon.

"They like you," Ahmose says as he sits beside me.

I give a playful scoff. "They just think I have a treat for them."

"And I," Ahmose says, looking back to where Beket bounces toward us with a tray and a wine jug, "have a treat for you."

"Oh, I can't drink anymore wine."

"The wine will be sufficiently diluted, I assure you. I certainly had my share of strong wine last night."

Beket sets the tray on the bench next to me.

"Are those figs?" I ask.

"Baked," Ahmose says with satisfaction. "With honey. Just the way you like them. And with fresh yogurt, too."

"How did you know to prepare them?" They're still steaming. Without hesitation, I dip one in the yogurt and take a bite. It's even better than the ones at the banquet; it melts in my mouth.

"I . . . hoped that perhaps you'd find your way here tonight. And if you didn't, then I would have quite the new year's treat to share with my staff." He gives Beket a reverent nod. "That will be all."

"In peace, Lord Ahmose." She gives a quick bow and disappears into the villa again.

Ahmose pours a sheer red liquid from the jug into the two cups and hands me one. One sip is tart enough to pucker my mouth, yet sweet like dates.

"Pomegranate," Ahmose says after taking a sip of his own. "From my own gardens. But I'm assuming you aren't here only for my figs and wine."

Oh, how I wish I were here only for his figs and wine. To indulge in these luxuries with him, without a care about what dangers lurk outside these walls. I take in the idyllic surroundings and imagine what that would be like. My wistful daydream vanishes into the air as I let out a resigned sigh.

"Unfortunately not," I say.

"It's about the general, isn't it?" he asks.

I devour my second fig and give a solemn nod. "I thought he only wanted to have his war, but I fear it's much worse."

"Worse?"

"I suspect he's behind everything. The attack on the *Nebkhepri*. The assaults in Men-nefer. And he has his eyes on the Horu Throne. He wants to name himself as Bull of the Two Lands."

Ahmose curses under his breath. "We knew he was planning something, but we didn't know what, or how."

"I know how. He's calling on Apep."

He stops mid-sip, jaw dropping. "The Chaos Serpent? Why would he do such a thing?"

"I know it sounds absurd—"

"Not to me," he says. "The general has been clamoring for the throne since Ramesses first sat upon it."

"Why would he think he has any claim to the throne at all?"

Ahmose lets out a little grumble. "Most people don't know—only those of us at court and the extended royal family—but the Wasir King Seti had two sons. Each from a different wife. And Setankh is the younger."

"But if Setankh is the younger son, he has no right to the throne."

"He claims he can trace his blood back to the previous dynasty. Through his mother. A tenuous claim at best. But if it is true, then he has more royal—and therefore divine—blood than Ramesses himself."

The revelation makes me pause. Such a lineage would give him a legitimacy that the Good God himself could only dream of. "Do you believe him?"

He answers with a lift of one shoulder. "Even if it were true, the Wasir King Seti named Ramesses his heir. And that should have been the end of it."

Ahmose pours more wine into his cup and fills mine again to the top.

"If he's courting the Serpent, he has no right to the throne," I say. "He became a traitor the moment he considered it."

"Perhaps he believes calling on such destructive forces is his only recourse."

My spine prickles. "He's a monster," I mutter.

"More than any of us suspected." Ahmose looks up at the stars, then swirls his wine. "What *isfet* lurks in the heart of a man so hungry for power and adulation, especially a man who thinks he's right?"

I wish I knew the answer. And I wish I knew how to stop him.

"Tjati Hatiay has been trying to uncover the general's plans for years," Ahmose says, facing me again. "And you do it in mere weeks? How?"

I give a little shrug. "You asked me to open my eyes and ears to anything suspicious, so I did. And today, Rahuti and I followed those shadow men I told you about, this afternoon, into a storage chamber beneath the Temple of Sutekh."

"Underground? Here, in the delta?"

I nod. "The temple is built on an outcropping of stone."

"And the waters have been low."

"They met with a priest who led a prayer to the Serpent. He called on them to prepare their men and gather their weapons."

"Did you recognize anyone there?"

"Commander Hani."

Ahmose's jaw tightens. "General Setankh's loyal pet. What is he getting out of this arrangement?"

"A promotion, apparently."

"All this treachery for a promotion?"

I take a big sip of my wine. "More than just a promotion. The priest said they meant to capture you on the *Nebkhepri*."

"At least now we have confirmation," Ahmose says, his voice edged with anger.

"But he also said they have more valuable prey to hunt. If what I overheard on the last day of Shemu is true, they plan to take the Horu Throne on Nebet-het's birthday."

"The last of Sekhmet's days, when the court is most vulnerable. After five days of wine and indulgence. And when the waters of *isfet* are high." Ahmose bolts to his feet, a fresh determination on his face. "I need to tell the Good God to arrest the general now."

"Wait!" My hand reaches out for his. "No, you can't."

"The sooner the king apprehends the traitor, the sooner he can restore *ma'at* to his domain."

A rage builds in him, tensing the muscles of his neck, but he doesn't understand how tenuous my place in all of this really is.

"This plot," I say, "it runs deep. Setankh's men probably infest the entire length of the Iteru."

"We best get started," Ahmose says, his voice gruff. He tugs on my hand to urge me to stand with him. But I don't move.

"Please, Ahmose," I say. "If his followers find out I'm the one who revealed their plans . . ."

"Then I'll hire the king's most trusted Medjay to protect you."

"I fear that won't be enough."

When he sees the apprehension I'm sure shades my eyes, he loosens the pull on my hand and sits beside me again, the determination in his face softening. "What would you have the king do?"

Anything we do now will reveal me as a spy. The general knows I went to the banquet at the Great Hall. If the guards at the garrison gates last night were working for him, then he knows I went with Ahmose. And why would he let me see his arsenal of weapons if he didn't know I'd risk telling Ahmose everything? The general is trying to trap me.

But he probably doesn't know Rahuti and I followed Hani into the cellars. He doesn't know I recognized the daggers. In fact, the general thinks I'm daft; naive, he said. And Ahmose said he thinks the general underestimates me.

"What if we let Setankh think he has the advantage?" I say. "Let him believe he's more clever than us. Than me, than you, than the king himself."

Ahmose's brows lift with a cunning curiosity. "Play into his feelings of superiority and hunger for power."

"Exactly."

"But how? We only have three days."

"The general wants his battle, yes, so why not give him one?" I say. "Tell the Good God to be ready for the general's incursion. Have his most trusted Medjay and his most well-trained guardsmen posted at the Great Hall. But don't call any soldiers from the garrison. Who knows how many of them the general has infected with his delusions?"

"And when the general arrives with whoever is foolish enough to follow him, the Medjay will crush him."

"The king himself will cut the head off the snake."

We share a moment of conspiratorial hope, even as dread grows heavy on my shoulders. If the Good God is victorious, the general's devotees will still slither in our cities, with or without a head. And if they don't come for me because I've betrayed the general, they'll come for me because of my blood.

I can't smooth the worry on my brow. My fingers fidget with my pendant. This pendant that may well cost me my life. "I just pray to all the gods it works. Because if it doesn't . . ."

"It will. It has too."

"But it won't change what I am." The words jump from my mouth before I even know what I've said. But I've said too much.

"What do you mean *what* you are?" Ahmose asks incredulously.

"I mean, who I am," I say as quickly as I can.

Ahmose flicks his hand in the air, as though he were brushing away the apprehension in my words. "I may not know everything about you," he says, sliding closer to me on the bench, narrowing the space between our thighs. "But I do know this: You're from Men-nefer. You're a military captain's daughter. You're a fighter. A healer. You're the only woman I've known to survive weeks of grueling training in the king's military."

My heart swells at his words, fluttering and racing. Or does it race because I've opened a door I can't close, and now I must lead Ahmose through?

He brushes his fingertips along my jaw, turning my face to his. "I know I've never met anyone like you in all of the Two Lands."

My heart drops, but I should be dancing amongst the stars. He must still think I'm from the Two Lands, like he is. Perhaps I should be thrilled he doesn't seem to suspect otherwise, that I've been able to blend in so well. To him, I might as well be from the Two Lands. And if that's so, then what does it matter where I was born or where I'm from?

Curse these conflicted feelings, of wanting to be so close to him and yet feeling like I have to hide this part of me.

I turn away, and my teeth set, with his touch still lingering on my skin.

"What's wrong?" he asks.

"I'm not . . ." My voice is little more than a squeak.

A battle erupts within me. One side urges me to tell him. Let him know the truth. It tells me I have a kindred *ka* in this nobleman, he has given me no reason to doubt him, and he has been kind to me because he is a *ma'at* man. The other clamors, trying to pull me back from the precipice, warning me I can't trust him. It says Ahmose has only been kind to me because of my access to the general. It says I can't trust anyone in this cursed place, and if I reveal to him all I am, he'll reject me, or worse, suspect me as working for the Nine Bows themselves.

I let his fingers turn my face toward him again. He has traveled all along the river, to the farthest reaches of the king's domain. He's seen all manner of people, from Tanehsu to Hatti. Surely, he must see Retenu in my features. By Sutekh, he must know Aya isn't from the Two Lands either. And if he does, and hasn't even so much as mentioned it, what am I so afraid of?

A thin trail of light streaks across the milky band of stars above and flashes in a burst of blue and green. Our heads turn together to catch a glimpse, and just as quickly, it vanishes.

The might of the stars.

"You're not what?" he asks, his voice assuring and soft.

I take a breath more deep and full than any I ever have. I try to calm the tremble in my lower lip. The wine in my cup shimmers with my shaking hands.

Ahmose takes my hands, setting my cup beside him.

"Whatever it is, you are safe here with me." He intertwines his fingers with mine, and my prickly defensiveness slowly dissolves.

"I'm not..." Go on, just say it. "I'm not Kemeti. I wasn't born here. I was born outside of Qadesh. My father saved me from a village the Hittites destroyed." I can't even bear to look at him, to read his reaction.

He tilts his face to me. "Is that all?"

I search his expression for any trace of anger or betrayal. Or worse, hatred. "You're not angry?"

His smile is a drink of cool water at the height of a Shemu day. "By Wadjet, why would I be angry?"

Relief floods over me, and I can breathe again. Thank Sekhmet. Thank Ptah. Thank Nefertem. Thank all the gods.

"Because," I say, "my whole life I've always felt out of place. And now, with what's been happening in Men-nefer, with the general, even with what the king carves into his own walls about his enemies..."

"The general may be motivated by his hatred, but the king's walls are all for show," he says, as though it's the most obvious thing in the world. "As long as you are loyal to the king and devoted to *ma'at*, he doesn't care where you were born. And you—you're not just loyal. You're risking your life for him and *ma'at*."

"But the general. I think he knows." Even though the night is warm, I shiver.

"How?"

"He must have been there, at Qadesh. He asked about my necklace. It belonged to my birth mother. I think he recognized it, which means he knew my father."

"Even if he does know, we'll make sure he faces the king's justice, together."

I know he wants to assure me, to make me feel safe and protected. I suspect I'll never be either of those things, but I want to believe him.

He looks into my eyes with a fierce determination and squeezes my hands.

That tantalizing warmth from last night returns. I inhale the scent of cinnamon and myrrh, of lily blossoms and jasmine blooms and honey swirling around us. I remember how safe I felt, with Ahmose's arms around me and my head on his shoulder. That was real. I want to feel that way again, and I let myself lean closer to him.

He brushes his palm over my cheek, letting his fingers trail down the nape of my neck.

"My dear Sati . . ." he whispers as he tilts his head. My name sounds like date syrup in his mouth. Sweet, rich, and thick with yearning.

May all my fears be devoured by Ammit, because I can't resist the lure of him anymore.

I press my lips to his, and that glowing, radiant warmth surges through my entire being.

He pulls me into him, threading his fingers through my short hair, as though he's dreamed about this moment for as long as I have. Perhaps longer. My lips part against his, yielding to his mouth, sweet like honey and pomegranate.

For a brief, precious, fleeting moment, nothing else matters. Not my bruised skin and aching muscles. Not 'Awi's flies nor Hani's insults. Not even the general's plan to pull us all down into *isfet*. If face them after tonight, I'll face them knowing Ahmose sees me for who I am and not what he fears me to be.

All that matters now is his touch, his presence, his breath.

I melt under the heat of his palms and lose myself completely in him.

Then a piercing scream shocks us apart.

CHAPTER TWENTY-FOUR

"Intruders!" Nehemet screams, bolting out of the villa. Her sandals slap against the stone as she runs.

Ahmose dashes to her.

"They're looking for you, lord!" she pants, and tears stream down her cheeks in black streaks. "They threatened to slit Beket's throat if you don't go to them!"

Dear gods. I shouldn't have come here. What if they followed me? What if they know Rahuti and I were in the cellar today? Oh no. Rahuti! Will they go after him too?

"Those sons of *kerbetu*!" I say, grabbing Ahmose's arm. "They said they wouldn't come for you again!"

"And they won't have me," Ahmose growls, drawing a dagger from beneath his leather waistband.

"They certainly won't." I draw my own dagger, the anticipation of a fight like lightning in my veins.

"No!" Ahmose turns to me and clasps a hand around my upper arm.

"But they'll take you! They'll kill you!" Fire roils in me, twisting and fighting with the frosty terror in my spine.

"If they are Setankh's men, they can't find you here."

"But what if they're here because of me?" I'm about to protest further. I'm about to wrestle myself away from his grip.

But he's right. I can't be seen in this place. Because then the general will know I've been spying on him.

"You need to get out of here." He pulls me in and kisses me again, deeply. "Escape through the back gate. I can't lose you."

Sekhmet help me, for I might very well lose him.

He releases me and charges toward the patio. Nehemet chases after him.

Please, Powerful One, protect him. Don't let them send him to Duat. Not after tonight.

I watch as he disappears into the villa, and I feel as though all my life and breath, my *ka* and *ba*, have abandoned my body.

I resign myself to leaving the deceptive tranquility of the garden, calling on all the gods, the stars, to Geb in the earth and Nuit in the sky to protect Ahmose and his household.

As I open the door at the back of his courtyard, a woman screams.

I shudder. My flesh feels as though it's being pulled into the villa, while my *ba* knows I need to fly from here.

But how can I leave?

A crash of pottery bounces off the walls.

I curse and pound my fists against the wood.

A man cries out in pain.

I press my back against the door.

A woman sobs.

I slump to the ground.

And I wait.

○ ○ ○

The villa is eerily silent. Even the crickets in the bushes and the frogs in the pond have stopped their singing.

I creep past a broken acacia bench. A gilded table is splintered into two, its sides leaning in against each other. A shattered wine jug spills its rich liquid across the tiles, filling the room with its pungent, sour spice. I nudge a round mehen board on the floor with my toes, and the game pieces tumble away from me. The once impeccable flower arrangements now lie scattered along the walls.

I find Ahmose's dagger by my feet.

"Ahmose?" I call out as I pick it up. No one answers.

I wipe the blade on my *shendyt*. I try not to think the worst, but it leaves a dark carnelian stain on the creamy linen. I slip it into my belt.

"Ahmose . . . ?"

A trail of blood leads into the heart of his home.

My breath stops. My hand sweats so much I fear my dagger will slip from my hand. If those snakes are still here, I'll destroy them.

I slip into a breezy side chamber and call his name again. But I receive no answer.

Footsteps pad behind me, and I whip around, weapon ready.

"Nehemet?"

She runs to me and wraps her arms around me. She's sobbing, heaving, almost coughing.

"Nehemet, what happened? Where's Ahmose?"

She pulls back and wipes her tears away from her face with the heel of her hand. Streaks of kohl smear her cheeks.

"They . . ." She sniffs. "They took him. They bound his wrists and took him."

My heart fills with all the terrible things I want to do to those *isfet* men.

"And Beket?" I ask.

"They let her go, praise Hat-hor, but she's closed herself off in the servants' quarters."

I point the tip of the dagger at the streak of blood on the tiles. "Whose is that?"

"One of theirs, I think." Nehemet's voice shakes. "Lord Ahmose did put up a good fight."

I suppose that's something. Perhaps at least one of those *desheru* men will face Ammit tonight.

"There were so many of them," Nehemet continues. "Maybe ten, fifteen."

"How did they get through the villa's guards?"

"They said they were here on order of the Good God."

Like the Scarred Man did when he barged into the Per-seshen.

"What were they wearing?"

"Tan leather tunics. Pectoral necklaces. They were a bit plain for the Good God's men, but the gold . . ." She stares at the mess of a broken vase for a moment. "Hat-hor's horns," she says, shaking her head in horror, "we invited them in without a second thought."

My face goes hot. Those cursed liars. Vile, cursed liars.

I pace in the entrance of Ahmose's villa while Nehemet stands aside.

Through my haze of rage, a panic threatens to overwhelm me.

No, breathe. It's what Iti would tell me to do whenever I started to lose a skirmish.

Just breathe.

What am I going to do?

My first impulse is to return to their cellar and lie in wait for them, unleashing my fury on them. I want to render them all lifeless, limbless, and to scatter the bloody pieces of them to the farthest reaches of the river.

But even as my thirst for vengeance grows, I'd stand no chance against them. Sure, I could take Hani again, but I can't take ten Hanis.

So, if I can't destroy them myself, then what?

Find Ahmose. But I could search the entire city and still have little hope of finding him. I have no idea where they've taken him, and or even if they've deigned to keep him alive. No, he's alive. He must be. I can't let myself believe otherwise.

And without him to tell the Good God of the general's plan, how will the Great House be prepared to fight on the morning of Nebethet's birthday?

Everything is in Ammit's teeth, and I can't pry it out.

I don't know my way to the garrison, especially now with Re so deep in Duat, and Khonsu's moon hasn't risen above the rooftops. And what would I even do at the garrison?

I need to tell the Great House of Setankh's plan. If I don't, then *isfet* will consume us all. And it will be my fault if I do nothing to stop it.

But I can't just show up at the gates of the Great House and demand to speak to the Good God, especially so late, and wearing a *shendyt* streaked with blood. The Medjay would toss me into the Great Prison, and no one would ever hear from me again. And the general would still storm the Great House, releasing Apep on us all.

Besides, even if I did go to the Great House, the Good God and his court are likely throwing yet another celebration, likely more exclusive and guarded than last night.

Think, Sati. Think.

Wait. Ubenu!

I can write to the Great House and warn the court and have Ubenu deliver the message. But who do I address it to? The Good God or the *tjati*? Both men would be far too consumed with the rituals and ceremonies of Wepet Renpet to read anything from me.

To Aya, then? Ah, yes, greetings Aya, you might be my long-lost sister, and General Setankh is planning to attack the Great House, so could you please tell the Good God to prepare?

No, that won't work at all. I don't even know if she can read.

Then the answer becomes obvious. The Great Royal Wife!

Ever since I arrived here, she's taken an unusual interest in me. She not only advocated for me in the Great Hall, but also spoke to me in private at the banquet. If I address my letter to her, and if she sees my name signed at the bottom, surely she'll read it without hesitation. And if I write it in Akkadian, even fewer people will be able to read it, if it falls into the wrong hands.

I pray to Djehuty it will work. It has to. I don't have many other options.

"Nehemet, where's Ubenu?"

She starts like a frightened rabbit. "Oh, I think he's at a party."

Hes. I need him now.

"But he never stays too late. He should be back soon."

I suppose I can wait here until he returns. It's the best plan I have right now. In the meantime, I'll prepare my message.

"I need to write a letter," I say. "Where does Ahmose keep his papers and inks?"

○ ○ ○

Nehemet lets me sit in Ahmose's office while I wait for Ubenu. She tends to a still terrified Beket and offers me a clean *shendyt* before retiring for the night. It smells like Ahmose's perfume oil.

I open my senses, listening for any further incursion. Any sign that Setankh's men might come back to look for me.

Through the high windows, I watch the stars move across the sky in their incremental march, and I trace the silvery light of the moon on the painted tile floor.

Right when sleep threatens to take me, a knock sounds from the doorway.

"What in Duat happened here?"

I jolt awake. A man's voice.

"Where's Ahmose?" he asks just outside.

I run to him in the hall with my letter. "Ubenu! Thank Djehuty you're back!"

Ubenu looks like he's seen Apep himself, the creases at the sides of his eyes even deeper than usual. "What? Why are you here? And Lord

Ahmose? What happened to the entryway?" Panic sharpens his voice. "Why is everything destroyed? Is that blood?"

"I can explain, but first I need you to deliver a message for me. To the Great House."

"You . . ." He points an accusatory finger at me. "Did you have something to do with this?"

I step back. How dare he even suggest such a thing? I restrain my resentment. Seeing as I can smell the wine on his breath, he might not be entirely in control of his wits.

"No, please, listen," I say. "I know who did it. They took your lord, and if you deliver this letter to the Great House, we'll be able to find him and bring him back." That last part might not be true, but I pray to Wasir it is.

I hold the curl of papyrus before us, hoping he'll take it. But he only stares at it—and me—in shock.

"Please, Ubenu. The sooner you go, the sooner we can bring justice to the men who attacked."

His brows release, and he scrubs his hand under his wig. "I told him to keep his toes out of trouble, but he never listens."

"In this case, trouble came to him," I say.

He sighs and plucks the paper from my fingers. "The Great House you say?"

"Yes. To the Great Royal Wife."

Ubenu glances at the windows, where the sky outside turns amethyst with morning light. "Her Highness will *not* like being disturbed so early."

"Tell her attendants it's about what she told Sati on Wasir's birthday."

He gives me a skeptical look. "Just know I'm not doing this for you, but for my lord."

After turning on his heels with a little huff, he rushes out of the office.

I don't care who he thinks he serves right now, as long as the Great Royal Wife receives my warning. Now, as Re's barque rises in the east, it's time for me to find my way back to the garrison. Back to the Temple of Sutekh, where perhaps I can uncover where Setankh's men are keeping Ahmose, if they've kept him alive at all.

CHAPTER TWENTY-FIVE

I don't dare disturb Nehemet or Beket before slipping out through the back gate.

If I can just trace my steps from last night, then I can get there. But it's still so dark.

On our way here, Djedi led us north, so I keep the sun on my left and follow the path between the cluster of walls belonging to the elites.

Yes, I remember this building, this dip in the earth, this muddy pathway, that grove of persea trees.

The gamey stench of the stables meets my nostrils, and I heave a sigh of relief. I'm close to the barracks. From there I can find my way to the temple.

The triangular flags of the pylons slither on the breeze over the soldiers' quarters, and a slender cat trots past me on its morning hunt.

When I reach the temple walls, a few wigged noblewomen in gold jewelry saunter toward me, chattering like birds.

Oh, *hes*. It's Sutekh's birthday today.

I need to get inside and into the storage chambers before the services begin. The priests are probably already there making the preparations. Somehow, I'll have to get past them, too.

I push open the gates, dash across the courtyard, and knock hard on the tall double doors.

One of them creaks open. A man with a prominent nose, bald head, and a leathery face glares at me.

"You are early," he grouses and rolls his painted eyes. "The morning service does not begin until Re has fully risen over the eastern horizon."

I can't wait that long. "Please, your holiness. May I sit inside?" I press my hand to my forehead, as though I'm feeling last night's wine, which, today, isn't true. Ma'at forgive me. "My head hurts so much from last night."

The elegantly dressed ladies pass through the gates behind me.

"Please," I say, "let me rest in the god's presence on his birthday."

The priest lets out a sharp exhale. "All right, but be quiet. We are quite busy."

He opens the door, and I slip inside. I sit against a column halfway between the entrance and the farthest end of the hall and rub my forehead again, hoping to convince them of my wine ache.

He and two other priests bathe and anoint the life-sized figure of Sutekh by the altar. They drape long lily stalks along the base, muttering prayers as they go. How will I get back to the cellar now?

A knock at the doors interrupts the priests' preparations, and to my relief, all three of them shuffle to the entrance. They open the doors wide, giving the two richly-dressed women friendly greetings and kisses on the cheek.

I grumble. The priests don't make them wait outside but welcome them in gladly. When I see what they're carrying, I realize why. One of the women gives the priests an enormous basket overflowing with bread. The other brought a basket of fresh, green lettuce—Sutekh's favorite. The priest thanks and blesses them. As they talk together, I know this is my only chance.

I dart back behind the altar, crouching as low as I can before peeking around the corner. The priests and the noblewomen continue their chatting. Apparently, those service preparations weren't all that important after all, not when there are highborn women with baskets full of offerings. No matter. I won't even be here when they start the opening prayers.

I pluck an oil lamp from an offering table and lift the trap door. Thankfully, opening it this time is easy, and I sneak down through the floor. After shutting it, I hold the single flame up into the darkness. The black goes on forever.

My body tenses. One slip on this narrow stairway will send me tumbling down. And if Hani and his men are here, they'll kill me on sight. Then they'll kill Ahmose, if they haven't already.

But I can't go back now.

I take my first step, then another, and another into the muddy air.

At the bottom, I pause, listening for any footsteps or murmuring in the next chamber.

Men's voices. They're chanting. Chanting in Apep's name.

Gooseflesh crawls over me like spiders, and I blow out the lamp. I can't risk them seeing it, even if I fumble in the dark again.

I creep on my hands and knees to the passage between the two chambers. There, I'm met with a wall of men in long robes, standing opposite another holding a scepter. He must be the priest. They raise their arms as their voices crescendo, then fall into a final, foul hum.

The priest raps his scepter on the stone floor.

"Sons of Apep, I have called you here on the occasion of Sutekh's birthday because I hear you have disobeyed me. Is this true?" His deep, resonant voice fills the chamber like smoke.

The men respond with humiliated mumbling.

"Let me explain, *wabuir*."

Hani. Curse him. Curse his heart, his *ka*, his *ba*. Everything about him.

"With him out of our way—"

"I told you all to leave him be!" The priest bellows with all the might of his lungs. "You have risked revealing us too soon!"

The men snivel and shuffle their feet.

"But, *wabuir*," Hani says after a disturbing silence, "he consorts with the girl."

My heart stops. It was only a matter of time before they'd see my pieces in this cursed senet game.

"Girl?" the priest snarls and steps forward, his shrouded head better illuminated by the lamps. Yet shadows obscure his face.

"The one who serves the general in the afternoons, *wabuir*," Hani continues. "Afif and Piy said the negotiator drove her home after the Wepet Renpet banquet."

My breathing goes shallow again; I was right about those guards. They *were* working for the general. How many spies does the general have at the garrison or all throughout Per-Ramesses?

Hani's voice races. "He secured permission from the Great House for her to go with him, *wabuir*."

"And the general agreed?" the priest asks.

"He did, *wabuir*."

The priest makes an ominous, thoughtful sound.

"I think she told the negotiator about us," Hani says. "About the general's plans and—"

"Silence!" The priest shoots up his scepter. "The general was wise to allow her one last unwitting indulgence, but you were fools to act without my blessing."

The men mutter weak apologies.

"But all is not lost," the priest continues, striding in front of the cluster of hooded heads. "The general's suspicions about the girl were correct: a nuisance, but a nuisance to be eliminated nonetheless. A single thorn can fell the swiftest warhorse."

I grab the hilt of my dagger in a vain attempt to stop my shaking.

The priest stops in front of Hani. "Perhaps your little guest will prove useful after all, Commander."

He points the end of his scepter at a man at Hani's side, and the man steps forward without hesitation.

"Can you bring the girl to us?" the priest asks. I go cold. It's not a question. It's an order.

"Yes, *wabuir*," the man answers in an airy voice. "I can bring the girl to you."

I can't believe my ears. Despite my impulse to deny it, that melodic lilt is unmistakable.

It belongs to Djedi.

CHAPTER TWENTY-SIX

Time itself suspends in the smokey darkness.

No wonder he brought me washbasins with fresh water and clean linens. No wonder he fussed over me and teased me and took an interest in my correspondence with Ahmose. So he could earn my trust, so I'd consider him a friend. And now I know why he was so eager to lead me to Ahmose's villa. So he could confirm Ahmose was home, so he could tell Hani and his men to strike.

That slimy, loathsome, vile piece of *hes*.

I've heard enough. If I don't leave now, I won't be able to contain my impulse to cut his heavy heart from his ribs. By Duat, I'll break them too.

Besides, if I reveal myself, Hani and his men would make quick work of me. And who knows what dark *heka* that priest wields through his communion with the Serpent. This cellar might well become my tomb, and I'm not at all ready to meet Djehuty at the scales. I have to stop an insurrection. And deal with a double-crossing scribe.

I slip back toward the entrance and crawl up the stairs as fast as I can. In the darkness, I imagine all the ways I'll make Djedi regret everything. I'll make him tremble in fear at the sight of me.

At the top, the ceremony honoring Sutekh's birthday is already in urgent, tumultuous fervor.

May Ammit devour everything.

The temple is full of worshippers, and the priests will see me for sure. But I have no choice. With as much might as I can muster, I throw my shoulder against the door. It opens enough for me to thread my fingers through the notch, and I squeeze through the narrowest opening I can manage.

The sweet scent of frankincense engulfs me. In the center of the temple, the figure of Sutekh floats over the crowd, the priests carrying it on their shoulders as they process down the great columned hall. The revelers clap with their arms raised, chanting, singing, and adoring the god. Women cry out with high-pitched ululations. And in their rapture, not one of them seems to see me.

I thank Sutekh for his protection, for hiding me from their sight.

As I slide along the wall toward the temple entrance, the rhythm of the drums fills me with its trance. The air grows warmer. Maybe it's the heat of dancing, chanting bodies, or Re's sun attacking from outside. Or it's my anger simmering within me.

The *heka* wraps around me like river grass at my ankles.

I try to resist it. Now is not the time.

But it entices me, seducing me with its intoxicating call.

I need to get out of here before the *heka* takes me. Just sneak out the front while the revelers distract themselves with promises of blessings from the Good God's protector.

A voice says something to me, right into my ear.

Stay.

I turn, but no one is near me. Surely I couldn't hear anyone speaking to me above the crowd, the blaring trumpets, and the cacophony of the sistra and drums.

Stay, the voice says again. She sounds vaguely like Mawat, but I know that's impossible.

The heka *wishes to speak to you. Don't fight it.*

I don't want to stay. I need to get back to my quarters and wait for Djedi so I can give him the justice he deserves.

Justice . . . or vengeance?

"What's the difference?" I say out loud.

A laugh. A purr. A growl. It's not Mawat at all. The Powerful One has found me again.

Oh, my foolish child, you have so much to learn.

"Why don't you teach me?"

The roars of a thousand lions boom, bouncing off the walls, echoing into eternity.

A wall of flames erupts in front of me, tossing me back against the wall.

Baring her fangs, the goddess Sekhmet emerges from the fire and growls. Her mane radiates out from her feline face like the sun itself.

I crawl back, away from her, and my palms find something warm and wet. When I hold up my hands, blood runs down my fingers. It rises around me, reeking of its metallic scent. The rusty carnelian curls up the hem of the Powerful One's dress.

You need to learn patience.

"How can I be patient? Djedi is going to offer me up to that *isfet* priest, and they've taken Ahmose! What if I'm too late, and they've already killed him?"

Her whiskered cheeks pull in a grin.

The girl's heart leans to another. I assure you, the nobleman is unharmed.

She bends down and offers me her hand. When I take it, it shifts in between the fierce paw of a lion and the soft hand of a woman.

Remember, I could have sent anyone, anyone at all, in your place.

"Why did you send me?"

The priests say I act in the role of a man. I only act according to my true nature. But you, child, also play the role of a man.

"Is that all? Because I wanted to become a soldier like Iti?"

You have become exactly who I need. Because I seek justice of my own against those who conspire against Horu on His Throne.

"Justice . . . or vengeance?"

The goddess lets out a hearty, growling laugh.

Very good, child. Now you are beginning to learn.

My feet drag through the blood as she leads me to the entrance of the temple. It flows against me but parts before her steady paws. Flames rise along the walls, thundering in my ears, drowning out any trace of the drums, trumpets, sistra, or the wailing cries of the worshipping crowd.

Before we reach the doors, the goddess stops and faces me.

Righteous wrath simmers in you. It feeds you. Sustains you. Nourishes you so you can be my eye. But it will ruin you if you let it intoxicate you.

"How do I stop it? How do I stop the general?"

Wait in the tall grass until the gazelle passes.

"Like a lion."

No. Like a lioness.

She grins again, sharp teeth gleaming, and the flames swirl and storm toward the altar. I try to shield my face from the hot dust with my arms, bracing against the biting sands.

After the wind dissipates and the fire burns out, I uncover my head.

Date palm fronds shuffle above me in the breeze.

The sun hovers over the western horizon, casting a pink glow over the sky. Evening already. The goddess certainly does mean for me to be patient.

I turn to find myself outside a two-story mudbrick building. I know this place. My quarters. I open the door.

On the table, my papers and ink palette sit neatly, right where I left them before going to Ahmose's villa. I retrieve my staff, weighing it in my hands, ensuring that it's real.

"Djedi?" I call sweetly up the stairway.

He doesn't answer back.

Good. That means he isn't here. And I have time to plan my attack.

The goddess' voice echoes in my ears. Be patient. Wait in the grass until the time is right.

So I stretch myself out on my bed, like a cobra on warm sand, like a cat on a stone in the sun, like the lioness herself in the blazing heat of midafternoon, and I wait for Djedi to return.

○ ○ ○

The sound of the door closing jerks my eyes open. The silvery light of Khonsu's moon streaks across the floor mats. Djedi has been out all evening, either with Tay or with the Apep cult. I hope for his sake and the sake of his treacherous heart it's the former.

I pretend to sleep as he strikes a flint to light a lamp. His sandals flap against the earthen floor, then up to his quarters. When the footsteps cease, I draw my dagger.

Just enough moonlight illuminates my way as I stalk him up the stairs, feeding that fire within me. I worry for a moment I'll lose control of it. That it will destroy him or even destroy me.

But this betrayal is too much.

Djedi wipes the kohl from his eyelids, mirror in one hand.

"How could you?" I hiss, holding my dagger out to my side.

His eyes widen in the reflection, and spins around on his short stool, knocking over a little glass bottle of oil. It shatters on the floor.

"Have you been working with them the whole time?" I clench my teeth to stop myself from outright yelling at him. I can't risk attracting any unnecessary attention from passersby.

"What? No!" He scrambles back over his stool.

"You told them everything, didn't you?"

"I promise I didn't." His voice breaks. He drops his bronze mirror and flinches when it clatters to the floor.

"They took Ahmose last night." The rage sputters in my throat, raw and bitter. I try so hard to keep it under control, but it fights me. "But you know that already, don't you?"

"I swear on the girdle of Iset, I had nothing to do with it!" He shakes his palms at me, as though that will be enough to stop me from cutting his throat.

"Tell me where he is." I prowl toward him, forcing him into the corner.

"I swear on my *ka* I don't know!"

I hold back the rage with all of my might. "Don't pretend to be stupid. I heard your voice yesterday. You told them you'd bring me to them."

"How? How did—"

"Did you read my letters? His letters?"

"No, I promise you I would never! How a woman gives her heart is of no concern to me."

"How can I know for sure?" My voice is a guttural, lethal growl. "If you've tampered with our letters, I'll cut you."

"I swear—on everything I love! On my life, on Tay's life."

"But you still promised to deliver me to those snakes!"

I shove him against the corner, holding the edge of my blade a hair away from his cheek. I could kill him, yes, but for him, marring his elegant face and flawless skin would be worse than death.

"I thought you were my friend," I snarl. "But you only pretended to be my friend, because you've been working for them!"

He whimpers as I press the blade against his cheek, just shy of breaking his soft, pampered skin.

"You wish to lead me to my death?" I say. "How could you? I trusted you!" The fire inside me verges on spiraling out of control as I unravel every way Djedi might have betrayed me.

"I swear by Iset and Wasir and Min and all the gods I never meant you any harm!"

"Liar. *Desher* liar, like all the rest of them! You were there! Praying to Apep!"

"Hani forced me! On the general's orders. He threatened to kill me if I didn't go with them!" His eyes moisten, and his upper lip shakes. "He threatened to tell my commander about Tay."

A gut-wrenching vulnerability washes over his face. A vulnerability too painful to be just an act. Something softens in my heart, but I can't let him see.

"I told them what they wanted to hear," he says.

"How can I trust you're telling me the truth?"

"I was going to tell you their plan, so you could tell Ahmose."

"Well, it's too late for that, isn't it?"

He darts panicked glances between the blade and me. "I'm sorry," he says, his lips quivering. "I never meant for that to happen. But we still have time."

"Time for what?"

"To bring him back. To stop the general."

I glower at him. He gives me a stare as round as serving platters. With one hand still pinning him to the wall, I pull the dagger from his cheek.

His mustache twitches. "Remember how I warned you to bring your staff to the meal hall your first night here? The general had me fight one of his commanders when I first arrived, too. When I lost," he swallows and shudders, "they took me out back and beat me. Called me a disgusting little *puhuyt*."

His story sounds exactly like something Setankh and Hani would do. My sympathy for him battles with my sense of betrayal, and I think it's winning. My rage slinks back to my belly, still churning and begging for a fight.

"For the four years I've been here,"—his voice shakes with fury—"I've wanted my revenge."

I search his face again, and a simmering thirst for vengeance reflects from his glistening eyes. Perhaps he's telling Ma'at's truth after all.

"When Hani ordered me to go with him," he says, "I thought I finally had my chance."

"By promising to deliver me to them?" I rasp, wanting to believe him, wanting to trust him. "How is that revenge for what they did?"

"Please, Sati." His jaw quivers. "Together we can make them pay for what they've done. To you, to me, to Ahmose. To everyone."

A tempting offer. With one hand still pinning him to the wall, I pull the dagger from his cheek. I release him, not daring to look away. He rubs the mark the blade made on his skin, and I allow him a moment to catch his breath.

"And how do you suggest we do that?" I ask.

He flashes a glance at my necklace.

CHAPTER TWENTY-SEVEN

Djedi and I spend the afternoon scheming, and he gives me no new reasons to believe that his alliances lie with Setankh, that priest, and those men who call themselves the Sons of Apep.

Even still, part of me fears I've made a mistake in trusting him again, and he'll call in Hani to send me to Duat when I'm most defenseless. But the harrowing flash of terror in his face when he mentioned his *ibib*, and the venomous contempt in his eyes when he told me about what Setankh did to him, and the shaking in his jaw tells me he speaks *ma'at*. He has waited far longer than I have to bring justice to Setankh and his men.

Justice . . . or vengeance?

○ ○ ○

Before dashing off to another new year gathering, Djedi assures me that I'll be safe tonight at the meal hall. He claims Setankh wouldn't order an attack on me with so many witnesses or so many men who might risk defending me.

I tuck my dagger in my waistband anyway.

As I sit at the corner table, I stay vigilant, hoping Rahuti will join me soon. The other soldiers come and go, some lingering at their tables over half-eaten bread rolls and empty cups of beer. The mood here remains as light as it was the morning after Wasir's birthday, with my fellow soldiers laughing and recalling the previous night's indiscretions.

The crash of a platter on my table startles me to my feet, and my hand flies to the hilt of my dagger.

"Ai! It's just me!" Rahuti says, backing away with his hands in the air.

I rub my eyes with my free hand and sit again. "Oh, thank Sekhmet."

"Where were you this afternoon?" he asks as he sits beside me.

I swirl the remaining beer in my cup. "I can't tell you here," I say in a low voice, even though I want to. "But a lot more has happened since yesterday."

"Well, I promise I haven't told anyone about"—he hushes his voice to a whisper—"well, you know."

He digs into his meal of bread and soft cheese. After a moment, he makes a confused face at me. "No Hani or the general today?"

"I haven't seen them or 'Awi and his flies."

His lower lip quirks. "Do you think they're . . ."

I reply with a tiny nod, and he hunches over his plate. Keeping watch on the meal hall, I wrap several rolls in a length of cloth.

After Rahuti finishes his final bites of bread, I turn to him. "Something big is going to happen on Nebet-het's birthday. And I need your help."

○ ○ ○

That night, I force myself to close my eyes, hoping I can rest at least a little. In my dreams, I chase after Setankh and Hani, beating them senseless with my staff, then drawing my father's dagger. But as I'm about to deliver the fatal slice across their treacherous throats, my arm catches, like a plow on a heavy rock. At that moment, I wake up, both relieved I haven't spilled blood and furious at my incompetence, only to return to my dreams to try again.

After Re rises in the east, I call up the stairs for Djedi. He doesn't answer. He must still be out, hopefully preparing to do what we've planned. My gut twists with apprehension, and I reach for my necklace.

But today they find nothing.

Soon, Djedi will return to the cellar, offering my lily pendant as a promise to the Sons of Apep. He knows how risky it is, showing up without me, but it would be riskier still if I went with him. He swore he could convince them that he forced me to give it up, and he trapped me in our quarters, bound and hobbled. If Djedi returned with me in binds—poorly tied ones, of course—the Sons of Apep surely wouldn't hesitate to take my life right there. A chance neither of us wanted to take. No one would even hear us scream.

When the priest asks why Djedi came without me, Djedi will say, "Why not bring her to the Great Hall, so the general can kill her in front of the king? Wouldn't that be a far more worthy sacrifice for the Serpent?"

Then Djedi will show them my pendant as proof, which the priest will swipe from Djedi's slender fingers.

The thought of it makes me feel like my *ka* is being torn from my body. I don't even know if it has happened yet, or if it will happen. And if it does, will I ever see my precious flower again?

For all our planning, the Sons of Apep might kill Djedi anyway, before they come for me, knowing I'm captive in my own quarters.

I shake away the possibility with a shudder. Djedi will be all right. He may play the fool, but he's clever and quick-witted. The Sons of Apep will take the bait. Setankh won't let them refuse it.

But this waiting gnaws at me from the inside, even if the Powerful One told me I must wait in the tall grass for my prey to appear. Today, the tall grass is my quarters.

When I can't stand sitting still anymore, I push my mattress against the wall and pull my fighting staff corner where it's been for weeks. If everything I planned with Djedi works, I will need to be prepared.

The wood feels foreign in my grip.

I begin with basic forms, the weight and rhythm of the weapon slowly becoming familiar again. But again and again, I hit the walls, smacking away chunks of mudbrick. This room is too small and the ceiling too low.

If only I could go outside!

But I can't risk any of Setankh's men seeing me. Djedi promised them he took me captive, so captive I must remain.

What would Iti tell me to do?

He'd tell me to be flexible, to adapt to my surroundings, to move with intention and focus. Every battlefield is different, he'd say, every opponent a unique balance of strengths and weaknesses.

I adjust my stances, the lengths of my lunges, and the range of my strikes. Within moments, a lifetime of rehearsed movements surges through my veins.

My staff is an extension of my hands again. I hear Iti's lessons in my ears. I feel them in my heart. Every attack, every move. Should I succeed tomorrow, my victory will be for him.

Before long, sweat runs down my temples, along my spine, dripping onto the floor mats. With every breath, my lungs draw the fierce air into them deeper and deeper, sharpening my senses, filling me with life. My arms and legs pulse with that delicious ache of effort telling me I'm moving with the precision and intention I'll need tomorrow. That when tomorrow comes, I'll hit my marks with aggressive ease, that I'll show my opponent no mercy.

Because my opponent deserves no mercy.

○ ○ ○

That evening, Djedi returns with fresh bread from the scribe's hall, and a generous portion of dates stuffed with a soft cheese. A peace offering, perhaps, but it's one I'll take. As I fill my empty belly, he assures me that the Sons of Apep accepted his offer, albeit not without suspicion.

They'll be waiting for us—for me—outside Setankh's offices tomorrow. The wheels are in motion.

Even though tonight might be my last, I fall into a sleep deeper and darker than Duat. In my dreams, my hand doesn't catch over Setankh's neck. I revel in the savage satisfaction of blade against skin even after Djedi shakes me awake.

If I didn't know better, it feels like any other ordinary morning. The birds sing their cacophony of calls, taking over for the chorus nighttime creatures. The faint glow of sunrise looms in the sky.

After changing into my uniform, I splash my face in the washbasin and run my hands through my hair. Djedi offers to kohl my eyes, which I accept; he paints the lines with the accuracy of an architect. When I look at my reflection in his mirror, I imagine them to be like the patterns adorning a falcon's face or the cheeks of a wildcat. For today, this makeup isn't to beautify me. It's to transform me into the predator I'm supposed to become.

And sometimes the predator must lure its prey with deception.

"Are you ready?" Djedi asks with a tinge of hesitation. He holds up a length of finely spun rope and a strip of linen.

"We don't have a choice." I turn my back to him, holding my wrists together behind me, and say a silent prayer to Sekhmet that Djedi won't betray me. I think I feel her warmth against my cheek.

"Just remember to struggle once in a while," Djedi says with a wink as he finishes the knot.

After wrapping the linen around my eyes, he brings me to the garrison gates.

CHAPTER TWENTY-EIGHT

"The worm came through, after all." Setankh. It must be.

His rough hand grabs my shoulder and pulls me closer to him.

Just beneath the linen blind, I see his sandaled feet prowl around me. He pats my waistband with a familiarity I've never allowed him. I try to pull away, but he wrenches my hips toward his. My skin squirms at his violation.

"*Imyr!*" Djedi blurts out, interrupting Setankh's inspection. "I assure you, she is unarmed."

Setankh huffs and steps back. "One can't be too sure." I can still feel his eyes on me, slick like eel skin.

Around me, the footsteps of a few men grow to those of ten, maybe twenty. I wish I could see how many, to know what we'll be up against in the Great Hall. A cruel, murderous hunger permeates the air, along with the clattering of spear shafts and sharpened bronze blades.

I keep an eye on Djedi's manicured feet, wrapped in his fine reed sandals, but I can only see what's immediately under me. He promised to stay close, and he better not abandon me now.

A gentle hand grasps my upper arm, and a quick glance under the blind tells me it's his. I resist, hopefully enough to be believable, and he jerks me toward him again, with perhaps a little more force than necessary. We need to maintain the ruse, and we need to stay together.

"Where's Hani?" That voice doesn't belong to Setankh. Perhaps

Wefer? Or 'Awi? I wouldn't put it past him to align himself with these pieces of *hes*.

"He had . . . an urgent assignment." Feet crunch in the sandy dirt. Setankh again. "He'll join us soon." I can hear the sneer in his reply, and I sense him leering at me.

Just when I think he'll touch me again, he steps back at the sound of more footsteps approaching from behind me.

"Ah, good," he says with a smug satisfaction. "Our guest of honor. My brother will be so pleased to see you."

Instinctually, I try to look, only to be met with the blankness of the linen. My nose picks up a sour, unwashed stench, laced with stale urine and feces. Beside me, the feet of a man barely touch the earth, dragged along by two others at his sides. At first I think it might be Ahmose, but he wears a colorful, embroidered tunic that tangles in his toes. A tunic that wasn't dyed or woven here in Kemet. I've never seen patterns or colors like that. A purple deeper than any amethyst radiates through the thick layer of dirt. Or is that blood? Probably both.

A lump forms in my throat when I put the pieces together. Could it be?

I tug against Djedi, a silent accusation. *Did you know about this too?* But of course he doesn't understand, and he only responds with a tight yank.

Setankh takes a deep, confident breath, letting it out slowly. "The time has come, men. Time for our appointment at the Great Hall."

Djedi keeps me close as we follow Setankh from the garrison. The gamey stench of the stables yields to the dusty, incense laced air of the palace grounds. I breathe deeper, readying myself for whatever greets us there.

But when we walk along what must be the avenue of ram's headed sphinxes leading to the gates of the Great House, Djedi hasn't given me the signal we agreed on yesterday. I tug away from his arm again, hoping he'll figure out what I mean. He's playing his part all too well. A burr of distrust buries in my heart. Does he sympathize with the Sons of Apep, and he's been toying with me all the entire time? Like a hunting dog with a duck?

Djedi jerks me to a stop.

"General Setankh." A man's voice. A guard? How many of them are there? If only I could see, then perhaps I could determine whether the Great Royal Wife read my letter.

Feet shuffle in the sand. More guards?

"I'm here to meet with my brother," Setankh says with derision.

"My apologies, *imyr*, but..." The guard hesitates. "The Good God has refused you and your men an audience today."

"Oh," Setankh says, "that's a pity."

Setankh's men step closer to the guards and vocalize in a low, rumbling tone. Several others chant something strange and twisted. It's not our tongue. Djedi pulls me backward and hugs me closer. His fingers shake against my skin.

"What's happening?" I whisper.

"I don't know," Djedi says with a genuine panic in his voice. "The king's men aren't fighting back. They're just standing there."

The men hum and hiss, growing louder and louder, culminating in a beastly growl.

"That will do," Setankh says. "Perhaps now my brother's guards will welcome us to the Great Hall."

A few of Setankh's men rush forward. Metal squelches through flesh, followed by a few agonized moans, and the collapse of bodies to the ground.

Djedi flinches, yanking me back. "How can they—"

"Come on, worm," a man grunts, pulling me and Djedi with him as we pass through the doors.

Once we're inside, Setankh's men chant again. I hear a few of the king's guards fight back as Djedi and I keep walking forward.

Setankh doesn't even give orders to his men. They know exactly what to do. And somehow their chanting has made the king's guards unable to fight. The sickening sound of blades slicing through skin comes from everywhere.

Djedi's fingers tremble.

"Stay strong," I say, trying to convince him as much as myself. "We'll be all right." At least he isn't in binds.

But he squeals in horror as we keep moving, and I step in something warm and sticky. The rivulet of blood stretches far beyond my sight.

"Get used to it, worm," a man's voice says. With a smack of palm against skin, Djedi gasps in pain and lurches forward, pulling me with him.

As we go, I pretend I can't see anything at all. What I can see chills me to my *ka*.

Dozens of the Good God's guards lie scattered about the hall. Some appear unharmed, as if they were merely sleeping. But others sprawl lifeless on the floor, blood pouring from yawning wounds, entrails spilling out on to the painted tiles.

"By Min's member," Djedi says shakily.

"Keep up, worm, or that will be you!" Setankh bellows at Djedi, and we're close behind him again.

The entire time, Setankh's men sing their nightmarish song and do their grisly work in the next hall, and the next.

Even if the Great Royal Wife received my letter, nothing I could have said would have warned her of whatever dark *heka* Setankh's men wield with their voices. Dark *heka* they must have learned from their priest of Apep.

Now we're in a room that feels smaller. The footsteps don't echo as deep, the morning birdsongs more muffled. We're in the antechamber.

There, Djedi squeezes my arm three times. The signal!

Rahuti isn't far behind.

PART FOUR: THE SERPENT'S NEST

◐ ◉ ◑

I listen for the standard-bearer, but he's either absent or Setankh's men have killed him too. I just hope Rahuti holds back far enough, so he doesn't go to Duat in the same way.

The foreign man's stench grows suffocating. He groans as his captors drag him closer enough for me to see his long matted hair stuck to his bearded face.

The longer we wait here, the more the nauseating, metallic scent of blood and viscera threatens to bring up my last meal.

"All right, men," Setankh rasps. "This is the moment we've all been preparing for. We'll give my brother one final chance to give us what we want. Only attack on my order."

His fighters respond with low grunts and a round of muffled, "Yes, *imyr*."

"You." Setankh's feet stop in front of me and Djedi. "Stay with the girl. She might prove valuable in our . . . negotiations."

"Yes, *imyr*." Djedi must be terrified, but he has calmed the shaking in his hands.

"If either of you dare try to run," Setankh warns as he takes another step closer, "my men will fell you faster than you can say your own name." His breath is hot against my face, and his gaze oozes over my skin again.

A chilling anticipation courses through me, and I remind myself to breathe. I won't be able to do anything if I don't breathe.

"Let's go," Setankh says, and we're moving again.

A door opens, flooding the antechamber with a choking fog of incense.

As we cross into the Great Hall, Djedi kicks something long and wooden out of the way. A battle axe with a half-moon shaped blade. He clears his throat a little louder than necessary.

"Quiet, worm," one of the men scolds.

"Sorry, *imyr*. It's just the smoke."

The man grunts. But it's not the smoke. The axe is for Rahuti. Djedi's squeeze on my arm tells me he's not far behind.

We keep walking until I think we're near the center of the Great Hall.

Wood raps against tile, followed by the shuffle of weapons in every direction.

"General Setankh," a deep, silvery voice booms. "We've been waiting for you."

CHAPTER TWENTY-NINE

"I knew you wouldn't listen to my entrance guards," the voice taunts. It must be the Good God himself. No one else could speak with such calm and command in the face of Setankh's armed insolence.

"I cut through your guards," Setankh says. "And I could do the same now with everyone in this hall."

The Good God grunts as the hall buzzes with rushed whispers. Leather and feet rustle in front of us; there must be a wall of Medjay guarding the dais.

"But I will spare you, for now, because you have something that should have been given to me," Setankh continues. "And I have a few things you'll want given to you."

"Bring them forward, half-brother." The Good God's voice is like poisoned honey.

"Brother." Setankh is too quick to correct the king. "I'm your brother. We are of the same blood."

"Ah, but only somewhat." I hear the derisive smile on the Good God's lips. "For we are not of the same womb."

Setankh makes a low, frustrated sound as Djedi leads me forward. After a dozen paces or so, a rough hand throws me to my knees. Bones crack against the floor next to me, and I smell the foreign man again.

Someone rips the linen from my eyes. I squint into the sunlight streaming in through the windows like dagger blades.

Setankh's men surround us. I don't recognize most of them, but a few faces are detestably familiar. Wefer. 'Awi. 'Awi's pathetic flies. They're all armed with the weapons from Setankh's office.

'Awi sneers at me as Wefer tosses Djedi away. I try to reach for Djedi with my bound hands, but it's best he isn't here with me. If Setankh orders his men to attack, he might be able to escape.

And still no Hani. No doubt, he'll be here soon, but I fear what he might bring with him when he arrives.

Setankh looms over me, his hulking form blocking the sunlight. "I want you to know that no matter how much you try, you can't stop me." His breath steams against my cheek. "You're just another pathetic beetle under my feet. And today I will crush you."

I choke back the urge to bite off his nose as he moves to the man beside me and removes his blind.

When my sight adjusts to the light again, I look at the poor wraith at my right.

The colored robe. His long hair. The beard. He isn't from the Two Lands at all.

After scrutinizing him for a moment, the Good God stands and crosses the royal crook and flail over his heart and bows. "Your Highness, Prince Mursili, the third of his name, Urhi-Teshub, son of King Muwatili the Second and my worthy foe, deposed ruler of the Kingdom of Hatti."

A hush falls over the Great Hall. It *is* the Hittite prince. Ahmose said that Setankh underestimates me, yes, but I fear we all underestimated Setankh. For Setankh has been holding this man captive all this time, right under our feet.

The Good God sits back on his golden throne. If he's shocked or surprised, nothing on his face shows it. In fact, it's almost as if he suspected Setankh has been behind the Hittite's disappearance all along.

"What a favor you have done for me, half-brother," the Good God says. "Now we can assure King Hattusili, however illegitimate he may be, that his nephew is safe here in our care, a guest of my court."

Setankh snarls. "He's a Hittite dog and my hostage."

"Not your hostage for long." The Good God slides his focus to me. His face darkens with recognition. "And who is this beside him?"

"The girl you assigned to spy on me," Setankh says.

"Spy?" The Good God raises his sharp brows. "Oh, I asked nothing of the sort."

It's true. The Good God never commanded me to report on Setankh's affairs; the Great Royal Wife did, and she's notably absent from the Great Hall this morning. And so is Aya. But I would have done it anyway once I suspected his treachery.

"Liar," Setankh spits. "You claim to be the *ma'at* of Re, yet you lie about everything!"

The Good God rolls his eyes. "Everything?"

"You've been lying about Qadesh for sixteen years."

"Ah, Setankh," the Good God says in a sarcastic purr. "Were we not young and foolish then?"

"You are foolish now, and have been for the twenty years you have sat on that throne." Setankh wags the end of his *khopesh* at the king. The Medjay take one step forward, weapons up, but Setankh stands firm. "Your feeble attempts to regain the northern borderlands have failed us time and time again. You continue to deceive with your extravagant temple walls. You shouldn't even *be* king! And now what will happen when the Hittite king discovers you've also been lying to him about the whereabouts of their little dog?"

"Hand him over," the Good God orders with a practiced poise. "The girl, as well."

"Not without an exchange."

The Good God leans forward, boring a dark stare into his half-brother.

"I'm giving you a choice," Setankh says.

"You?" The Good God lifts his sharp chin in condescension. "Giving *me*, the Bull of the Two Lands, a choice? I am the one who gives. And I can just as easily take."

Setankh takes another step forward, unfazed by the Good God's subtle warning. "Step down from the throne and the Hittite is yours."

"Absolutely not," the Good God says. "My Wasir father, and his Wasir father before him, named me as heir to the Horu Throne. You are a traitor for even suggesting otherwise."

Setankh flicks his fingers at the cloaked men behind him. They rush to his side, including that rat 'Awi. Wefer hovers his dagger over me like a kestrel ready to strike, but I don't acknowledge him with even a glance. Somewhere behind me, Djedi gasps. I wiggle my fingers against the ropes. Still loose enough for an escape.

"Very well," Setankh says. "Then I'll kill the Hittite. Right here. And we will send messengers to King Hattusili saying you did it."

If Setankh's threat disturbs the Good God, he shows no sign at all. He must believe Setankh is bluffing, but I can't afford to be so sure.

The prince doesn't even look up. His head hangs off his neck, as though it's not a part of his body anymore. Sending him to the beyond to join his gods would probably be nothing but relief for him.

"And the girl?" he asks.

"We'll relieve the girl of her *ka* while we're at it."

Djedi gasps, but I keep my eyes on Setankh, becoming ever aware of Wefer's weapon closing in on my neck.

"Without the Hittite as your key to wretched peace," Setankh says, "and without the girl to get in my way, I'll finally return us to the glorious battlefield. When the Hittite king receives word that the armies of the Iteru march to Qadesh, he will have no choice but to meet us there with his men. And I will finish what you couldn't. Because the blood of my divine ancestors flows through my veins!"

The Good God glowers at Setankh, his looming presence filling every corner of the hall. "I once hoped you would abandon your boyish ways," he says with a disappointed sigh. "That if I gave you noble responsibilities, you would grow into them. But you are still the boy on the battlefield. You still think victory is a numbers game. You ask, 'How many of the enemy have we slaughtered? How many of their hands have we collected for our records?' To you, as long as we eliminate more of them than they of us, we have triumphed. What you have not yet learned is true victory is far more complex. While you have been training men for *my* wars, to defend *my* kingdom, I have been strengthening this land you claim to love so much through trade and diplomacy and image, which will serve us all far more than war ever will."

The Good God gives Setankh a wily squint, then bores into him with an iron stare.

"It is no wonder my father chose me," he says, "a son born only of a military family, over you. Despite your claim to royal blood."

"My blood flows with the power of the gods!" Setankh rattles his *khopesh* at the dais. He's beginning to lose any control he has over his temper. "And yours is poisoned with that of our northern enemies! That's why you allow, no, you *invite* foreigners to live here. While they suck at the teat of Iset! Eating our grain. Drinking our beer. Living on our land!"

My skin goes cold and bumpy again, even in the rising heat of the morning. Everything I've suspected about him is true. It's all true. Setankh wants more than a decisive victory over the Hittites. He wants to exterminate anyone he believes to be foreign, and he's willing to drag us all into a bloody, chaotic war to do it. He must know I'm foreign, too, which is why he's all too eager to send me to Duat. And now he works with that *isfet* priest, calling on an evil more dangerous than any man should wield.

Please, Sekhmet, protect us all from this man and all who dare to follow him.

The Good God remains composed as he leans forward again, his eyes never straying from Setankh. "You always failed to see the larger picture, the potential of what one sacrifice now can sow for the future." He sits back, rapping his fingers on the armrests of his throne. "You love a kingdom that no longer exists, that perhaps never existed. Indeed, your view of this world is quite . . . old-fashioned. The future is not the mere shooting of arrows, but projecting a diplomatic and imperial might so fierce that our foes won't dare tempt us to the battlefield at all."

"Your northern blood has poisoned your heart."

"Hatred and resentment have poisoned yours." The Good God's voice grows louder and more resolute. "How do you plan to greet the Assessors of Ma'at with a heart as heavy as yours? You are an insolent, violent man, acting in rage. Unhand Urhi-Teshub and the girl and deliver them to my guards."

A rage seethes in the Good God's dark eyes as Setankh loses control of his own.

"Give me the throne, or give me my war." Setankh's voice thunders through the hall.

"Even if I were foolish enough to abdicate to a traitor," the Good God says with contempt behind his teeth, "your deceitful, blasphemous heart will still burn in the lake of fire."

"Then the Hittite dies." Setankh raises his *khopesh* over the neck of the prince and yanks him up from his collar. The poor man dangles from his clothing. "And the girl goes with him!"

Wefer grabs my tunic and pulls me to my knees. As he holds his dagger—plain, like all the others—against the base of my throat, I try to put a hair's distance between my skin and the blade. Djedi and I planned for this moment, with me only a flick away from death. But I'm not so sure we planned well. My shaking fingers test the knot binding my wrists.

"I won't stop," Setankh bellows, "until I've killed all who remain loyal to you and dare come here from foreign lands to live amongst us. Step down now, before the river runs red with your incompetence!"

The Good God settles in his seat again, pursing his thin lips. I hope he knows what he's doing. The sharp edge of Wefer's dagger threatens my pulse, but I can't pull away anymore.

"You think me as unwise as yourself," the Good God says. "I know you'd still do those very things anyway." With unwavering resolve, he opens his arms, gesturing to the hall. "You have no legitimate claim to any of this. You should be grateful for all I've already given you." He speaks with a tight mouth and a venomous tongue. "In fact, you have everything you could possibly want, for a son of a concubine."

I see now what the Good God is doing. He's pushing at Setankh's insecurities, to make him appear—and even feel—weak in front of his own men.

"I deserve more." Ire oozes out of Setankh's every pore. "You gave golden flies, land, and iron weapons to your most valiant warriors after Qadesh." Setankh's rage gushes from his mouth. "What did you reward me with? You made me command an army full of foreigners and peasants. You think that's an honor? You think that's what I—a royal descendant—deserve? It's a punishment, and you know it!"

"It *is* an honor," the Good God states. "One of the highest. This is the land you live in now. No matter where our soldiers come from, if they pledge their loyalty to this land and to me, then you must train them to be the mightiest warriors the world has ever seen."

"For what? So we never need to use them?"

"Precisely." The Good God sits as still and commanding as the colossal statues carved in his likeness, betrayed only by the false beard shifting beneath his grinding jaw.

In the silence, the tension between them roils like a sandstorm.

I search the hall for any sign of Ahmose, my sightline obscured by a dense field of Medjay and Setankh's men. But he's not here. I suspect why Hani continues to be absent. He has Ahmose.

It's time to prepare for the worst.

My fingers work at the ropes again, slowly, as to not attract attention from Setankh's men standing behind me, or from Wefer who wants nothing more than to draw his blade across my throat. Through a narrow window of Medjay, Djedi risks a glance at me. At seeing I'm nearly free, wriggling my thumb under and around the knot, he flashes me the smallest of relieved smiles.

His smile crashes to the floor when he sees something behind me. It takes everything in me not to look. If I even so much as turn my head, Wefer will make his move. Whatever has caught Djedi's attention, it can't be good.

"Excellent," Setankh says, sucking his fury back into his lungs. "One last gift for my brother."

CHAPTER THIRTY

"Sati!" Ahmose calls as Hani yanks him toward me. He struggles against the ropes binding his wrists behind his back. His torn *shendyt* is smudged with red dirt. Dried blood has crusted on the corners of his mouth, and a fresh cut on his head drips down his cheek. The sight of it sends a burning rage bursting into my throat.

But I can't move now. Not with Wefer's blade pressing ever harder against my skin.

"Commander Hani," Setankh says with a cruel satisfaction. "You're right on time. The king has, predictably, refused our offer. Perhaps killing his new pet negotiator will change his mind."

Hani holds his *khopesh* against Ahmose's neck, and my rage chills into a boulder in my chest.

The Good God stands, a lightning bolt against the rising dark. "I order you to release them!"

Setankh laughs as Hani pulls Ahmose forward.

I pretend to resist the ropes no longer holding my wrists. "Let him go!" I cry through my tight jaw.

Shut it!" Wefer growls, bearing his cracked teeth.

Ahmose shakes his head at me as a warning. But I can't let Setankh and all his *isfet* men bring the Great House to its knees, all because he collapses under the weight of a granite grudge he has quarried himself.

I stare at the king, whose own vitriol bleeds like red ink over his painted face. I want nothing more than for him to see the pleading in my eyes, to know he just needs to give the order to his men. Just command the Medjay to attack and end Setankh's violent betrayal.

The hall falls so still I think I can hear the footsteps of the beetle trudging past me, oblivious to the giants above him.

Setankh hovers his sandaled foot above it before flattening the creature with a sickening crunch.

My blood goes cold.

Ahmose's resolve cracks for an almost imperceptible moment. His throat bobs as he swallows.

I'll get you out of here, I want to say to him. We'll return to your villa, where we'll have figs and wine and all things luxurious and *nefer*.

My focus darts between Ahmose and the dais, then to Setankh, whose face has lost all its color, his skin a sickly grey. The Serpent runs through him. And it won't let go. He locks eyes with the Good God, the two like rams, with neither intending to yield. By the scales, they'll take us all down with them.

Please, Your Highness, give the burning order!

The Good God's upper lip curls, but I can't wait anymore.

Forgive me, Ma'at, for acting without your king's blessing.

I fall back on my elbows.

Before Wefer can bring his blade to me again, I kick it out of his hand and roll farther from his oafish reach.

Someone calls my name. Rahuti!

He slides my staff to me along the floor. I swipe it up as he does the same with my dagger.

Wefer lunges for me, but he's too slow. I'm already on my feet. I shove my dagger into my belt and jam my staff under Hani's crooked chin.

"Let him go," I growl.

Hani scoffs. "One flick of my hand, and he's gone." He jerks his *khopesh* at Ahmose's throat. "And how I'll relish watching you crumble when I do."

"Behind you!" Ahmose tries to warn me through clenched teeth. Before I can turn to see why, Wefer holds his blade against the soft place right under my ribs.

I steady my staff in my shaking hands, my breath quickening.

Still, the Good God does nothing. But if he did, these blades would end me and Ahmose before the Medjay even had a chance to pull Hani and Wefer from us.

Ahmose stops fighting against his binds. "I'm sorry," he mouths.

No. No sorrow. No regret. Not now. And not over these men and their treachery. These snakes will meet the unflinching justice of Ma'at.

He holds my gaze, firm and defiant. Nothing in his face appears to fear meeting Anpu at the scales.

Despite my hope we'll escape with our lives, I fight back hot, welling tears.

Oh Sekhmet, where are you now? You can't possibly have planned for me and Ahmose to be one swipe of a blade away from death. Is this your price? They sacrifice Ahmose to *isfet* so I can do your work?

Sweat makes my hands so slippery my staff might escape my grip. My feet stick to the floor. I'm a lifeless block of mud.

A tear runs down Ahmose's kohl and blood smeared cheek.

"I'll wait for you in the Field of Reeds," he says, looking right into my eyes.

"How touching," Hani says with a rotten sneer, his *khopesh* quivering in the morning light.

Do it, Sati. Jam the staff under his jaw and be done with it!

As I thrust my weapon forward, I can barely watch.

Djedi's squeal echoes against the columns.

Ahmose falls forward as Hani's *khopesh* clatters to the ground, followed by a shower of desert red blood. When I see the dripping axe hovering above me, I flinch and curl myself into a ball, awaiting its fatal blow.

Only then does the Good God order his men to attack.

○ ○ ○

I roll out from under Hani's lifeless form, and chaos erupts in the Great Hall.

The tempest of noise means I'm not dead, but blood soaks my clothes. Whose blood?

Ahmose! Where's Ahmose?

A large hand reaches for mine and pulls me up.

"Thanks for the axe," Rahuti says proudly. Bits of flesh still cling to the blade.

"Oh thank the gods, Rahuti!" I give him a firm embrace. My legs are shaking so much, and I'm gasping for air, heaving as I pull back.

"Sati!"

I whirl to see Ahmose scrambling to his feet, wrists still bound. I struggle to steady my trembling fingers as I try to cut through the ropes. The moment I'm able to slide the blade through and unwind the ties, Ahmose throws his arms around me and holds me close, but we are as vulnerable as ducks in a pond.

Rahuti pulls Ahmose's dagger from his belt and hands it to him with a toothy smile.

The surrounding melee grows louder with the grunts and clashing metal of battle. The Medjay rush toward us, an unstoppable stampede, fending off Setankh's men.

"Get out of here!" one of them says, grabbing my upper arm.

Another pulls Ahmose toward him. "You too, nobleman."

"No," Ahmose says, his voice fierce and resolute. He dips to retrieve Hani's fallen weapon and pulls back near Rahuti. "We all need to stop Setankh."

The bellowing orders of the Good God resound against Setankh's own increasingly desperate commands.

"This is your last chance to get out of here," the officer says. The three of us confer and shake our heads.

His fellow Medjay circle around us, fending off any of Setankh's men who dare approach. Over their shoulders, I see more Medjay and guards slashing against the enemy.

How are there so many more fighting for Setankh now? Weren't there only twenty or so when Setankh dragged me and the Hittite here?

The Hittite.

"Where's the Hittite?" I ask.

"We grabbed him. He's safe," the Medjay closest to me says.

I hope he stays that way.

Rahuti, Ahmose, and I pull closer, backs pressed together. As the Medjay contract around us, something warm and wet seeps under my toes.

Sprawled on the tiles a footstep away, Hani's lifeless body oozes, his head so mangled by Rahuti's axe he doesn't look like a man at all anymore.

My mouth fills with a blistering hatred. I risk a step closer to him and hover the end of my staff over his maimed face.

No embalmer will be able to reconstruct him if I let my weapon succumb to my vicious impulse. I crushed that man's ribs on the *Nebkhepri* without a second thought. And I can—no—I need to do it again. After all Hani has done to me, to Rahuti, to Djedi, to Ahmose, the feather demands it.

Ahmose glances back at me. I wait for him to chide me, to stop me, to tell me it's not worth it.

But he doesn't.

"What are you waiting for?" he says.

Instead of unleashing my betrayal on Hani, I withdraw my weapon.

Let the Devourer have him. There's no sense in fighting a dead man. I leave the traitor to Ammit and the lake of fire.

"We can't keep them away from you all much longer," one of the Medjay says.

"Then don't," Ahmose says, a wild determination on his face.

"But, lord—"

"Look!" Rahuti yells, pointing to the dais.

Through the barrage of bronze against bronze, of blood and the groans of battle, I see Setankh. He strides toward the throne, where the Good Good himself now holds a *khopesh* of his own behind the Medjay shields.

Setankh slashes his weapon against a pair of Medjay. For a moment, the two officers have distracted him, but his deathly stare never deviates from the Good God.

"He's getting too close," I say back to Ahmose and Rahuti.

"Let us out!" Ahmose commands the Medjay whose leather now pushes against us as Setankh's men advance. But they don't budge.

If they won't move for us, then we'll move around them.

"When I give the order," I call back, "drop to the floor and crawl out. Hold your weapons tight. Setankh's men won't notice us if they're engaged with the Medjay." At least, I hope not.

I pause, doing my best to survey the brawl, seeing only flashes of skin, leather, and blood. "And let me have Setankh."

"What?" Rahuti asks. I can't see his face, but I'm sure his eyes have gone round.

"We'll cover you," Ahmose says with confidence.

"Good." I glance at Setankh as he battles another assault of Medjay. May the Powerful One protect me. "Setankh is mine."

In the corner of my vision, Ahmose raises his dagger. "For the glory of the Good God!"

Rahuti holds up his axe. "And for the Two Lands."

My heart swells with courage. "On my count of three," I say. "One..."

The mass of Medjay jostles us sideways.

"Two..."

Another blow from the opposite side nearly topples me.

"Three!"

We drop to the ground and the Medjay collide against each other, staving off wave after wave of Setankh's men.

CHAPTER THIRTY-ONE

It's almost like being underwater in a storm. The surface above churns and seethes. Down here, the three of us maneuver between sandaled feet and bloodied legs, quiet and undetected.

We crawl our way toward a clearing in the forest of limbs and help each other to our feet. Several paces away, Setankh pushes back another of the king's guards with a roar.

He hasn't noticed us, even as we advance.

I know he's so much stronger than me. He's so much more experienced and driven by a lust for blood.

Instead of fear, a predatory impulse comes over me. A lioness stalking her prey. I can hunger for blood, too.

All the fury and haste of the morning stands still as I place one foot in front of the other. I sense Ahmose and Rahuti close behind me, beating back the chaos so I can pounce.

With each step, call on the Powerful One. She who brought me here. She who entrusted me to root out Setankh's treachery and deliver her righteous justice.

That now familiar spark ignites in my belly. I nurture it. I fan it. I feed it. And it nourishes me in a way I didn't know possible until this moment.

The spark grows to a flame, and the flame into a fire. I savor its destructive power, reveling in the divine wrath of the lioness, of her sisters, her brothers. I feel her presence within me, coursing through my blood, along with the *heka* itself.

Her satisfied laugh echoes and roars between the columns and against the walls.

Behind me, Ahmose and Rahuti fend off those who dare come for me, for us, their blades striking swift and true.

I step closer to Setankh, my hands gripping the leather wrappings of my trusted weapon. When I'm a staff's length away, he spins and swipes his *khopesh* at me.

The whistle of the blade cuts through the air above my head as I duck.

"You?" Spit foams at the edges of his mouth. His bloodshot eyes bulge out of his skull, dull and empty, as though his *ka* has abandoned him. "I'll kill you before you can even get close to me, you vile *shema't*!"

Shema't. The word hooks in my ears. If I had any doubt before that he knows who I am and where I'm from, it has evaporated into the oppressive heat with a single insult.

I swing, hitting the soft spot at the back of his knees. His legs crumple, and he limps forward.

"It was you," I say as he regains his stance. "Your men came to the Per-seshen, threatened my family. Your men attacked Tahir! For what? More violence? More death?"

His sneer is all the confession I need. "Stupid little girl."

We lock on each other, circling, like two cobras, hoods open, venom ready.

"The Serpent blessed me when you walked into my office wearing that necklace. Or should I say, your *shema't* mother's necklace?"

He reaches into his waistband and pulls out my pendant, dangling it before me in a cruel taunt. Before I can grab it, he whips it away and shoves it back in his leather. May Sekhmet plague him if I never get it back.

"You should have seen the fear in her eyes when she begged me to spare her life."

A sickening twist in my belly doubles me over. "What? Iti said the Hittites destroyed the village." Iti wouldn't have lied to me. Not about that.

Setankh smirks. "I'm not surprised Paser would raise a child as ignorant as he is."

"Keep my father's name out of your *hes*-filled mouth!"

I can't stop my next desperate, unaimed volley. Setankh slashes at me again, once, twice. The third catches my leather tunic at the side of my waist, sparing my skin.

My heart reels as the two of us fall back and catch our breath. Why didn't I figure it out earlier? Setankh killed my birth parents. He sacked the place where I was born. The Hittites had nothing to do with it.

"Your real father is just another dead *shema'* man from Retenu. Another locust in an endless swarm, robbing the Black Land of what is ours."

"You're worse than *isfet*," I say, holding my staff between us, tears threatening to cloud my sight.

"I could have been satisfied with killing those two spies who told us the Hittites were too far away to fight. But I thought, 'Why not destroy their entire village?' It's their fault we lost the battle. Because of them, we had to retreat. They left us looking like impotent cowards." Saliva sprays from his mouth. His face grows scarlet, veins bulging in his temples.

I toss my shock aside and take the chance to provoke him further. "But you were too much of a coward to kill a baby girl," I say with a proud sneer of my own. "You have no right to the throne. You're a liar. A murderer."

As we circle, I keep enough space between us to avoid the next strike. Sweat streams down his stubbled cheeks, and a thin trail of blood escapes one of his flaring nostrils. When he wipes it with the back of his arm, it smears across his upper lip.

"And," I say, jamming my staff at his chin, "you're no son of a king!"

My weapon finds only air when I arc my staff at his head, and my momentum throws me around. I spin so far I don't know which way to face.

"I should have smothered you when I had the chance," he says to my left. "You and that *shema't* sister of yours."

He must see my mouth twist in confusion, then realization. Aya. He means Aya.

"And when I'm done with you," he says, "I'll find her and crush her, too. No more foreign vermin in my court."

"May Ammit devour you." My fire turns white hot.

"She'll have you too, once I do what I should have sixteen years ago."

His *khopesh* comes for me out of the corner of my eye, and I spin to block it. It catches in the wood of my staff.

No matter how hard I try, I can't release my weapon from his.

Setankh yanks his blade toward him, lurching my captured staff and me forward with it.

He brings his sweaty, bloody, grey face close to mine. His breath smells of decay and rotting flesh.

"It's such a shame you weren't here long enough for *khopesh* training. A shame for you, anyway."

"I won't need it," I snarl, resisting him. It's more a wish than a threat.

When I finally wrench my weapon from his blade, a chunk of wood flies into the air.

Dear Sekhmet, no!

I risk a glance at my staff as I stumble back. A gaping wound yawns from the middle, where it needs to be its strongest. If I attack again, it will certainly break. But I need to keep fighting. I need to end this. I need to end him.

If I'm to be disarmed, then so will he.

I aim for Setankh's *khopesh*.

It flies from his hands and clatters to the floor behind him, too far back for him to retrieve it.

He rushes toward me and grabs the end of my weapon with both hands. He pulls on it with all his might. I grip as hard as I can, but the leather wrappings slip against my sweaty palms.

"No, I won't let you have it!" I try to make myself heavy, but his hold is so strong he drags me along the floor.

"What good is a broken weapon to you?"

"My father gave it to me!" The words leap out of my mouth.

"Better reason for me to destroy it."

Setankh shoves his foot into my belly, and my staff escapes my tiring hands.

CHAPTER THIRTY-TWO

I catch myself from falling on my rear as Setankh holds my staff in both hands. He lifts his knee and twists his lips in a cruel smile. And he snaps my precious weapon over his thigh.

I hear myself cry out for it as the splinters suspend in the air.

Something inside me snaps with it, as if Setankh has just broken my arms.

He flings the pieces aside in triumph, and they clatter to the floor. I instinctually reach for them, but I stop myself.

What good is a broken weapon?

I need to let it go. This part of me I brought all the way from Men-nefer, that Iti gave to me as a child, with the memory of so many spars with him on the edge of the fields, day after beautiful and idyllic day, is shattered. It's gone. That life, who I was, is gone.

Setankh turns to me and laughs from the depths of his belly, his voice channeling a darkness I've only heard in my nightmares.

He runs for me.

Please, Sekhmet, let me do it right.

I hunker into the floor, crouching, watching.

Time slows as his hulking body gets closer.

Wait for the prey. When the gazelle passes, attack.

He opens his arms, fingers splayed, murder in his eyes.

Just before he makes impact, I dip and grab him by his legs.

He wails as he tumbles on my back, and my knees threaten to crumple under his weight.

I push my feet into the floor, sending him falling behind me. His body hits the tiles with a sickening thud.

He's several paces from me, coughing as he scrambles, unable to find his footing. I only have a few moments to catch my breath before he attacks again. Sweat pools in my waistband.

As he bares his teeth at me, he heaves. "Curse you!"

My little victory banishes the fatigue thickening in me. Setankh isn't invincible. And I might be the one to end him. I know now why I'm here. Why Sekhmet gave me this mission.

I call on the might of the stars. I call on the fire of the Powerful One, on the storms and spears of Sutekh, on the Iteru cataracts and arrows of Satet, and on the justice of Ma'at.

I draw my father's dagger from my waistband.

Setankh pulls his dagger from his side.

I don't hear the fighting and shouting around us. Not the Medjay, Setankh's loyalists, or even Rahuti and Ahmose.

I draw on the last gasps of my strength, searching deep within my *ka* for the power to defeat him.

In Setankh's eyes, I see no *ka* left at all. The darkness has poisoned him, eating away at him like maggots in a carcass. There's no more life in him, only death, killing, chaos, and oblivion.

I charge and slash at him. He returns the volley and catches my shoulder. Pain bursts down my arm along with my blood. My fire dwindles, gasping for fuel. The fatigue in my limbs grows heavier.

Setankh laughs.

I can't let him win. I refuse to accept it's my time to enter Duat.

He attacks again, drawing his blade above my knee. I double over, and the blood soaks my leg, seeping into the linen of my *shendyt*. Like Sekhmet's dress.

I swing at him, but my arm slows and falters. I only nick him. He swipes his blade under my ribs, slicing through my leather tunic.

White hot pain flashes up my side, blurring my vision. I wrap my arm around the wound, my blood pouring over it. My head goes light and adrift.

If I die today, I'll do so knowing I was *ma'at*. That I was with the gods. That I was with the Good God himself. That I've been true. That I kept my heart light. That the beast won't devour me at the scales, and my heart won't burn in the lake of fire. I will enter the Field of Reeds, having lived a good, honest life. I'll live in eternity knowing I fought the Serpent. That I tried to push back the primordial Chaos.

But I will not die today. This is my last chance.

With all my might, with anything I can summon from my injured, fatigued body, I hurl myself at Setankh.

I slam into him, and we hit the tiles. Blood pools around my knees and over his tunic as I try to pin him under me.

I hold my dagger to his throat for the final, lethal cut.

Setankh snarls and pulls me over, tossing me on my back. A fresh, nauseating wave of pain nearly overtakes me.

He presses his knee into my belly, and a million terrible things cross my heart as his slippery grin slips its way over my neck and chest.

My breath betrays my lungs as I struggle against Setankh's sheer power. And I can't find enough of my own to escape. When I wriggle against him, he only holds me down harder.

He brings his face close to my ear. I twist away from him as the scent of his breath sends bile into my mouth.

Then I feel the cool edge of his blade against the front of my throat.

"It was a mistake to spare you."

Setankh's voice slips into my ear like rancid oil. The metallic smell of the blood from his nose mixes with his rotten sweat, both dripping on my chest and cheeks. It makes me want to tear off my skin.

His rough lips brush against my cheek. "And I'll do what my cowardly brother could not," he hisses.

I can't quiet the tremble in my jaw as my sweat stings my eyes. My heart races, thumping against my bones. I try to fill my lungs with my shallow, jagged, futile breaths.

I pull on what little might I have left. But I'm only embers.

I think of Iti. Of Mawat. Of home. I need to see them all again. This can't be how I face death. I didn't even tell Iti and Mawat goodbye.

Then a hot wind caresses my cheeks.

What are you going to do, my child?

I don't know!

You must find a way out.

Tell me how. I did everything you wanted.

Remember what I told you.

Remember what? You've told me so much.

The might of the stars.

Setankh snickers as he presses his dagger against my neck.

As he revels in your fear, he's giving you a chance to fight back. End him.

I twist my fighting arm against his unrelenting hold and wind the tip of my dagger between his hips and the floor. And I plunge my star-fallen iron into his side, tearing through the linen and leather.

He roars and releases me for a moment just long enough for me to roll out from beneath him.

On my knees, I slash at him again, slicing through the muscle at the base of his neck.

He scrambles back from me with a savage yell, slipping on the blood-soaked tiles, gripping his wound with his free hand.

I barely find my feet, my legs now shaking under my weight.

When I do, Setankh already stands, staring down at me.

The dagger feels as immovable as a limestone block. I slash it without aim with all the force I can muster, catching the skin by

Setankh's navel. It drags through the flesh, and the wound spills forth its carnelian reward.

He must fall now. He has to.

But he still stands, with that terrible, monstrous sneer on his lips. Blood pours from the gash in his neck, yet he doesn't seem to notice.

The edges of my sight swirl with darkness. I can't feel the pain of my wounds. I don't feel anything anymore.

Setankh drops his weapon and lunges for me, his hands catching around the side of my head.

My feet leave the floor before I can tear at his grip.

I see the sparkle of golden stars on the ceiling.

My dagger hovers above me.

Setankh laughs.

Ahmose calls my name.

The back of my skull hits the tiles with a crack. A searing, blinding pain spills over my head, through my neck, down my arms, my fingers, my legs, my feet.

Setankh's hulking, bleeding body tumbles down beside me, and the sight of him fades into a choking blur.

I think I hear Rahuti. I think I hear the clatter of his axe as he drops it on the tile. He's struggling against Setankh, and with a deadening thud, Setankh's grunting fades away, too.

My vision fuzzes, and the form of Ahmose's body hovers over me. I think I smell a hint of spice and feel his hands on my arms. I try to say his name, but no sound comes forth from my throat.

Inky darkness slithers into the sides of my vision. I fight against it, resisting its pull. It sinks its fangs into my shoulders, my chest, and it drags me down. Its venom runs through my veins. My heart slows. I gasp for air. I'm drowning in it.

Then the darkness swallows me.

PART FIVE: THE RETURN

CHAPTER THIRTY-THREE

A warm palm presses against my forehead.
"Mawat?" My voice creaks through my burning throat. I can't open my eyes.

"Shh..."

I feel a cool, damp cloth against my neck and smell lilies, resin, and honey.

When I try to open my eyes again, I squint and blink into the light. Everything is so blurry. As my surroundings come into focus, a mural of a grand garden surrounded by fluffy trees greets me.

A woman in a plain dress wearing a necklace of large turquoise baubles holds a bowl and a folded square of linen.

I'm not home. And that's not Mawat.

I need to get out of here. I need to go back to the Per-seshen.

I try to sit up. An excruciating pain in my side pins me down.

"Oh, my dear, no no no," the woman says as she catches my head. The pressure of her hand sends a dull ache through my sight. But I begin to trust my eyes and my ears.

"Nehemet?" I ask. It's more of a dry croak.

"Yes, little kitten," Nehemet says. "You're safe now, but you need to rest." She eases me to the bed and pulls a large strip of linen from the bowl. After wringing it out, she curls it behind my neck, and I relax, even if she isn't Mawat.

She feels my cheeks and forehead with the back of her hand. "Your fever is finally gone. Sometimes it's not good to keep the fire of the Powerful One in your heart."

Fever. My injuries. How many times did Setankh's *khopesh* catch me? Too many. Far too many. I struggle to look at my left shoulder. A crisp white bandage wraps around it and my upper arm. I touch the side of my waist and find wide strips of linen there too, as neat and tidy as Wasir himself. Even though I can't see the gash above my knee, the pain of it flashes up my thigh. My stomach churns. I hope I don't vomit.

"I was beginning to worry you'd never return to us. We all were." She pulls a stool next to me and sits, examining me with motherly eyes.

Motherly. Mawat. I need to tell her what happened. I need to tell her I'm all right.

"Ahmose managed to get to you just in time. And the larger man. What's his name?"

"Rahuti?" I say.

"Yes, Rahuti. Good heart, that one, even with that axe. He carried you here as though you were nothing more than a baby!"

I don't remember Rahuti carrying me. I can't remember anything after I hit the floor. Nothing but a terrifying and overwhelming darkness. And the shreds of what I can remember feel like a dream, a hallucination. Dear Ptah, I must have been on the edge of entering Duat.

I try to prop myself up on my elbows, but my ribs cry out in agony.

"No, no," Nehemet chides, scooping her arms around my back and setting me on the bed. "That gash in your side has just started to heal. After the care I put into those stitches, I can't have you opening it up."

"How long have I been here?" I ask.

"Well, Nebet-het's birthday was two days ago."

I've been unconscious for two days.

And I'm starving. My belly gurgles, and Nehemet giggles.

"Well, that's a welcome sound. I'll be right back."

She returns quickly with a small tray of plain bread and a blue ceramic cup. "We were able to wake you enough to give you a bit of beer with a few drops of poppy milk to ease your pain. And thank Iset. I feared you might fade from us completely."

I grab a flatbread and tear into it. The nausea threatens to return, but I'm too ravenous to care. The nourishing grain eases the emptiness in my belly.

"Ahmose was so pleased to hear you're awake," she chirps.

"Where is he? Can I see him?" I immediately take a second flatbread as though I'll never eat again in my life.

"He'll be in shortly." She leaves the tray on the bedside table. "I'll get you more bread, and perhaps a little cheese as well? Keeping up with both of your appetites will prove impossible. He's been just ravenous since he returned home."

The door creaks open on its wooden hinge, and Ahmose peeks through the opening. "Can I come in?"

"Of course," I say. My chuckle sends another pummeling pain through me, and I hold back a groan.

Nehemet gives me a scolding glance as she stands. "I'll let you two have some privacy."

After thanking Nehemet for her care, Ahmose presses a lingering kiss on my lips and sits on the stool beside me. As he takes my hands, my heart lightens, but something about him feels burdened. The usual rich color of his face has faded, like his blood has been drained. If he looks so pale, I must be like bleached linen.

For a moment, we sit quietly in the presence of one another. A soft breeze wafts in through the high windows, sweeping away some of the heat from my neck.

"I prayed all night to Wasir and Anpu," he finally says, running his thumb over my knuckles. "So they wouldn't take you. I thought . . ."

He keeps his head down, pressing his lips together and shaking his head.

"Thought what?" I ask.

When he looks at me, his eyes glisten with tears. "We'd have to call the embalmer."

I squeeze his hands tight. "I don't plan on going to Duat any time soon. And Nehemet made sure of it."

"I don't know what I'd do without her." Something harrowing lurks behind his half-smile. I want to ask what troubles him, but I don't want to ruin the peaceful moment. "I visited quite often," he says. "Or, at least, as much as my own injuries would allow. And every time, she was in here tending to you."

"I hope I can properly thank her. But what do you do for someone who's saved your life?"

"How soon you forget the *Nebkhepri*." His cheeks pull into an admiring smirk. "Speaking of saving lives. The man who fought with us and brought you here. Rahuti? He has the lightest heart of anyone I've ever met."

"Where is he? Is he all right?"

Ahmose gives me an assuring nod. "He returned to the garrison, but only after I promised to tell him when you woke up."

"Did you?"

"Ubenu is on his way there now," he says with satisfaction. "The garrison may be infested with Setankh's loyalists, but Rahuti . . . I don't think anything could corrupt his heart. We fought back Setankh's men after you fell. He swung his axe with all the force of a seasoned warrior."

I knew Rahuti had it in him; he's far more fierce than he knows. He could have stood up to 'Awi and his flies long ago. He just needed to trust himself and have something beyond himself to fight for. "Would you believe he's afraid of the dark?"

"I would, actually."

We share a chuckle, and we let the silence embrace us as he rests his forehead against mine.

After a while, I say, "I'd wait for you, too."

"What do you mean?" he asks.

"In the Field of Reeds."

"I thank Wasir that you don't have to. Besides, how could the Field of Reeds be any better than this, right now?"

I glance at my bandages. "I can think of at least one reason."

"When our injuries heal, then will this be better than the Field of Reeds?"

"Much better," I say.

A warmth brushes over me. Not tingling or exciting like when he took my hand at the Wepet Renpet banquet or when we first kissed, but soft like kitten fur, as though nothing in the world can harm me, harm us. For now, at least.

After a very long time, not wanting to break this moment of peace, I speak. "Can you write a letter for me? Mawat and Iti need to know what we've done."

○ ○ ○

Ahmose tells me he has delivered my letter to the Great House's own messengers. That night, Nehemet brings me a bowl of broth with duck meat and freshly baked bread rolls to soothe my ever more grumbling belly. Helped again by Nehemet's precise blend of beer and poppy milk, I fall asleep soon after, while Ahmose sits on the stool by my side.

I wake the next day with a renewed sense of strength, although judging by the angle of Re's light beaming through the windows, I'm not sure it's morning anymore. Today I can shift my weight to my elbows and sit up without help, and with far less pain than yesterday.

When Nehemet brings me my first meal of the day, she scolds me and tells me to sit back, but I want nothing more than to feel the sun on my face.

She cocks her wigged head at me and folds her arms. "All right," she says reluctantly. "I really shouldn't let you be up and about so soon."

"Please, Nehemet."

Not long after, she returns with Ahmose. "You're looking much better!" he says, his own face brighter and less sickly than yesterday.

He and Nehemet help me upright with care. I cringe at the pain, but with each little movement, it subsides. I sit at the edge of the bed, letting my legs dangle. My vision swims with shooting stars. And I remember that night by the pond, the star blazing across the sky. I need to be there again.

"You best be careful with those bandages," Nehemet says. "Beket and I worked so hard to get them right."

"I promise I'll be gentle with her," Ahmose jokes as he wraps his arm under mine. "Please tell Beket to bring out dates and pomegranate juice."

Nehemet responds with a single nod. As she leaves, she shakes her head, like Mawat does when she knows she can't stop me from getting into trouble.

I let Ahmose bear my weight as he helps me to my feet. The wound in my leg burns as I hobble with him to the garden.

As soon as Re's light hits my cheeks, I forget I was ever in pain at all.

A gentle breeze rustles through the leaves of the tall sycamore and bushy pomegranate trees, fresh and cooling. The waters must be returning. I can smell it. I can feel it in my *ka*. And my *ka* is still in my living body to see another flood.

Ahmose brings me to the patio overlooking the sparkling pond and lush greenery. A pair of ducks skim into the water, their feathers glistening in the sunlight. Beket has already left a spouted jar and matching cups painted with lily flowers and and a tray of dried dates on a low table.

After sitting me on a long chair with a high backrest, he sits beside me and interweaves his fingers with mine. I rest my head on his shoulder and let out a contented sigh.

"We did it," I breathe, not realizing I've spoken out loud. "It's over."

Ahmose turns to me, his peaceful expression falling to one of regret.

"What's wrong?" I ask.

"I don't think it's over," he says, squeezing my hands.

My stomach drops. "But Setankh's dead, right? He must be."

"He... survived."

"He what?" I sit up too fast and groan at a fresh surge of pain, and Ahmose darts his arm under my back to help me recline. "How is that piece of *hes* still alive? I jammed my dagger so hard into his side." The memory of his blood spilling over my hands turns my fingers to fists.

"You did enough for the Medjay to arrest him," Ahmose says as he sits. I pat the bandages around my waist to make sure I haven't disturbed them.

"I suppose that's something. Does the Good God know what his men did to the guards outside the Great Hall?" I ask.

"Killed them all," Ahmose says grimly. "But how?"

The harrowing sound of their voices invades my memory. "Chanting. In a strange language. It seemed to paralyze the guards so they couldn't fight back."

He sucks his teeth in disgust. "Dark *heka*... The king's investigators have their work cut out for them."

In more ways than any of us know. "Where is Setankh now?"

"The Great Prison, waiting to face the king's justice."

"And having his wounds tended to while he awaits trial," I scoff. "He doesn't deserve it. The king should let him rot."

"The king will want to make an example of him," Ahmose says.

"What about the others? Wefer and 'Awi? Were they arrested too?"

"The Medjay arrested everyone they could."

"All of them should be cowering in fear in the presence of Ammit," I mutter. "Not sitting in the Great Prison."

"I doubt they'll be enjoying themselves. The prison guards won't be kind to any of them, especially Setankh. And he'll be nursing those wounds you inflicted for some time. I've never seen so much blood."

"Good," I say, folding my arms. If only I'd struck sooner and drawn my dagger across his throat before he toppled me. "I hope he's just as terrified as I was when he held his *khopesh* to my neck."

Ahmose unfurls my arms and takes my hand again, and the rage in my throat retreats.

"The king is grateful for everything you've done. We're all grateful. And because of your courage, Urhi-Teshub is now safe in the Great House, recovering from his imprisonment."

"Does that mean we're closer to a treaty?"

Ahmose makes a hesitant face. "Somewhat. Now the king will have to explain to King Hattusili why it took so long to find his nephew, without looking ineffectual and incompetent. And surely word of Setankh's insurrection is well on its way to Hatti already." He heaves a weary sigh. "I'll likely be spending much of the coming weeks convincing the Hittite delegation that their king doesn't need to worry about what happened. But if the Good God doesn't stop raging, that will be impossible. He hasn't even opened an investigation."

He pinches the bridge of his nose.

"I still don't know where Setankh held us," he says. "His men blindfolded me."

"I tried to find you. I went to their chamber under the Temple of Sutekh."

"We were never there," he says. "I would have recognized the scent. Wherever we were, it smelled musty, like rot and mold and urine." He takes a deep breath and looks out at the pond. "But I wasn't alone. I lost count of the different accents and dialects, even languages."

"A prison for foreigners," I murmur.

"It seems so. And likely not the only one."

Even with the confirmation that Setankh and his men have been kidnapping foreigners, a glimmer of hope sparks in my heart. Perhaps

Kala and Asata were there, and maybe Tahir, too. Maybe they're all still alive, waiting for the Medjay to find them.

Seeing the haunted look on Ahmose's face, I don't ask him about whether he might have heard my friends in that terrible place. But I hold fast to my hope that we'll find them and bring them home.

I reach for my pendant, and my heart drops.

"Ahmose," I say with dread. "Setankh doesn't still have my necklace, does he?"

He shakes his head. "But I know who does."

CHAPTER THIRTY-FOUR

Four days after I failed to send Setankh to Duat, I sit on Ahmose's garden patio, reveling in the scent of the blossoming flowers and the breeze brushing my face.

As the heat of midday subsides, I sip my pomegranate wine and close my eyes, savoring the tartness on my tongue, and hoping the memory of my night with Ahmose will drive away the terrors of battle on Nebet-het's birthday. While I want to heal quickly so I'm no longer in constant pain, part of me wants my body to take its time, so I can enjoy more languid afternoons like this one.

Yesterday, after inspecting my bandages, Nehemet deemed me healed enough to receive visitors. I knew exactly who I wanted to see.

"I would have come sooner," an airy voice says behind me.

"Djedi!"

The ache in my side stops me from leaping up to greet him.

Djedi's face blanches with concern as he rushes to help me sit again. "Oh, *bitbit*, I didn't realize you were so injured." He shakes his head with a *tsk*. "They told me, but . . . It's a wonder you're alive at all!"

"You should have seen me a few days ago," I say, trying not to chuckle too hard.

"I wish I could have visited." He pulls a chair nearer to me and sits. "But the *tjati* held me for questioning. Can you believe it? For two days!" I can't tell if he's exaggerating the offense on his face.

I raise a brow at him. "You *did* arrive at the Great Hall with me in binds."

"Yes, but you escaped!"

"Only because you tied a terrible knot."

He waves my teasing away. "A plan that worked, by the way. Surely the Good God noticed. Besides, I kept myself as far from Setankh and Wefer as I could. That should have been the Good God's first sign I wasn't truly aligned with those brutes. Besides, they reeked of sweat and newly tanned leather." He holds an offended hand to his heart. "I could *never* live like that."

He reaches for the wine jar on the nearby table and helps himself to a cup.

"I admit," I say tentatively, "I wasn't sure I could trust you. Not after I discovered you in the cellar with Hani—do they really call themselves . . ."

"The Sons of Apep," he answers with a nod of disgust. "And I hope I've redeemed myself enough for you."

"More than enough," I say.

He takes in the painted columns and lush greenery, then lifts his brows at me. "So, you get to hide out here for a few days, and with your *ibib*. Where is he, anyway?"

"He had business at the Great House. The treaty negotiations continue, in spite of Setankh's efforts."

The corner of Djedi's mouth stretches into a grin. "You're never returning to the garrison, are you?"

I pat his hand, which is only slightly less spotted with ink than the first day I met him. "Oh, I will. But only when Nehemet says I'm well enough."

"Not a terrible fate to recuperate here, if I say so myself. I'd want to stay here as long as I could."

"It'd be far more enjoyable if I weren't so beat up."

"Well, even with all these"—he twirls a finger at my bandages—"I'm sure you'll be in fighting shape again soon. And you'll need to be."

"Why?"

"The *tjati* let it slip that the Good God will begin his investigation soon, and I can't imagine he'd proceed without you in his employ. We still know so little about who Setankh works for."

"But you know who they are, right? That priest, the one you called *wabuir*—he must have a name."

He shakes his head with regret. "I'm not sure he even has a face, let alone a name."

Before I can ask him more questions, the sound of footsteps inside the villa draws our attention.

"Look who I found on his way to see you," Ahmose says, strolling toward us.

Behind him, Rahuti approaches with his arms open wide. A rough bandage wraps around his upper arm, and quite a few scrapes mar his round face. He gives me a tentative embrace, but I pull him in tight.

Ahmose offers him a seat and Djedi a warm greeting, then gives me a kiss. Djedi throws me a suggestive look, and I reply with a roll of my eyes. After ensuring our cups are full, Ahmose pulls up a chair of his own next to me.

"I guess we won't be wrestling again anytime soon?" Rahuti jokes as he sits.

"No, definitely not," I chuckle and point at his own bandage. "Not that you should be rolling in the dirt, either."

"Good thing I don't need to," Rahuti says. "We haven't been training much since the attack. The Good God hasn't named replacements for Setankh or Hani."

"Oh, I do wish the Good God had just let you kill both of them," Djedi grumbles.

"What do you mean, 'let' us?" I flash Rahuti a wide-eyed glance. His gaze drops to his hands, as though he can't comprehend how they came so close to ending a life. Even the life of someone as corrupted as Setankh. "The Medjay stopped me and detained him right there."

"That's when Ahmose swept in," Djedi adds. "I saw little else except Rahuti scooping you off the floor and following Ahmose out of the Great Hall. By then, the Medjay killed or arrested enough of Setankh's men that the remaining ones surrendered. They arrested me, too, I'll add."

"But you're here now," I say.

Ubenu appears in the doorway.

"A message for you, lord," he says with a tight bow. "From the *tjati*."

Ahmose calls him forward and takes the small coil of paper. After unfurling it, he scans the writing. He reads it several times, surprise blooming on his face.

"They found it," he says.

"Found what?" Rahuti asks.

"Where Setankh held us."

My heart swells with hope. If the Medjay found where Setankh's men held Ahmose, they might have found Asata and Kala. Perhaps even Tahir.

"The Medjay discovered an abandoned mudbrick building, across a river channel, north of the city." Ahmose's face pinches with confusion. "But it seemed so much larger. There were so many of us."

"Is there anything about the others?" I ask.

He flips the page over. "Released," he says with relief. "The king's own physicians are attending to them."

"Oh, thank Iset!" I say.

He, Djedi, and Rahuti shoot me puzzled stares.

"You seem strangely invested in people you've never met," Djedi says to me.

"Ahmose," I say, ignoring Djedi as excitement and anticipation tumble in my belly. "Did they find a family? From"—I almost say Tanehsu—"from Men-nefer?"

PART FIVE: THE RETURN

○ ○ ○

As we still await any sign that my friends might be among those rescued, I don't give up hope.

And I don't stop trying to pry out the whereabouts of my necklace from Ahmose. Every time I ask, he replies with a frustratingly smug smile and, "You'll find out soon."

Five days after the battle at the Great Hall, on a morning as clear as spring water, Nehemet inspects my bandages and finally declares me well enough to leave the villa. Likely at Ahmose's insistence, because today, he says, I have a very important appointment.

Nehemet and Beket don't let me go before they paint my eyes with kohl, crown my head with a braided wig, and dress me in a fine linen sheath with turquoise and green embroidery along the hem. Just weeks ago, I couldn't stand wearing such things.

Ahmose helps me into his chariot, and we return to the Great House.

Instead of entering through the antechamber, as I did my first day here, he leads me to the tall cedar doors reserved for royal officials, courtiers, and foreign dignitaries.

"Am I allowed?" I ask.

"You're the guest of honor today."

Before I can ask what he means, the doors swing open with a blast of trumpet fanfare.

The overwhelming fog of incense and haze of perfumes can't cover the lingering metallic and sour scent of blood. My heart stops at the memory of it, with Setankh's rotten face flashing behind my sight.

I blink the images away and approach the dais with Ahmose, trying so hard to hide my limp. Only a few courtiers line the walls, and to my surprise, they regard me with admiration. Some throw lily blossoms at our feet, calling out, "*Ankh, udja, seneb.*"

"That's not for me, is it?" I whisper to Ahmose.

"It is, *ibty*."

I keep my head down as we walk to the center of the hall, and the Fan-bearer raps his standard against the floor.

Just as I lean my weight into Ahmose so I can kneel before the Horu Throne, the Good God and the Great Royal Wife hold up their hands to signal me to stop.

"Please, stand and look upon us," the Great Royal Wife says, "Sati of Men-nefer."

I give Ahmose a confused glance. He replies with an enigmatic smile.

The Great Royal Wife settles in her throne, and the Good God inclines his crowned head to me. Behind them, Aya stands with her hands folded in front of her, her gaze never straying from me.

"Sati of Men-nefer," the Good God says. "We invited you here because you accomplished a remarkable deed for the Two Lands."

"Because of your letter," the Great Royal Wife says, "we knew of the general's incursion. And while much blood was shed on Nebet-het's birthday, your keen ear and intuition were critical in protecting the throne. Our fiercest fighters met him in this hall with dignity and honor. And now he languishes in the Great Prison, along with all who accompanied him."

I'm unsure if I'm allowed to speak, but I start anyway. "Your Majesty..." Neither she nor the Good God tell me to stop. "I regret I knew nothing of the dark *heka* Setankh called on to send your guards to Duat."

The Great Royal Wife and the Good God share a glance, a moment of silent communication.

"We cannot know everything all at once, can we? Even the gods do not know all." A muscle in his jaw feathers. "But you, Sati of Men-nefer, are a woman of *ma'at*, loyal to the Two Lands." He pauses, as though he's about to share a secret. "Regardless of where you were born."

I go cold, taking Ahmose's hand for reassurance. "What does he mean?" I ask under my breath.

"You'll see," he says.

The Great Royal Wife gestures to Aya. The handmaiden holds a box no bigger than a mouse between her palms. The Great Royal Wife takes it with a grateful nod and lifts the lid with her henna-painted fingers.

"I presume you would like this returned to you?" She plucks a leather cord from the box, a gold lily pendant hanging from its center. Relief sweeps through me at the sight of it.

I barely feel the playful nudge of Ahmose's elbow as I watch Aya's face burst with recognition. She covers her mouth as her eyes dart back and forth from my pendant to me and back again.

She looks as though she wants to run to me. Aya leans toward the Great Royal Wife, who responds with a lift of her hand. *Wait*, it says.

"Lord Ahmose, if you please," the Great Royal Wife says, summoning him forward.

After making sure I'm steady enough to stand on my own, he retrieves my necklace and the box, itself plated with gold and jewels.

"A reward for your devotion to *ma'at*," the Good God says with pride.

As I turn the embellished box over in my hands, Ahmose ties the cord around my neck. I'm complete again, now reunited with this tiny token of my past.

"For the girl rescued from the frontier lands," the Good God adds. "The gods sometimes work in hidden ways."

He knows. That means the Great Royal Wife knows, that Aya—

"You see," the Good God says, sitting taller, "I recognized the pendant the moment you came to petition. And you so resemble my Great Wife's esteemed handmaiden, which only confirmed my suspicions that you are, indeed, Captain Paser's daughter."

"Adopted, Your Majesty," I say.

He tilts his head in question. I avert my gaze, hoping I haven't been disrespectful.

He makes a thoughtful sound, and at Ahmose's soft squeeze of my hand, I lift my head.

"While blood may determine who sits upon this throne," the king says, patting the gilded arm rests, "it does not determine who is loyal to the king who sits upon it. Your valiant actions have more than proven that."

I bow my head. Was I valiant? Or only fulfilling the vow I took in the presence of Sutekh?

"When you have recovered," he says, lifting his chin, "it would please me greatly if you were to return to the Garrison of Sutekh to continue your service to me and the Two Lands."

"Yes, Your Majesty," I say without hesitation. "It would be my honor."

"But that is not the only reason we've called you here today," the Great Royal Wife says. "Please, Aya."

Aya takes a hesitant step forward and off the dais. She hastens toward me and stares in disbelief, holding out her hand like she wants to touch me.

"Idra?" she whispers. "Is that really you?"

I nearly ask her what she means before I realize . . . Idra is me.

"It's me," she says. "Your sister. Don't you remember?"

I shake my head. I don't remember. As she embraces me, I wish I could.

Something about her feels so familiar. It awakens an early, distant, deep memory. An uncanny connection I've been seeking my entire life, but never knew I was searching for. I let myself wrap my arms around her in return.

After a long moment that leaves us both sniffling with tears, she pulls back. "I couldn't believe it, when you first stepped into this hall. But here you are."

She takes my pendant between her fingers, also stained with henna in delicate geometric patterns. "I thought I'd never see this again."

She gives me another embrace, and I grapple with what it might mean to have a blood sister. A sister I'll never share a childhood with, because Setankh and his men stole it from us. I wonder if Aya knows what really happened in our village or if the Good God even knows. If not, I'll have to be the one to tell them. But not today. Just enjoy the peace that today offers, for it could all end tomorrow.

CHAPTER THIRTY-FIVE

Aya and I say a teary goodbye, knowing this is only the first of many reunions.

As Ahmose and I leave the Great Hall, I turn the jewelry box over in my hands. By the looks of it, the wood is cedar. Cedar from Retenu, the only place in the Good God's realm where the trees grow. I remove the lid. On the inside are the name of the Good God and three symbols—*ankh, udja, seneb*—overlaid with gold. Like me, it's both foreign and of Kemet. I wonder if the Great Royal Wife insisted that the Great House reward me with such a gift.

In the columned entrance hall, I thread my arm through Ahmose's. "How much did you know about this morning?"

He grins and draws me closer. "Most of it. A few days ago, the *tjati* told me that the Medjay found your necklace in Setankh's belt as they arrested him. He suggested I return it to you in private, but I said that perhaps a royal meeting might be more fitting. As I expected, he wasn't keen on the idea; he values protocol above all. But I convinced the Great Royal Wife otherwise, and the king enthusiastically agreed."

Guards at the gate nod at us as we exit into the bright late morning sun, where a horse groom awaits with Ahmose's chariot. Ahmose greets the animals with a pat on their necks, and they respond with friendly snorts.

After thanking the groom, Ahmose helps me step into the cab and takes the reins. With a click of his tongue, the horses stretch into an eager walk. I grip the front rail, feeling even a little stronger than this morning.

As we leave the grounds of the Great House, my thoughts return to Aya. I've had a sister all this time, and she's been in the capital the entire time I've been in Men-nefer. Perhaps that's why I felt drawn here. Not just to become a soldier, but to reunite with the only person alive with whom I share blood.

I turn to Ahmose, who revels in the wind against his face as the horses speed to a canter. "Did you know Aya was my sister?" I ask.

"Not at all! Although, I'm not sure how I didn't see the resemblance. Maybe the Great Royal Wife did when you arrived to petition the king. She took an interest in you right away. I've never seen her do that with anyone before."

Indeed, she seemed to favor me, giving me guidance when I hadn't even asked. The advice she offered at the Wepet Renpet banquet returns to me. *A woman who has the ear of a man of noble birth has great influence.*

I never intended to capture her attention or Ahmose's ear. Somehow, I have both.

The tall date palms lining the road rustle above us in the breeze, the sunlight twinkling in their fronds. Just beyond, blue and green temple banners sway like river grass, all blissfully unaware of our recent fight for *ma'at*.

Ahmose slows the horses as we approach the avenue of ram's headed sphinxes, where ladies in their finery stroll again, servants beside them with woven sunshades and feather fans, all signs of Setankh's treachery now erased.

As we drive, I think of all the questions I want to ask Aya. What was she like as a young girl? What were her favorite toys and stories and songs? Did she have anyone like a mother to raise her? How often did she ask about me, if she did at all? When the soldiers brought us back from Qadesh, why couldn't we stay together?

"Something troubles you?" Ahmose asks as he turns the horses down the avenue of villas, the riverbank at our side.

"Aya called me 'Idra,'" I say. "I don't remember being called Idra."

Ahmose meets my gaze with his own.

"Does that mean I have two names?" I ask. "I'm not sure I want two names."

"It's not often someone has more than one name," he says. "That's an honor usually reserved for the Good God and his closest family."

Another reason I don't want to be both Sati and Idra. While I thought Sat-reshwet didn't fit me, Sati fits me far more than Idra, a word in a language I don't speak. I don't even know what it means. Another question to ask Aya when I see her again, which I hope is soon.

"Before I came here," I say, "I thought I wanted to be called something other than Sat-reshwet."

"Like what?"

I shake my head and let out a self-conscious chuckle. "I never decided. Not that Mawat and Iti would have approved if I did."

With the long leather reins in one hand, he wraps his free arm around my waist, trusting the horses to lead our way back to the stables. "I'll call you any name you choose."

I lean into him, remembering how he said my name that night in the garden. Oh, how I want to hear him say it again, sweet like dates and honey against the sparkling sky.

"Sati," I say with confidence. "Sati of Men-nefer."

After returning to the villa, I collapse on to my patio chair. Ahmose must see the strain on my face, because he rushes to my side.

"I think I've been up too much today," I say, my wounds aching. "Just don't tell Nehemet."

"Your secrets are safe with me," he says. "Are you well enough for a grand celebration feast? I warned the kitchens that I might have a few extra guests tonight." He flashes his rakish, enigmatic grin. The one that means he has a surprise for me.

"How many extra guests?"

"More than just Rahuti and Djedi."

My heart swells with hope again. "Does that mean the Great House replied to your message? About my friends?"

He only replies with a smile as serene as the full moon. At least I know him well enough now to understand it means, "Yes."

○ ○ ○

"Sati! Sati!" A young girl's familiar voice rings out in a joyful cry.

I can't stop myself from jumping from my chair and rushing to catch her as she hurls herself at me.

Beket chases after her. "Oh, Kala, be careful!"

Tears fill my eyes as I kiss the crown of the girl's head, now covered with thin braids.

"Kala," I say as I gently pull back, taking in the excitement on her face. "Where's your *mawat*?"

Kala points back to the villa where Nehemet walks into the garden alongside a woman with skin like river silt. Tahir, however, doesn't follow, and my heart breaks.

I wrap my arms around Asata in a tight embrace while Kala clings to our legs. She holds me close, in that way mothers do. I don't want to let go, for fear that Setankh's men might take her again, so far away that the Medjay will never find her.

"I'm so sorry," I say, holding in a sob against the crisp linen of her dress. "I wanted to stop them."

"Oh, Sati. I know. I saw you." She rubs my back with her comforting hands. "You did what you could."

"It wasn't enough." Tears cloud my vision, and several sobs break free from my throat.

"Being here is enough," Asata says, her own wise eyes welling. "And now Kala and I are safe."

She urges Kala to the pond to look at the fish, which she does gleefully. I shudder, thinking of how long Setankh's men held her and Asata, how dark and confining and terrifying it must have been. No wonder Kala delights in leaning over the edge of the water, trying to grasp at fish too fast and slippery for her little hands. She probably felt no joy at all for weeks.

As Asata and I sit, I hesitate to ask about Tahir, but I must. With a deep breath, I draw up the courage.

"Will . . . Tahir be joining us?"

Grief darkens the hollows beneath her high cheekbones, exposing Setankh's mistreatment of her and her fellow prisoners, twisting my belly with hatred.

"I'll find everyone involved," I say, putting my hand on hers. "I'll make every last one of those *isfet* men face the king's justice."

Asata pats my shoulder. She's seen me have my share of tantrums when I was Kala's age; she knows me nearly as well as Mawat does.

We sit in silence for a long moment, watching a giggling Kala run her fingers through the water, the carp greeting her with their moon-shaped mouths.

"Does Kala understand?" I ask after I've quelled the simmering vengeance in my heart.

Asata sniffs and wipes her cheeks, somehow not smudging her kohl, and nods. "Some days are easier than others."

Ahmose returns to the patio but stops short.

"My apologies, ladies, if I interrupted." He must see our tears. "Is it all right if the servants prepare the patio for the evening meal?"

"Yes, of course, please," I say, after looking at Asata for her tacit approval. A lavish meal won't satisfy my hunger for revenge, but it will help heal my injured body.

Servants carrying a large table and chairs soon emerge, while Ahmose directs the placement of the furniture under the shade of the awnings stretched overhead.

"When will you return to Men-nefer?" I ask Asata.

"I don't think we will," she answers.

"But Mawat—"

"I know Mereyet will miss me," she says. "But the Great Royal Wife offered me a position as a Chantress of Amun. For which Ahmose has my eternal gratitude."

He excuses the servants and sits beside me. "Asata sang prayers to the gods every day we were captive. Her voice is as pure and true as the sun itself. Her songs gave us hope."

Kala races up the stairs, a fresh lily blossom in her hand. "Look! Look!"

Asata takes it and tucks the stem behind the girl's ear.

"Besides," Asata says, "What do we have back in Men-nefer?"

"Your home, your neighbors, Mawat . . ."

She shakes her head. "With Tahir gone, and us now under the protection of the King's Wife, I have no doubt we should remain in Per-Ramesses. Going back would bring me nothing but nightmares. And here, Kala will train as a priestess when she's old enough."

"No!" Kala chirps in defiance. "I'm going to be a warrior!"

"Oh, are you?" I say, tapping her lightly on the nose. "I'm not sure your *mawat* would approve. Being a warrior is dangerous."

"I'm brave like you," she says, putting her hands on her hips and taking a wide stance.

"Like me, hmm?" Kala never knew me as a soldier, only as the daughter of her mother's friend who sometimes practiced staff fighting with Iti. I squint at Ahmose. "What did you tell her?"

He gives a little shrug. "After hours and hours in the dark, Kala would get so scared."

Kala punches her tiny fists in the air. "I wasn't afraid! I'll smash Apep!" She stomps her bare feet against the stone.

The three of us try not to laugh at her show of innocent courage.

"She would cry for hours, utterly inconsolable," Asata says, drawing Kala near. The girl's demeanor flips from tiny warrior to gentle child. "I would hold her close, telling her everything would be all right. No matter how hard I tried, I couldn't console her. Then Ahmose said he knew a brave woman from Men-nefer, and that Kala needed to be strong and courageous like her."

"Girls deserve stories of bravery and defending *ma'at*," he adds.

Asata unwinds a trio of Kala's braids twisted around the lily stem. "And when he mentioned your name, I almost didn't believe it."

"Then I said you have green eyes, of course."

Asata smirks at him. "No, what you said is that Sati's eyes are as green as the sea on a calm day, as the budding figs of the sycamore, as the malachite in the..."

"All right, all right. That's enough." Ahmose says as he tries to hide his flushing face behind his hand.

"You did, did you?" I tease.

Asata pats Ahmose's shoulder. "Your stories were the only thing that stopped Kala's tears."

I raise an eyebrow at him. "I hope you only told her *ma'at* and *nefer* things."

"I told her about how you fought the attackers on the *Nebkhepri*," he says, "that you tended to my injuries, and you probably saved my life."

I fidget with my necklace and glance at my feet. He makes me sound so valiant.

"And I told her you were fighting for *ma'at*. And you would save her, too." He shrugs in an unconvincing show of humility. "And I might have exaggerated some details."

"The details don't matter," Asata adds with a motherly calm and looks at me. "What matters is whatever you did, whatever you risked, ensured we could be here together again."

But not all of us. I wish Tahir could be here, to see his daughter run off again to delight in the lilies and fish, to see the sun sparkling in the glass beads of her braids. May he live forever.

"My apologies, ladies," Ahmose says, "but do you mind if I tell the kitchens we're ready for them?"

I defer to Asata who dips her head, and Ahmose strides back into the villa.

After he has gone, Asata takes my face in her hands and kisses my forehead. "Mereyet and Paser will be so proud of you."

Not long after, Djedi and Rahuti return, and along with Asata and Kala, we sit ourselves around the table where Ahmose's cooks have laid out a grand spread of fresh breads, baked fish, and slices of juicy melons. Rahuti shifts uncomfortably in his seat, as though he might never have eaten at a formal table before. Djedi, however, sits with confidence, and Kala bounces on the two plush cushions in her own chair to make her tall enough to see over her dish. Nehemet and Beket join us, too, sitting across from me, near enough to fuss over me should I exert myself too much.

I nearly ask Ahmose about the one last vacant chair when a voice sounds from the entry.

"I hope you weren't waiting on me."

Aya walks toward us, the hem of her light green linen dress swaying with her steps. She twists her hands together, looking unsure of herself.

I rise to greet her, but I'm not sure if I should embrace her. She, however, doesn't hesitate, pulling me close as though she's always known me. I introduce her to everyone else, and my *ka* rejoices with so many people dear to me in one place.

Ahmose offers Aya the chair to my left before sitting to my right. She thanks him with a gracious nod, a gesture refined through years in the Great Hall, attending to the most powerful woman in the land. She feels so familiar and yet so distant. How do I get to know my estranged sister, torn from me by the horrors of war?

After the attendants have filled our cups with wine, Ahmose stands and holds his cup high.

"Thank you all for your presence here on this beautiful evening," he starts. "For your loyalty to the Two Lands and to the Lord of the Sedge and the Bee. And let us thank the woman who has brought us all together." He gestures to me, and I give him a look as everyone else cheers in agreement.

"I'm serious!" he says. "I don't dare imagine what might have happened on Nebet-het's birthday if it weren't for your tenacity and finding the right people to assist you in your efforts."

Djedi and Rahuti beam with pride.

"So," Ahmose continues, "let us praise the gods for blessing us with this moment. For devoted friends, for family reunited, for the preservation of *ma'at* in the Two Lands, and for the abundance of the returning river."

We respond with enthusiastic agreement—Rahuti's and Kala's the most boisterous of all—and sip our wine before filling our bellies.

As the frogs and twilight insects strike up their songs, our conversations and laughter grow louder and more familiar. The rift that time carved between me and Aya shrinks as we share stories of our childhoods. When I ask, she tells me that Idra means "fig tree," and Ahmose laughs. I forget about my injuries as my heart grows ever more full, and all my fears of feeling out of place vanish into the indigo sky.

CHAPTER THIRTY-SIX

Over the next few days, fortified by Nehemet and Beket's care, regular and hearty meals, and the peace of the garden, I regain much of my strength.

Just after sunrise, I take short strolls through courtyard. I can nearly put all my weight on my injured leg, even if it still aches at the end of the day.

Aya returned to visit yesterday, regaling me with tales of growing up in the Ipet-Nesew—the royal women's quarters—and helping raise the king's many children. She brought tiger nut cake, which we dipped in a gooey date syrup, laughing like little girls as it smeared all over our fingers and faces. Even if Setankh robbed us of our childhood together, these moments are just as joyful. Maybe even more so, because we don't take them for granted.

During the days, Ahmose meets with diplomats and delegates at Great House, keeping them entertained and pacified as they barrage him with questions about what happened on Nebet-hct's birthday.

On the tenth day of the first month of Akhet, the season of flood, Ahmose and I eat our evening meal on the patio, as we have every day since I convinced Nehemet my wounds were healed enough to do so.

Today, he slumps into his chair, the frustration of the day still on his breath.

"Every day," he says, filling my cup with beer, "I try to convince the Hittites that the Good God intends to fulfill his promises, but they suspect we're not being entirely honest about what happened a week ago." He picks a bit of meat from the wing of the roasted duck on the table but doesn't eat it. "And they're right."

"What *do* they know?" I ask, scooping up a heap of lentils and cucumbers with a pinch of bread.

He sighs. "They know Urhi-Teshub is, indeed, here, and in the Good God's care. Most of them are grateful he's well and no longer a prisoner."

"But he's safe, and that should help to finalize the treaty, right?"

"Only so much. It's one thing for the Good God to accuse his own general of holding a foreigner hostage. He and the *tjati* advised me to frame the whole fiasco as a petty political ploy, a prank by a bitter brother gone too far." Ahmose takes a drink and sets his cup down with an irritated thud. "But it's another entirely for the Good God to admit Setankh nearly took the Horu Throne for himself. We can't afford for him to appear so weak. Not when being the Strong Arm is so vital to our success."

After a long exhale, he takes my hand and threads his fingers through mine.

"Today, the king threatened everyone who was there that day with imprisonment, even death, should we speak of Setankh's incursion with any of the foreign delegates. But rumors fly faster than a falcon on the hunt. Besides, the Good God won't give the prince up to the Hittites until their king has ratified the treaty. And as it stands, neither of them agrees with what we have now."

He slumps against the back of his chair, under the weight of his responsibilities.

I squeeze his hand. "I'm sure the brother kings will agree to something soon."

"I hope you're right."

Sandaled footsteps draw our attention to the doorway.

"Ubenu," Ahmose says with an inviting nod, and his page strides toward us, holding a small roll of papyrus.

"A courier just arrived, lord," Ubenu says with a bow. To my surprise, he hands the papyrus to me. "It's addressed to Sati."

Ahmose and I give each other puzzled glances.

"The courier said it's from Men-nefer," Ubenu clarifies.

My heart bursts with sunlight as I examine the fine cord and clay seal. The figures spell out Iti's name.

"Mawat and Iti must have received my letter!" My fingers fumble with the knot in excitement. I break the seal and unroll the paper.

I scan the words.

And they eclipse the radiant light in my heart.

Out of the corner of my sight, I see Ahmose excuse Ubenu.

"Is everything all right?" Ahmose says, standing to put his arm around my shoulder.

"I'm not sure."

I read the message again. It's certainly in Iti's hand. I would recognize it anywhere. But it's shaky and crooked, so unlike the sure hand of the lessons he wrote for me in the weeks before I left.

> *Our dearest Sati,*
>
> *We have received your letter, and we are overcome with joy at tales of your brave deeds. Mereyet and I are so proud of you. But you must come home to us. I need to see you. I can't wait. Time is running short. Mereyet and I both miss you so very much. May your hearing be beautiful, and may your journey be swift.*
>
> *Your Iti*

An ache for home, one I've been ignoring, seeps into my bones. What's worse is that something seems very wrong.

"He . . . he rarely writes so formally with me," I say. "And his writing . . ." I point to Iti's name at the bottom. "It's so messy."

I coil and uncoil the paper in my hands as my belly goes cold with worry.

Ahmose pulls me closer to him, and I lean into his embrace. "It sounds like you need to go back to them," he says.

I do, but I'm also needed here to serve the Good God. As soon as I'm well enough, I'm sure he and his *tjati* will put me to work as they investigate Setankh's crimes. And I want to. I want to be here when the Good God gives the order to bring his axe down on the traitor's neck.

But this letter . . . I left Iti and Mawat without saying goodbye, and now they're calling me home without anger or resentment. Only pride and love.

I don't notice my brows furrowing or the tight frown on my face until Ahmose turns my chin to him with a gentle nudge of his fingertips. "If I could see my mother and father one more time, I would. And from what you've told me, you're closer to your father than I ever was with mine."

I glance at the letter again. My worry darkens into dread.

Perhaps the Scarred Man remembered his promise. He said if Iti made his heart heavy with a lie, he'd return. And Iti lied about me.

I swallow back the thought. I can't let myself imagine the worst.

"Can you get me on a ship tomorrow?" I ask.

He grins. "It just so happens I ran into Khefer this morning. He asked if I would travel with him again, help negotiate a few trades, and he's sailing upriver at sunrise."

"Does that mean you'll come with me?"

His grin flattens as he shakes his head. "For the first time, I told him I'm needed here. I need to stop running from my duties and do what's *ma'at*. Peace and our prosperity depend on it. But you . . . Your family needs you."

PART FIVE: THE RETURN

"They do." I curl the paper, furling and unfurling. Tears bubble in my eyes as I stare at the rough edges and shaky script.

Ahmose presses a long kiss on my forehead. "I'll be here for you when you return," he says, crouching beside my chair and taking both of my hands in his.

"I don't know how long I'll be away."

He releases my hands and twists off the gold ring that never leaves his smallest finger.

"Give me your hand," he says. When I do, he drops the ring in my hand and folds my fingers over it.

"What? No, I can't." I hold out the ring to him. "I've never seen you without it."

When he doesn't take it back, I slip it on the first finger of my left hand. I run my thumb over the symbols on its crown. An ibis, a crescent moon, and a star.

"Is this a promise?" I ask, hoping he can't hear my skepticism.

"Yes," he says without hesitation. "A thousand times, yes."

○ ○ ○

That night, I write to Aya and Djedi telling them I'll be leaving tomorrow, and I'm sorry I won't have a chance to say a proper goodbye. I ask Djedi to tell Rahuti where I'm going and why, because he wouldn't be able to read my message even if I were to send him one of his own. I send another letter to Asata, promising to tell Mawat all about her new position in the Temple of Amun and that Kala is well and healthy. And I assure them all I'll write to them as soon as I've arrived safely at the Per-seshen.

During a night of fitful sleep, my heart races as I imagine all the terrible things that might have happened to Iti and Mawat while I was gone. Beket wakes me as the morning songbirds begin their calls. Nehemet inspects my remaining bandages and reluctantly declares me well enough to leave her meticulous, if not fussy, care. I try not to cry as I give them farewell embraces, thanking them for everything they've done for me. But tears run down our cheeks anyway.

At the entrance of the villa, Ahmose waits with me for the chariot that will take me to the docks. He wraps his arms around me, his skin warm against the morning mist.

"Why not drive me there yourself?" I ask, hoping for a few more moments with him before I leave.

"If I go with you," he says, pulling back to look at me with dark, glistening eyes, "I might never return to the Great Hall." He lets out a soft chuckle. "Besides, I wouldn't dare let Khefer and his crew see me cry. They'd never let me hear the end of it."

The chariot arrives too soon, driven by one of Ahmose's horse grooms. If I don't leave now, I'll miss my best opportunity to sail home.

I draw Ahmose as close as I can, breathing in the scent of him, hoping my heart will remember it when I'm gone. He kisses me so deep I want to let my palms wander down the curves of his back, around his waist, pulling us into the privacy of the villa. Just as Ahmose winds his fingers up my neck and into my hair, the groom clears his throat.

We reluctantly separate, and he helps me into the cab, his hand still holding mine.

"Write to me," he says.

"Of course," I say. "As soon as I can."

After Ahmose steps away, the groom clicks his tongue. The horses stride forward, taking me to the ship that will sail me home.

○ ○ ○

As Re's sun barque peeks over the eastern horizon, I stride down the canal path toward the *Nebkhepri* once again.

I'm wearing the *shendyt* and tunic I wore when I first arrived, washed and pleated by Nehemet and Beket, with my shawl wrapped around my shoulders and my iron dagger at my hip. The ragged incisions

PART FIVE: THE RETURN

in my side, leg, and arm from Setankh's blade have nearly healed, but his red eyes shock me awake from my dreams. Even with these souvenirs of battle, I'm stronger now. Perhaps a little more wise. And certainly much less alone.

I twist Ahmose's ring around my first finger and look out over the burgeoning riverbanks. A flock of ducks skims across a new channel of water, settling themselves in the reeds. An elegant white egret stalks beside them, plucking a silvery fish out of the shallow waters. Relief flows into the delta from the thirsty cities upriver. The gods have blessed us with the life-giving Iteru for another year.

On the docks, Khefer coils his ropes, like he did on the day we met. But today, he greets me as though I were an old friend.

"What a joyful surprise," he says as he holds out his rough, calloused hand, and I take it. He dips his head to me. "My *ka* rejoices in your return to the *Nebkhepri*."

"May you live forever, Khefer," I say. How different this encounter is from to our first meeting.

"No Ahmose this morning?"

I shake my head.

"Just as well. The boy has fancy sandals to fill, and it's time he did. But with you aboard, we won't have to worry about defending ourselves, if the stories I'm hearing from the Great House are true."

I'm not as sure about that as he is.

"May Hapi protect our journey," I say, gazing up at the gilded mast.

"Aren't you missing something?" he asks as I turn toward the ramp. "Your staff. You didn't forget it, did you? Not like you."

"Ah, right, my staff." As I pivot to him, my words choke in my throat as I remember watching the splinters of my beloved weapon fly into the air. "I, uh, lost it."

He shrugs. "Ah, well, perhaps the gods mean for you to get something better."

I hope he's right.

He points to my hand and gives me an insinuating smile. "Maybe that's something better?"

My cheeks heat, and I pull my hand behind me, as though Khefer hasn't already seen Ahmose's ring.

Khefer pats me on the back. "Don't need to explain. But I knew he had a liking for you the moment he saw you. Too bad he isn't coming with us."

I twist the ring around my finger again.

"Well, we'll get you to Men-nefer quickly, even with the river currents as strong as they've been. And back again to that boy. Now, go get yourself settled. We'll be leaving soon."

I walk up the ramp to the now familiar decks of the *Nebkhepri*.

"Our journey is blessed now," one of the crew declares.

"The Protector of Re is aboard!" another declares, greeting me with a hearty handshake.

I thank them, not sure what to do with their confidence in me. In my heart, I know what I did took courage and strength. But I did what I had to do, what was right. I did what the Powerful One called on me to do, to protect the Horu Throne, to defend *ma'at*.

Any *ma'at* man would have done the same.

Khefer pulls the last ropes aboard, and he orders the crew to take their positions along the side of the ship. A few uncoil the sail from the center mast, and it inflates in the wind.

"All right, men," Khefer calls out in his gruff, weathered voice. "Let's go."

The crewmen chant as they push the oars in a synchronized rhythm to their song, and the *Nebkhepri* departs from the glorious port of Per-Ramesses.

In a way, this city has become home to me, despite all I've been through. A wistfulness passes through my heart as the golden capped obelisks, the pylon flags, and the slanted limestone walls of temples shrink and vanish behind the fluffy tops of papyrus. I have no idea how long I'll be gone before I can return to my friends, my sister, to Ahmose.

Our pace quickens as the waters widen, and we're greeted with the low hills of the red desert just beyond the banks.

In the distance, I hear a rumbling purr.

A warm wind rushes against my face as I head to the lily-capped bow of the ship.

I close my eyes. I breathe it in. Fresh and green and teeming with life.

And like Sanehat returning from Retenu, I am going home.

GLOSSARY

Instead of the classical and more contemporary terms for deities, places, and other aspects of ancient Egypt, I use terms derived from the ancient Egyptian language. Proper nouns are capitalized and not italicized; all other Egyptian words are italicized.

Akhet: Season of Flood, approximately August through November.

Ammit: Monster with the head of a crocodile, forelegs of a lion, and backside of a hippopotamus. She devours hearts that Anpu/Anubis finds to be heavier than the feather of Ma'at and therefore heavy with misdeeds.

Amun: Chief god of royalty, known as the "Hidden One."

Ankh, Udja, Seneb: "Life, Prosperity, Health." Originally used as a benediction for kings, the phrase also became a way to say goodbye or farewell as well as a general blessing of good tidings.

Anpu: Anubis, jackal-headed god of death and the afterlife.

Apep: Apophis, the Chaos Serpent, embodying disorder and darkness. One of Re's greatest enemies.

Astarte: Canaanite goddess who became relatively popular in Ramesside Egypt.

Ba: An aspect of the human soul, often depicted as a bird with a human head.

Benret: Sweet, used here to mean "sweetheart," "dear."

Bes: Protective deity for households, mothers, and children.

Bitbit: Honey, used here as term of endearment.

The Black Land: Ancient Egypt; the fertile land along the Nile. Also called Kemet.

Deben: Measure of weight used to determine value of bartered items.

Desher: Red, evil. Feminine Deshret can refer to the "Red Lands" beyond the fertile riverbanks. Plural *desheru*.

Djehuty: Thoth, ibis-headed god of writing, wisdom, and magic.

Duat: The underworld the deceased must pass through to reach the Field of Reeds.

Field of Reeds: The afterlife. Also called Aaru.

Geb: God of the Earth.

Good God: Title for the king, pharaoh.

Hapiu Bull: Apis Bull, sacred animal worshipped in Memphis.

Hat-hor: Hathor, cow-headed goddess of love. Counterpart of Sekhmet (see below).

Heka: Magic.

Hes: Excrement, used here as an equivalent to "shit."

Hiyu: Monster, beast. Feminine *hiyut*. Interestingly, the hieroglyph spelling of this word includes the determinative sign for "foreign."

Horu: Horus, falcon-headed son of Iset/Isis and Wasir/Osiris.

Ibib / Ibty: Sweetheart, dear. From *ib*, meaning "heart."

Idet: Vulva, womb, used here as derogatory.

Imyr: Sir, commander, overseer.

Ipet-Nesew: Women's quarters in the palace, a bit like an Ottoman harem.

Iset: Isis, wife of Wasir/Osiris, mother of Horu/Horus.

Isfet: Chaos, evil. The opposite of *ma'at*.

Iteru: "The River;" the Nile. Literally, it means "blue."

Iti: Father.

Ka: Somewhat equivalent to the soul, which leaves the body upon someone's death.

Ka't: Vagina, used here as derogatory.

Kemet: Egypt. Literally, "black," and refers to the black fertile soil on the banks of the Nile, and not necessarily the lands beyond the Nile valley also under pharaonic rule. Depending on the context, I use this term interchangeably with "the Two Lands," as the ancient Egyptians did.

Khonsu: God of the moon, son of Amun and Mut.

Khopesh: The sickle-shaped sword used by New Kingdom soldiers.

Kerbetu: Bitches. Singular *kerbet*. (I admit I took liberties with this one, particularly because it's so similar to the Arabic word for dog: *kalb*.)

Ma'at: Truth and justice as a concept and guide for living a good life, symbolized by an ostrich feather.

Ma'at: Goddess of truth and justice. Note that *ma'at* as a concept is italicized, while the goddess' name is not.

Mawat: Mother.

Medjay: Once a nomadic Nubian group, by the New Kingdom, the name no longer referred to an ethnic group, but to the king's elite police and protective forces.

Mehen: Ancient Egyptian board game in the shape of a coiled snake.

Men-nefer: The ancient city of Memphis. Literally, "Enduring and Beautiful."

Mheti: Northern/northerner. Feminine *mehtet*. Plural *mhetyu*.

Min: God of fertility, depicted as a man with an erect phallus.

Nebet: Lady, "ma'am."

Nebet-het: Nephthys, daughter of Geb and Nuit, sister of Iset/Isis.

Nefer: Goodness, perfection.

Nefertem: Son of Sekhmet and Ptah associated with the blue water lily.

Nu: Primordial darkness from which the rest of creation rose.

Nuit: Goddess of the night sky.

Per-Ramesses: "House of Ramesses." The capital city in the eastern delta of the Nile.

Peret: Season of Emergence/Growth, approximately December through March.

Ptah: Creator god, consort of Sekhmet, father of Nefertem. Sometimes called the "Beautiful Face."

Puhuyt: Anus, used as derogatory.

Punt: Ancient kingdom in the Horn of Africa that exported gold, incense, ebony, ivory, and other valuable commodities to ancient Egypt.

Ribu: Ancient Egyptian name for Libya.

Re: Falcon-headed god of the sun.

Rekhyt: Collective term for the common people under the pharaoh's rule.

Rem: Fish god who fertilizes the land with his tears.

Retenu: Greater Canaan; the wider Syrian region.

Sa: A symbol of protection.

Satet: Satis, goddess from southern Egypt associated with the annual Nile flood, war, and hunting. Her name means "to shoot" or "to pour forth."

Sekhmet: Lioness-headed goddess of war, plagues, and healing, also known as the Powerful One. Sometimes manifests as the Eye of Re who defends the king against his enemies.

Shema': Disease demon, foreigner, used as derogatory. Feminine *shema't*.

Shemu: Season of Harvest, approximately April through July.

Shendyt: The linen kilt worn by men of all social status in New Kingdom Egypt. Plural *shendytu*.

Senet: Ancient Egyptian board game.

GLOSSARY

Shuyit: The shadow aspect of a living person. Sometimes used to refer to statues of people and deities. Plural *shuyitu*.

Sopdet: Sothis, goddess of the star we call Sirius.

Sutekh: Set (Seth), brother of Osiris. God of the deserts and storms, but also protector of the king.

Tanehsi: Nubian.

Tanehsu: Ancient Nubia.

Tawaret: Hippopotamus goddess who protects women and children.

The Two Lands: United Upper and Lower Egypt, the Nile Valley from the delta to Nubia. Depending on the context, I use this term interchangeably with "Kemet," as the ancient Egyptians often did.

Tjati: Vizier, the king's second in command.

Wasir: Osiris, god of fertility, death, and resurrection. Sometimes referred to as Wennefer, meaning "the Beautiful One."

Wabuir: Priest, used as honorific. For the purposes of this book, I combined *wab* and *imyr*, which, coincidentally is similar to Egyptological *Wbr*, meaning "Apep as a hostile serpent."

Wadjet: Cobra goddess of northern Egypt, associated with the Eye of Re.

Waset: Ancient Thebes, in current-day Luxor. Literally, "City of the Scepter."

Wepet Renpet: New Year. Literally, "Opening of the Year."

AUTHOR NOTES

NOTES ON LANGUAGE

As you flip through this book, you might notice two things: the hefty glossary and the lack of more familiar terms for ancient Egyptian gods and cities.

Because my main character, Sati, tells her story in first person present tense, I've tried to use names and terminology that are closer to the original ancient Egyptian when it seemed most appropriate. As with any foreign language, ancient Egyptian has words and terms for which there aren't direct translations in English. In addition, everything the reader sees is through the perspective of someone who doesn't know the modern names for her cities or gods. (For the record, I tried writing this book in third person past and first person past, but Sati is stubborn and didn't like either of them.)

The Egyptian names that most of us are familiar with come from Greek interpretations, but aren't always what the ancient Egyptians particularly those living in the 13th century BCE—would have used themselves. So, you won't see "Egypt," "Nile," or even "Pharaoh;" you'll see their equivalents of "Kemet" or "the Two Lands," "the Iteru," and "the Good God," respectively. Nor will you see the common names for Egyptian deities such as Isis, Osiris, or Thoth; instead, I use Iset, Wasir, and Djehuty. If words are proper nouns, I do not italicize them.

So, "Mawat" and "Iti," meaning "Mom" and "Dad" are not italicized, but words like *tjati*, meaning "vizier," are italicized.

I also wanted to avoid using English language swear words. It felt weird for Sati and her contemporaries to say words like "shit" as they're so specific to English (and often Germanic in origin). This led me to imagine what the ancient Egyptians might use instead, leading me to make some educated guesses and create some curses of my own. I did the same for terms of endearment, which I pulled from literal translations for "sweet" and "honey."

Please see the Glossary for a comprehensive list of names and terminology.

NOTES ON HISTORICAL INTERPRETATION

This story takes place during the reign of Ramesses II, often called Ramesses the Great, fifteen years after the famed Battle of Qadesh. As a student of political history and international relations, a former intelligence analyst, and a life-long Egyptophile, I've been fascinated by the Battle of Qadesh and its aftermath for some time.

By the time Ramesses II had taken the throne, Qadesh, a strategic city at the very northern edge of Egyptian influence (near what's now the Lebanon/Syria border), had fallen under control of the Hittites, a rival kingdom based in the Anatolian Peninsula. In his early twenties, only five years into his reign, and eager to prove his might as king, Ramesses led his troops into battle against the Hittites to claim this long-contested city. Ultimately, the Hittites out-maneuvered the Egyptian forces, and even fed them misleading intelligence, the truth of which the Egyptians uncovered far too late to adjust their battle plans. While Ramesses claimed victory over the Hittites at Qadesh—most famously in the reliefs on the walls of his temple at Abu Simbel—in reality, the battle was more of a stalemate. This stalemate led to the world's first known parity treaty, known as the Treaty of Qadesh or the Silver Treaty, ratified some sixteen years later.

Despite a number of military campaigns in Syria and Nubia in the first decade of his reign, it seems that for the fifty years after the treaty, Ramesses chose a more diplomatic approach to relations with his rivals. He refrained from explicit saber rattling (or should I say *khopesh* rattling?) and war-mongering, instead covering the Nile valley with his image and cartouche, building his famed temple at Abu Simbel and developing his new capital city—Per-Ramesses—in the eastern Nile delta. He looked inward to his domain, ensuring that everyone under his rule—Egyptians and foreigners alike—knew he was watching them.

While some scholars (and rightfully so) point out his arrogance and the propagandistic nature of the monuments he had built during his reign, I also see a man who understood that the benefits of some semblance of peace with his neighbors far outweighed the accolades that constant warfare in the hinterlands could potentially bring him. He was not a war-hawk, seeking glory in the physical subjugation of his enemies abroad. Instead, he preferred to portray himself as trampling the foreign enemies of Egypt primarily in image, as a warning of what could befall those who challenged or disobeyed him. And it seems to have worked.

As I researched his reign, I started to wonder: What if Ramesses commissioned so many monuments and statues to counter an internal threat to his power? What kind of threat would spur him to take almost extreme measures to counter it? And what did the foreigners living under his rule in the Nile valley think about so many violent portrayals of their king smiting their brethren? Those questions led to the creation of *Daughter of Sekhmet*.

Despite years of research, I take some liberties with the documented history. After all, this is a work of fiction. A work of fiction told through the perspective of an impulsive, independent, and fallible teenager. And I fully acknowledge that the premise of this story—that an unknown half-brother of Ramesses II plans a coup—is made up. That said, if such a thing did happen, do you think Ramesses would have allowed it to be documented anywhere? And it just so happens that Ramesses III—who ruled barely twenty years later—*was* the victim of a coup; his mummy shows a clear and gaping wound in his throat.

Now, about the Egyptian calendar. Those of you more familiar with the complexities of the ancient Egyptian calendar might remark that my dating system isn't exactly correct, because of the whole 365 days and no leap year thing in the Egyptian civil calendar. In the year this story is set—sometime around 1258 BCE—the first day of the civil calendar would not have been the first day of the heliacal rising of Sopdet/Sirius. That said, it made more narrative sense to align the annual flood, the rising of Sopdet/Sirius, and the start of the new year, especially in a culture so reliant on the cycle of the seasons.

When it comes to gender roles, I understand that I play a little fast and loose. It's true that women in ancient Egypt had more "freedoms" than their Greek or Roman counterparts, but the entire premise of a woman becoming a solider is, I know, a bit far-fetched. That said, the concept of a woman entering a man's world would not have been completely unknown to the ancient Egyptians, having seen queens Hatshepsut and Sobeknefru rule over the Two Lands well before the reign of Ramesses II. And there are bits of evidence of royal women being associated with military power, such as queen Ahhotep, who was buried with a gilded battle ax and the golden flies of victory. Archeologists and historians have found evidence for warrior women all over the world. Why would ancient Egypt be an exception? I don't think it's unreasonable to imagine that at least one girl in ancient Egypt's three-thousand-year history dreamed of joining her king's military. After all, we know that the images the ancient Egyptians left behind were highly idealized, not only told through the eyes and agendas of not only the wealthy and powerful, but also of men.

Interestingly enough, there is a *shabti*—a figurine buried with the dead to act as a servant in the afterlife—from the 18th Dynasty in the Brooklyn Museum of a woman called "the Lady Sati," and she is depicted as having male features. I didn't even know about her until I was well into finishing the first draft of this book. See the Further Reading section for a link to the page at the Brooklyn Museum about her.

Ultimately, this is the tale I wanted to read when I was a teenager and could never find. And it's the culmination of years of a hobbyist's enthusiasm for a world long since passed. I hope it brings you joy and you love this world as much as I do.

FURTHER READING

THE BASICS
If you're looking for accessible introductions to the history, people, and culture of ancient Egypt, I recommend these books.

Brewer, Douglas J., and Emily Teeter. *Egypt and the Egyptians*. Cambridge University Press, 2007.
Mertz, Barbara. *Red Land, Black Land: Daily Life in Ancient Egypt*. Harper Collins, 2011.
———. *Temples, Tombs, & Hieroglyphs: A Popular History of Ancient Egypt*. Harper Collins, 2009.
Ryan, Donald P. *A Year in the Life of Ancient Egypt: The Real Lives of the People Who Lived There*. Michael O'Mara Books, 2022.
———. *Ancient Egypt on 5 Deben a Day*. Thames and Hudson, 2010.
Shaw, Ian. *The Oxford History of Ancient Egypt*. Oxford University Press, 2003.
Silverman, David P. *Ancient Egypt*. Oxford University Press, 2003.

DEEPER DIVES

For those who want to explore beyond the basics.

Brooklyn Museum. "Shabty of Lady Sati," https://www.brooklynmuseum.org/opencollection/objects/3973.

Candelora, Danielle, Nadia Ben-Marzouk, and Kathlyn M. Cooney. *Ancient Egyptian Society: Challenging Assumptions, Exploring Approaches.* Taylor & Francis, 2022.

Cooney, Kara. *The Good Kings: Absolute Power in Ancient Egypt and the Modern World.* Simon and Schuster, 2021.

———. *When Women Ruled the World: Six Queens of Egypt.* Simon and Schuster, 2018.

David, Ann Rosalie. *A Year in the Life of Ancient Egypt.* Pen and Sword, 2015.

Dean, Rebecca. *Warfare & Weaponry in Dynastic Egypt.* Casemate Publishers, 2017.

Graves-Brown, Carolyn. *Dancing for Hathor: Women in Ancient Egypt.* Bloomsbury Publishing, 2010.

Hare, Tom. *ReMembering Osiris: Number, Gender, and the Word in Ancient Egyptian Representational Systems.* Stanford University Press, 1999.

Healy, Mark. *New Kingdom Egypt.* Bloomsbury Publishing, 2013.

———. *Qadesh, 1300 BC: Clash of the Warrior Kings.* Greenwood, 2005.

Montet, Pierre. *Everyday Life in Egypt in the Days of Ramesses the Great.* University of Pennsylvania Press, 1958.

Pinch, Geraldine. *Egyptian Mythology: A Guide to the Gods, Goddesses, and Traditions of Ancient Egypt.* Oxford University Press, 2004.

———. *Magic in Ancient Egypt: Revised Edition.* University of Texas Press, 2010.

Romer, John. *Ancient Lives: The Story of the Pharaohs' Tombmakers.* Weidenfeld & Nicolson, 2003.

Shaw, Garry J. *Egyptian Mythology: A Traveler's Guide From Aswan to Alexandria.* Thames & Hudson, 2021.

———. *War & Trade With the Pharaohs: An Archaeological Study of Ancient Egypt's Foreign Relations.* Casemate Publishers, 2017.

Shaw, Ian. *Ancient Egyptian Warfare: Tactics, Weaponry and Ideology of the Pharaohs.* Casemate Publishers, 2019.

Tyldesley, Joyce. *Daughters of Isis: Women of Ancient Egypt.* Penguin UK, 1995.

———. *Judgement of the Pharaoh: Crime and Punishment in Ancient Egypt.* Orion Publishing Company, 2001.

———. *Ramesses: Egypt's Greatest Pharaoh.* Penguin UK, 2001.

Von Dassow, Eva. *The Egyptian Book of the Dead: The Book of Going Forth by Day - The Complete Papyrus of Ani Featuring Integrated Text and Full-Color Images.* Chronicle Books, 2008.

Wilkinson, Toby. *Lives of the Ancient Egyptians.* Thames & Hudson, 2013.

———. *Ramesses the Great: Egypt's King of Kings.* Yale University Press, 2023.

———. *The Rise and Fall of Ancient Egypt.* Bloomsbury Publishing, 2013.

———. *Writings From Ancient Egypt.* Penguin UK, 2016.

PODCASTS

Cooney, Kara, Jordan Galczynski, and Amber Myers Wells. *Afterlives of Ancient Egypt.* https://ancientnow.substack.com/.

Perry, Dominic. *History of Ancient Egypt Podcast.* https://www.egyptianhistorypodcast.com/.

FICTION

Women-centered novels set in ancient Egypt I think you'll enjoy.

Hawker, Libbie. *The Sekhmet Bed*. Running Rabbit Press, 2014.
McGraw, Eloise Jarvis. *Mara, Daughter of the Nile*. Penguin, 1953.
Moran, Michelle. *Nefertiti*. Crown Publishers, 2008.
———. *The Heretic Queen*. Crown Publishers, 2008.
Thornton, Stephanie. *Daughter of the Gods: A Novel of Ancient Egypt*. Penguin, 2014.

ACKNOWLEDGEMENTS

This book wouldn't have been possible without so many people.

First to my wonderful partner and collaborator and favorite person, Tim Rayborn. Thank you for encouraging me to let you read my first draft and for believing in me and in Sati's story. I'll never forget the enthusiastic look on your face when I came home from teaching my dance class and you'd just finished reading my first chapter. Without your input, support, and inspiration, I'm not sure I would have ever finished writing it.

To my parents, who indulged my interests in Mediterranean antiquity, starting when I was a young girl. Thank you for letting me drag you through the British Museum's Egyptian collections when I was ten, and for sending me to Cambridge in the summer of 1997 to study with Toby Wilkinson. And thank you to Mom for suggesting we take a tour in Egypt together in 2024. It's exactly what I needed.

Maryann Karinch at Armin Lear Press and Thousand Acre Books: your trust in my work is invaluable, and I'm so grateful you took a chance on this story to add it to your catalogue. Also, much gratitude to the design and typesetting team for the beautiful interior.

After I finished my first draft of this novel in January 2021, Elinore Eden Edge offered to create the cover art, long before she even knew what the book was about. But I knew at that moment she would be the perfect artist for the job. Elinore, thank you for bringing Sati to life in such vivid color.

My beta readers—Ziah and Ava McKinney, Linda Alila, Heather Harvey, Cynthia Caton, and Benita Hartwell—for your invaluable feedback and encouragement. Also to Jo Wallis for answering my many questions about being a woman in a military school; even though your experience is contemporary, people are people and assholes gonna asshole.

To my former co-workers and managers at the Central Intelligence Agency who taught me so many skills I've used in creating this book: understanding the psychology of tyrants, the fragility of treaties, and the fine art of ruthless editing. You are some of the best thinkers, writers, and editors in the world. Too bad you can't bring home writing samples to prove it.

To all the Egyptologists whose work I've drawn from through the years, but especially Dr. Kara Cooney for her no-nonsense examinations of ancient Egypt through a clear sociological and political lens. I admit that some of the questions I've asked on the Afterlives Discord server have been research for this book (and future books). And another special thank you to Dr. Toby Wilkinson for the mini-course on Egyptology I took with you so long ago at Queen's College, Cambridge. I still have your letter of commendation. I also need to mention Dr. Christian Casey for offering free courses in the ancient Egyptian language and Coptic, and for the calendar spreadsheet you've shared on Google Sheets. Your generosity is not without notice. And to all the other experts whose books fill my home library: thank you.

Without music, this book absolutely would not have taken shape the way it did. I need to mention all the musicians and bands whose music I binged while writing, helping me give depth, voice, and texture to Sati and her world. Special mention to Peter Gabriel, Paula Cole, Dream Theater, Destiny Potato, Envy of None, Fair to Midland, Fiona Apple, Haken, Noa, Ani DiFranco, TesseracT, Saga, Scardust, and

Rush (of course). A few specific albums saw me through the completion of the first full draft: Devin Townsend's *Empath* and Lunatic Soul's *Through Shaded Woods*. And a shout out to *Mannequin* by Kyros for helping me power through the rewrites and revisions. Thank you all for providing the soundtrack to my writing sessions.

A special thank you to the crew, hospitality staff, and indefatigable guides (Hanan, Hanan, and Nesrine—I will reach out to you the next time I'm in Egypt) of the Viking *Osiris*. You helped me fall in love with Egypt—its past and present—all over again.

And, of course, all my heartfelt appreciation to you, dear reader.

ABOUT THE AUTHOR

ABIGAIL KEYES has lived many lives, including professional belly dancer, intelligence analyst, and college professor. Her passion for ancient Egypt and the Middle East led her to earn a degree in Near Eastern Studies from Princeton University. She has written several books on 20th-century Middle Eastern performing arts and is an experienced freelance writer and blogger. Abigail is currently a book coach and editor, and lives in Vancouver, Washington, with her partner and their cat, Mingo.

Milton Keynes UK
Ingram Content Group UK Ltd.
UKHW020055061124
450708UK00006B/714